A Copper Town Summer

To
Mike & Joann,
I hope you enjoy
the book.

A Copper Town Summer

Derek Sailors

Library of Congress Control Number: 2008909033
ISBN: Hardcover   978-1-4363-7565-8
                 Softcover   978-1-4363-7564-1

To order additional copies of this book, contact:
Xlibris Corporation
1-888-795-4274
www.Xlibris.com
Orders@Xlibris.com
53676

Dedicated to my parents, my sister Shelley and my dog Jade

In memory of my good buddy Danny Rhodes

PROLOGUE

Like a firefly in search of its mate, the flickering orb levitated from the unmarked corner grave. Having taken the form of a faintly glowing ball of light, the nocturnal spirit of the Slavic miner bobbed over the tranquil cemetery grounds that rested on a hill on the eastern edge of the sleepy town.

If live human beings had been present in the cemetery during the middle of that cloudless night, they would have smelled a pungent, rotting odor seep from the unmarked grave of Goran Divanevic. They may also have detected a shadowy mist near the cold plot where the miner's life-form chose to remain for the past decade.

After transforming from the vapor, the orb floated with the gentle breeze like a leaf down a slow-running stream toward the direction of the town. Free to drift above the mountain and through its canyons, the spirit was bound to the mining town that had so wrongfully taken its physical life in a lynching years before.

Goran was one of several Slavs who made their way to the mining town of Jerome, Arizona, and its railroad at the turn of the century. After the railroad was completed, he found work in the copper mine. Like so many others who performed the laborious, backbreaking work deep inside the veins below the town's core, at the end of a long day buried in the blistering heat, he was thirsty for beer—a beverage which had been enjoyed by his Slavic ancestors for well over one thousand years.

After slugging down several beverages with his countrymen in one of the town's several saloons, he hungered for female companionship to which there was an abundance. A short man in stature, he was neither handsome nor homely looking. He had cash in his pocket. That was all that mattered.

Late one Saturday evening, Goran was seen leaving the Mineflower Saloon with Janie Bailey, a popular lady of the evening, after a heavy night of imbibing. After accompanying the woman to her place of residence—a brothel in the Tenderloin District on Main Street—he was soon struck by the effects of his overindulgence and collapsed, unable to perform the act that he had saved his pittance for and had so longed to accomplish.

He found himself in an alleyway behind the brothel late the next morning, lying in a pool of vomit and urine, which may also have been his. He had no recollection of the events that occurred on the previous evening. When he attempted to pick himself up, an excruciating pain pulsated from the side of his head, where a tender lump had formed under a bloody, matted-down patch of hair. He soon became aware that his pocket watch was gone. Only an empty silver chain remained attached to his trousers where he once kept his most prized possession. The pockets of his trousers had been rummaged through and were now empty. He thought that he had started the evening with ten dollars but couldn't be sure. His Case pocket knife was also missing. The only thing that he was fairly certain about was that he had been clubbed over the head and robbed.

Once he was able to steady himself on his feet, a nauseous wave overwhelmed him, and he vomited on the ground and the shoe he was wearing. After all the contents of his stomach were spilled, he looked around but didn't see his other shoe or any of his other possessions. His first thought was to march into the brothel and demand to speak with the madame. After he staggered from the alleyway, he stopped and looked down at himself, a pitiful sight.

With a pounding headache and smelling like a filthy bathhouse, he decided to limp home to his room at the boardinghouse that he shared with a few of his countrymen. He would return to the brothel later in the day when he was not so ragged and demand some answers.

When he arrived at the boardinghouse three blocks away, he stripped out of his soiled clothes to his long one-piece woolen underwear. Luckily, he found an empty narrow cot and promptly lay down. His head pounding, the room slowly spun as if orbiting around him.

Hours later, he was rudely awakened by the heel of a boot to the side of his stomach. He opened his eyes and stared at two angry men glaring down on him. His head still hurt, and his empty stomach now ached as well.

The men threw a rope around his torso and pulled him from the bed onto the floor. Despite his protests, they dragged him down the back stairs and into the twilight of the early Sunday evening. For some reason, none of his countrymen were present. Tied to the saddle of a large black horse, he was dragged through the dirt streets for several blocks until the rider stopped among a group of men standing under a lone juniper tree near Deception Gulch. Bloodied from head to toe, he fell in and out of consciousness. One of the men threw the rope over a thick branch and secured the other end in a noose around his neck before spitting tobacco juice in his face. Goran was lifted and placed backward in the saddle by two of the men while another man tied his hands behind him tightly, ripping the flesh from his forearms.

His cheeks were swollen. Blood and sweat stung his eyes. Looking up at his captors, he couldn't tell if he saw four or five men, all wearing handkerchiefs over their faces with their hats pulled down low over their raging faces. Goran was able to make out some English words but could not understand what all was being said. The men clearly had hostile intentions.

Before he left the physical world so violently, one of the men pulled out a small knife, the knife that had been taken from him, and held it out before him. "This here's the knife you used to stab Janie to death, you sorry bastard! Now you've met your judge and jury. The verdict is unanimous! You better say your prayers cuz your soul's gonna rot in hell!"

With that said, one of the vigilantes slapped the horse hard on its hind end. Goran dropped a couple feet before the rope pulled taut, leaving him hanging by his neck to the thick tree branch. He remained alive for only a few moments before he stopped swinging, and death welcomed him.

His limp body was found the next morning and was cut down from the tree where it hung. His fellow countrymen who had known Goran knew he was not capable of committing such a violent crime. The marshal assured the men that the girl's death would be thoroughly investigated, but nothing ever happened. He also promised to track down Goran's killers. Again, nothing ever happened.

The men passed the hat among the Slavic community and gathered a few dollars, enough to bury their hardworking comrade in the cemetery with a small unmarked headstone. A traditional Slavic funeral included a huge feast that had been prepared and brought to the cemetery where it was eaten. A portion of the meal was left for Goran. He was welcomed into the afterworld by Volos, the god of the herds. Yet his tortured spirit refused to move on and stayed behind.

On this starry evening, the spirit of Goran was able to sense a malevolent presence. Just as the spirit was able to sense the horrific events that had transpired since the arrival of the newcomer into the peaceful mining community, its attempts to prevent the horror met with futile results.

The aura that radiated from the newcomer cast a powerful negative energy that could be felt throughout the spirit world. Goran had never sensed such an evil feeling, while alive or dead.

Without the presence of this guardian spirit, the following story would not be told.

1

July 1921

Three crows were perched in a dead mesquite tree that cast a long shadow in the late-afternoon sun. Like sentinels, the black birds watched over the body's spirit with fervid curiosity. The black birds were creatures of the underworld—omens of prophecy, magic, war, and death. They stared at the mangled corpse that lay crumpled, wedged between the jagged rocks at the bottom of the steep ravine. The lifeless limbs of her blood-spattered body were contorted unnaturally. A heart-shaped locket on a sterling silver chain dangled from her twisted neck.

Like trash discarded from the winding roadway high above linking the mountain town of Jerome with the town of Prescott forty miles to the southwest, the body of the once-vibrant doe-eyed beauty now lay dead where she was thrown to the centipedes, scorpions, and rattlesnakes in the rocky canyon below. For so many men, all hopes of a tryst with the dark-haired beauty now lay dashed upon the rocks hundreds of feet below.

Along with the smell of the expensive perfume that emanated from her body, never again to drive men insane, a faint odor of decomposition began to manifest. Insects feasted on the recent arrival to their habitat. Tattered remnants of her blue satin dress blew in the summer monsoon wind that swirled down through the canyon depth.

A beautiful young woman who had shared her most intimate company with only the wealthiest men around Jerome died a horribly painful death. Euripides and Shakespeare both would have been challenged to have written a sadder tragedy. Swung into the canyon from the grips of a strong man, she bounced off the canyon wall thirty feet down from the edge, careening off solid rock three times before bounding another one hundred feet. The impact of the fall crammed her petite frame into a narrow crevice at the bottom between a mass of brush, gravel, and boulders.

Her profession was considered by the more virtuous as a less-than-honorable profession. In spite of that, it was necessary for obvious reasons. Her privileged clientèle included the owner of a large Prescott ranch, two local business owners, executives of the mines, a surgeon, an attorney, and the town mayor.

While her clients were few, her admirers were many. She was one of the most beautiful woman in the booming Arizona mining town, venerated for her elegance, grace, and kindness. Annabelle James would be greatly missed.

During the days following her disappearance, a search party, led by Yavapai County Deputy Sheriff George Thompson, scoured the Black Mountains for any clue that would lead to her or two other missing young women. While hopes remained that Annabelle had just left town on a whim without telling anyone, this was not something she had any history of doing. She wasn't the first woman of her profession to have been reported to the town marshal's office as missing lately.

The marshal's office heard complaints about a couple of young women who had disappeared from the Cribs, a district of ill repute that made up in numbers of clients what it lacked in class and prestige. However, it wasn't until one of the ladies from the Parlor House disappeared that the law started to pay attention. The women in the Parlor House earned more money, wore more finery, and took care of themselves better than any of the girls at the Cribs; and their clientèle was influential enough to exert pressure on the marshal and the sheriff to look into the matter.

During the search, a group of volunteers slowly and deliberately walked around the edge of the ravine while Sheriff Thompson studied the canyon with a pair of high-powered German binoculars, a souvenir from the Great War.

At one point, members of the team stepped over the very place at the edge of the roadway where the young woman had vanished over the cliff's edge. However, the heavy monsoon wind and rains had washed any sign of footprints, tire tracks, or any other significant evidence of foul play down the canyon—never to be uncovered.

Deputy Sheriff Thompson wore a pained expression on his weather-beaten face. His bushy dark eyebrows matched his thick dusty mustache perfectly. The wide brim of his Stetson was pulled low over his forehead. His keen eyes alertly scanned the horizon with a fixed stare, scrutinizing the vast Verde River valley below and the majestic Mogollon Rim escarpment that surrounded it.

As dusk was drawing near, he removed a fresh plug of tobacco from a small rawhide pouch that he kept in his shirt pocket and stuffed the wad into his mouth. To his immediate right, Jerome town marshal Big John Williams and one of his three deputies, Billy Ray, surveyed the canyon walls.

Marshal Williams strolled over to where Sheriff Thompson was standing. Lifting the brim of his hat so it sat awkwardly on top of his head, he gazed over the vast valley below, scratching the side of his neck. Finally, he stated, "You don't suppose Miss James's disappearance has anything to do with them other two girls, do you? I mean, Miss James has some class. She looked like something out of a fairy tale. Them other two girls were just a couple of two-bit whores. No disrespect intended, but who knows some of the men them girls rode with if ya follow what I'm saying."

After pondering the question for a minute, Thompson turned his head away from the marshal and spat a chunk of his chew to the ground, "I reckon nobody knows for sure. Hell, they ain't been found either. Until a body turns up, I reckon we just need to ask the townsfolk who she was 'sociating with and go from there. All the rain we been getting this past week makes it hard to find anything of value to our investigation. By the way, how well did you know her?"

At six feet four inches tall, the marshal was an intimidating presence. He was well liked since he came to Jerome two years earlier, earning the respect of the townsfolk. Even some of the criminals whom he had apprehended respected him for his fairness and humanity. Most of the criminal activity involved drunken miners or cowboys who got into brainless and mostly harmless acts of violence over women or gambling. This was his first experience investigating the disappearance of young women. He suspected foul play but remained hopeful that a few young women, all prostitutes, who are not returning to their regular beds may still be a coincidence with a logical and peaceful explanation.

Since the end of the war in 1919, the town of Jerome grew swiftly in size. Like any Western boomtown or any other community that experiences sudden, rapid population that was flush with money, there was a noticeable influx of degenerates from all over the country who had decided to make Jerome their home, or base of illicit operations.

The price of copper experienced a slight decline in 1920. This caused the townspeople to fear that a major shutdown of the mines and smelters of the district may be inevitable, especially since the Verde United Copper Company, one of two large mining operations in town, reduced their workforce by two-thirds.

The entire country struggled through a postwar recession in 1921, but this did not prevent the Jerome Town Council from improving living conditions. Among the civil projects they approved was a paving project which, when completed, would result in the paving of cement sidewalks running parallel to the streets throughout the entire center of the town. Outside town limits, the rut-filled dirt roads became a thick boggy mess whenever it rained, making any form of travel slow as molasses in January.

"I only met her a couple of times, once at the company store and another time when I was at the opera house with Shirl." He then allowed himself a slight grin and added, "My girl wasn't real happy with me that I knew who she was. Must have been jealous or something."

The town marshal had been going with Shirley Hudson since shortly after arriving in Jerome. She was one of the three daughters of the Verde United Copper Company's general smelter superintendent, Thomas Hudson. A former deputy, he was promoted to town marshal after his predecessor was gunned down in front of the Bank of Jerome following a botched robbery attempt the previous year.

"She was one hell of a perty lady." He caught himself using the past tense, then stated, "I highly doubt that she killed herself. Those girls at the Parlor House are taken care of perty good. Sure would hate to see something bad happen to her though."

"Yeah, me too," Thompson replied. "I don't believe any whore, or any respectable woman for that matter, should be treated like an animal, but the town has got a lot of shady characters mixed in with the good folk these days. Prohibition ain't changed anything. Some of that hooch men are drinkin' makes them plum loco." He turned his head and spat.

The sun began to set over Mingus Mountain to the west, casting long shadows over the weary men. The wind picked up, and dark thunderstorm clouds began to roll in. Lightning could be seen in the distance. It felt like a heavy rain would soon be falling. "I reckon I better get started back toward Prescott. John, why don't you speak with Paige and find out what you can. Maybe she can provide us with a list of men Miss James was . . . friendly with. Might want to send your deputies around town too. See if they can dig up anything. I'll be back over in a few days."

Thompson walked up to the side of the road where his black Ford Model T was parked. He took another second to scan the area, wondering if there might be something he missed. After spitting another glob of tobacco juice from his mouth, he got in his patrol car and closed the door with its emblem, a big gold star, painted on its smooth inky surface. He then drove away on the newly paved road toward Prescott.

After Thompson's vehicle had disappeared around the winding road, the marshal gathered Deputy Ray and the three other townsmen who volunteered for the search. Those three men were Clarence Schneider, owner of Schneider's Drugstore; Roy Olson, the bartender at the Mineflower Saloon; and J. R. Wilson, who worked at his father's business, Bill's Garage, as a small-engines mechanic.

Once all the men were together, the marshal stated, "Thank you, men, for your efforts today. Tomorrow I'd like to search the gulch on the other side of town by old Chinatown and north of the Mexican section. Y'all gonna be able to help out?"

After the men all nodded their heads and voiced agreement, he added, "Good. We'll meet jist west of the New State Motor Company around ten o'clock. Now, I'm going home to get me some dinner. Come on, Billy, let's get back to town."

The other men crawled into Clarence's Ford Model T pickup and followed the two Jerome law enforcement officers back into town.

When the men arrived in the town center and found a place to park their vehicles, the dust and debris were blowing around wildly. The sprinkle that began to fall soon became a heavy downpour. Spectacular bolts of lightning zigzagged across the blackening sky. Sporadic, yet earsplitting, thunder boomed over Jerome. The noise from the thunder had people covering their ears, but it was not new to a town where dynamiting at the adjacent open pit mine was an everyday occurrence.

The few people that were still outside ran for cover from the storm, ducking into various businesses along Main Street. Clarence ran into his drugstore shouting, "Holy Jesus. It's raining pitchforks." The lawmen ducked into town hall while Roy and J. R. sprinted across the street where they sought refuge in the nearest saloon.

The chaos from the thunderstorm momentarily drew everyone's attention away from the disappearance of Annabelle James. The melancholy that had settled over the town in the past week, like the dark clouds of the monsoon, was blown away as the spectacle of the storm held captive the passing thoughts of those who were concerned for her welfare.

Everyone, that is, except one man. Looking out from the second-floor window of his rented apartment at the New State Boardinghouse on lower Hull Avenue, the man watched the deluge of rainfall over the Black Mountain hamlet. He took a swig of moonshine from a dirty tin cup while he looked out toward the north and the now-hidden San Francisco Peaks on the horizon. His eyes then wandered nearer through the clouds, down over the mammoth smelter in Clarkdale, and then to the huge mansion owned by one of Jerome's wealthier families. Their estate sat on a hill overlooking the Little Daisy Mine for which they were the principal proprietors. To the south of the mine was the Little Daisy Hotel. It housed the mine workers and, up until last week, he himself. Four or five magnificent homes of the mine executives dotted the nearby hillside to the west. He was thinking that one of these days, he may have to take a closer look at those homes on the side of the hill.

He drained his cup, actually an old red Hills Brothers coffee can, and poured more hooch from a ceramic jug into it. Gulping down another swallow of the foul-tasting swill, he took his left hand and methodically ran it over a two-inch scar on the right side of his face. His sandy-haired beard was starting to fill in, but the gouge on his cheek was still noticeable. He hoped to return to his job at the Little Daisy Mine in a few days, not that he needed the money. He was merely a mucker, a laborer who hand-shoveled ore from deep inside the mine into mine cars.

Hoping he would be able to return to work with no questions asked, he would lie and make up some tale that he scratched his face while laying barbed wire as side work at a Verde Valley ranch, in case somebody asked. If the mine didn't allow him to return to work, then "to hell with them anyways." He still had plenty of money left over. His job, that he was lucky to get, provided some cover as he tried to blend in with the surroundings. He had no real friends.

He preferred the privacy of his boardinghouse room to the hotel where all the mine workers lived. His jug of hooch was about empty, and he needed to find a new bootlegger. Along with finding another jug of hooch, he had other things that he wanted to do.

2

July 2001

Rhonda, a short, fat, ogreish woman in her late twenties, pushed C. W. into an open space at the far table in the dining hall. Her permanent scowl permeated through her thick, fleshy "hide" all the way down to her bitter core. For the ninety-seven-year-old, her presence reminded him of an old fairy tale his grandmother told him when he was a small child. It was no longer clear, but he remembered it had something to do with goats attempting to cross a bridge. To him, she was the evil troll that lived under it.

C. W. was not confined to a wheelchair; in fact, he was rather spry for a man of his age. While walking in his room on the Fourth of July, he tripped and bumped his hip on a wooden dresser, leaving a good-sized bruise. He was a little stiff and sore but thought he would appease the medical staff at Desert Winds by taking it easy for a few days.

The Desert Winds Assisted-Living Center was a retirement community for low-income seniors located in Cottonwood, Arizona. Some of the senior residents were cranky and confused. The underpaid staff was generally very professional and hospitable. Rhonda was a noticeable exception.

C. W. was a quiet person but was well liked by the staff members and most of his fellow residents. He moved into Desert Winds shortly after his ninetieth birthday with little fanfare. Seemingly in good health for a nonagenarian, he enjoyed the assisted-living arrangement over more restrictive nursing-home care. He would have preferred the independent-living arrangement, but at ninety-seven, he had to depend on others to help him get around. Not as much physically, but he was beginning to forget things. He never complained and considered himself lucky to have people to cook for him and talk to.

A pleasant gathering had been held in the park behind the center to celebrate his ninety-seventh birthday a month earlier. The staff at the Desert Winds had brought a German chocolate-layer cake to the event where many of the senior residents and staff members attended. He has no living family members.

On the "campus" where C. W. shared a small room with his roommate, Dwight, meal times were the highlight of each day for the senior residents. C. W. admired the few people who worked in the Food Services Department. He even considered them his friends.

Breakfast at the Desert Winds was described as an "expanded continental" that was self-service for the assisted-living residents and was served between 6:30 and 10:00 a.m. It included a selection of cold cereals, two kinds of hot cereal, fresh fruits and juices, assorted donuts, muffins and bagels, toaster items, yogurt, prunes, and coffee, tea, milk, or cocoa to drink. On Wednesdays, the food service staff provided a "featured hot item of the week," usually ham or a few slices of bacon. Saturday mornings featured Belgian waffles, "made to order."

Lunch was served from 11:30 to 1:00. Along with a salad bar, the daily lunch menu included cold sandwiches on your choice of wheat or white bread with potato chips. Other sandwiches were grilled chicken breast fillet, grilled or poached fish, hamburgers (either beef or vegetarian), and hot dogs. There was also a C. W. favorite, macaroni and cheese. In addition to the lunch selection, Food Services offered two choices of soup, many beverage choices, and fine desserts.

The dining hall was open between 4:00 to 7:00 for dinner. For C. W., and most of the other senior residents, this was the most special event of the day that they, literally, lived for. There were three designated seating times: 4:00 to 5:20, 5:20 to 6:10, and 6:10 to 7:00. Each evening meal featured four items of either meat, poultry, fish or seafood, and a vegetarian dish. Then there was also the "chef's daily special."

C. W. never complained about the food or the service provided. He was grateful and felt blessed to have good-tasting nutritional food three times a day. He was able to remember that at one time in his life, when he was a boy being raised by his grandfather, food was never so plentiful. He paid no attention to Lena, Maude, and Albert's bellyaching, which was a much-too-often occurrence. There were a lot of residents to serve, so sometimes some meals were lukewarm by the time he ate, but it was nice to have a well-cooked meal. Some of the ladies liked to complain, remembering their own cooking, but most of the men were easier to please. To him, Albert was simply a doddering old man.

Every holiday at Desert Winds was recognized with a special menu. On holidays, family and friends were welcome. Guests were always welcome, and their meal prices were fair. Certainly, the people in the Admin Department wanted their residents, and the people paying for their room and board, to remain happy and contented. For the most part, they were.

For about as long as C. W. had been there—or at least, as long as he could remember—Food Services employed two or three friendly young ladies who worked as waitresses for the senior residents during lunch and dinner. C. W. was particularly fond of Heather. She was of average height, but slim with an olive complexion. Her dark brown hair was usually pulled back in a small bun on the back of her head. He had seen her before when she was off work and let her long hair hang down her back. She had a sweet face that needed no makeup. Her eyes were like chocolates and complemented her disposition which was always warm and friendly. She smelled fresh and clean, making C. W. glad that his sense of smell still had not deserted him. She reminded him of someone from his youth, but he couldn't put his finger on exactly who it was.

C. W. always ate dinner at the 6:10 seating designation. He ate breakfast at 7:00 and lunch at 12:00. It wasn't that he made a conscious effort, but he had slipped into a routine in the twilight years of his life. Now, he was temporarily incapable to get around without the medical staff mandate that he only use his wheelchair and that someone from the Nursing Department assist him. Rhonda was oblivious to his routine and would come and get him whenever she got around to it. Still, the good-natured man never complained.

On this evening, following dinner, he asked Rhonda to be wheeled into the game room, where he usually met up with Dwight for a game of checkers before turning in for the night. Her reply left him with a disappointed frown on his face. "Not tonight, it's my little boy's birthday, and I'm getting off early because I still have some things to do. Why don't you just lie down on your bed or watch some television?" She began to roll him back to his room. C. W. didn't protest but clearly wasn't happy that this woman, like the troll in the nursery rhyme, whom he didn't even know until a few days earlier, suddenly had so much control over his life.

3

The men in the search team all gathered west of the New State Motor Company around ten the following morning. Billy Ray stayed at the jail while Deputy Dave Zalensky, a young man of twenty-seven years old, and Deputy Jim Evans, the mayor's son, age twenty-six, took over in his place.

Several of the townspeople were walking about town, tending to their daily business. Miners who had worked the night shift were going into the English Cafe or down the street to the Nevada Cafe where they could get a solid breakfast before heading back to their boardinghouse or hotel rooms for some much-needed sleep. Some of the miners went into one of the saloons to play poker, shoot billiards, or to cozy up next to some of the female companionship that was always within reach.

Like an eagle's nest, the town of Jerome sat perched high on a cliff, clinging boldly to the north side of the Black Hills mountain ridge in central Arizona. Along with its prosperous copper mines, it loomed approximately six thousand feet above the vast Verde River valley below. The copper that was extracted from below its homes and businesses had been a high commodity, especially during the war. It was now refined at the smelter ten miles down the mountain in the small town of Clarkdale.

The fourth largest city in the newly formed State of Arizona, Jerome exuded a vibrant energy. A cultural mix of immigrants, who arrived from all corners of the world, their presence in the town added an eclectic flavor to the melting pot. They came in search of a steady-paying job and, for some, dreams of a quick fortune.

The former mining camp was given its name in 1883 after a wealthy New York financier, who never paid the town a visit after it was named after him. Jerome was devastated by a series of fires during the late 1800s. Due to its propensity for fires, town ordinance now dictated that all residential and business structures be built of masonry. It later became known for its saloons, gambling houses, and brothels. Jerome had earned a reputation, given the notorious title in 1903 of the Wickedest Town in America by a back east publication.

Many of the more puritan locals attributed the ravaging fires to divine retribution. In Jerome, there was likely more illegal drinking and gambling, along with narcotic use, than in a town several times its size.

Jerome had enjoyed a steady growth in the past twenty years. The 1920s had brought a new decade full of hope and opportunity. After Henry Ford began the production of his Model T automobile, the horse and buggy suddenly became a thing of the past. Feed and livery stables were moved from the center of the business district to outside the town.

In addition to the American-born miners, cowboys, and business owners, there were Mexicans, Chinese, Irish, Italians, Russians, Slavs, and Croatians among other immigrants in Jerome. Most worked in the mines except the Chinese, who owned restaurants and laundry parlors. The Chinese also brought opium into the town. Many of the immigrant women kept boarders to supplement family income as miners' wages were meager.

Jerome now boasted a population of nearly fifteen thousand people. Civic groups had been formed leading not only to the pavement of some roads and sturdier foundations but also to the forming of a firefighting brigade and a municipal court to handle its mounting legal affairs. The sheriff's office had four deputies along with the town marshal. As a flourishing mining town, Jerome provided business opportunities for anyone who wished to take advantage of them.

A vertical town, the streets of Jerome were narrow, and the hills were steep. The streets were a maze, especially at night, with the dark alleyways winding into the dark from the commercial district down, around and behind them, toward the outer shacks of town. Buildings, large and small, clung to the hillside with a vengeance, as if they could topple over without constant vigilance. The dynamite blasts from the mine rumbled across the land daily, and though the residents became accustomed, the homes shook slightly from the onslaught.

A few years earlier, mine executives decided to improve their mining technique after a fire started in the upper level shafts and worked its way down nine hundred feet, killing six miners. Everything that was on top of the mine—including the smelter, business offices, shops, and homes—had to be moved. The smelter was relocated down the hill in the newly established town of Clarkdale, named after the former Montana senator and millionaire William A. Clark, who acquired the Verde United Mine in the late 1800s.

Mine executives brought in the Marion 300 steam shovel that had been so successful in building the Panama Canal. The massive steam shovel dug out a large open pit over the site of the mine. It dug out the open pit and loaded the ore onto railroad cars. The steam shovels sat on mobile rail tracks and were able to revolve 360 degrees. They had incredible moving capacity. Quite an impressive sight.

Open-pit mining brought dynamiting to the town. This new technique, called tunnel blasting, consisted of packing entire mine shafts between 25 and 130 tons of dynamite. It was then detonated in a single blast. An entire section of the mountain side would collapse into tons of movable rubble.

One day a couple years back, the "scoop" of the steam struck part of a tunnel blast that had failed to detonate. The explosion that immediately followed was devastating. Three of the four crewmen died in the blast. Pieces of the mangled shovel flew for several hundred feet. One large piece of torn steel narrowly missed striking the back porch of a home in the gulch east of town. Falling rocks and steel fell like hail for several intense, heart-stopping minutes that turned into hours of fear and horror.

The blasts rattled the hills, cracked buildings, and caused several buildings to slide down the hill. Many people's homes, including the homes of mining engineers, were condemned and declared unsafe to live in. The families were forced to relocate. During the monsoon season, heavy rains would wash down the barren mountainside, turning the streets and the gulches into flowing rivers, often causing much property damage. But the mine owners were fair men who tried to compensate all the families for the loss of their homes.

On this morning, the marshal gathered two of his deputies and the volunteers together. "Men, let's fan out and search down below all the way down past the hotel and the Mexican quarter. I know it's kinda muddy, but there's a chance last night's rain may have washed something out from under something that might give us a clue to what the hell's been goin' on around here."

With that said, the men took off down the hill and began their search, walking through mud that would be dried up by afternoon. The sound of the mining operations around the Little Daisy Mine was distracting at times. Then there was the occasional *boom* from the mammoth open pit above them.

Distracting as it was, by noon the men had made their way past some boarding homes and were searching the area around the Little Daisy operation. The mine superintendent had been informed by the marshal of their business and offered to help out in any way that he could. The only thing the marshal asked was to keep the nature of their search under his hat so there was no attention drawn to them.

The men were branched out approximately fifty feet apart as they systematically hunted for any sign of a clue that would lead them to finding Annabelle James or the other two missing women. The sun was beating down, and the humidity was thick as fog. Clarence Schneider—a single man, forty-one years of age, and owner of one of the three drugstores in town—was situated at the farthest west of the men below the railroad tracks that ran along the east side of a hill to Perkinsville.

Clarence had stopped to rest for a moment, taking a handkerchief from the back pocket of his trousers, wiping the sweat from his forehead and off his brow. Along his waist, an M1910 U.S. Army—issued canteen was attached to his belt. He removed the canteen and unscrewed the cap. The canteen once belonged to his younger brother who perished in the war. As he guzzled a drink of water, his eyes began to focus on an area where the heavy rain had formed a narrow furrow not fifty feet to the west of where he was standing.

He replaced the cap to the canteen and began walking in that direction, thinking what he had seen was merely a sheet or someone's laundry blown from the line on the day before. However, as he came closer, a malodorous smell hit him like a manure truck. He placed his handkerchief over his nose and mouth and cautiously inched forward to the object, a human torso that had been wrapped in a white sheet with a badly bruised and decomposed arm partially exposed from the torn cloth.

Thousands of flies buzzed around the decaying flesh. He began to gag at the sight and the smell, trying hard to remain composed. After a few seconds, he turned and walked a few feet away from the shocking sight. He turned to the east where he saw one of his search team members, head down, kicking his way through some tall grass. He cupped his hands around his mouth for amplification and bellowed, "Hey, over here!" He waved his arms over his head frantically. "Over here!"

Deputy Evans finally turned toward Clarence, hearing the commotion and quickly alerted Roy Olson, who was the search team member on his immediate east side. The two men ran to where Clarence was excitedly waving his arms.

When Deputy Evans and Roy arrived on the grisly scene, a wide-eyed Evans gasped, "Holy Shit!" He looked at an equally rattled Roy who also had never seen such a sight. "Go get the marshal and have him hightail it over here."

Roy ran off to the area where the marshal and the other men were searching. Deputy Evans took his cowboy hat off and tried to fan the putrid stench away from under his nose; then he spoke without removing his eyes from the figure wrapped in the sheet, "Well, it looks like we found one of our girls."

4

From the window of his rented room, he looked down to where several men appeared to be searching for something, or someone, over by the Little Daisy Hotel. He took a pull from his cigarette and studied their movements. From his vantage point, the men would disappear and then reappear again over a hill from time to time, heads down toward the ground. Every once in a while, one of the men would bend over and pick something up and examine it only to toss it back to the ground.

He had overheard two of the men in his boardinghouse talking about a search party that the town marshal had organized to look for the whores that had gone missing. Now as he watched the marshal's men tromping through the mud and grass, he thought to himself, *Go ahead and find 'em. Over there, they'll figure one of them Mexicans did it.*

He poured himself another tin can half-full of his home brew. A crooked smile broke across his face, thinking, *It'll be a cold day in hell before these half-wits can catch a wily Texas coyote like me. I'm way too smart for ya.*

Joseph Pazrosky was very mentally disturbed and a dangerous man. Born on his family's small sorghum grain farm near Littleton, Texas, in June of 1887, he recorded his first arrest at the age of eleven for being drunk and disorderly. By the time he was fourteen, he had developed into a violent alcoholic like his father, repeatedly in trouble with the law enforcement authorities, most often for burglary and various thefts. He was caught by his father committing degrading and immoral acts with farm animals on the property, and after severely beaten, he lost much of his hearing in his right ear.

He ran away from home at the age of sixteen, catching a train east where he finally made it to New Orleans. His only attempts at making an honest living were working various jobs cleaning toilets and washing dishes in the

French Quarter restaurants. Constantly drunk of stolen liquor, he was gang-raped by a group of thugs in the Storyville District as a seventeen-year-old.

He was a prolific and pitiful drunken thief who was often apprehended and incarcerated. As defiant as he was stupid, he always ignored the jailer's orders and got into one-sided fights with the guards. This always resulted in getting punished and soundly beaten.

By the time he reached adulthood, he had been in and out of numerous jails in Louisiana and Texas, even escaping from a jail in Houston. He had no desire to reestablish any contact with his family. He had gained several aliases and committed his first murder at the age of twenty-two, strangling a prostitute after she demanded more money after he forced her to perform a perverse act.

He found work on the Southern Pacific Railroad but was red-lighted after a couple of months for being drunk all the time. He then burglarized another home. He was arrested a few weeks later when he attempted to sell the stolen items to a relative of the victim. For this crime, he served seven years at the Texas State Penitentiary in Huntsville.

After spending much of his sentence abandoned to solitary confinement, he was finally released in 1916. He hopped an Atchison, Topeka, and Sante Fe freight train to El Paso where his drunkenness and violent rages left him to wake up on the street. He was always bigoted toward Mexicans and other races. Anyone who wasn't a red-blooded white American was considered less than human.

He arrived in El Paso during the Mexican Revolution where Juarez was the focus of intense fighting that occasionally sprayed out into El Paso. The violence didn't bother him at all. And he hated women, especially prostitutes.

With the arrival of World War I and Prohibition, he crossed the Rio Grande and spent his time in Juarez saloons and gambling halls. With his criminal record, mental health issues, and transitory lifestyle, he was able to dodge participation in the war even though he considered himself a devoted American citizen. He murdered two Juarez prostitutes in a matter of eight months and threw their mutilated bodies into the river.

After the war ended, he immediately returned to El Paso in search of legitimate work. He got drunk one afternoon with a soldier from Fort Bliss who was AWOL and killed the man after an argument. He later stole the man's money, gold watch, and automobile. Driving north out of El Paso, he soon buried his body in a shallow grave in the New Mexico desert. He had spent too much time behind bars and vowed never to return to prison.

He decided to change his name again. He filled the stolen automobile with gasoline and headed toward Tucson, Arizona.

In November of 1920, he robbed the home of the wealthy Tucson businessman Sterling Warner, stealing a large amount of silver, jewelry, cash, and bonds as well as the businessman's .45-caliber handgun. Tucson was a large city, and the authorities were hot on his trail. Soon after, he drove to Phoenix but thought the authorities may have got wind after he hocked some of the stolen items there. He continued his trek to Jerome where he planned on laying low for a while, perhaps finding work in the mines.

Upon his arrival in Jerome, as Henry Joseph, he became enchanted with the town's rowdiness. He got a room at the Valley View Hotel and walked the streets late at night. It wasn't long before he wandered into the Tenderloin District, then discovered the Cribs on Hull Avenue. Through his burglary in Tucson, he had pocketed several thousand dollars. He meant to meet some of Jerome's girls, and figured with all that money burning a hole in his pockets, he had the means to do it.

On his first weekend in Jerome, he popped into the Club at the Boyd Hotel up the street from his hotel. The patrons were established regulars who, he felt, were noticeably unfriendly toward him. The bartender, for some reason, didn't like the looks of him and wouldn't serve him an alcoholic beverage. He didn't care too much for the men in there whom he considered stuffed shirts. Fuming, he left the bar before he caused a scene. The last thing he wanted to do was to attract attention to himself. He adjusted his gray Northbrook dress hat and left the fraternal order where he was not welcome. He mumbled to himself, "There ain't no women around there anyway."

He crossed Main Street and entered a crowded saloon. He discovered that most of the men in the establishment appeared to be dirt-caked miners shooting billiards. This time, there were a few women scattered around but not many. He struck up a conversation with a short man around fifty years old who was standing by himself and drinking from a glass mug. He lit one of his Chesterfields, took a long drag, then said, "How's everything, old boy? You know where I can see a man about a dog?"

The short man had a disheveled appearance with streaks of gray running through his unkempt black hair. When he opened his mouth and attempted to smile, he exposed a mouth half-full of dirty, rotting, yellowed teeth. It quickly made sense to why he was not too popular with other men in the saloon. He obviously hadn't had a bath in several days. The man appeared to relish in the fact that he was approached by someone, likely a newcomer to the town, who was amicable toward him.

The short man looked around, but no one was paying the least amount of attention to him. Removing a flask from his hip pocket, he held it out. "The name's Homer, I ain't seen you before. You new to these parts?"

Taking the flask and downing a swig of the harsh-tasting hooch, he wiped his mouth with his shirtsleeve, grimaced, and lied, "Yeah, it's a long story. My wife died of influenza over in Texas, so I thought I'd get away, put some distance between me and some old memories, hoping I might find some work in one of the mines up here." Extending his right hand, he added, "The name's Henry."

The two men shook hands. Homer began to speak, "Good luck. Things are starting to pick up a little I reckon, but I don't know if they're taking on any newcomers or not." An inebriated young man, tall and scrappy looking like a wild dog, with a glass in hand, separated himself from two men he was talking loudly to. Steadying himself with the wall, he interrupted the introduction with a distinctive Irish accent, "Hey, Ethel, who's that you're sharing that coffin varnish of yours with?" He bellowed an obnoxious laugh, and his two partners both laughed aloud as if this were the funniest thing they had heard in a long time. It seemed to Pazrosky that this wasn't the first time poor old Homer had been picked on.

The drunken Irishman staggered over toward Homer and Pazrosky in a menacing manner. He looked at a terrorized Homer, whose hand holding his drink was now visibly shaking, "I seen ya share some of your rotgut hooch with this party crasher." He asked intimidatingly, "Now why do you want to do such a thing?"

The drunk then turned his nose down at Pazrosky, who viewed the drunken miner as nothing more than a nuisance, and said to him in a demanding tone, "Give me a cigarette."

Pazrosky broke into a wide smile, not the least bit afraid of this slightly bigger man, patted his full pack of Chesterfields in his shirt pocket, and curtly replied, "I'd love to, but I'm afraid my mother taught me never to share anything with a stinkin' blarney spittin' Mick."

The stirred-up Irishman's face quickly turned red as a tomato. He awkwardly lunged toward Pazrosky and raised his right arm back in preparation to throw a devastating blow toward the newcomer's grinning face. Like a rattlesnake striking a rodent, Pazrosky's left fist struck out and connected solidly with the large man's nose, buckling the man from Dublin.

The Irishman's nose burst, and blood flowed down his face. Broken glass flew everywhere as he dropped his tumbler. In a flash, Pazrosky instinctively threw two more quick solid blows to the drunkard's head, knocking him to the floor. The crowded pool hall went quiet as men stopped shooting pool in midstroke to watch what had just happened.

Pazrosky then calmly looked at the fallen man's partners and said, "Is there anything I can help you, ladies, with today?" They just stared with mouths agape. He looked at the startled group of men who made their way to the disturbance and turned his head. Before he strolled out toward the nearby front door, he shot a glance at the stinky short man and said, "It was a pleasure to meet you, Homer. I'll be in contact."

5

C. W. was lying on his bed with the TV on when Dwight returned to the room shortly after 8:00. Dwight had a worried look on his face when he saw C. W. lying on the bed. "You all right, C. W.? I almost came back here to check on you, but Ol' Fat Ass said you were just going to take it easy tonight. I asked her what she was talkin' about, that I seen you tonight and you were fine. She said something about your dinner not digestin' too good."

While he was much more quiet and demure than his eighty-year-old roommate, he thoroughly enjoyed the talkative Dwight's company. The two old men always got along splendidly, looking after each other. They shared war stories of their youth, although C. W's memory was starting to fail him. He admired the brash, outspoken man.

C. W. struggled to sit up from his prone position on his bed. When he had finally got himself straightened up, in his usual soft gentle voice he said, "Nah, everything's fine I guess. She had something to do at home, didn't feel like bothering with me too much."

Dwight was noticeably angered at the perceived mistreatment of his roommate and best friend. "First thing in the morning, I'm going to talk with Miss Spokes and tell her 'bout that bullshit. That ain't right, lying and tellin' me that you weren't feeling well and everything." He paused for a moment to catch his breath, then continued, "That ain't what we pay these people for. Besides, she's about the most unfriendliest fat-mouthed pig I've seen in the five years that I been here."

C. W. lay back down. Dwight continued to carry on, clearly more upset with the situation than C. W. Both men paid no attention to the small TV and an episode of *Animal Kingdom* that was on the screen. Dwight had an opinion about everything, and to him, he didn't watch TV because he thought the elderly characters were always the butt of jokes and portrayed in too disrespectful light.

His bickering on behalf of his best friend finally made him tired, and he fell asleep only minutes after lying down on his bed, next to C. W.'s.

C. W. got up from his bed and walked over to the window. Looking out, he saw the lighted parking lot. He watched as Rhonda waddled her way out to an old Chevy station wagon. C. W. glanced over to the clock that sat on the small table next to his bed. It was 8:40. She would have had plenty of time to wheel him across to the west wing where the activities room was. He frowned and shook his head while Dwight snored loudly on his bed nearby.

C. W. picked up a brochure next to the clock that a volunteer had left behind the previous week. The brochure had larger print to benefit the senior citizens. C. W. didn't read much anymore. He had reading glasses, but he seldom read anything anymore as the print was generally too small and caused him to strain and get headaches.

A few days earlier while sitting in the lounge area of the activity center, Dwight found a newspaper article of interest in the *Cottonwood Tribune*. The *Tribune*, usually all of five pages, came out twice a week. He used to enjoy reading the *Tribune*; but in the past year or so, he was content to sit back and rest his eyes while Dwight or Richard, the assistant activities director, read him anything they found to be of significant interest. Page 5 of the *Tribune* included the obituary section. It was in this section where he had seen the names of two of his comrades from Desert Winds listed in the last few months. He accepted that it probably wouldn't be too long until he, too, would have a paragraph on the back page detailing his life.

He grabbed the brochure and sat on the edge of his bed. He remembered when the young volunteer from the Baptist Church came over. A nice, pleasant man. The brochure was about artificial human companions. There were articles that related to assisting the elderly in maintaining an acceptable standard of life. A gerontologist from an eastern university wrote that a study had shown that most senior citizens tended to live alone and had a limited social network. These people had an increased risk of developing depression and dementia. They also had a shorter life span than more socially connected seniors.

At first, C. W. scoffed at the idea when it was read to him by the volunteer. After all, he considered himself to be in pretty good health for a man who had been on the planet for ninety-seven years. He attributed his health to a clean life—free of alcohol and tobacco. He had had very few vices. He wasn't a man who got too worked up over the adversities of day-to-day life. He tried to live his life with a low amount of stress and was very successful at doing so. However, he remembered how lonely he was for years before he decided to move into Desert Winds.

The article continued by stating that gerontologists, the scholarly people who studied the behavior of senior citizens, had suggested for some time how pets, cats, and dogs particularly helped prevent depression in the elderly.

C. W. couldn't remember everything about the article other than the part about pets, but there was also something about television. According to the article, watching TV represented a large percentage of how seniors spent their waking hours. That percentage increased directly with age. However, a harmful cycle was created when seniors, who typically watched TV to avoid loneliness, limited their social interaction at the same time by watching too much TV.

Judith Spokes, the director at Desert Winds, was a bright, attractive lady who was kind to the residents and was always having their interests in mind. She was always accessible, often making the rounds, asking the residents when they were in the privacy of their rooms, what changes they would like to see made. Dr. Spokes was also a gerontologist, but she refused to implement the ultramodern technology that some of the other senior centers with much-bigger budgets had began to utilize. Such as robots or digital pets, and computer technology like artificial interfacing and chat bots.

The staff at Desert Winds made sure the residents were offered plenty of activities during the day such as exercise sessions, bingo, Scrabble, Pinochle, and a visiting reader. Every Tuesday, some of the residents would compete in a pool tournament. The staff was careful that residents weren't spending too much time alone in their rooms watching television.

Only recently did Desert Winds implement a program where volunteers would bring in pets to visit with the residents. This was a winning situation for all as the residents adored the furry creatures. The pets loved all the attention they received from the residents. Of course, the pets were carefully screened before they were allowed to be companions for the residents. So far, no one had been bitten or scratched, although a few residents experienced allergic reactions to the pet's fur and were restricted to limited contact.

C. W. smiled when he thought of Bozo, a beautiful chocolate lab that would spend time with him one afternoon a week. The dog was so lovable and basked in the attention she received from C. W. and Dwight. Bozo, like many of the other dogs that came to Desert Winds during the "Dog

Day Afternoons" as they called it, was a shelter dog that was housed at the Cottonwood Humane Society.

Why no one came and gave this wonderful animal a good home was a mystery to C. W. and Dwight. Its heartwarming smile, tender disposition, and passion for life were remarkable qualities. Bozo also brought back memories of the loyal dog C. W. had long ago when he was a teenager. He remembered that that dog was the best friend he ever had.

C. W. put the brochure back on the nightstand and got ready for bed. He didn't stir Dwight who was sleeping soundly, as someone from the medical staff would be around shortly and get him into bed. C. W. lay in bed for a few minutes before he too joined Dwight in slumber land for another night of dreamless sleep.

6

The afternoon sun beat down on the backs of the five men who circled around the dead woman's body. Marshal Big John Williams was in charge of the investigation. He directed Deputies Evans and Zalensky to return to the jail and contact Sheriff Thompson in Prescott by telephone. Evans was to return to the horrific scene with a camera as soon as the Yavapai County Sheriff's Office was contacted so photos could be taken. Zalensky stayed at the jail. He escorted Sheriff Thompson to the scene when he arrived three hours later.

Before the body was exhumed from its shallow resting place, the remaining men were ordered to carefully back away from the scene by tracing their own footsteps. The marshal figured that the heavy rains that ran down the small canyon where the body was found had likely washed away any footprints anyways, but the volunteers, in their haste to see the body, further contaminated the scene of the crime.

The men congregated approximately thirty feet away from the body. Most of them had removed their hats and were wiping sweat away from their necks and faces. After allowing a few minutes to collect his thoughts, the marshal said, "Good job, men. I don't want to do too much until the sheriff gets here." Pointing up the hill toward the Little Daisy Mine and the surrounding buildings, he was glad that they were partially obscured from view from the hundreds of workers who were employed there by their position in the canyon. "I don't want no word of this to get out to anyone, understand? There's already been enough people wonderin' what the hell we're up to."

After thirty minutes passed, Deputy Evans came back to the area where the men were standing. He trudged down the embankment with a blanket rolled under his right arm. He handed a camera to Marshal Williams. "We were able to contact Sheriff Thompson after a few tries. He's coming this way immediately. He wanted me to advise you to cover the body with this blanket and keep any curious onlookers away."

With a brief nod of affirmation, the marshal started back toward the body. He stopped for a moment, looking up at the boarding homes and private residences that were to the south. "You men should head back into town. Stop by the jail later, and we'll talk. I just don't want anyone up there getting wind of what we found. The town will be notified all in good time. But before you go, I want to thank you personally for your help. We found one of our girls, and hopefully we'll find the other two real soon. I know some of the townsfolk are scared to death that some lunatic is running around, but we can't be too sure until we decipher any evidence we might find on the deceased. And, men, I know none of ya's married, 'cept you, Roy, but let's don't tell a soul about this. We may have got lucky in that none of them Little Daisy people up there seen what we found, and I sure would like to keep it that way. I know I'm the one to enforce the law round here but I sure wish I could buy you all a beer."

With that said, the tension broke for the four volunteers, and they headed back into town on foot. The marshal and Evans continued toward the body. When he was five feet away from it, he pointed the box camera, an Eastman Kodak No. 2A Folding Pocket Brownie Camera to be exact, to where the victim lay. This was a rather rudimentary camera in 1921, purchased by the town council for the marshal's office in 1915 for $7, but nonetheless, it was an adequate camera for their purposes. Despite the word "pocket" in its name, this was a large camera. Only the deepest pocket was able to accommodate it. It produced images two and a half inches by four and a half inches.

When he was done taking photos from various angles of the scene, the marshal pulled at the silver chain that his pocket watch was connected to, extracting it from his shirt pocket. It was 2:20, and the hot afternoon was starting to get muggy. Temperatures were likely over ninety degrees and close to one hundred in the valley. He hoped that Sheriff Thompson and Deputy Zalensky would get there soon in case the monsoon rains come again later that afternoon. He and Deputy Evans wiped the sweat from their foreheads and stared at the victim, now covered in the jail blanket. "Let's look around the area some more, maybe we'll find a knife or something. Thompson ought to be here pretty soon. We need to get in contact with Dr. Newman too. Ain't nothing he can do for her now, but at least when we get her out of this grave, we'll have a place to put her. Need to get her out of this hot sun too."

Deputy Evans spoke, "You don't reckon that's Miss James, do you?"

Without looking up from the blanketed corpse, the marshal replied, "You know, I don't think so, Jim, but I reckon we'll find out perty soon. Sheriff Thompson should be here in an hour or two."

After futilely looking for evidence around the scene of the unearthed grave in the sweltering heat, Deputy Evans turned around to see two men coming down the hill. Deputy Zalensky was carrying a miner's pick and a small shovel. Sheriff Thompson was at his side. Evans took off his damp felt hat and wiped his face with his shirtsleeve.

"Howdy, fellas," Thompson said. "It looks like you found one of the missing ladies. Good work." As he neared the scene, he got a whiff of the smell of decaying flesh. "She been here awhile."

The Jerome lawmen listened as Thompson continued, "John, did you get some pictures taken? I appreciate y'all waiting for me to get here. Find anything around in the area that might help us before we get her out of that hole?"

"Nah, we looked, Sheriff but yesterday's downpour washed everything away, I reckon. My volunteers had to run over and see for themselves not helpin' the matter."

Thompson spat out a wad of his tobacco, being courteous to spit the glob away from the other three men, "I don't think they hurt nothin'. You're probably right about the rain washin' any clues away. Besides, I betcha a silver dollar she's been here for a little while anyways."

In a matter of moments, ominous dark clouds formed over the heads of the men, and thunder grumbled. Thompson looked over at Deputy Zalensky. "Deputy, better hand me that shovel. Let's get her out of there."

7

Pazrosky awoke hungover and nauseous, trying to shake the cobwebs from his pounding head. He slowly wavered over to the window and opened it. The morning air wasn't fresh, but it still felt good. He needed to find a drink, the hair of the dog that had bitten him. After he used the toilet at the end of the hall, he would find Homer and get another jug of his hooch.

He was getting tired of laying low. Like so many other places around the country, the postwar spirit was still fresh in everyone's minds. The new decade brought hope and promise for a better way of life. Jerome had so much excitement to offer. There were more women out there, and he still had a bunch of coins in his pocket. The Roaring Twenties were alive and well in Jerome.

The mine still owed him sixty dollars for a month's work. He would go by the payroll office and get that money. He was going to get fired for not showing up in over a week, but he didn't really care. Hell, he thought, he's been fired from better jobs than this one. He now had plenty of money. Blending in with the townspeople might be the difficult matter.

He knew one thing for certain, and that was he did not ever want to return to prison. If they ever caught him for the girls he had killed in Jerome, he would surely hang at the Arizona State Prison in Florence. The death penalty had recently been restored a few years earlier. He didn't think it was fair to be hung just for ridding a community of its vermin. He was also thinking that it may be time to get the hell out of Jerome. Maybe he would head west to San Francisco.

He had taken a bag of his dirty clothes to the Chinese laundry on Main Street on two previous occasions, but the thought of these yellow people handling his personal property was repulsive. He resorted to washing the three pairs of socks and underwear he owned in the sink at the boardinghouse ever since. He had purchased a pair of trousers and a couple of shirts at the men's store on Main Street a few weeks earlier. After a drunken evening with one of Jerome's girls that he met near the Cribs, he was forced to throw some of his clothing away after they got soiled.

Now sitting in "his" Model T, he was wondering if he had done an adequate-enough job of cleaning it up. There was no blood or anything, but the car still had a spoiled smell after he kept one of his dead victims in the small trunk area for five days before he got rid of her.

He needed to go by that hovel where Homer lived and get another jug of hooch. He was disgusted with himself for not being able to find better-quality liquor. He heard that down in the valley, he could get in his hands on some "white mule" at a home near Peck's Lake that was much better than the swill he got from that old fool Homer.

First things first, he drove to the gulch east of town where Homer lived on a steep incline. His home was a small isolated run-down shanty that was formerly an outbuilding for a small family slaughterhouse operation that since moved to its present location in Deception Gulch. Approximately fifty feet away from the shanty was a small storage shed where Homer kept his still. Both buildings were a half mile off the main dirt road that curled through the gulch.

Pazrosky parked his car near the small wooden building. A wooden gutter ran along the edge of the roof into a trough where Homer collected rainwater for drinking water and his weekly wash. Behind the small shack about fifty feet set an old rust-covered buggy. Behind the buggy was a crooked outhouse.

Pazrosky walked in through the open front door that was swung open and swinging on its bent hinges. The small one-room shed was partitioned into two sections by two sheets that were nailed to the ceiling. In the front room, a small black pot-bellied stove with a kettle half-full of some kind of stew sat next to the entryway. The ashen remnants of three or four burned-out pieces of wood spilled from the front door of the stove. The front area of the home also had a rickety wooden table with one chair. The place smelled stagnant and of body odor.

Pazrosky pulled the sheets back that acted as a divider between the kitchen and the bedroom and rudely greeted the diminutive wretch of a man who was asleep on a dingy small mattress half-covered by an old blanket, "Time to get that one foot out of the grave and get out of bed, old-timer. I got some business to conduct with you."

Homer was sleeping off a wicked drunk from the night before and was slow to awaken. After a minute, he realized that his dream of walking down Main

Street being warmly greeted by many of the townsfolk was just that. Groggily, he got to his feet. He was wearing worn trousers and a dirty undershirt from the night before. The blood rushed from his head; everything started spinning. He burst past a gloating Pazrosky and fell to his knees outside the front doorway, vomit gushing from his mouth and nose. He hacked and threw up for another few minutes before an impatient and unsympathetic Pazrosky spoke in a demanding tone, "You're pathetic. I thought *I* was feeling ill this morning. Get up and fill my jug so you can go back to sleeping the day away."

Homer was on his knees with both palms pressed firmly to the ground. With his head facedown inches from the dirt, he resembled a goat grazing in a field. He rolled over to where he sat on his rump, with his short legs straightened out in front of him. He was truly a pathetic sight. He wiped his eyes and mouth with his right forearm, then tried to focus on where "Henry" was standing. "Sure, Henry, I'm sorry for that. Just give me a minute to get my shit together."

Pazrosky shook his head and bent over to help the humbled man off the dirt ground. He allowed himself to have a fleeting sense of compassion for the man as he brushed dirt off his back. In a friendlier yet still sarcastic tone, he said while eying the pot of stew on the stove, "I'm sorry you're not feeling so well this morning. Maybe it was something you ate."

After Homer began to get his bearings, both men walked back into the shack. He said, "I don't remember walking home, but I went into town last night to look at some of the ladies. I wish you could give me a few dollars so I could buy an hour with one of them ladies I seen last night. I can't remember the last time I had the pleasure of a woman's company."

"Them ladies ain't no good for nothing anyways, old-timer. You'd be better off without them," Pazrosky replied. "Wouldn't hurt if you wiped some of that stink off you once in a while. Now, if you don't mind, I need a drink."

"I got a jug in the back, help yourself, but I need some money, Henry. I got a barrel of mash fermentin' in the shed, and it'll be ready tonight, but I only got enough ingredients for one more batch," Homer said. "The price of malt and corn's been goin' up lately. Besides you, I only got three or four regular customers."

The two men started walking toward the small toolshed that resembled an outhouse. A hole was cut in the top of the shed to allow smoke and steam out. In it, Homer had constructed a small still out of a converted copper washtub. The washtub had a removable lid with a winding coil extracted from an old automobile radiator connected to a copper kettle to hold cold water. This kettle had a drip from another coil into a filtered bucket. Much of the home brew was dangerously high in lead salts causing lead poison for the heavy imbibers.

A copper still was better than stainless-steel stills at removing toxins, due to its natural acidic nature.

Homer's old family recipe for white lightning was very simple. He used cornmeal, sugar, yeast, and water. He typically made his hooch from grain, generally corn that was ground into meal, but sometimes he used rye. One a few occasions, he used white sugar instead of cornmeal, when it was cheaper, but this was rum, not whiskey. He preferred whiskey.

Homer also used a secret family ingredient, Jamaican ginger extract. He learned about Jake from his grandfather. It was commonly used in the mid-1800s as a medicinal agent reputed to relieve nausea and diarrhea. After the Volstead Act was passed in 1919, medicinal products that contained alcohol were still permissible under law. Jake had a 70 percent alcohol content. It was available at all corner drugstores and relatively cheap. In addition to being mixed in with soft drinks such as Coca-Cola, Dr Pepper, or Canada Dry ginger ale, it was added to moonshine and bathtub gins to hide the harsh acidic taste of the hooch that was ready to drink, or sell, immediately after it was produced.

Moonshining was a family tradition for Homer. Both his father and grandfather distilled moonshine from their home in the Ozark Mountains of southern Missouri, bootlegging their product to their fellow hillbillies in the surrounding hills. Like Homer, neither his father nor grandfather were particularly astute men. After his last arrest, Homer's father was given the standard four-year sentence in a Missouri prison. Prison guards generally didn't feel that bootlegging was too serious of a crime and treated bootleggers pretty well in prison. But Homer's father ran his mouth too much and was stabbed to death nine days before he was to be released.

Homer quit his job as a mucker in the Little Daisy Mine the previous year when Prohibition went into effect and legal alcohol was no longer available for the average Joe. During the start of Prohibition, it was hard for a person to find a drink. Most people felt that Prohibition caused more trouble than it ever hoped to prevent.

The distillation process required heat to boil the alcoholic liquor from the "mash" and produced a considerable amount of smoke and steam that could be visible for miles if it was done in the daytime. Homer slept during the day and concocted his hooch in the middle of the night in his attempt to avoid detection from the local authorities. He lived high on the farside of a hill and was generally left alone.

Pazrosky grabbed a jug and took a swig. After a few more swigs, he began to feel better. He could feel his headache start to go away. "Homer, my good man, I'll not only give you some coins, I'll drive you into town so you can buy what you need, and tonight, you can whip up a new batch of your world-famous hooch. Besides, I've got some business of my own that needs to get done. Now, go wipe some of that stink off you, and let's get into town."

8

C. W. slept soundly until six thirty the next morning. He and Dwight walked to the dining hall shortly after seven for breakfast. He wasn't about to wait for Rhonda or anyone else to come and push him in a wheelchair that he felt he never needed. He regretted that he ever mentioned that he bumped his hip to anyone in the first place. Someone was sure to talk to him like he was a six-year-old, but if necessary, he would speak to the medical staff and be firm with them. He was tired of other people controlling his life or what was left of it. Besides, he felt fine, and the short walk would do him good.

He and Dwight saw an opening at a table with eighty-eight-year-old Spenser and his wife of sixty-four years, Rita, a woman four years his younger. Spenser and Rita were the only married couple in the assisted-living wing of Desert Winds. They were, after all these years, still a delightful couple who doted on each other as if they were newlyweds. Desert Winds celebrated their wedding anniversary a few months earlier in April with a nice celebration in the dining hall. They had been well taken care of in their old age by their only adult child, but she had passed away, a poor widow, a short time ago, it was necessary that they move into a retirement community. They had no grandchildren.

After C. W. and Dwight had returned from the self-serve breakfast bar and were seated, Spenser looked at C. W. and in a gentle hoarse voice said, "I see you lost your chariot. You and your girlfriend must have broke up." Rita shot her husband a loathing look of disgust but knew he was only trying to get a charge out of the even-keeled C. W. It was well-known between the four friends how much C. W. had despised using a wheelchair and the tech who had been pushing him around in it the past week.

C. W. smirked and said, "Maybe I'll get lucky, and it's her day off."

After several minutes of listening to the sincere chatter voicing her concern, he was able to persuade Rita that his hip really was feeling better and that he was fine. They all then sat in silence while C. W. finished a bowl of Cheerios, and Dwight chewed on a piece of toast with his favorite marmalade.

Around 7:45, the heavyset tech walked into the dining hall with an angry look on her face. As C. W. and the others were getting up from their table, she saw C. W. and with short steps, swinging her chubby arms from side to side, approached him, "And what do you think you're doing? I went by your room to pick you up for breakfast. I haven't seen any paperwork from the nurses saying you've been cleared to be walking around without your wheelchair."

Rita was quick to come to C. W.'s defense, "Oh, he's feeling much better today, getting along real well."

With an offensive air of superiority, Rhonda glared at Rita. "Thank you, Nurse Rita, but I would much rather hear that from one of our own professional staff members," Rhonda said, accentuating the word "professional." Some of the other seniors overheard the sarcasm, looking up from their tables at the disruption.

Rita was undeterred by the harsh rhetoric of the malicious tech. "He's a grown man. If he doesn't want you pushing him around in a wheelchair, then leave him alone." For some reason, Dwight remained silent. Rhonda wasn't used to senior citizens putting her in her place, especially such a sweet woman like Rita. She softened her tone as she saw Dr. Spokes enter the dining hall.

Dr. Spokes looked at Rhonda curiously. "Rhonda, is there a problem?"

"No, ma'am," she answered stiffly. "I was just asking C. W. here why he wasn't using his wheelchair today. I hadn't seen any paperwork from the medical staff clearing him to walk around on his own just yet."

Dr. Spokes looked at C. W. and asked politely, "Is this true, C. W.? Are you supposed to be on your feet? I know that you hurt your hip last week."

C. W. looked at his shoes like a boy that had been caught stealing. "My hip feels better," he answered in his typical short sentence.

Dr. Spokes smiled at Rhonda and then back at C. W. and said, "I see. You folks understand that Rhonda was just doing her job and only has your best care in mind?" After her hypothetical question went unanswered by the four residents, she continued, "Personally, I'm all right with it, but for good measure, I'm going to have the medical staff give you a quick checkup just so everyone is sure that you're back to your old nimble self. After all, I'm no medical doctor."

After Dr. Spokes dismissed herself, C. W. and the others started shuffling slowly out the dining hall. Spenser was assisted by a walker. Rhonda exhaled a deep breath and under her breath muttered, "What am I to do with you folks?" Looking up as she exited the dining hall ahead of the foursome, she smiled pretentiously and said, "I'll be here if any of you need me. I'm off at 5:00 today."

Now Dwight decided to speak up after holding his tongue during the confrontational exchange between the tech and Rita. "You let her know who's boss here, Rita. That's the way to stick up for C. W.," he said, shaking his fist. "I'm glad Dr. Spokes showed up when she did before I let her have it too."

C. W. appreciated the support of his friends. He said gently, "Thanks for your help. I hope they don't make me ride in that blasted wheelchair." Changing the subject, he asked, "Where's everyone going?"

Rita answered, "I have my weaving class at 9:00, but I don't know . . ." Looking at her husband, she asked, "Spenser, what are we going to do until then?" She had to repeat the question a little louder as Spenser wasn't paying close attention and failed to hear it. "Spenser, C. W. asked us where we were going now."

"Oh, I thought I'd go watch that exercise class and look at the pretty girls," he joked.

Rita rolled her eyes and said, "Oh, if you only knew what to do."

Dwight laughed and looked at C. W., "What do you say, C. W.? Should we go see the morning paper, maybe play a game of checkers? You can hide out from what's-her-name."

While C. W. pondered Dwight's idea, Spenser said, "You fellas go ahead. Me and Rita will catch up with you."

C. W. and Dwight walked down to the activity center. Another resident had beaten them to the lounge area and was reading the newspapers from the previous evening, so they sat down at a card table that had a checkerboard set up. In addition to a pool table and a dartboard, the activity center had a few card tables set up with games like checkers, Parcheesi, backgammon, and playing cards. On the west side of the room, there was a couple of couches with newspapers and magazines spread out on a coffee table. Both men enjoyed relaxing here after their meals. There was also an adjacent room where an exercise class and other activities were held and a small lounge area for employees with soda and snack machines.

C. W. and Dwight were playing a friendly game of checkers when Richard walked out of the employees' lounge and saw the men seated at one of the card tables. Richard was a large heavyset man. He reminded Dwight of the opera singer Pavarotti. A single man, he was warmhearted and sociable. He was a favorite of both Dwight and C. W. He enjoyed spending his off-work hours playing Texas hold'em at the Casino Montezuma on a nearby Yavapai Apache reservation and often bragged about his poker playing skills.

He hollered across the room at C. W., "Hey, C. W., I just read where they're tearing down an old building up in Jerome." Holding the *Cottonwood Tribune* in his left hand, he walked toward where the men were seated. "Says here a demolition crew is coming up from Phoenix in a couple of days and will have the whole building smashed into a pile of dust by Friday."

Richard pulled up a folding chair to the table, sliding the chair next to where C. W. was seated. "I found this story buried on the back page of the newspaper. Would you like me to read the article to you?" A little weary after breakfast and a game of checkers, Dwight went to set down on the couch that was recently vacated. Looking at the newspaper in Richard's hand, C. W. nodded.

Richard began to read the article aloud, struggling with the word "dilapidated." "Once the sight of a wild and boisterous saloon, the Mineflower Saloon & Gambling House thrived with exhilaration and excitement during the early 1900s. A victim of a suspicious fire in 1907, the structure was rebuilt in 1910 and enjoyed its peak years after World War I in the 1920s. It was one of only a few saloons unaffected by the Prohibition era in the old mining town of Jerome."

C. W. straightened up in his chair and leaned in, giving Richard his undivided attention, listening intensely to every word as Richard continued, "Even though valiant efforts were made to save the precious ruin from the wrecking ball, a private contractor, who has owned the property since 1982, has opted to tear down the building and build a bed and breakfast in its location."

Richard held the newspaper close to C. W.'s face, showing him an grainy old black-and-white photo. The caption under the photo read, "This photograph, taken circa 1916, is provided courtesy of the Town of Jerome." The photo showed the saloon in its heyday before Prohibition. It had several men and women standing outside its front entrance. There were both automobiles and horses tied to hitching posts in front of the establishment. Richard could sense that C. W. was genuinely moved by the article. "Isn't that where you grew up? Did you ever win any money playing poker at this place?"

C. W. stared at the photo for several minutes. A gentle and somewhat-confused frown then began to form on his face. He was a quiet person who rarely spoke. Now, with the innocence of a person ninety years younger, his somber eyes looked up to the heavyset man as he said in a hushed tone, "Richard, is there anyway you can take me up there one last time, please?"

9

In the July 20, 1921, edition of the *Jerome Mining News*, a small article could be found in the bottom right-hand corner of the biweekly publication:

> *Emma Mae Lewis, aged twenty-four years and native of Butte, Montana. Time of death unknown. The immediate cause of death appears to be by asphyxiation according to Town Marshal John Williams who found the remains of the deceased on July 14 in a shallow grave just northwest of the town center. Foul play is suspected. Miss Lewis was reported missing by friends in May. She is survived by a sister, Mabel Armstrong of Billings, Montana. Mrs. Armstrong is en route to Ash Fork to accompany her sister to her final resting place, interment at the Butte City Cemetery. R. J. Sanford, undertaker, yesterday prepared the remains for shipment which will take place today. Deceased resided in Jerome for two years. Her occupation was formerly as a waitress at the Nevada Cafe.*

Upon reading the article, Shirley Hudson exclaimed, "Waitress? That girl hasn't worked as a waitress in well over a year. It sounds like the good people at the *Mining News* didn't have the indecency to print what she was really doing in Jerome."

Sitting on the porch swing in front of the entryway to the Hudson family home that sat on the hill overlooking the town, Marshal Williams patted his fiancée's hand and said, "Yes, dear, I'm sure the whole town knows how that poor girl made a living. I think it's the right thing to do in respect to how she was killed and buried in the dirt so the coyotes and all the other varmints could get to her."

"That's a disgusting thing to say, John Williams." Shirley Hudson was the middle daughter of Thomas and Anne Hudson. She was twenty-seven years old and had been teaching school, like her mother, at the new primary school on Main Street for the past four years. She was a lot of things John Williams wasn't. He was big and rugged; she was petite and dainty. He was messy and disorganized; she was neat and orderly. While he thought carefully before speaking, she spoke her mind without pretext.

They were a charming couple engaged to be married the following summer. The Hudsons were very fond of John Williams but were hopeful that he would soon one day change his occupation. In a town where violence had become rampant, they didn't want to see him suffer the same fate as the previous town marshal. He died after he was shot five times on Main Street.

The death of Emma Lewis didn't help matters as she wasn't the only girl in Jerome who had "gone missing." The Hudsons had three daughters, two of whom were schoolteachers and the other, the oldest and married, a nurse at the Verde United Hospital. They were respectable women, and the girls who were missing, and now one found dead, were single women known to earn their livings as prostitutes. And Emma Lewis's death was clearly a homicide.

Shirley cuddled up next to John, then grabbed his big right arm, and teasingly swung it around her neck and shoulder. John immediately took his arm back from around Shirley's shoulder and moved a few inches away from her. "What are you doing?" she whispered, suddenly moping as if her feelings were run over by a locomotive. "You know how much Daddy likes you."

John replied politely, "Yes, dear, I know he does, and I'd like to keep it that way."

A few minutes later, Thomas Hudson walked out the front door, patting his stuffed stomach and lighting a cigar. His faithful black Labrador retriever, Smokey, was at his side. Looking over at the couple on the swing, he said, "You're a lucky man, John. My girls all learned how to cook from their mother. You're going to end up a fat old man like me someday." The couple both laughed respectfully. Changing the subject, Mr. Hudson asked the town marshal, "You lawmen find any clues to how that hussy got herself killed?"

John removed his hat and set it in his lap. "Well, sir, we haven't found much to go on. My deputies have been asking around, and I got 'em going out at night in their regular clothes to see if they can get some scuttlebutt, but unfortunately, most of the townspeople know they're deputies and clam up when they see 'em coming. Or if they got hooch on 'em, they sneak out before my men can talk to 'em. I wish the sheriff in Prescott or the feds could bring me a couple of good men. Seems everybody's busy chasing the bootleggers, and there ain't any lawmen to spare. Trying to find these women is like looking for a needle in a haystack. We got perty lucky finding one so close to town. Who knows where the other girls are or even if they're dead or alive."

"Well, you men did a good job finding that girl's body," Mr. Hudson replied. "You know, some of these girls come here to find honest work or a husband. They get into drinkin' or smoking opium, start running with unsavory types. No family to run home to. Then they end up dead and buried in a hole. It's kinda sad when you think about it. All the more reason to thank the good Lord for blessing us. Anyways, I'll leave you two lovebirds alone. Got any plans for tonight?"

Shirley spoke up with excitement, "Yeah, Daddy, John's taking me to the movie theater to see a Buster Keaton movie. We've been courting for two years tomorrow, so we're celebrating."

John joked, "Yeah, I guess I can splurge and pay thirty cents for balcony seats since it's a special occasion and everything."

Mr. Hudson stepped off the front porch walking out toward the side of the house, puffing on his cigar. "Been two years already? Congratulations. I hear that Keaton fellow is pretty funny. You have fun but be careful. It's Friday night, and there will be a lot of hopped-up folks out, I imagine." Looking at John, he added, "I guess you'll be safe since you got the marshal looking after you." He gave his daughter a soft hug and said, "I know you two haven't been out for a while with John keeping busy at the jail. OK, your mother and me are going to go out for a drive, so we'll be seeing you later."

Mr. Hudson disappeared around the side of the house with Smokey, where the "apple of my eye," as he called it, his red 1920 Packard Roadster was parked under a metal carport. He was a member of the exclusive Automobile Club and took great satisfaction in his ownership of such a lovely automobile. He enjoyed taking Mrs. Hudson for rides to Prescott now that the roadway was finished. He and his wife would also drive down to his office in Clarkdale and into the town of Cottonwood for Sunday picnics after attending church.

John pulled his watch from his pocket and saw that it was almost 7:00. "Hey, we better be going so we don't miss the picture. I jist want my deputies to know where I will be."

The attractive couple strolled off the porch after saying their good-byes and headed down the street to the town center and the Lyric Theatre. The Hudsons' home was in an area known as Company Hill. It got its name from the number of engineers and executives of the Verde United Copper Company that had beautiful homes there. The Hudsons were fortunate in that their home had a solid foundation and did not slide down the hill like a few others had as a result of the dynamiting at the open-pit mine which was only a mile away.

The marshal and Shirley loved going for walks in the evenings. They had been forced to stay inside recently as the monsoon season brought evening rain showers. That and the fact that he was spending more time at the jail.

Unlike the Verde Valley below with its small towns of Clarkdale, Cottonwood, and Clemenceau, Jerome cooled down at night and made summer evenings nice and relaxing.

As they entered the town center arm in arm, the happy couple stopped in front of the jail, "only for a moment" as he insisted to check in with his deputies. It was hard for him to walk right in front of the jail, where he had a small apartment in the back, without stopping to see if his deputies had anything to report. Shirley waited outside. Less than a minute later, he came back out and said, "Everything appears to be in order, let's go see the picture."

10

Pazrosky and Homer drove into town late Friday morning. Homer didn't ask Pazrosky why his automobile had such an awful stench. Living in an old slaughterhouse shack, he likely didn't notice or wasn't bothered by it. Before dropping him off near the Jerome Market, Pazrosky reached into his pocket and gave Homer $25 and a list to buy supplies. Homer was told to look for him in "about an hour."

Pazrosky continued into the center of town, which was crowded with people tending to their personal affairs. He finally found a place to park the Model T near the Valley View Hotel, where he once rented a room for a short while. He got out and began to walk up the north side of Main Street. One thing he wanted to do this morning, he once considered a luxury beyond his means.

He saw the freestanding seven-foot-high red-white-and-blue barber pole outside the small establishment and went inside. Skip's Barbershop was considered modern and was a source of pride for the men of Jerome. A one-chair barbershop, men could go in, have a shave and a haircut. A man could also take a shower in the back of the building. If customers wished, their clothes could be pressed while they were in the shower by Skip's barber boy.

Pazrosky hadn't ever been in a barbershop except the one at the prison in Huntsville. In fact, the barber chair, with its black leather seat, headrest, and metal footrest reminded him of a chair he had once seen in a solitary confinement cell. But this chair didn't have straps to hold you in. This chair had wooden armrests capped on each side with porcelain and a revolving porcelain base. A hydraulic lever under the right arm adjusted the chair's height.

Skip's workstation had a large rectangular mirror bordered by two shelves on each side. A glass Herpicide jar containing combs sat on the countertop along with a hand mirror. In addition to the jar, brushes, razors, shaving mugs, and several bottles of various tonics adorned the shelves. A leather strap used to keep the razors sharp hung from the workstation. A square candle burned a musky masculine scent as a ceiling fan turned above.

Benjamin "Skip" Arnold had a successful business as one of two barbershop owners in Jerome. As was fashion after the war, men began to move away from the close-cropped military haircuts into a different style. While long hair was fashionable before the war, with extensive beards and mustaches, it virtually disappeared after the war. The unsanitary living conditions of trench warfare had sparked a cultural change for American men. Facial hair was now a rarity.

Pazrosky needed to get his newly grown beard trimmed up nice and even. His dark blond hair needed to be cut as it was almost below his collar. He waited in a chair and looked through the newspaper as the barber had one man in the chair and another ahead of him. He didn't mind the wait. Somehow, he felt like he was just one of the men here—a feeling he wasn't accustomed to, hard as he tried.

Pazrosky had a full head of hair that he wore long on top and combed straight back with a part down the middle. His beard had filled in to where the scratch on his lower right cheek was barely noticeable.

In the bottom corner of the newspaper, he saw an article referring to the death of Emma Mae Lewis. *Ummm*, he thought to himself. *It looks like they found Emma. Probably won't be too long before they find the other ones.* He skimmed through the rest of the newspaper and its ads for Chesterfield cigarettes (his brand), a cigar store selling ten-cent cigars, car sales at the New State Garage, and "Chamberlain Tablets—A Cure for Stomach Trouble."

The barber finished shaving the man in the chair. After he paid and left, the man waiting got up and sat down in the vacant chair addressing the barber, "Howdy, Skip. How is everything?"

The barber smiled and replied, "Just fine, Mr. Schneider. How is everything at the drugstore?" He then placed a white cloth over the customer and tied a handkerchief loosely around his neck.

"Well, Skip, not too bad I suppose. I am a little worried about Dr. Starr. It seems that he has come down with some kind of ailment. He's been home for the past two weeks. He's one of the best doctors in town, so I hope he gets better soon. And . . . huh just a little trim, same as last time."

"Oh yes, Dr. Starr, I haven't seen him myself in quite a while." The barber grabbed his scissors off his work station and looked up at the ceiling for a moment. "He's getting up there in age. I suppose he's in his late sixties. Hell of a nice man."

Skip snipped away in silence for a while, while Clarence Schneider sat in the chair half-dozed with his eyes closed. After a few minutes, Skip said, "I read in the paper this morning that they found one of the missing girls last week. That's a crying shame what someone did to her. I'll never understand how someone can be so cruel and inhumane." Pazrosky continued to look through the newspaper, unmindful of the men's conversation.

Clarence abruptly opened his eyes and stated with importance, "Hell, I was the one who found her." He looked over at the bearded man reading the newspaper, wanting him to hear, but the man continued reading the newspaper, apparently not interested in such important information or his heroic efforts. "Me and some other fellows were part of the marshal's search team. That was the most vile, repulsive, sick thing I have ever seen in my entire life. The girl had been strangled with some kind of cord or something, you could see the marks around her neck. She was probably pretty, but you couldn't tell by looking at her. All black-and-blue and puffy. Whoever it was who killed her just threw her body in a shallow hole and threw a little dirt and some rocks over her like he didn't care if she was found or not."

An astonished Skip stopped what he was doing and took a step back. He finally said, "You don't say! Well, I'll be a . . . so you was the one who found her."

Pazrosky put the newspaper down and saw that both men were looking at him, expecting some kind of response. He shook his head and said, "It's hard to believe that someone would do such a thing."

Clarence continued, proud that the bearded man had now joined their conversation, "There's two more girls out there that ain't be seen in a while. I sure hope the same thing hasn't happened to them too."

Pazrosky just shook his head and said crassly, "I hope there ain't some crazy person going around killing off Jerome's ladies of the evening. I was hopin' to make my acquaintance with one of them. I hear there's a whole wagon full of beautiful young ladies in this town."

11

Exhausted, C. W. rested his lanky frame against the trunk of a tall cottonwood tree. He struggled to gather his breath as he looked up at the late-afternoon sun. He reckoned it wouldn't be too much longer before the hot sun would begin to set over the western edge of the mountains, casting a welcome shadow on the town below. On this day, the heat and altitude teamed up to rob the nonagenarian of nearly all his strength and energy.

Earlier that afternoon, C. W. and his three most respected friends were driven the peaceful twenty-minute drive from the Desert Winds Assisted-Living Center to Jerome. Now, slowly, he exhaled through his dry, cracked lips as a soft breeze blew through his wispy white hair. His feeble fingers grasped a cotton handkerchief, limply dragging it from his right front shirt pocket.

He looked out over the expansive Verde River valley below. In the valley, the Arizona sun had reached a sweltering 103 degrees that afternoon, according to the weather report he had heard on the radio while riding in the activity center van from Cottonwood.

Mopping the sweat that began to bead on his forehead, he glanced over at Dwight, Spenser, and Rita, who were watching him from the sanctuary of the air-conditioned van with concern. Richard was lighting a cigarette a few feet away from the others on the other side of the van, finding refuge from the heat in the shade of a large juniper. He kept a close eye on C. W. He wasn't going to let him stay outside in the heat for much longer.

C. W.'s sunken eyes squinted as he returned his attention to the event for which they were all there. For a ninety-seven—year-old man, he was still blessed with fairly decent eyesight. But while he was in relative good health for a man of his age, clearly, his hearing and eyesight were not as acute as they were at one time.

At the moment, he stood approximately 150 feet away from the main attraction where several other people—curious or just there to pay their respects to the precious historical monument—had gathered to watch the demolition of the Mineflower, one of Jerome's most infamous "ruins."

Two large screeching cranes swinging massive iron wrecking balls had already knocked the north and west walls down to a pile of dusty rubble on the ground. The dirt and dust hovered over the remains of the Mineflower foundation like a thick cloud. Even standing several yards away, the ear-shattering noise created by the two cranes, the wrecking balls, a bulldozer, and three monstrous dump trucks that hauled the fragmented debris away from the area could be heard. It would have seemed deafening to someone standing any closer.

Ignoring the harsh dissonance of the heavy machinery, C. W.'s thoughts began to drift away. After several minutes had passed, he felt a slight tapping on his right shoulder. Awakened from his trance, he turned and looked into the thoughtful eyes of his friend Dwight. Dwight grabbed his arm delicately and gently escorted him back to the van. No words were ever exchanged.

Richard finished his cigarette and waited for the two men to walk back to the van. He carefully assisted the eldest of the two into the van, then got back behind the wheel. He pulled the van out of the tiny parking area after making sure that his four passengers had latched their seatbelts securely. Heading down the hill on U.S. Route 89, the sun began to set over Mingus Mountain.

C. W. closed his eyes. He reminisced about a nearly forgotten time in his life. While tears welled from his eyes, he thought about a time in his youth he had buried inside of him for all these years. A time when he was young and hopeful. A time when he had a family and a dog. A time when he loved a beautiful girl and she returned his love. There was also something evil about that time that he had trouble recalling. The Mineflower was the place he had dreamed of for so many years.

Once the van pulled back into the Desert Winds' parking lot, Richard helped the four out of the van in front of the entryway. They all quietly walked inside, Spenser assisted by his walking chair. C. W.'s friends, including Richard, could easily sense that their friend was deeply moved, and perhaps a little upset, by the day's events.

"We'll see you at dinner, gentlemen?" Rita asked.

Dwight answered, "See you at 7:00." C. W. nodded his head and, with Dwight trailing slowly behind him, returned to his room to lay down for a much-needed nap.

A little after 7:00, Dwight stirred C. W. from a restless nap. Still tired, he walked with Dwight quietly to the dining hall where they accompanied Spenser and Rita at a dinner table. After nibbling at his dinner and not saying much, C. W. excused himself and returned to his room. After he left the dining hall, Rita asked, "I wonder why that building getting torn down bothers him so much."

Dwight removed a spoonful of mashed potatoes from his mouth, swallowed, and answered, "I sure as hell don't know, but he paid more attention to Heather tonight than he did his dinner. He was making her uncomfortable. It was like he couldn't take his eyes off her."

"Something don't seem right," Spenser added.

C. W. returned to his room and sat at the edge of his bed. Something on his mind was clearly troubling him. He bent over and removed his shoes and lay down on his back. The trip to Jerome had shaken some old memories away from where they had been stored in a safe place. Some pleasant and some sad. After a few minutes, he fell into a deep sleep.

12

The marshal sat with his large frame leaning back in his chair. His boots were up on his metal desk. In the seat in front of him, his jailer, Deputy Will Burns, was explaining about a small ruckus that had occurred the night before in the Jerome jailhouse. The jailhouse was a small concrete building, approximately ten feet by twenty feet, that sat on the south side of Hull Avenue. It held as many as six or seven inmates. The jail itself only had a small isolation cell, approximately sixty square feet.

On the previous Thursday, the marshal and Deputy Evans were called to the scene of an automobile wreck on the switchback from Clarkdale. The marshal discovered hooch being transported in the wrecked vehicle. Fifteen gallons of moonshine and the Ford were seized. Two occupants, brothers from Camp Verde, had been arrested and incarcerated in the jailhouse. The offenders were unable to come up with the $250 bail and remained incarcerated.

The jail itself occupied the first floor of the town hall. Because it just had the one small holding cell, it was often necessary to segregate certain prisoners such as women and teenage offenders from some of the men that were housed in the jailhouse. The more ruthless offenders were transported to Prescott, to the county jail which was much-better equipped to handle them.

Deputy Burns was explaining how on Sunday night the two men were getting each other riled up about whose fault it was that caused their accident and the subsequent loss of their hooch. Adding fuel to the fire, they asked what it would take to get out and get their daddy's Ford back and were told that the Ford will be sold in a town council auction. This sparked quite a brawl between the two brothers, which left one with a swollen lip and cut face, the other with two black eyes. The sheriff's office in Prescott was called to come pick up the men before the town magistrate returned from a personal commitment in Phoenix and decided what to do with them.

The marshal had, at one time, requested that the board of supervisors fund a new jail facility. He had reported to the board, at a meeting held in the town hall that March, that the jail and jailhouse down the street were unfit for the number of prisoners they received.

The Jerome town marshal's office consisted of five full-time employees and a few other part-time deputies. The board of supervisors had authorized that the town marshal receive $3,750 annually. The three full-time deputies received $1,500 and the jailer, $1,250. This wasn't great pay by any means, but it was stable income with job security. The low pay could have been grounds for corruption, which it was in Chicago and other big cities during the day, but Jerome's law enforcement officers were honest and just men. Previous law enforcement officers of Jerome were not always so fair and just.

In addition to his law enforcement duties, the marshal was the keeper of the jail, in charge of the jailer and the deputies, courts, and services of civil process. He liked his position and the respect that he had earned in the two years that he was town marshal. He had no aspirations for higher office as some of the townspeople had suggested to him. He lacked a formal education, only completing six years of schooling, and thought that even though he considered himself to be a wise man, this may come back to haunt him if he were to run for an office against a more articulate adversary.

He was happy in Jerome. He had a loving girlfriend whom he intended to marry within a year. She was from a well-respected, wealthy family who supported the work he was doing and didn't care about his lack of education and that his grammar wasn't always proper. He rarely drank alcohol, even before Prohibition, and had no history of sharing the company of the town's infinite ladies of the evening.

There was one thing that tugged at him and kept him awake at night. Someone had killed one of the town's prostitutes, leaving her body to the elements. Two other prostitutes—one of particular ill repute and the other, well respected—were missing. He understood that the most prudish of the local townspeople, usually members of church groups, thought it was sinful and punishable by eternal damnation to give one's body to another out of wedlock for the sole purpose of financial gain. He never paid a penny to have a woman but understood that some men needed to.

But prostitution was not an illegal activity. In 1905, women were prohibited from entering saloons. Later that year, prostitutes were ordered to abandon their places of business and leave town. However, a year later, after a new town council was elected, they were allowed to return as long as they registered and reported for physical exams twice a month. A red-light district was even established on North Hull Avenue and several brick buildings, some three stories in height, were erected. This area came to be known as "the Cribs."

Prostitutes were kicked out of town again at the start of the war. A lot of the girls left, but some remained and continued their business under clandestine conditions. Prostitution was seen to threaten the health and hygiene of the town. Venereal diseases among servicemen in the war had become a serious problem. In some states, laws were passed legalizing the quarantine of thousands of men and women with venereal diseases. The idea was widespread disease cost the army in terms of lost time and medical treatment. There had never been an epidemic of this nature in Jerome.

By the end of the war, the Jerome Town Council lifted the restrictions. There was much opposition to having the red-light district so near the center of town. Despite the opposition by various church and civic groups, it was 1921—the Roaring Twenties was in its infancy. They were allowed to be there and perform their nefarious services.

The marshal wasn't nearly as concerned about prostitution or illegal acts against prohibition as much as he wanted to find the person or persons responsible for the murder of Emma Lewis and the unexplained disappearance of Annabelle James and Jenny Richardson.

13

Pazrosky's comments about the dead woman did not endear himself to Skip the barber or Clarence Schneider. There was little conversation between him and the barber as he got a haircut and his shaggy beard trimmed. Clarence quickly left the barbershop when Skip had finished cutting his hair. Pazrosky didn't care. He was now as well groomed as he could ever remember. He considered himself a devilishly handsome man. Looking at himself in the large mirror, he wished his hair was darker. He almost asked the barber a question about it before he caught himself.

He walked out of the barbershop and headed to the parked automobile. He wanted to drive by the payroll office at the Little Daisy Mine and get the money they owed him. As he got back in the vehicle, he wished there was something he could do to get rid of the dreadful smell. Oh well, he would worry about that later.

He drove out to the payroll office, parked, and went inside. He walked up to the man sitting behind a desk in an anterior office. He told the man who he was, "Henry Joseph." And he also told him that he had been down with what he was afraid may have been consumption and has been away. Even though he said a doctor told him it wasn't consumption, the man was quick to pass him on to the payroll clerk.

Consumption was a disease known to be the result of germs being passed through the air and contagious. The man thought it was unlikely that Joseph had consumption as he appeared rather healthy and had only missed a couple weeks of work. He thought it was more likely that Mr. Joseph was just a drunkard.

Pazrosky knocked on the door marked Payroll Clerk and entered after a man behind the door yelled for him to come in. He told the clerk who he was and that he was here to pick up four week's pay that he was owed. The clerk, a small man wearing thick eyeglasses, shuffled through a mountain of paper on his desk until he came across the one he was searching for. "Oh yes, Henry Joseph." He crunched some numbers on another piece of paper; then without looking up, he said, "I'm afraid with the slowdown, we can't give you your job back. Copper prices have been tumbling down faster than an old man falling down a hill, but we can pay you what we owe you, $74." Then he filled out a banknote and handed it to him, saying, "If you take this to the Bank of Jerome in the Bartlett Hotel, they will give you $74 silver for it. If things pick up, come back and see us."

Pazrosky feigned a look of discouragement, exhaling heavily, then said, "Yes, sir. I understand. Thanks." He walked out, and a smile broke on his face when he left the building. He still had enough money to last him for a long time. He was tired of the hard, dirty work of a mine mucker. He had a plan he was going to run by Homer. He wanted to increase the volume of hooch that he had been brewing. Expand Homer's little business.

He had a fresh haircut, a nice trimmed beard, money in his pocket, an automobile. He thought he would take himself out to dinner, treat himself to a nice meal, perhaps a big steak and potato. Then he would finish the night off in the company of one of Jerome's finest ladies. Not like those first two whom he ran into off Hull Avenue, openly flaunting their sex to him like he was some kind of leper who was not capable of getting a woman without having to pay for it. No, he would pay $100 for a sweet-smelling beautiful woman. Like the fine-smelling gal that he met in the clothing store. He didn't have to kill. If she allowed him to be himself, then no harm would come of her.

He didn't know where his hatred of women, particularly prostitutes, came from. He had once fallen in love with a woman as a young man in New Orleans. He accused her of prostituting herself when he was locked up for thirty days for a burglary. He had strangled her to death. She was a two-bit whore that deserved to be punished.

Perhaps his hatred of prostitutes stemmed from displaced anger from the love he never received from his mother. Or the fact that she, too, was a whore. He remembers her locking the door to the bedroom with his uncle and a delivery man when he was just a kid and his father was doing time in a Lubbock jail. She was drinking plum wine and laughing with Uncle Bob—and she wasn't wearing all her clothes. He remembers how confused he was at the time. He thought that she should be sad because Poppa was away, but he had never seen her happier.

He remembered the day he saw his mother with Uncle Bob in his parents' bedroom. He was so angry. He didn't know how to control it. He went outside and swung the cat by its tail and smashed its head on the ground. Then he cried because he really loved Fluff. But after that day, he didn't cry anymore.

14

Ashley sat in front of the beveled mirror, running a sterling silver hairbrush through her thick auburn hair. The Olde English hairbrush was a gift from a wealthy Prescott rancher whom she had "befriended." The scallop-shaped mirror, adorned by soft white roses, hung from a copper nail above her mahogany dresser.

Running a brush through her luscious long hair, keeping a written diary of her daily events, and saying her prayers were part of her evening rituals. The roman numerals of her key-winded mantel clock indicated that it was 10:45. The end of a rather long day was coming to its merciful end. She was looking forward to a good night's rest.

She set her brush down, got up from the chair, and walked barefoot across the carpeted floor of her bedroom toward the French doors that opened out into a tiny front balcony area. While she longed for a deep breath of fresh mountain evening air, this would not be the night. On this evening, there was no welcomed breeze.

Her spacious bedroom was on the second floor in the southeast corner of the establishment. She unlatched the glass doors and walked out onto the balcony overlooking East Avenue and Main Street. Lost in thought, she was oblivious to the lust-filled stares from the sidewalk below. The hoots and hollers of the drunken men carousing the town street fell on deaf ears.

Breathing clean, crisp mountain air in a booming copper-mining town like Jerome was a rare event. Nothing like where she was from. While the gigantic smelter and its three towering smokestacks, once located on the edge of town, was relocated down in the valley to the town of Clarkdale a few years before, the acrid smoke that ascended from the valley below made life malodorous.

On extraordinary occasions, when the air was clear, Ashley was able to look up at the nearby mountain range that surrounded Cleopatra Hill.

Once covered in ponderosa pine trees, the hills that wrapped around Jerome were now barren. The noxious fumes from the copper smelter poisoned and suffocated plant life. Years of timber use for wooden structures, including the mine shafts, had stripped the hills of the rest of its vegetation.

Ashley had loved the smell of the pine trees, which reminded her of her family home near Payson. But on this warm night, a sulfuric cloud hovered above the town. With no breeze, the haze struggled to disperse over the vast Verde River valley below.

She pulled the drawstrings around her robe tighter and looked down on the street. It was still abuzz with the jubilant sound of inebriated men yelling and automobiles honking.

Ashley had arrived in Jerome six months earlier, shortly after her first Christmas spent alone. The town she left behind had been a day's travel by coach. The Verde Valley Stage Company had cars leave and arrive morning and afternoon at the Union Depot.

The past fall, her beloved mother finally lost her long battle with Spanish influenza. Ashley still felt the painful loss of her mother's soft voice and loving presence.

She thought of how her mother met her father in Las Cruces, New Mexico. It wasn't long before the couple realized they were perfect for each other. After their wedding, they moved to Payson, Arizona. Sometime in the late 1800s, they decided to have a child. They lived humbly, never wasting a penny. They made a hard, honest living and provided their daughter with everything she needed. Devoted members of the Catholic Church in Payson, they were very protective of her. Ashley hadn't been in a church since her mother's funeral. She now felt an urge to attend the Holy Family Catholic Church in Jerome for spiritual repose.

Ashley softly closed her eyes and enjoyed a pleasant reflection of her father. She enjoyed as close a friendship with him as she did her mother. He was born and raised in the small New Mexico town of Ruidoso, one of five siblings. As a young man, he herded cattle along the Chisholm Trail from San Antonio, Texas, to Caldwell, Kansas. He would rise before the sun and work all day. After herding cattle for others, he collected enough savings to start his own herd. Very careful with his earnings, he never wasted his money on booze, gambling, or women. He managed well and survived the panic years of the early 1890s. He later moved to west Texas to be near his ailing mother. Having cattle business in Las Cruces, he met Ashley's mother, Maria, there.

In a terrible blow for Ashley, he died three years earlier, at the age of forty-nine, after he fell from a windmill tower he was repairing on their Payson ranch.

Ashley closed the balcony doors behind her and reentered the bedroom area. A colorful twenty-four-inch square oil canvas of a horse drinking from a mountain stream hung on the east wall near her brass bed. The rest of her bedroom furniture consisted of a marble washstand and ladies' parlor desk. A small opal glass oil lamp burned on her nightstand, providing soft lighting and a relaxing ambiance. In the southwest corner was a cast-iron pot-bellied stove, which she had little need for another few months. The stovepipe went directly up to the roof. Fuel for the stove was stored in a small woodshed behind the house. The wood for the home was often donated by the clientèle.

Her wardrobe was full of many fine gowns, dresses, and robes. She loved wearing her French-embroidered silk robes. She also had a Chinese cherry-print silk robe that she often wore. Both were gifts from men who held her in high esteem. Much of her wardrobe remained Western style. Although she rarely rode horseback anymore, she still enjoyed wearing one of her several brushed twill riding skirts. She had no interest in the fashion that was beginning to be so popular back in the eastern part of the country.

In the postwar fashion era, for some reason, it seemed like girls wanted to look like little boys with their bobbed haircuts. Women wore longer dresses that were loose and shapeless. While the bust was flattened to nonexistence, the waist completely disappeared and shoulders became broader. All womanly curves were eliminated.

Born in February of 1900, the twenty-one-year-old beauty stood nearly five feet and six inches tall. Her slender frame barely carried 120 pounds. Since she had been a young teenager riding horses on her family's ranch, she tried to hide her girlish figure by wearing baggy cowboy clothes. She inherited much of her mother's Mexican features: smooth olive complexion, coffee-colored eyes, and beautiful auburn hair. But unlike her teenage years, she was now proud of her appearance.

Ashley never married. Nor did she ever have serious marital intentions with the only man she was ever intimately involved with. Poor Edward had died shortly after he returned from the war. He had contracted diphtheria, as did several of his fellow soldiers, in the rat-infested trenches of Western Europe. He was never the same man she knew and loved when he returned from the war. Although he never spoke about it, Ashley always wondered what it was he must have seen as witness to the worst displays of war's traumatic brutality.

She tried not to think too much about what her mother would think of her now if she were still alive and knew of her current profession. She had come to Jerome with the sole intention of being a proper lady with aspirations of singing and dancing. With her elegance and attractive looks, it didn't take long before she was dancing in one of Jerome's classier dance halls. She always maintained a passion for dancing and singing cowboy ballads. She also cherished some of the old folk songs from Mexico that she learned from her mother.

For a young woman, Ashley had already experienced the deaths of both of her parents and a man she once loved. She could not deny that in a self-centered way, she had been cheated. She was only seventeen years old when her father died. She dreamed about returning to her Payson home, hugging her parents and riding horses on the ranch. Deep down inside, she hoped that her metamorphosis from a reserved ranch girl, who loved the Wild West shows, to the most desired woman (along with Annabelle), in a bustling mining town where 70 percent of the population was men, was the right thing to do.

But Ashley felt that it was now time to move forward. She had money in a bank account—a rarity for women—and it was growing at the Bank of Arizona. In a few years, she would start her own ranch near Payson or in the Verde Valley. She was overwhelmed by the attention she now received from men and envious women alike. She enjoyed being admired. She delighted in the company of the other girls with whom she shared a residence. She didn't let any emotions get in the way with the men that she encountered. She had no remorse for what she was doing. She loved how life in Jerome had made her feel. Even though she missed her parents, she was independent and having the time of her life.

But she was also worried about Annabelle. They lived in the same house and had become close friends in the few months before she disappeared. While Annabelle often spoke about returning home to her family in Omaha, Nebraska, she would never have just left without saying good-bye to her or Paige or the other girls in the Parlor House. Her room was just as she left it that late afternoon when she went out to buy a bottle of that perfume that she was so fond of.

Ashley thought about how badly she missed her friend and what could have happened to her. She was such a beautiful and friendly girl. She wouldn't have hurt a flea. Who would possibly want to cause her any harm? She walked over to the French balcony doors and did something she had never done before—she locked them. She then took off her robe and slipped into bed.

15

He walked out of Miller's Drugstore where he had just enjoyed a rare indulgence of a chocolate ice cream soda. The ice cream soda was an extravagance that he treated himself to with his allowance money once every month or two.

He was very grateful that his grandfather gave him a monthly allowance of $5 for doing chores around the home that he would have gladly done anyways. He routinely washed his and his grandfather's clothes, collected and chopped wood for the stove, went into town to pick up supplies, and took care of Jake, their loyal and beloved dog.

Charles Winston Taylor, or C. W., as his grandfather liked to call him, was a tall, slender kid. For a boy who had just turned seventeen, he had been forced to grow up fast. In the course of the past four years, he lost his mother to the Spanish influenza and his father in a mining accident.

Since his mother's death, his life had been turned upside down. He didn't know what he would have done if it hadn't been for her father, who quit his job panning gold in Crown Point and came to Jerome to take care of him and their small piece of property, which he was able save from foreclosure.

Now standing on the corner of Main Street and Jerome Avenue, he was thinking about what he wanted to do next. He had purchased some groceries the day before, so he and his grandfather were OK with enough supplies to last them for a while. He just stood there basking in the afterglow of his ice cream soda.

C. W. quit going to school the year before so he could help his grandfather around their small house. He was offered a job as a delivery boy for the Safeway Store, but he and his grandfather thought for the time being, it would be better for him to help around the house. Now that he was seventeen years old, he wanted to find a job. He would talk to his grandfather about it.

C. W.'s grandfather, Barney Parker, had always worked with his hands digging for iron, coal, silver, gold, and now copper. He had the calluses on his rough, dirty hands to prove it. With his thick white beard, he resembled ole Saint Nick after he just climbed down a soot-filled chimney. He had friendly blue eyes that twinkled when the sun shined in them just right. His Levi Strauss overalls were always caked in dirt or mud from the mines.

Born in 1864 in Hibbing, Minnesota, he was now a man of fifty-seven years. He got his first taste of mine work after extensive iron ore deposits were discovered in the hills of northeast Minnesota. He loved the hard work and physical rewards of working in the mines. He enjoyed being near his daughter until her death four years ago. Eighteen months later, he lost his son-in-law when a steam shovel detonated dynamite that had failed to explode during a tunnel-blasting operation. The blast killed him and three other men. He came to Jerome to be near his only kin, his thirteen-year-old grandson.

Like his grandson, Barney was also left without parents to raise him as a young man. When he was just an infant, his father died in the closing days of the Civil War. His mother died during a three-day blizzard in the winter of 1873 when he was only nine. He moved in with an aunt and uncle but was on his own by the age of fifteen. He married a Canadian woman when he was nineteen. They traveled and lived together as he worked the mines of Minnesota, Montana, and Colorado before settling in Crown Point, Arizona, to pan for gold in the late 1880s. He had one daughter but lost his wife during childbirth.

Now all he had was his grandson, C. W., and all C. W. had was his grandpa and their lovable hound, Jake. Although their home was just a small one-bedroom wooden house in the Mexican section, he fought tooth and nail to keep the greedy bankers at the Bank of Arizona from filing a foreclosure notification. He currently worked as a mucker at the Verde United Mine, keeping rocky debris cleared away from the work site so the drillers and tappers could drill the holes for the next round of blasting.

Barney worked the second shift at the mine, usually returning home around ten thirty every night. He loved his grandson and was always good to him. He didn't demand anything. All he asked was that the small home be kept nice and clean as possible, and that there was a can of beans or stew ready for him to eat when he returned from work. Clean laundry was not a priority for Barney as he knew as a miner, his clothes were going to get dirty. But C. W. did his best, and the two got along wonderfully.

C. W. took the death of his parents very hard. But Barney took him under his wing, coming to Jerome, the only place the boy ever knew as home. He was struggling in school, although he could read well, so Barney took him out and gave him a small allowance for doing the household chores. Barney worked hard, stayed out of trouble, and expected the same from C.W.

C. W. and his grandfather were huge fans of professional baseball. They adored the mean-spirited Ty Cobb and remained faithful even through the Black Sox Scandal of 1919 when the Chicago White Sox were paid by gamblers to lose the World Series against the Cincinnati Reds. They each had baseball mitts and would play catch sometimes before Barney had to go to work. Now their favorite player was Babe Ruth; the once-dominant pitcher of the Boston Red Sox, he was traded to the New York Yankees and hit fifty-four home runs the previous season.

Locally, they would watch baseball games between a team from Jerome against their heated rivalry from a team in Clarkdale. These teams were formed by the Verde United Copper Company to keep the young men entertained and so they would stay close to home. Often the games were so heated that fights would break out. Nonetheless, there was a lot of baseball talent on the field, and their games were fun to watch.

C. W. and his grandfather also enjoyed boxing. They worshiped the Manassa Mauler, Jack Dempsey. Before Independence Day that summer, he fought Frenchman Georges Carpenter in front of a New Jersey crowd of ninety-some thousand people. The fight was broadcast by RCA nationwide. Barney's shift foreman, Pete Smith, had a homemade radio set in his home and invited a small group of men, including Barney who brought C. W. with him, to his home where they listened as the bigger and stronger Dempsey administered a brutal beating to the Frenchman, knocking him out in the fourth round.

C. W. was enjoying the summer of 1921. He wanted to go to work now that he was seventeen. He would speak to his grandfather about this. He didn't think that his grandfather would mind after they discussed it. He knew how worried his grandfather was that something might happen to him where he could get hurt or worse, like his father. But he was all grown-up and strong for his lean frame. He thought while he was in town, he would go by the Safeway Store and see if Mr. Baker still needed a delivery boy. He could still get his household chores done and bring in a little money so he and his grandfather could live a little better or at least eat a little better.

He was walking down the north side of Main Street in front of the Bartlett Hotel when he bumped into two large men coming out the hotel's front entrance wearing badges. He couldn't help see the six-pointed star with "Special Deputy U.S. Marshal" that was pinned to one of the men's swollen chest. "Whoa, excuse me there, partner," he said. "Be careful, you almost knocked me down," he joked.

C. W. muttered, "Sorry, sir." And he continued walking down the street, turning around to look at the federal marshals, who were impressive in their confident swagger, big guns in holsters at their side. He wondered what they were doing in town but supposed they were there to make sure the saloons or gambling halls weren't serving alcohol to anyone. He watched as they crossed the street and headed toward the town hall.

He was thinking how Marshal Williams was also a big man who commanded a great deal of respect. Maybe someday he would be a lawman, perhaps even a U.S. marshal, when he got a little older. He enjoyed hunting for birds and rabbits and considered himself a pretty good shot with a rifle. His father had taught him to shoot a rifle when he was eleven years old. He had never shot one of those heavy pistols that the lawmen carried though. Although he just figured he would end up working in the mines like his father and grandfather, he imagined himself as a U.S. marshal traveling around the state and staying in fancy hotels.

While the primary duties of U.S. marshals during the war were to protect the home front while American soldiers were fighting in the trenches of Europe, their duties also included arresting enemy aliens and draft evaders. It wasn't long after the Armistice was declared in 1918 that the Eighteenth Amendment was ratified, prohibiting the manufacture, sale, and transportation of intoxicating beverages. U.S. marshals were the principal enforcing agents of the Prohibition laws. They arrested bootleggers, seizing all their equipment—cars, trucks, breweries, and storage facilities. C. W. knew that there was a lot of bootlegging going on around Jerome because he heard his grandfather talking about it once.

He crossed the street, which wasn't too busy, when he saw the beautiful woman coming out of the Boyd Hotel. She literally took his breath away. Tall, dark, elegant, with an aura of class about her, C. W. couldn't help but just stand there and stare at the beautiful lady. She pulled a handkerchief from her purse and was about to wipe something from here eye when a large gust of wind whipped through the buildings and blew the handkerchief from her hand. Her mouth opened in surprise and then a quick look of disappointment as she realized that the wind was blowing her handkerchief several feet up the street.

C. W. dashed between the parked cars and was able to chase the handkerchief that was whirled away by the summer breeze. He was able to catch up to it near the Chinese laundry. He retrieved it from the ground and walked briskly back to the young woman, handing her the feathery linen.

Taking her handkerchief from the boy, she stated delightedly, "Oh, nice young man. You are so kind to chase this down for me. This mop is my favorite. A gift from . . . my mother. I am so thankful to you for doing that." Looking down at his dirty clothes and fresh chocolate ice cream stain on the front of his shirt, she asked, "Is there anything I can get for you, a sandwich, Coca-Cola, are you hungry?"

Feeling a little embarrassed and smitten by the women's beauty, C. W. replied, "Oh no, ma'am. Thank you for offerin', but I'm fine. Thank you. I'm glad I was here to help." Rambling, he finally broke away from the trance he had fallen under, unable to resist the woman's captivating charm, "See you around." He then scurried around her and into the Safeway Store.

Tom Baker was preparing a produce display just outside the front entryway when he saw C. W. enter the store. "Hey, C. W. Everything all right? You look like you just found a $100 bill or something. Calm down a minute and take a deep breath, son." Baker took a peek just up the street and saw the statuesque woman still standing in front of the hotel. He finally peeled his eyes away and refocused on the still-panting boy. "So, C. W., what can I do for you?"

16

In the small office in the jail, Town Marshal Williams greeted the two federal marshals, "Welcome to Jerome, gentlemen. What is it I can help you with?"

The smaller of the two strapping special deputies spoke up, "Nice town you got here, Marshal. The drive from Prescott left my partner here a little queasy, but you got a good-lookin' town here. I'm Special Deputy Martin, and this is Special Deputy Forest. As you may have already surmised, we're U.S. marshals. We're based out of Tucson. First time I ever been here. We just got in awhile ago and got ourselves rooms at the hotel across the street."

"Thank you," the marshal answered. "It's an awful good-lookin' town, but we get our share of characters that come through now and then. I take it you're here to investigate some bootleggers or gambling?"

"Matter-of-fact, Marshal, we're looking for someone who robbed a businessman's home in Tucson back around December. The victim was Sterling Warner, a real estate mogul. We got an old picture of our lead suspect from when he was doing time in the Texas State Prison in Huntsville. We were informed he was in the state and might still be around somewhere." With that said, Special Deputy Martin reached into his coat pocket and pulled out a grainy photo of a light-skinned, beady-eyed man with close-cropped hair and a clean-shaven face.

Perusing the photo for a minute, the marshal slowly shook his head and said, "I don't reckon I've seen this character about town. I've got my deputies that are currently on duty somewhere. Maybe they've seen this guy around town. Can I keep this for a while?"

"Sure. We've been in Prescott the past couple of days. We'll be headin' back to Tucson tomorrow late afternoon. We wanted to speak to you and poke around a little bit if you don't mind."

Nodding his head, the marshal asked, "So what's this fella's name?"

This time, Special Deputy Forest spoke up, "Marshal, his name is Joseph Pazrosky. He's a bohunk from a small farm in West Texas. We think that he may have killed a former girlfriend in Louisiana. He did some time in Huntsville for home burglaries, then made his way west through New Mexico. Authorities just found the body of a dead GI, AWOL from Fort Bliss, buried in the desert near the town of Las Cruces. One of our deputies got together with some military policemen in Fort Bliss to assist in their investigation. He allegedly was last seen with this guy Pazrosky getting stone drunk in some El Paso bars. Some witnesses claim to have seen the two men arguing about a woman or something. They got suspicious when the now-deceased man quit coming around the bar. I guess he was a quite a regular who had made some friends there. He had some family in Texas who was sending him money and bought him a Ford. We think this fella Pazrosky killed him or left him for dead in New Mexico and likely stole the man's roadster."

Marshal Williams scratched his neck and was digesting what the man was saying. "You men think he's somewhere in Arizona and maybe around these parts, huh?"

Special Deputy Forest continued, "Marshal, we've been showing that picture around Prescott without too much luck, but one young man who worked at a filling station there thought he may have recognized the man in that photo. Said he was driving a Model T and had him look at the engine. This fella asked about Jerome and if he knew whether he could find work. I guess what reminded him was when the man paid him, he had a fistful of money. Now we know there's thousands of black Model Ts all over the country and men who don't trust the banks and keep their life savings in their stockings, but this is all we got to go on, so that's one of the reasons why we're here, I reckon."

Marshal Williams fumbled with a lead pencil on his desk, looking at each special deputy in the eye. "It sure sounds like you men have spent some time and effort on this Pez . . . Paz . . ."

Special Deputy Martin now took his turn, "Pazrosky, Joseph Pazrosky. But he also goes by Jefferson Davis, Jeffrey Davis, Jeff Davis, Jeff Rhodes, Jefferson Baldwin, Jack Allen, John King, and John O'Leary. So his name is not going to be that important. Hell, he probably doesn't remember what his real name is hisself since he uses so damn many aliases."

At that moment, Deputy Ray walked in. He saw the badges on the men seated in front of Marshal Williams and unhooked his waist belt and his holstered heavy pistols, setting them in a small gun locker. "Howdy, Deputies, I'm Deputy Billy Ray. What brings you to Jerome?"

Marshal Williams spoke up, "Billy, these here are U.S. marshals from Tucson. They been lookin' for a fella who burglarized a man's home in Tucson back toward the end of last year. They talked to a filling-station worker in Prescott who may have recognized the man from this photograph." He held out the photo, and Deputy Ray took it, holding it up to the afternoon light coming through the window. He looked at the photo for several seconds, then handed it back to the marshal.

Finally, after a moment, Deputy Ray frowned and said, "I don't know if I've run into that fella or not. Looks kinda familiar though. Y'all think he might be up here in Jerome?"

Special Deputy Forest answered, "Well, we're not sure. The boy at the garage said he was asking about Jerome and if he knew about any jobs here. We know that he has worked in saloons and restaurants as cook and kitchen help. He worked for the railroad in Texas for a little bit. He grew up on a farm. He's always been a drifter, so it's just too hard to say if he's here or not. We're sure he still gotta have a whole pocketful of cash. The man whom he robbed in Tucson didn't believe in banks. He got away with several thousand dollars. I'm sorry we can't be of more help to you, men."

Deputy Ray looked at the marshal. "I can ask around town at the pool halls and some of the mine workers, I reckon. Did you men speak with Sheriff Thompson when you were in Prescott?"

"We didn't get a chance to. He had some business in Phoenix, we were told. Spoke to a couple deputies but they didn't know anything," Forest said.

Marshal Williams continued to sit behind his desk stone-faced as Deputy Ray asked, "So this fella, what did you say his name was?"

Martin spoke, "Pazrosky, Joseph Pazrosky. But we were tellin' Marshal Williams before you came in that his name doesn't matter much. He likely hasn't used his real name in years. In fact, he uses several aliases. He might be drivin' a black Model T 1919 roadster, but that don't help you men too much either, I know."

Deputy Ray continued, "So he's a home burglar, you're saying? Sounds armed and dangerous too."

Special Deputy Forest took the floor, "He sure is. He's certainly a thief for one thing and a fall-down drunk too. But, Marshal, yes, there is something very dangerous about this man. We want him for the home burglary in Tucson, the murder of the GI in El Paso, the theft of an automobile during the commitment of a capital offense, driving said automobile across two state lines."

He looked over at his partner with the U.S. marshals before continuing, "I reckon what we ain't got around to tellin' you is that he hates women, particularly saloon girls or whores. He has a history of choking them to death."

17

Pazrosky picked Homer up along Main Street. He was sitting a few feet away from the street with a boxful of supplies. Homer placed the box in the backseat and jumped in the front. "I was afraid you forgot about me. I got them things you asked for and supplies to make another batch of our finest scotch tonight."

Pazrosky was in a good mood but hated it when Homer tried to play up to him. Homer commented on how neat Pazrosky looked, noticing the haircut and that his beard was trimmed, "Man, ain't you the big cheese. Looks like you're ready to find yourself a nice doll and go out dancin' or something."

Pazrosky ignored the compliment. "Homer, I want you, with my supervision of course, to brew up some more of your hooch. I'm going to drum up some more business so it just ain't me and a couple other guys. We need to raise your price a little, and I bet we can make a little kale."

Homer voiced no opposition to Pazrosky's plan, "I ain't got no problem with that. As long as the cops don't get the goods on me. I seen a couple of feds walking around town today. Big bulls. I'm sure they're lookin for some big fish to fry. They'll leave me—I mean, us, alone."

Pazrosky quickly responded to what Homer had just said, "What's that? You say you seen a couple of bulls walking around? How did you know they were U.S. marshals?"

"I seen their badges. They walked right by me. Big silver stars says 'U.S. Marshal' on 'em."

Pazrosky regained his composure. "I'm sure they're just walking around making everybody nervous. We'll just have to lie low for a couple of days. That's all. Let's get this jalopy up to your place. I'm ready for another drink."

Homer replied, "I'm all for that. Hey, is it just me or does your car have kinda a bad smell to it?"

"Yeah," Pazrosky answered. "I just noticed it myself. I think I must have run over a raccoon or something. The guts are still reeking through the floorboard."

Pazrosky drove the Ford up the beaten dirt road, then turned onto the trail that led to Homer's place. He grabbed the box of supplies and ordered Homer to pour him a drink while walking inside the small hovel that was Homer's home. Placing the box on the table, he pulled out the sack of malt, cornmeal, sugar, yeast, a can of beans, some bread, and bottled water on the table. He took the box back out to the Ford with shoe polish, cleaning agents, some fruit, and a few toiletry items still in it. He hurried back in where Homer had a cup poured and waiting for him.

Pazrosky took a big swig from the cup, then wiped his mouth with his sleeve. "Now that ain't bad. It ain't good, but it ain't bad either."

Homer pulled the sheets aside that separated the front kitchen area from the "bedroom" area and sat on the edge of the small bed drinking from a tin can. "So, Henry, how do you figure you're going to be able to find us some more customers?"

Pazrosky poured another cupful of hooch from the jug. "Well, first, we got to wait until them feds go back to Phoenix or Tucson or where the hell they came from. I'll hit a few of the saloons and pool halls in town, and one by one, I'll quietly get the word out that I know where they can find hooch good as that hooch that they're brewing in the valley. I know my onions, so trust me."

"I'm sure you know what's best. It sure would be nice to have some more dough around here. You hungry? How 'bout if I heat up them beans for lunch?"

Pazrosky thought for a minute, then said, "Yeah, go ahead and heat up some lunch. I'm going to walk around a little bit outside."

Homer opened the can of beans with a rusty can opener and poured the beans into an old pan. He lit some firewood in the pot-bellied stove and soon had a small fire going. The smell of the burning wood helped drowned out the stale smell of body odor that lingered about the small hovel.

Pazrosky walked around to the small storage shed. He stopped long enough to light a cigarette, content that he was on his way to a good drunk. He looked down over the hill to the town of Jerome. What Homer had said about being two federal marshals in town bothered him, but he didn't want Homer to know of his concern. He felt safe up here, away from town and the townspeople. He didn't know what the feds wanted and chastised himself for worrying that they might be looking for him. He knew that he was still on the lam and reminded himself not to do anything stupid. But were they here about that home he robbed in Tucson or the woman who was found dead and others missing? Were they here about the car or the drunken soldier he buried in New Mexico?

Pazrosky finished his cigarette and started back to the home, smoke escaping from a stack on the roof. He shook the worry aside and walked back in the hut. Homer was stirring the beans on the stove. "I got a clean bowl off the shelf for ya. Why don't you sit down, Henry, make yourself at home and have another drink. I want to hear what you been thinkin' about as fer as us getting a little business going."

Pazrosky pulled the wooden chair up to the small table and poured himself another drink, feeling the effects of the moonshine. "I was just thinking that we'll need to buy some more jugs and supplies, and if we can brew more hooch and store it somewhere, like in an oak barrel, allow it to age for a little while, we only need a steady clientèle of ten or twelve regular customers, and at $20 a jug, we'll be doing all right. We just need to keep the law off our backs. I ain't never been in any trouble with the law before," he lied.

Homer poured beans from the pot into the clean bowl for Pazrosky, then sat down, and ate the remaining beans straight from the pan. "I ain't been in too much trouble myself, a night or two here and there. I once did a week in county for fightin', paid a pretty steep fine, but never been in trouble for brewing hooch."

Pazrosky downed his bowl of beans and got up from the table. "Pour some for yourself and let me take the jug with me, and I'll be back sometime tomorrow late morning."

Homer did as he was told, pouring himself only a few cups of hooch in his tin can, leaving most of what was left over of his last jug for Pazrosky to take. He didn't care. He had a belly full of beans. After Pazrosky left, he was going to lie down and take a nice, long nap. He needed to sleep because he would be up all night brewing a new batch of hooch.

18

One block north of Main Street near the town center on Hull Avenue was where most of the town's brothels were located. The Cribs were comprised of rows of shacks with alleyways filled with young girls.

The Cribs was a block-long district commonly known as the "Tenderloin District" and less commonly known as "Husband's Alley." The mostly brick-lined alley was lined with small narrow dwellings overhung with a single white lightbulb over each doorway. The south side of Hull Avenue was lined with double-deckers where the street-level cribs were surmounted by a second tier of cribs accessible by a wooden staircase.

The women who worked the Cribs typically wore bright-colored and short-skirted dresses. Some were equipped with call boxes for ordering food or drinks from a nearby restaurant owned by a Chinese man.

Deputies Evans and Zalensky spent a good part of the morning and early afternoon walking around Jerome asking the townspeople questions about the two missing girls, Jenny Richardson and Annabelle James. By two that afternoon, they had made their way up to the Cribs District. They knocked on doors of the Cribs and were either greeted warmly or coldly. There was no middle ground. The district was rather quiet at this time of day. Most of the girls were inside "working" or resting up for a busy night. A few stood in their doorways and greeted the men who would venture down their street.

Most of the men seen at this time of day were miners who weren't expected at work until the graveyard shift or those who were just finishing the first shift and were "edgy." The deputies saw a local business owner who appeared to twirl like he was on ice after seeing the two lawmen walking down the street. He quickly proceeded down the way he was coming as if he had forgotten something.

Jenny Richardson made her home in one of the cribs. They hoped to speak with the young woman who shared the crib with her. Her cooperation, as they would explain, could only assist them with their investigation and perhaps point them in the right direction to finding her assailant.

Knocking on the door at 462 North Hull Avenue, they were greeted by a young woman with strawberry blonde hair. Upon first contact, she smiled warmly, apparently not seeing the badges on the men's white cotton shirts. However, when the men introduced themselves as deputy marshals, oddly, her eyes brightened, and the corners of her mouth opened slightly, "Oh, you men are looking for Jenny. I was wondering if you were ever going to come by. Please come in."

The deputies entered the small one-bedroom apartment. Upon entering, both immediately detected a faint smell like burning hemp. Neither of the men wanted to sit down on the bed, so they remained standing. The young woman acted a little strange as she introduced herself as Lilly Rogers. The young deputies just assumed she was nervous to be in the presence of two local lawmen.

The crib was scarcely furnished. Besides the two small beds, a Victor Victrola hand-cranked phonograph sat near a small wooden shelf that contained three or four phonograph records.

Deputy Zalensky spoke first, "Miss Rogers, we're here because we want to see if there is something we can find out about Jenny that may help us find out what happened to her. Can you tell us when was the last time you saw her and what she was doing?"

"Well . . . I think it's been just over a month. It was a Thursday night. We saw a Jack London picture . . . *The Little Fool* at the Lyric Theatre. Yeah, that was it. That movie was darb. We both really liked it, I remember."

"Did you come home right after the picture, or did you stop somewhere?"

"Well . . . let me think. No, we stopped by the English Kitchen on our way back here. Jenny used to work there. We ate a bowl of soup. Wait a minute. There was some drugstore cowboy hanging around us that night. I didn't talk to him, but I think Jenny did. He had on glad rags and was acting like he had a lot of dough or something."

"Miss Rogers, what do you mean by 'or something'?"

"Oh, I don't know. I think he had some dope. I can't remember if it was just reefer or if it was something else. I was tired, so I came home and went to bed—alone. I think she stayed out. I don't know, we were both pretty hopped up."

"OK. Miss Rogers, what can you tell us about the man? Was he short, tall, fat, skinny, dark, light? Did he have a beard? Mustache? Was he a foreigner? A Mexican? A white guy? Did he have an accent? What can you tell us?"

"It's like I said. He had on a nice suit. He was just a regular palooka. Nothing out of the ordinary. Average height, average weight. No beard. No mustache. Blondish. I thought he was just a regular cat. He was certainly no sheik, if that's what you're after."

"OK. Did she go somewhere with the man? Do you remember if he had a car or truck?"

"He said his car was parked around the corner. I walked home. She went with the fella. I guess that's the last time I seen her. We were all dolled up because we were going to go dancing. She had on her brand-new dancin' shoes too. I was a little upset when she never came back for me. I really didn't think that anything was wrong. He looked like he might have had some dough, you know? Maybe he took her to Prescott or Phoenix. Maybe she got tired of the lifestyle. I keep thinkin' she's going to come home. We drank from the same glass. You know? I mean we were close, like sisters. You don't think what happened to that other girl . . ."

Lilly was beginning to be visibly upset. She started sniveling and soon lost all composure and began to cry. "You don't think anything bad happened to her, do you? She wasn't taken for a ride, was she?" She sobbed uncontrollably for several minutes while the deputies stood in silence. Then she continued, "Her face was so beautiful. Her beautiful blonde hair. She was waterproof. She was such a beautiful person. I'm sorry. I guess I was holding everything inside. I miss her."

After a few moments, Deputy Evans caught Deputy Zalensky's eye and jerked his head toward the door. "We're sorry to upset you, Miss Rogers. We just want to find out what's been goin' on around here. If there is a man that's been kidnapping the women of Jerome, then we want to find him and lock him up. You've been very helpful. Please be careful. You may be seeing us again."

The deputies left the crib and began walking toward the center of town. Deputy Evans spoke first, "That gal needs to lay off the reefer, but I guess she has a reason to get upset like that. I reckon we will be speaking to her again sometime soon. I want to know how well she knew the dead girl, Emma."

"Yeah. I think you're right. There's a few more questions to ask there. I hope she's not in danger because she may have seen the man responsible for the girls that have gone missin'."

"Hell, I didn't even think about that. We'll need to keep our eyes and ears open, especially around here in Husband's Alley."

"Ready to get back to the jail and let the marshal know what we got?"

"Just about, Dan. Marshal wanted us to speak to Madame Cheavant. I'm kind of curious. I don't know about you, but I've never been to the infamous Parlor House before."

"No, me neither. I ain't got that kind of dough."

19

C. W. hurried home after he spoke with Mr. Baker. He was excited that Mr. Baker still had an opening for a delivery boy. The pay was $6 every two weeks, plus any tips that he may receive. He would have to run the idea past his grandfather but thought that he would be in favor of it since he was now seventeen.

On the way home, he couldn't stop thinking about the beautiful young woman who was so sweet to him on the street near the grocery store. He wondered what her name was. How old she was. She was so attractive and smelled so good—like lavenders or some other flower—he couldn't put his finger on it.

His encounter with the good-looking woman brought back thoughts of his mother. She too was a sweet woman whom he thought was the most beautiful woman in the world. He really missed her. She had been a laundress at the Montana Hotel until it burned down. Then she worked at a beauty parlor until she got sick. She was sick for several weeks before she finally died. C. W. didn't like to think about those days.

He hoped that someday he would meet and marry a woman like his mother. He had never been on a date or anything. He had no real close friends to think of. The only girl he had ever talked to was the daughter of an Italian family who had a small restaurant in town. Her name was Chiara, and she was about his age. He was shy, but the two would talk outside the restaurant until her father would yell for her to come back in to wash dishes or mop the floor. It seemed like her father would make her do anything just to get her away from him.

He meant to walk by there today but got distracted after he bumped into the tall U.S. marshals, the woman, and his positive meeting with Mr. Baker. He thought about retracing his footsteps back to town in hopes of seeing

Chiara but figured he better continue on home. He had to clear their small yard of weeds and wanted to clean up the kitchen before his grandfather came home. He still wanted to take Jake out for a walk down the gulch too.

When he finally made his way back home, Jake bounded out from his shelter under the porch. He grabbed an old rolled-up sock and immediately insisted on playing fetch with C. W. "Not now, Jake, I've got some work to do in the yard first." Sensing the dog's disappointment, he added, "We still have a few hours before the sun goes down. I promise you we'll play before then."

He walked into the unlocked house with Jake nipping at his heels. He drank a cup of warm drinking water, then went out to the shed to grab a hoe. Their home was small and quaint. He slept in the bedroom while his grandfather slept on the davenport in the front room. The home was near the Mexican section off Diaz Street between the two enormous mines.

He cleared the yard of its weeds and shoveled Jake's dog poop into the wash that bordered their property. Jake was pestering C. W. to throw his ball, and C. W. would comply to the dog's wishes. He took a brief break from his weeding and tossed the ball errantly into some creosote bushes that ran alongside their property near the wash. When Jake scampered off to retrieve it, C. W. would get back to work, muttering to the dog that he was preventing him from getting his work done.

All of a sudden, he heard the unmistakable resounding buzzing of an irritated rattlesnake in the vicinity of where he had thrown the dog's ball. "Jake!" He ran toward the wash and saw Jake, with the hair along his back raised, barking loudly. "No, Jake!" C. W. then saw the reptile curled up, ready to strike at the dog for invading its territory. The buzzing of the snake's rattle sounded like a million cicadas, except this was a more horrifying noise. C. W. dropped his hoe and aggressively pulled Jake away by his neck before either creature could strike. "No, Jake!" He was able to wrestle the dog into the house and close the door, still unsure if the dog had been bitten. Adrenaline pumping, he ran back outside and grabbed the hoe. The snake was still rattling, but its buzz had quieted somewhat. With one solid swing of the hoe, the narrow sharp blade chopped the snake below its head, nearly severing it from the rest of its body.

C. W. took a few steps back from the scene, watching as the venomous serpent wriggled grotesquely before it died. Feeling no sympathy for the dead snake, he ran back into the house to see if Jake had been bitten by it. He entered the home to find the dog still in an agitated state, wanting desperately to return to the scene and administer his own punishment to the slithering creature who had interrupted his play with his master. This was a good sign. C. W. got down on both knees and carefully examined the dog from head to toe, relieved not to find any bite marks. "Are you OK, buddy? That snake didn't bite you, did it?"

After a few minutes, C. W. was able to relax a little, although he was still a little worried about his dog. He would watch him closely in the next few hours. He didn't know what he would do if anything happened to the dog. His grandfather still wouldn't be home for another four or five hours. He would just have to sit and wait. He wanted to cry. Jake was his best friend. If anything were to happen to him, he would just die. He said a prayer and hugged his dog while the sun disappeared behind the mountain.

A little after ten, Barney walked in the door. He was greeted in the usual warm manner by Jake, alleviating C. W.'s fears that the snake may have bitten him. He tossed his hard hat aside and washed his dirt-caked hands in a washbasin. C. W. had a pot of pork stew heating on the cast-iron wood-burning stove. The stove served two purposes—as a cooking range and as a heating stove. It stood nearly five feet tall and kept the home warm during the cold winter months.

Barney sat down at the table and ripped a piece of bread from the loaf, dipping it into his bowl of stew. "Thanks, partner. You'll make someone a good housewife someday." This wasn't the first time C. W. heard this; in fact, it was quite repetitious, but he didn't mind. He loved and respected his grandfather and knew he was a hard worker. "Well, partner, tell me, how was your day?"

C. W. didn't know where to start, but he eventually reeled off the events of his day, omitting the part where he chased down a beautiful woman's handkerchief, ending with the excitement in the wash with the rattler.

"Jeepers creepers! Boy, it sounds like you've had quite a day. I'm glad you cut the head off that varmint. You don't want to futz around with them poisonous critters. Old Jake doesn't look like he's any worse for wear. If that thing would have bit him, I think we would know by now."

Barney took a few more bites of his dinner and took a swig from a bottle of root beer. "If you want to work for Mr. Baker, it's OK with me. He's a fair man. The work would probably do you some good. Old Jake's going to miss having you around, but I'm here during the day, and you'll be here during the evenings. What are you going to do with all your money?" he joked.

"Grandpa, you won't have to pay me no allowance no more. I'll still do my chores around the house, but I thought maybe you and I could just live a little better."

"Live better than we're doing now? I thought we was doing pretty good."

"We do live good, Grandpa, thanks to you taking care of me and Jake. I just thought if I were working, maybe we could have a steak every so often with all the fixin's or eat out at one of the fancy restaurants in town once in a while."

Barney ate the rest of his stew and mulled over the conversation he had with his grandson for a while before he spoke again. He was a kindhearted soul who never lost his temper, at least not around C. W. Finally, he broke the silence, "Well, it looks like you're growing up. I suppose one day you'll have to take care of your old grandpa. But right now, we're living good. Thank the Lord."

20

Pazrosky didn't sleep well. He tossed and turned until he had a dream that rocked him from his sleep and his bed. He dreamed that he was asleep in a prison cell, only to "wake up" to find out he had a Mexican cell mate. The Mexican cell mate was demanding to know what happened to his sister in Juarez, and that he was going to kill him because he knew he was responsible for her horrible death. Pazrosky kept lying that he didn't have any idea what the man was talking about. The man pulled a huge metal shank from his sock and was in the process of jabbing it in Pazrosky's eye when he woke up, wide-awake in a cold sweat in his Jerome boardinghouse bed.

"Shit!" Pazrosky was breathing heavily. He could feel his heart thumping in his chest. His sheets were wet from his sweat. He was immediately wide-awake and got out of his bed. He turned on a lamp and grabbed the stolen watch from his trousers pocket. It was 4:12 AM.

He had nightmares before, but it had been awhile since he had one as vivid and palpable as the one he had this evening. As a child, he had nightmares regularly. In these nightmares, he was always attacked in a sexually conflictive nature. During his childhood, he had several deep-rooted emotional issues—he was a bed wetter until past the age of ten, which he was always beaten for, he was cruel to animals and other children, he was a daydreamer, and he was a chronic liar. He would often self-mutilate himself by using a knife to carve deep gouges in his hands and feet.

As an adult, he would select an intended victim—generally a prostitute or young woman—and fantasize about the murder until the fantasy was no longer enough to arouse the pleasure, so he would then commit the heinous crime. He was very meticulous and would carefully scan the location, taking every precaution necessary so he wouldn't get caught. He would then seek out the victim and kill them. He often got a thrill out of extending the suffering of his victim, torturing her for several days in order to obtain as much pleasure as possible.

Such was the case with Jenny Richardson, a young prostitute whom he saw in the Cribs soon after he arrived in Jerome. He plied her with liquor and opium, then brutally assaulted her a few miles out of town. He kept her in the trunk of his car for five days, of which the first three days she remained alive, before he strangled her with one of her stockings.

At times, he hated himself and the life he chose to lead. He hoped that someday, someone would kill him and end the misery. It was addictive though, the pleasure and the thrill. It was like a drug sometimes, thinking about the lust, the blood, the pain on their face. It was something horrible and exciting at the same time. When he was young, he felt the rush from stealing and from torturing things. He progressed from animals to people—first in anger, then to feel the excitement, and to plunge into the rush of adrenaline. It wasn't long before he numbed the visions of his victims with alcohol; and throughout his life, he continued to steal, torture, and murder.

He poured the rest of the contents from the jug into his coffee can and looked out the window into the darkness. The nightmare bothered him. He thought it was a sign that the law was on to him, and his days on the outside were numbered. He refused to get caught. There was no way in hell that he would ever go back to prison where he would spend the rest of his life or be executed. He needed to get out of this boardinghouse. Maybe he would camp or build a shack on Homer's property. He still thought it was a good idea to find more customers for Homer's hooch, which really wasn't that bad after all.

He lay back down on the damp sheets and was able to fall back asleep after an hour. He awoke again around 10:00. He grabbed the jug off the floor and held it up to his lips, only to have the remaining few drops drip off his chin. He needed to get up to Homer's place. He was going to lie low for a while, real low.

After he returned from the communal bathroom at the end of the hall, he returned to his room and took a long look at himself in the mirror. He was glad that he went by the barbershop. His hair was longer than he ever had worn it, but it was neat. His beard was filling in nicely so where you couldn't see the scratch on his lower cheek unless you looked real hard at it.

Now was the time for his experiment. He removed the Shinola black boot polish from the grocer's box and opened the tin. With two fingers, he took a small glob of the polish and evenly spread the smooth pastelike substance over his beard. He ran a comb through his beard, then ran the comb through his hair. It was far from perfect, but it had achieved the purpose he desired. He thought about taking a towel and rubbing the boot polish off his hair and beard since the only plans he had for the day were to visit Old Homer but decided against it. He didn't worry about what Homer thought anyways.

He left the boardinghouse and got into his car with the foul stench that certainly wasn't going away. He thought he might air it out and try to clean it up a little while he spent the afternoon at Homer's. He knew one thing for certain, he needed a drink before he could think straight. He was still rattled by last night's nightmare.

He drove up to Homer's with the midday sun beating down. He pulled in front of the place where Homer slept and walked in the front door without knocking. Like always, the hovel had a dank, musty smell of sweat and body odor. There was a jug three quarters full of hooch on the table with Homer's cup next to it. He poured himself a drink and took a generous sip. Grimacing from the taste, he heard Homer snoring loudly but decided he would let the nocturnal man sleep a little longer while he surveyed the surroundings and had a smoke.

He liked the location of Homer's obscure piece of property. Like a strategic military position, it was located on the highest ground around, overlooking the eastern edge of town with a view of the Hogback. If anyone with bad intentions were ever to come up this way, they would be seen a mile away. He walked over to the shed and stepped inside. He saw that a clear liquid was dripping from the worm box out a tap into a large metal bucket that was nearly full. He shook his head, disgusted that if he hadn't come along when he did, their valuable product would be wasted and soaked up by the dirt floor.

He walked briskly back toward the shack and through the sheets that acted as curtains to Homer's bedroom. "Hey, wake up. You're about to spill our hooch all over the damn place. Get up." He began to shake Homer around the shoulders when he started to wake up.

"Huh . . . what . . . who the hell are you?"

Forgetting that he had darkened his hair and beard with black boot polish, Pazrosky replied angrily, "What the hell do you mean who the hell am I? I'm someone who's about to put this boot up your ass if you don't get your ass out of that rat's nest right now."

"Henry? Is that you? I didn't recognize you. What were you saying?"

"I was saying that you need to get out of bed before our hooch starts spillin' all over the damn mountain."

"Ain't there another jug out there by the bucket? Never mind, I'm getting up. What did you do to your hair? It wasn't always like that, was it?"

"Never mind my hair. Let's get out there and pour the hooch from that bucket. I don't want to spill a drop."

Homer's head was spinning as he sat up on the edge of the bed. As he followed Pazrosky out the front door, a six-inch lizard ran from beneath the bed, under Homer's feet to where the pot-bellied stove was located. Like it was a family pet, Homer didn't stir at the sight of the reptile in his living area. He stepped out into the midday sun and was temporarily blinded by the bright afternoon sky. His head was pounding, but he tried to keep up with the now-dark-headed Henry.

Homer followed Pazrosky into the former storage shed. He saw the bucket that was nearly full of clear liquid. "We weren't going to waste any. There's a jug right there under that tarp. Gimme a minute." He stepped back outside the shed and urinated. Walking back into the shed, he continued, "Here, gimme that can and funnel over there."

Pazrosky's temper began to cool off, but he didn't like Homer's imperious tone. Homer dipped the coffee can into the bucket, then poured the hooch through the funnel into the glass jug. "We're going to have to buy some more of these jugs if you're thinking about expanding our operation."

"Yeah, sure. How do you deal with your customers?" He was careful not to include himself as a customer as he considered himself a business partner now. "I mean, you don't have a means of transportation. Do they come up here, or do you meet them in town or what? What kind of fellas are they?" He was afraid that he was starting to sound a little paranoid.

"Oh, they're just some guys I knew when I was working in the mine. Just muckers like me. No big shots or nothing like that. There's Leroy, Otis, and Harry, that's all. Harry likes to drop in on me and should be here sometime soon, I imagine. I meet Leroy and Otis at the place where I met you, and they let me know when they need hooch. They know where I live, and they'll find a way to come up and see me. They all buy two jugs at a time. They don't seem to drink it as fast as you and I do. Come on inside, and we can sit down and have a drink."

They returned to the main shack and sat around the smal table. Homer grabbed a dry loaf of bread and ripped off a piece shoving it in his mouth. "I hope you've ate breakfast."

"Breakfast? Hell, it's lunchtime already."

"What time you reckon it is? I was up all night brewing hooch."

"It's after 1:00, I reckon."

As both men sat at the table, Homer grabbed a metal spoon and looked at Pazrosky. "Hey, why don't you give me a match. I want to show you how good the quality of this hooch is." He poured a small quantity from his drinking can into the spoon, then struck the match on the table. He lit the clear liquid in his spoon on fire. "See how that burns with a nice blue flame. Dirty moonshine burns with a yellow flame. This here is some mighty fine hooch, I'm tellin' ya, Henry."

Pazrosky seemed uninterested and a bit irritated, in Homer's attempt to show off about the only thing in the world he knew anything about. "I'm impressed, Homer. Just be careful so you don't burn Homer Hall down to the ground. Pass me some of that bread."

21

Deputies Zalensky and Evans decided to stop by the Jerome Parlor House and speak with Madame Paige Cheavant. Madame Cheavant was one of the wealthiest people—man or woman—in Jerome.

Paige Cheavant came to the United States from Quebec, via Syracuse, New York, before the turn of the century with her mother and father. She left her middle-class parents in New England to pursue a music career in Chicago. In Chicago, she met and was briefly married to a gentleman gambler. He was the jealous type who didn't allow her to sing in smoky nightclubs where she would be ogled by intoxicated men, and she soon became disgruntled with her arrangement.

After her husband died of suspicious causes in a fire that burned through their small home on the east side, she decided to make it on her own. She took the money which, oddly enough, was the only thing that managed to survive the decimating fire and purchased a train ticket to Kansas City. She spent some time here singing with ragtime bands and orchestras before she grew tired of this.

A beautiful woman with a heavy French accent, she found how she could supplement her measly income by entertaining gentleman callers who were smitten by her alluring features. She also had a good friend by the name of Micky Finn that added more coin for her purse.

Paige was an intelligent woman who had a keen sense of how to run a successful business. She used her good looks to dupe well-to-do men into buying her precious gifts of jewelry and furs, in addition to the money—and it was good money. But she had a bad habit of choosing men who were high profile and married. This soon led to her wearing out her welcome, especially with the prim Midwestern wives with whose husbands she was likely to have been well acquainted.

Paige later read about the opportunities that were becoming available in the west from an article in the *Kansas City Times*. She had clearly made a few enemies and had been threatened by one man in particular with gross bodily harm after he woke up one morning with little recollection of the previous night's events and $160 poorer. She heeded the article's headline of "GO WEST, YOUNG MAN . . . AND WOMAN" and once again proceeded to catch a train out of town. This time, she had a one-way ticket to Denver, Colorado.

In Denver, she found work, singing and dancing in the saloons and still managed to do a little side work. Wherever she settled, she always managed to make and save money. She also had a knack for finding trouble and was soon on her way westward again.

She arrived in Jerome during the fall of 1916 and purchased a small wooden-frame house on lower Hull Avenue. She handpicked a few young women whom she had seen dancing in the saloons and gave them room and board. Her "business" became an overnight success. The Jerome Parlor House was now the most-whispered-about place in town and one of the most luxurious brothels in all of Arizona.

Jerome was a town where the women often catered to men's needs. Whether it be cooking their meals, washing their clothes, or warming their bed, the women of Jerome were ambitious and hardworking. It was their robust appetite for a better way of life that helped make the town so fun and vibrant.

Paige's personal taste bordered on gaudy. She dressed in a different bright and colorful, yet beautiful, gown each day. Her clothing was the envy of all the women while always provoking long lustful stares from the men. She hid behind the charade of a more legitimate vocation, advertising her home as a boardinghouse. Still, everyone in Jerome knew what was going on there. Much to the dismay of Jerome's more "decent" women, Paige often flaunted her newfound wealth by cavorting down Main Street with her fine clothing, often wearing one of her elegant fur coats, in all kinds of weather.

Some of Jerome's wives and church groups complained that Paige and her girls were always in the stores shopping the same time they wanted to shop during the day. Town Marshal Williams attempted to regulate the shopping hours of the girls which would have allowed them to visit the stores only during "off-hours." John Nash, proprietor of J.C. Penney's general store, tried to calm the horrified women on both sides. He could not afford to lose the steady stream of revenue the girls provided his business. Paige could afford the best civil attorney in Jerome and often called on him to navigate her through any obstacles. She always attributed the townswomen's hostility to her and her girls' wealth.

Paige was doing so well that she moved her business to a larger brick building on the east side of town, not far from the Hogback District. She also made investments in real estate, forming business relationships with the town's wealthiest businessmen.

She never had more than five girls at one time live in her home. The Parlor House now was called home to five women, ranging from age twenty to twenty-five.

Throughout the community, it was well-known that Paige had a heart bigger than her bank account. She was always coming to the aid of those in poverty and the less fortunate. She often paid for medical care and food for those in need.

Paige was also one of the first women in Jerome to own and drive an automobile. She and one of her suitors drove to Jackson, Michigan, in April of 1920. Here, she purchased a Briscoe Motor Company touring sedan for $895. The four-passenger roadster sported a green body, cream-colored wheels, and had black fenders and chassis. It was a prominent and bold display of her success. Often, she was seen taking her girls with her for a drive through town or the two-and-a-half-hour drive over the bumpy mountain road to Prescott. They would go shopping or just get out of Jerome to breathe some fresh air.

Her girls were, by far, the most beautiful girls in all the brothels of Jerome. In addition to wearing fine clothing, her girls received medical exams and were compensated very well for their companionship. Paige spared no expense in keeping the Parlor House one of the finest establishments the town would ever know. The opulent dining room was decorated with imported wallpaper from Paris and furnished with the finest of hardwood furniture, expensive carpets, and crystal chandeliers. The building also had three bathrooms and telephone service.

The Parlor House provided what was desired to the most affluent gentlemen in the Jerome area. In addition, it attracted a rich clientèle from men as far away as Tucson. References and reservations were sometimes required of the guests. She charged $100.00 a night for services when $4.50 a day was considered a fair wage for a miner. Only the wealthiest men were able to afford a visit to the Parlor House.

The young deputies approached the front door and knocked. They were greeted warmly by an attractive woman, likely in her forties. She introduced herself as Paige and invited the men in when she saw their badges. She escorted the men into a living room off to the left of the entryway that was secluded by a small velvet curtain.

Before she asked the men to sit down, she asked, "Can I get either of you gentlemen a cup of tea, coffee, or anything? A chocolate fudge torte or a crepe, perhaps?"

The deputies politely declined, then took seats on a comfortable overstuffed couch next to a polished stone fireplace.

The cozy room had a warm elegance of a French library with its panels and fixtures imported from Paris. A walnut bookshelf sat next to the fireplace. French murals and framed photographs adorned the walls.

This time, Deputy Evans did the talking, "Ma'am, we were asked by Marshal Williams to come here to see if you might be able to help us in our search for Annabelle. We understand that she was living here at your . . . boardinghouse."

Paige's smile quickly turned into an expression of gloomy sadness. "Oh, my Annabelle." She grabbed a handkerchief and wiped her eyes that had begun to well. "So you are still searching for her? I guess you could be here for worse reasons. At least there is still hope that she is alive, oui?"

"We sure hope so, ma'am, we really do. Did she give some indication that she may have gone somewhere to visit a friend? Any chance that she may have gone on an extended vacation with someone? Any ailing family member that she needed to visit? Anything like that?"

"I'm afraid not. She is a very responsible girl, and I am much more than a boardinghouse owner who accepts rent checks every month. My girls and I are like a close family. We keep no secrets from each other." She again dabbed the tears from her eyes and sniffled. "I regret that I am to blame for her disappearance. As I'm sure you gentlemen know, my girls will provide companionship to an exclusive fraternity of men. They escort them to dinner . . . or the opera . . . or on picnics. They go for drives in the mountains or down in the valley. My girls are very independent minded but use only the utmost prudent judgment in the company they decide to keep. I carefully examine the resume of each man the first time he requests to seek the company of any of the girls who live here."

"Was there any man in particular that you had some doubt about? Can you tell us the name of the man she was last known to have . . . escorted?"

"That may be difficult. We sign contracts with our clients to protect their privacy. They, in turn, sign the contract, pledging that they will act as complete gentlemen and will treat the girls with the greatest amount of respect and dignity. My reputation is impeccable. Because for reasons that you intelligent men are certainly aware of, some men who visit my home don't want others to know that they enjoy the company of young, beautiful, and, if I may, classy young women."

Deputy Zalensky spoke, "We understand, ma'am. But is there any way you could look through your records, particularly where Miss James was concerned, and get back to us with any information that you may find that could help us in our investigation?"

"I can do that. I will do everything that I can to help you find our beloved Annabelle."

22

The next morning after a modest breakfast of toast and jam, C. W. took Jake out for a walk. Barney disposed of the dead snake so the carrion would not attract vultures or other predatory animals onto the property.

It was Saturday. C. W. didn't start working for Mr. Baker until Monday morning at ten. It was not unusual for his grandfather to work on Saturdays. In spite of the slowdown, Barney was one of the few who enjoyed relative job security as he was one of the most dependable, hardworking men most people had ever seen. Although he valued the time he spent with his grandson, he didn't mind working on Saturdays at all. To him, the money was good and the hard work spiritually rewarding.

C. W. enjoyed taking Jake down an arroyo that ran down past the Little Daisy Mines toward the slaughterhouse in an area commonly known as Deception Gulch. Just north of the Douglas mansion, not far from the slaughterhouse, was the portal of the Hopewell tunnel. The tunnel was at the base of Sunshine Hill's east side. Sunshine Hill was one of the few small hills that encircled the town. From here, smoke could be seen billowing from the colossal smokestacks of the Clarkdale smelter.

Jake loved chasing the rabbits and birds. He never seemed too flustered or upset that he never was able to actually catch one. He would always amble back to C. W., tail wagging, tongue completely extended, flopping in the breeze like Old Glory, seeking affirmation from C. W. for another successful job at running off the intruding creatures.

Yesterday's scare with the poisonous viper was still very much in the forefront of C. W.'s mind. He knew that the slithering vipers had a painful and often fatal bite and were in the washes, sunning themselves in the midsummer sun. He would be careful, but like his dog, he too needed to get away from the confines of their small home and the predominantly Mexican environs.

Although Barney and C. W. never had any problems with their non-English-speaking neighbors, the town of Jerome itself was a bubbling cauldron of racial strife. Most of the various ethnic groups lived together in blocs. These included the Chinese, Mexicans, Italians, and the Slavic immigrants who congregated in the lower Hogback District.

There was also Native American people who came to Jerome. While oftentimes everything appeared to be harmonious, there were times when the Apaches—much like the Chinese, Mexicans, and Slavs—were treated less than humane. But during celebrations, such as Labor Day or Independence Day, cultural and racial differences were generally set aside. Races and contests were held where everyone, despite of race, was allowed to compete.

C. W. and Jake made their way down the arroyo that sunny late morning. Halfway down, Jake rousted a desert-dwelling black-tailed jackrabbit from its shelter under an evergreen shrub and chased after the zigzagging hare in a valiant yet vain attempt. The jackrabbit's donkey ears flopped, and its tail bobbed as it raced through the wash. After a few moments, Jake gave up on his pursuit and began to run back to where C. W. was standing and watching his prancing pet.

C. W. waited for his dog to come back and get his congratulatory pat on the head for his efforts when the dog's attention was diverted. With his keen sense of smell, the dog followed its nose to a creosote bush and dug something out from under the bush. C. W. was overprotective of his dog and watched his actions from his position, fifty feet up the hill. Concerned that digging under a bush may dig up another rattler or the rarely seen, yet deadly, Gila monster, he shouted, "Jake. Get your butt back here."

Not wanting to come back to his master empty-handed, Jake had his newly found prize in his mouth as he hurried back to C. W.

"What's that you got in your mouth, silly dog?" He reached down and removed the object from Jake's grip. The object he pulled from his dog' s mouth was a ruby red woman's shoe. It had a pointed toe and a high heel. If it wasn't for a broken T-strap, the shoe was unblemished and could have been on a sales shelf at J.C. Penney's or one of the other stores in town that sold fancy women's shoes.

"Huh . . . pretty shoe. I wonder how it got down here." He thought about keeping the shoe and showing his grandfather; but after a moment, he tossed it to the ground, thinking it was probably not too important, although the shoe looked like it may be expensive and was brand-new.

"Come on, you sly dog. I'm hungry. Let's see if Grandpa has any lunch ready."

The dog understood by his master's tone that it was time to return home. Never short of having another toy to play with, or chew on, Jake retrieved the woman's shoe and kept it in his mouth as they returned up the wash, past the elegant homes of the Little Daisy Mine executives that sat on the east side of Sunshine Hill.

"You silly dog. I guess you can keep the shoe since you found it. Now let's go see Grandpa before he has to go to work."

23

Pazrosky left Homer alone and went outside. He had brought some of the cleaning supplies he had Homer purchase for him from the general store, including liquid chlorine and a deodorizing substance. He grabbed a scrub brush from Homer's sack and proceeded to scrub the trunk area which was the origin of the foul smell.

"What you up to?" Homer asked as he came outside to inspect what Pazrosky was doing.

"What does it look like I'm up to? I'm getting the flivver cleaned up. I thought I might go into town tonight and see if I can get a couple of dames to come up here and enjoy the stars and a few drinks."

"Really? I think that's a great idea, Henry. Maybe I should go inside and straighten up the place a little." Homer was excited at the prospect of Henry bringing some female companionship up to his home out in the gulch. He had never had any woman visit his home, and he had lived there for several years.

"Yeah, you go ahead and get the place straightened out, and I'll try to get this dead skunk smell out of my bucket."

"I thought you said you ran over a raccoon?"

"Raccoon, skunk, what's the difference? I just want to freshen it up a little, in case I get some dames in here tonight."

"Well, aren't you the big cheese? How 'bout if I go to town with ya?"

"I've got some things to do first. Then, I was thinkin', tonight I might check out the Cribs and see if I can sweet-talk a couple young broads into comin' up here to your place and do some celebrating. We can have a little party."

"I ain't never had a party up here. Maybe I should lock up the shed. Don't want any girls pokin' their head around our still."

"I hope you got some more mash fermenting. On Monday, I'll see about getting some more jugs so we can start bottling up some more shine."

"Sure thing. Now what about them broads you was talking about? Maybe I should get myself cleaned up. You know? A shave? Maybe a bath?"

"That's not a bad idea. I'm about done here. I'll leave you my liquid chlorine and deodorizer and maybe that'll help you get through the first layer."

Homer apparently had failed to see the humor in Henry's remark. "Ha ha ha. Ain't you a regular Eddie Cantor. Ever think about opening up your own vaudeville act? You'd make a million dollars."

Laughing, Pazrosky replied, "All right, wise head. I was only joking. I ain't promising a thing, but I'll be back, and hopefully I'll bring some skirts with me. Like I said, we'll celebrate our new business."

Still a little upset about Henry's comments regarding his personal hygiene, Homer waved him off and walked back into his house, muttering something under his breath.

Pazrosky, still laughing, walked off toward the car, taking two jugs of the hooch with him, one in each hand. The Ford certainly didn't have a natural smell to it, as the cleaning agents just added to the foulness, but Pazrosky wasn't too concerned. He'd air it out, maybe throw a few flowers or fruit in it. He thought he may even sprinkle some of the cologne in it that he bought at the men's store when he purchased his suit. *That would give it a masculine smell*, he thought. He wasn't going to worry about it anymore.

Driving down through the gulch, he passed another Model T going the other direction and wondered if that was one of Homer's customers. He would remember to ask him about it. He regretted that he got Homer all excited about the prospect of having women come up to his place for a party. He shouldn't have said anything. But he was getting that feeling again, a tingling sensation in his loins. He knew that he should lie low. After all, there were U.S. marshals in town, and as far as he knew, they may be there looking for him.

He pulled up next to the boardinghouse, and seeing nothing out of the ordinary, he parked the Model T near the house and walked up the stairwell that ran up the west side of the house into a second-floor entrance, carrying two jugs of hooch. He was feeling overly suspicious and more distrustful than usual. He thought that he would pay the landlady for one more week in advance, rather than the month in advance that he had been paying her. Rooms were hard to come by, and she would have no problem finding a new renter, but he was feeling the paranoia. He was being too nonchalant.

He thought about leaving Jerome, but he had really grown accustomed to the town. It was a tough town. He liked it and felt like someone important here. He had money, jewelry, and an automobile—albeit he had robbed and murdered to acquire such assets, but he bought a suit, cologne, a haircut and a shave; in Jerome, he had a job. Now, with the foolish little Homer, he could make a living selling moonshine if he played his cards right.

He opened the door to his room and went to his closet. His dark brown wool gabardine suit with his double-pleated slacks hung there. He then pulled the cigar box from between the mattresses and was assured to find the box there and all its contents undisturbed.

He was pulled apart as his conscious begged him to lay low, check out of the boardinghouse, and "take a bunk," get out of town. The other half told him to go out into the night and satisfy the urge that has been controlling him since he met the two pros outside the Chinaman's restaurant.

He wanted to experience the rush of excitement again that he experienced the one evening with the classy woman. She had been so gullible. For that, he paid $150. He got his money back. He doubted that her body would ever be found. He had given some thought to reliving that moment but feared that a woman like that would be missed while no one really cared about the girls that lived in the Cribs.

He didn't know what to do, but getting drunk and washing the Model T in the afternoon sun had made him tired. He was getting drowsy and wanted to lie down to take a nap. First, he rinsed the boot polish from his hair and beard so he wouldn't get it all over the pillowcase. He looked at the two full jugs of moonshine and put them in the corner of the closet, throwing some soiled clothing over the top of them. He had to be more careful. He was feeling good about himself, invincible. That was not always a good thing. If he left his guard down, he would surely be copped and end up dancing at the end of a rope in the Arizona State Prison.

24

The marshal got up and walked outside the jail to get some cool morning air. He had spent the previous evening at Shirley's house, where her mother had fixed a delicious pot roast with broiled potatoes and carrots and peas. In honor of Shirley's parents' thirty-fifth wedding anniversary, her mother baked an apple cobbler and an almond icebox cake with ice cream for dessert. He licked his lips and smiled as he reflected on how wonderful the meal was as he waited for a pot of coffee to brew.

Earlier on the day before, his deputies had told him about their meetings with Paige and the other girl, Lilly, who lived in the Cribs. He knew Paige. He actually had a fondness and respect for the woman. He felt that she had more guts and motivation than most of the men in town.

He showed his deputies the photograph the U.S. marshals gave him of Joseph Pazrosky. Neither of the deputies remembered ever seeing the guy around. They suggested that they take the photo to see if the girl from the Cribs could identify the man as the man whom her crib mate, Jenny, took off with. Perhaps Paige had seen the man around too. Marshal Williams agreed that they return with the photograph to the Cribs and the Parlor House.

He was wondering if the man responsible was in fact this Pazrosky fellow and if he was stupid enough to still be in town if he did kidnap or kill the two women still missing. The marshal had enough on his dinner plate, in addition to the death of the one prostitute and the disappearance of the other two. There was moonshine and bootlegging, illegal gambling; he knew the Chinese had "dens" in their establishments where they would smoke their opium. There was some friction developing with the foreigners as he called them, especially the Mexicans and Chinese, who were complaining about how the whites were treating them. There were the fights. A lot of fights.

He was a busy man and again wished he had a couple more deputies and a bigger jail, but what could he do? He went back into his living area of the jail and poured himself a cup of coffee. He grabbed the photograph of their suspect from a file and threw it on the desk. He then walked back outside. A large young Irishman with a crooked nose was half-asleep on the floor in the holding cell. He had been thrown in jail by Deputy Ray for fighting late-Friday night, after the marshal had left to go to Shirley's for that scrumptious dinner. Seeing the coffee steaming from the cup, the Irish lad regretted that his sense of smell could no longer get a whiff of freshly brewed coffee since some joker broke his nose five months earlier. He sat up and asked, "Hey, Marshal, how 'baht a cup of joe?"

The marshal ignored him and walked out on the boardwalk in front of the jail. There were quite a few people out and about early this Saturday morning. Several of the townsmen tipped their hat as they passed. The owner of the Cigar Store, Richard Kline, stopped to talk for a minute. The marshal asked how the business was doing and was given a complimentary cigar that he gladly accepted and put in his shirt pocket. Jacob Goldberg, owner of a small jewelry shop, also stopped and had a brief conversation with the marshal before he opened his store down the street.

The marshal was a well-respected man in Jerome. No one wanted his job. But they admired the work he was doing in spite of the widespread criminal activity that most felt was beyond the control of the marshal and his few deputies. He took another sip of the hot coffee and turned to go back inside.

He looked at the Irishman who was now sitting up on the floor of the cell. He said, "I've got to tell you, Mr. O'Leary, I'm getting awful tired seeing you in my jail every other Saturday morning."

The Irishman struggled to stand up. When he finally managed to stand up, he grabbed the steel bars and with an embarrassed expression replied with a stiff Irish accent, "Yessar. I don't blame yah much."

The marshal was feeling some compassion and sympathy for the big Irishman, a lad of twenty-one or twenty-two, whom he knew came to Jerome with his father a few years back. About a year ago, the old man died, and his son was alone. He started to run with some idiots, was drinking a lot, and was getting into trouble.

"Sean, as big and strong of man as you are, I can't understand why you have to prove it to everybody every Friday night. What you need is to find yourself a good woman, settle down a bit, and start respecting the law in my town. Still got your job at the mine, don't ya? Ya follow what I'm tellin' ya?"

"Right. There's a lot of truth to what yah say. Em . . . except I lost my job at the mine a few months ago after I got me nose brahken."

"I'm sorry to hear that. Now, I'm going to let you go home, Sean. But if I hear one more time that you're fighting or find you locked up in my jail like I did last night, then I'm going to nail you with a $50 fine and keep you locked up for a month, ya follow?"

"Right. I won't be a problem for yah. I'm leavin' town."

The marshal unlocked the cell and let the young man out. He fiddled with the lock with his back toward the large man as he walked past. The Irishman noticed the photograph of the man who had punched him that day in the pool hall, leaving him with a broken nose, a concussion, and a constant ringing in his ears that made him lose his job on the marshal's desk. Without breaking stride toward the front door, he spat at the photograph and snarled under his breath, "Wanker bastard!"

The marshal whirled around at the large man, "I beg your pardon, Mr. O'Leary."

Head down, the Irishman turned down the street where he vanished among a growing crowd of people who were getting their Saturday mornings started. Jerome had butchers, grocers, saloons, banks, dry goods, clothing, barbers, lumber yards, and several other small businesses that kept busy on Saturdays. Some businesses remained open on Sundays while some observed the Sabbath and were closed.

A few minutes later, Deputy Ray came walking up to the jail. He tipped his hat to the marshal, "Mornin', Marshal. I see you let Sean O'Leary out. I seen him walking home."

"Yeah. I gave him a long tooth lecture and told him I was getting plum tired seeing him in jail every Saturday morning. Ungrateful kid. We got bigger fish to fry than that fella."

"Are you thinkin' 'bout getting the search team back together next week?"

"Yeah. I think that's a good idea. I don't know if this man Buzrowsky, Patrowski, Patrosky, or whatever the hell his name is, is the man responsible or not for our missing girls, but we need to ask around and see if he's in Jerome or find out if he ever was here. With his history of strangling women to death, that girl we found last week was certainly strangled to death. Those other two missin' girls might have run into the same trouble. I got a feelin' we ain't gonna ever see them again. At least not alive."

"Want me to talk to Clarence and the others and see if they're able to help out? What are you thinkin'? Monday morning?"

"Yeah. If you would, Billy. I may stop by Paige's this afternoon. I think I'll show her the photo. I've always liked that woman. She's a real professional. For some maggot to get to one of her girls, he must be a perty serious criminal, the way I look at it. I know she's real careful about the men who get together with her girls."

"Sure enough. What is it you want me to do today?"

"Well, Billy, I think it's just gonna be you and me around here today. There's that mess down in the Mexican section between Jose Carlos and that other man he thinks spendin' too much time with his woman. If we ain't careful, that could boil over. He's already done six or seven years in Yuma when he was younger. He's ornery enough to stab another fellow to death. Those folks ain't real keen to me snoopin' around for some reason. Ever since I locked up Estevez last year and sent him downriver, they treat me like a dog that been skunked. Maybe you should see how things are goin', make sure ole Jose is thinkin' right."

"Yeah, that Mexican sure enough is an ornery old cuss. I don't think he likes me or anyone with a tin star too much. You remember they were celebrating on the Fifth of May, and I went down there to see what was going on. I thought they was gonna hang me on the tree like one of them pinatas and take to hammerin' some club at me."

"Well, since we found the dead girl down in their neck of the woods, we gotta be real careful. There seems to be a lot of racial tension with the work slowdown. I ain't got nothing personal with them folks, and I know you don't judge a man because where he was born either, but it's our job to keep the peace. Let's just don't get anyone riled up. I'm not expecting Jim or Dave to come in, unless we need 'em for something, until later tonight. I wanted to visit with them U.S. marshals before they get started back to Tucson. Maybe you can stay by the jail while I walk the streets, and then you can spell me in a few hours."

"Sounds all right with me, Marshal."

25

Ashley looked forward to this day. She got dressed and went downstairs where she joined Paige and the other girls—Gloria, Norma, and Marian—in the main dining room for the formal Saturday breakfast, which began every Saturday morning promptly at nine. Paige was a stickler when it came to meals, particularly breakfast, which she always harped about being the opening experience of the day.

She spent approximately one hour each evening with Cecile, her French chef and housekeeper, going over the meals for the following day. Cecile was blessed in that she was equipped with a cooking range more splendid than any of the finer restaurants in Jerome. The Magic Chef, as it was called, was a large pearly white gas range that featured six cook lids, two good-sized ovens, one broiler, a utensils drawer, a bread warmer, and a back shelf that held her spices and seasoning.

Cecile generally had the breakfast prepared in thirty minutes on each morning. After her evening meeting with Paige, she would spend time preparing the meats, greasing the pans, and measuring the flour so warm fresh bread was served the following morning.

Paige was so insistent that she and her girls be served the appropriate breakfast that she went so far to differentiate between breakfast in the summer months from breakfast in the winter months. For example, during the warm months, only the juicer fruits and iced melons were served wherein the winter months, only dried fruits, steamed figs, stewed prunes, and cooked fresh fruit were served. The dried fruits were often cooked into the oatmeal or cornmeal mush.

In the warmer months, the main breakfast course consisted of either whitefish, creamed chicken, or some other delicate meat wherein the winter months, more fats and more of the richer meats and fish were used.

Depending on the situation, she classified her breakfast menus in various degrees. Her breakfast menu for the girls was either light, moderate, or hearty. If they were formal, and they almost always were, she would have a different menu for a 10:00 company breakfast than her 12:00 breakfast. In addition to the cold weather and warm weather breakfasts, she had a particular breakfast menu for when lunch that day was uncertain, such as on days when she and the girls would go for a drive to Prescott or elsewhere. She also distinguished digestible foods from indigestible foods.

Like the town crier who made public announcements in the streets, but without the drum or hunting horn that were once used in her native France, Cecile would read the breakfast that was to be served to the girls once they had all been seated at the dining table. This formality only occurred on Saturdays, Sundays, and holidays.

On this morning, Cecile announced that the morning breakfast would be grapefruit stuffed with cherries, followed by broiled whitefish with sliced cucumbers, a savory omelet, potato puffs, fresh tomatoes, wheat muffins, hot rolls, cream waffles with butter, and crushed fresh strawberries.

None of the girls were accustomed to such lavish breakfasts before living at the Parlor House. They didn't complain and always allowed Paige to coddle them with her generosity. She wanted them to feel special, and they did. Cecile was always treated with respect and kindness, often receiving hugs from the girls in their appreciation of the heart and soul that she used in preparing each meal.

Part of her eccentric decorum was displayed in the linen Paige used for the breakfast table. She preferred a simple tablecloth of heavy muslin in gray or pink with hemstitched edges. But her choice of table linen also depended on the situation or her current mood. Table napkins that matched the cloth were always used.

The breakfast cloth always fell exactly to the edge of the table. Breakfast napkins were always smaller than dinner napkins.

Each girl was allowed a full two feet along the table edge. Care was taken so that the monogram that appeared on the plate, a large *P*, was turned in the right direction. The breakfast plate always sat exactly one inch from the table edge.

Paige enjoyed hearty breakfasts with merry conversations at the dinner table. One subject that they did not discuss however was Annabelle. This was difficult and sometimes awkward as a place was always set, with the appropriate silverware, at the dinner table for her for all meals, even though she had been missing for over a month.

Ashley finished her breakfast and, along with the other girls, excused herself from the dining table. She gave Cecile a hug and thanked her warmly for the wonderful breakfast before stepping outside. During breakfast, she had told Paige and the girls of her plans for the day. This was now customary in light of Annabelle's disappearance. She looked forward to her plans to go horseback riding with Lane Walker, whose family were wealthy and highly respected ranchers in the Verde Valley.

She was wearing one of her riding skirts and a full-sleeve cotton blouse. She had been out to dinner with Lane on two occasions. Strangely enough, Lane was rather old-fashioned and did not attempt to bed Ashley even though he paid Paige handsomely for her company. She liked him and found the tall rugged rancher very attractive. She was impressed that he had enormous wealth and more class than any other man she had met since she came to Jerome. With him, she had a difficult time adhering to her policy of not getting personally attached to the men she went out with. This is why she had only seen him twice. She was the only girl at the Parlor House that he called on. And while she hated to admit it, he reminded her of her father.

He appeared in front of the Parlor House at eleven sharp in his Cadillac Phaeton, a four-passenger vehicle with a gray body and slightly darker roof. It was obvious that he had it washed, for it looked like it just came off the assembly line. For a man of considerable wealth, he certainly didn't flaunt it. The Cadillac was a gorgeous automobile that he had paid $3,750 the year before. He could easily afford to pay much more for an automobile. On his family's ranch, they had an old Model T truck that he often used. But the Cadillac was a practical vehicle that he rarely used, unless it was to drive up to Jerome or drive his parents somewhere.

He jumped out and opened the passenger-side door for Ashley when she came out of the Parlor House. "How are you, my dear Ashley?"

She slid into the passenger seat of the open-air vehicle and smiled robustly as Lane walked around the back and opened the driver's side door sitting down behind the wheel. "I'm doing fine. It is so nice to see you again. I see you got your riding clothes on."

"Yes. I thought we would take Martha and Teddy out for a little ride today. You'll love them. They're both swell horses. Martha is a four-year-old Appaloosa. Very sweet disposition. Beautiful horse. She's bluish gray and looks like someone spilled a can of white paint all over her. I thought you could ride her. She keeps a real level head, and she's a nice, easy ride. And Teddy, that's my five-year-old palomino gelding. He stands over sixteen hands. He's a lovely golden brown with a white mane and tail and a white stripe down his nose. You know, I love those horses, I suppose, like some people love their children."

"Oh, Lane, I am so excited. I could barely sleep last night. I think it's been almost a year since I've gone horseback riding. Someday when I get back to Payson, the first thing I'm going to do is check with my babies. They're on a ranch not far from where we had our spread."

Lane knew that Ashley's family and the ranch near Payson were difficult subjects for her to talk about. She had explained during their first two times together how her parents had died. She sold her horses to some friends and came out to Jerome to sing and dance. He didn't judge her for what she was doing now. However, he still hadn't told his parents too much about her, other than she was a beautiful woman from a Payson ranch. He would think of something to tell his parents, but they were away for the week visiting his mother's brother's family in Ash Fork.

Lane was in his thirties. He lived on the Walker Ranch his entire life with his parents and elder sister Sally. He had a younger brother who died from an illness when they were both in their teen years.

On the twisting and turning road down Jerome to the Verde Valley, he asked Ashley, "How is Paige doing? I would have liked to have said hello, but maybe I'll have a chance when I drop you back off after our ride later."

"Oh, Lane. She is really hurting over Annabelle's disappearance, I guess like we all are. But you know Paige, she's the toughest lady I've ever known. It would be nice to have some closure with Annabelle. I mean, yeah, it would be nice if she showed up and apologized for leaving town without telling anyone, but I'm just afraid that's never going to happen."

"I know what you mean. I don't know what I would do if anything ever . . ." He broke off his sentence before he said too much about his feelings for Ashley, but she knew what he was trying to say.

Ashley reached over and grabbed Lane's hand for a moment, realizing that he needed both hands to navigate down the steep, bumpy roadway. Then she took her hand back and said, "I think a nice afternoon on horseback is just exactly what I need right now. Thank you so much for inviting me."

26

C. W. and Jake got back home just after lunchtime. Barney was sitting on the front porch as they came walking up. Seeing the red shoe in Jake's mouth, he asked, "What do you got there, fella?"

C. W. answered on behalf of the dog, "He was chasing this rabbit down in the wash and found this shoe. I tossed it back, but I guess he wanted to keep it."

Barney grabbed the shoe and examined it closely in his hand. "I bet some woman is missing this. It looks brand-new, and it's some pretty good craftsmanship too. Some cobbler did a mighty good job with this. Umm . . . it looks like the only thing wrong with it is this strap is broken." He scratched his head and gave the shoe back to Jake, who continued to beg for it to be returned to him. Then he reached back and, with a little force, took it back. "You know something? Where you just been walking wasn't too far from where they found that dead girl's body a couple weeks ago. Maybe I should ask Marshal Williams if the girl they found was missing a shoe. And another thing. They still haven't found those other two girls that have gone missing. Let's put this up somewhere for now. I got an old soup bone, so Jake will be all right."

"They found that girl's dead body down in the wash?"

"Yep. They sure did. The marshal and some of his deputies, I think. I wonder if that shoe belonged to her."

"I didn't know that they found that girl so close to our home. I wonder if one of the Mexicans killed her."

"Well, it ain't really fair to go pointin' fingers at someone just because they're not from here. These people that live all around us ain't ever given us any trouble 'bout nothin'. A lot of them just sit quiet in their homes and smoke that marijuana. They may have some problems between themselves like anybody else, but they ain't been nothing but pretty nice to us since . . . since it's just been the two of us livin' here. Now come inside and have a bowl of soup before I have to go to work."

C. W. walked into the house, and Barney threw an old ham bone out in the yard for Jake to chew on. C. W. sat down at the table where Barney had ham and bean soup prepared with some bread. Barney grabbed a couple of root beers out of the icebox and sat down at the table across from C. W. With a bottle opener, he put the open bottles on the table and said a quick prayer.

After a few minutes of silence, C. W. said, "So, Grandpa, who do you think killed that girl?"

"Well, that's the marshal's job. She wasn't exactly a girl. She was a lot older than you, a young woman really, I think twenty-three or twenty-four years old."

"And you said there were two more girls . . . or young women that gone missin'?"

"Yep."

"I wonder if that's why those U.S. marshals were in town that I told you about."

"Could be."

"So that means that there's maybe a killer on the loose in Jerome."

"Well. That's what some people may think."

C. W. slurped down the rest of his soup and pondered about the missing young women. He remembered the woman whom he spoke to in town that was so beautiful. He didn't tell his grandfather before but now said, "You know, Grandpa, when I was in town yesterday, I chased down this woman's handkerchief that got blown away by the wind. When I gave it back to her, she offered to buy me something to eat and was really nice."

Barney looked up from his soup for a minute. He had bread crumbs in his thick gray beard.

"Oh? An old woman or a young one?"

"She was probably in her twenties. And jeepers creepers, she was some kind of perty!"

"Oh yeah? What did she look like?"

"She had dark hair and a real perty face. And she was wearing some real perty clothes."

"Well, I reckon it's about time you start noticin' women for what they are. I think this doll may have been a little too old for you though. What ever happened to that little Italian girl you used to talk to?"

"Chiara? I ain't seen her in a while. Maybe after I start working for Mr. Baker next week, me and you can go in there and eat lunch or dinner sometime."

Barney chugged the rest of his root beer, then belched. "Well, maybe so. I hear their food ain't so bad. Might be good for you to see some girl about your own age. I hate to see them good looks you inherited from me go to waste."

27

Pazrosky woke up from his nap groggy and with a headache. He swung his legs around and pushed himself off the edge of the bed. Dizzy, he reached down into the small closet and grabbed a bottle of hooch. He held the jug to his lips and took a big drink from it.

He needed some air. He walked over to the window and opened it. He saw that it was getting darker as the sun was beginning to set behind him. He tried to shake the anxiety that he was feeling. He was hoping to awake from his nap refreshed and invigorated. But instead, he was still tired and full of angst and anger.

He was tormented not knowing what to do. He knew that he wasn't as invincible as he would have liked to think. He tried to calm himself down, pouring some hooch into his coffee can. He grabbed a cigarette from his deck of Chesterfields and lit one. He thought that he may move into a different boarding home.

Jerome was a much more boisterous town than little Clarkdale or Cottonwood, where he thought he could blend in with the high-spirited men and women more easily. He still had plenty of money. At least he didn't have to live in another flophouse for twenty cents a night, where a bunch of skid rogues shared the same room. *Don't be stupid.*

He also felt a craving. What was that whore's name? The friend of the girl he took for a ride, got all goad up on that Chinaman's opium, had his way with, and dragged down into the ravine. Now that was excitement! If he was going to kick the gong around with another one of them dope addicts, he would have to run by the Chinaman's place and get more stuff for the mud pipe.

The junkies were like taking candy from a baby. Show a gal you got a little dope, and it's like she'd do anything for it. Except that classy dish wasn't like that. In fact, when he started bringing the dope out, it was when she wanted to blow. That poor girl's addiction wasn't dope, but all the lettuce he was holding. But she sure clawed his face pretty good. Too bad she didn't know how to fly. He chuckled at himself and took another drag from his cigarette

He was lost in thought, but at least the cigarette and the alcohol were helping him start to relax a little bit. He may have to leave town for a bit, but with his well-groomed dark beard and hair, he didn't have to leave just yet. It was Saturday night, and maybe bringing a couple of whores up to Homer's place wasn't such a bad idea. He thought of Homer and sniggered to himself, "He'll probably cost me extra."

He knew one thing for certain. He wanted to get out. It was dark. Everything would be all right. He went down the hall to wash his face and use the bathroom. He wasn't so paranoid because he was already getting a little edge going. His headache had disappeared. He was glad that he didn't run into the landlady or any of the boarders.

He returned to his room and finished getting dressed. The suit stayed in the closet. He was too conspicuous with that on, although he liked how it made him feel. But he threw on a clean shirt and a little cologne. The last thing he did before he slipped out the side stairwell was apply some of the boot polish to his hair. He was careful not to put too much on because the stuff was greasy. He ran a comb through his hair so his hair was straight back and then ran the comb through his beard.

Before he left, he grabbed $100 from the cigar box he had hidden between the mattresses. He grabbed the hand mirror and admired himself one more time. He thought what a difference a year makes, remembering that last summer he was living penniless with a bunch of Mexicans in El Paso, Texas.

He went out the back door and down the stairs. He lit another cigarette and decided to leave the Model T parked where it was. It was a dark, moonless night, and the walk may help keep the anxiety he was feeling earlier away.

He began to walk up Hull Avenue, then thought that he would take the long way instead. He turned and headed east, past the Hotel Jerome that sat just to the west of his boardinghouse and toward the Hogback. He didn't know this area too well. He just passed by it on his way to Homer's. It was away from the town center and business district and much quieter.

It was still early. He passed some people on the street while a few cars drove by in each direction. He rounded a bend and came across a beautiful red brick home just off the main road. He continued his walk along the sidewalk that ran next to it. It was a two-story building with individual verandas extending from the rooms on the second floor.

As he got closer, an elegant roadster, perhaps a Cadillac, passed him on the street and pulled in front of the charming home. A tall man got out and walked around where he opened the passenger door for a woman. After she got out, she wrapped her arm around the man's arm, and the couple walked up the entryway. After pausing for a moment, the couple embraced and kissed each other passionately. They briefly exchanged a soft conversation that was followed by a girlish giggle, then the woman opened the door, and walked inside.

Pazrosky watched as the man got back in his automobile and started back onto the street out of the Hogback. It was dark, so he didn't get a good look at the woman, but she was intriguing. He wondered if this was her family's home. He continued to stand down the street from the house, smoking a cigarette. The passionate kiss and embrace had stimulated something inside him. He began to turn around and start back to the center of town when a light was turned on in one of the second-story rooms. A moment later, the same woman who got out of the roadster stepped out onto the small veranda.

Feeling rather conspicuous standing on the street corner all by himself, he casually turned and began walking back up the street toward the center of town. Seeing the woman on the veranda evoked a state of excitement inside him. He felt his heart beat a little faster. He took a glance over his shoulder at the woman who did not appear to notice him. In the dark, he could only tell that she had dark hair and a stunning figure.

He felt that tingling sensation and began to walk a little faster. He thought about stopping at the boardinghouse to pick up the Model T but chose to continue walking. As he got closer to the center of town, there were more people out. He was hungry and decided he would enjoy a nice dinner before continuing up to where most of the saloons and billiard parlors were located.

With the silhouette of the beautiful woman standing outside her room still in his mind, he entered the Grand Central Restaurant and was seated by a hostess. While fancy restaurants were a little out of his realm, his move to Jerome had done wonders for his self-confidence. Always told that he was worthless, from a young child to his adulthood, he now walked with a swagger.

Looking over the menu, he decided on the "Jerome cut" of beef with a side of vegetables. There were a few other patrons in the restaurant who paid him no attention. After he finished his meal, he paid the $1.50 and walked outside. After lighting a cigarette, he slipped into the crowd of people who had now filled the streets.

He walked past the saloons toward the Cribs District. He was very observant, on the lookout for the friend of the girl he knocked off the last time he was out in this area. He couldn't think of her name, but it was unimportant. There were girls, and men, everywhere, and the sound of jazz music could be heard playing from inside one of the cribs. He knew that the alcohol was flowing and longed for another drink as he was starting to lose his edge.

He thought about Homer. He was undoubtedly waiting for him to bring a couple of the girls up to his place for some partying. He was thinking that this wasn't a good idea as Homer's place was the only place where he didn't feel overly suspicious about people, and he could have some peace of mind. He didn't want to do anything stupid. He was a free man, and he wanted to keep it that way. This time, he wasn't flaunting his dough like the last time he was here.

He was now wishing he had stopped to pick up the Model T. The vehicle's smell bothered him. He thought with the money he still had, he could sell it and pick up another roadster, maybe something nice. He wondered why he hadn't thought of the idea before. Probably because he never had money before.

He continued to walk among the crowd when a petite gal, probably nineteen or twenty years old, walked out of one the cribs. She looked at Pazrosky with clouded eyes and said, "Hey, stranger, I ain't seen you around before 'cause if I did, I would have remembered you."

"No, I'm sure you haven't. This is the first time I've ever been up through here."

"Are you wantin' to have a little fun?"

"I was thinkin' about it. Know where I can find some?"

"Look no farther. Are you sure you can afford me? I'm a little more expensive than these other girls around here, you know?"

"Is that a fact? Well, miss, you can call me Henry."

"And you can call me anytime," she laughed.

28

The marshal had returned to the jail after spending a few hours walking around the town. He liked the townspeople to feel his presence on the streets. He hoped that his slow walk in front of their businesses and homes gave them an added sense of security. Of course, his presence in front of the saloons and pool halls always made some people nervous. But that was part of his job.

In addition to the assumption that there may be a serial killer on the loose, Jerome also attracted professional gamblers that would take the locals' money. They generally ended up getting run out of town, but some were jailed.

After Marshal Williams returned to the jail, Deputy Ray reported an uneventful shift while he was on duty at the jail and headed out for the street. Shortly after he left, Marshal Williams stepped back to the kitchen area and grabbed the pot roast sandwich that Mrs. Hudson had packed for him. He had been looking forward to tearing into that sandwich for the last few hours.

As he was biting into the delicious sandwich, an older man with dirty clothes, a bushy gray beard, and wearing a miner's helmet walked in. "Marshal Williams?"

Gulping down a bite of his sandwich, he walked into the main room. "I'm the marshal. What can I do for you?"

"Howdy, Marshal. My name is Barney Parker. I live with my grandson down on the end of Diaz Street. I've heard about the missing young women around town. I think you may have found the dead girl not too far from my house down in the wash. Well, the reason I'm here is my grandson and our dog were down in the gulch just north of the Douglas place this morning running around. The dog dug up a woman's shoe that looked darned near brand-new. Real fancy. It just had a broken strap. Had to pry the shoe loose from the dog, but I don't know if it's something you might be interested in or not. It might not be important at all."

"Well, Mr. Parker. It's mighty kind of you to stop by. I'm going to have to get the photos out that we took of the deceased girl to see if she was missing a shoe or both shoes or what. Come to think of it, I think we may have found the shoes that she was wearing. We are still investigating the disappearance of two other of our female citizens who been missing. Maybe that shoe could help us. What color did you say it was?"

"It was a bright ruby red, and like I said, it looked brand-new, except for the broken strap. Sure would be hard to walk around that wash in high heels, but you know, it may help your investigation. Anything to help find those girls or the one responsible, I reckon."

"Certainly, Mr. Parker. Myself or one of my deputies will probably be by your place today or tomorrow and pick that shoe up. Our search team will be back out on Monday. You said your grandson was down in Deception Gulch? You've been real helpful. Appreciate it."

"My grandson can show you where the dog found it, if you need him to help. He starts working for Mr. Baker at the Safeway grocery mart Monday around 10:00 though, as a delivery boy."

"Well, I'll be. Tom Baker is a good man." He walked Barney out the front door. "So how are things going at the mine?"

"That's where I'm headed." He nodded up the street indicating the Verde United Mine. "Hopefully, the copper market will pick up again soon enough so we can hire back a lot of the men, but there's still plenty of ore to be dug up."

"Thank you for dropping in, Mr. Parker. I'll be in contact."

Marshal Williams went to a tall black filing cabinet and looked through the files for a minute before he found what he was looking for. He pulled the photos taken at the scene where Emma Lewis's body was found. One photo clearly showed that she was only wearing one single dark shoe, but with the black-and-white photo, one couldn't tell the color of the shoe. But he remembered it wasn't ruby red. He remembered the shoe she was wearing to be navy blue or black, and it didn't look like it was brand-new.

He carefully looked over all the photos once more before slipping them back in the file. He got up and placed the file back in the filing cabinet. He still hadn't talked to Paige. He still wanted to ask her some questions about Annabelle James. Now he would ask if she owned a pair of ruby red high-heeled shoes. For that matter, the friend of Jenny Richardson would need to be talked to again also.

The marshal sat down behind a large gray metal desk and finished the rest of his lunch, washing it down with a cup of reheated coffee. There was a lot of activity going on in Jerome, but this was common for Saturday afternoons.

He wanted to get back on the street, but they were shorthanded, so he needed to stay near the jail in case someone else dropped by. He wondered if the information involving the shoe was going to be helpful. The search team would at least carefully look around that area on Monday morning.

At that moment, Shirley walked in. "Knock, knock. Is anyone home?"

His eyes lit up upon seeing his fiancée although he didn't always like it when she came by the jail, especially if he had a criminal locked up in the holding cell. At the moment, he didn't.

"Hi, sweetie. What are you up to this afternoon?"

"Nothing much. Are you here all by yourself?"

"Yep. Billy's out patrolling the streets. I'm not expecting Jim or Dave to come in until around six. Why? Did you have something in mind?" he asked suggestively.

"No, I certainly don't have anything in mind, John Williams, so get your mind off whatever it was you were thinking about. I just came by to see what time you were getting off duty. I was hoping we could go out and see a picture at the Lyric."

"You and your pictures. Ain't we already seen everything they made?"

She began to make a long, weepy face. "So does that mean you're not interested in seeing me this evening? Maybe I should make plans to go with my sister."

"Now, now, honeybear. I was just having some fun with you. Let me see when my deputies get here. I'll try to get away as soon as I can, I promise."

She smiled and walked closer so he could give her a hug and a quick peck. "OK. That's better. I just want to see you again. It's Saturday night. I better go help Mom with some stuff around the house. I love you."

"Yes, dear. I can't wait to see you tonight."

The long face returned. Pouting, she asked as if her feelings were suddenly trampled on, "That's all?"

He knew what she was after but played along, "What do you mean, sweetie pooh?"

"You know what I mean. Aren't you going to tell me you love me?"

"I'm the marshal, remember? You know that I do."

"Then say it. What does you being the marshal have to do with anything? There's nobody here but you and me."

"Yes, dear," he whined as if his mother had just ordered him to go wash his hands. He didn't mind telling her that he loved her because he truly did. He just didn't feel comfortable telling her in the jail. "I'll come by the house when I'm off duty. And . . . I love you."

Shirley turned and walked out, nearly bumping into Deputy Ray on the way out. "Hi, Billy. You fellas be careful," she said before she stepped out.

"I'm sorry, Marshal, I didn't mean to interrupt anything."

"No, no. She just dropped in to say hello. Ya mind stickin' around until I get back, I want to run this fella's photo by Paige, see if she remembers seeing him?"

The marshal grabbed his hat and headed out the front door. He had the photograph the U.S. marshals gave him in a large envelope in his left hand. But before he was out the door, Billy joked, "That's all right, Marshal. You don't have to tell me you love me"

The marshal stopped dead in his tracks without looking back. He pulled his cowboy hat down low over his eyes and continued walking.

29

Ashley was having the time of her life. She and Lane took the muscular horses down by the Verde River near the ancient ruins of the Tuzigoot Pueblo, a forgotten village of the Sinagua people who were thought to have left the area four or five hundred years ago. They rode the horses to where a group led by two archaeologists had begun to excavate the ruins from the desert landscape. The crumbly remains of the ruins sat upon a hilltop, like the crown on a king's head.

The land on which the ruins were located was now owned by the Verde United Copper Company. It was surrounded by the tailings pond of the VUCC copper mine, a pool of azure water that was pumped from the smelter in Clarkdale.

"What a beautiful pond," she said as she and Lane rode the horses near it.

Lane laughed, "It may be a beautiful pond, but we don't want to get any closer than this. There's nothing but poisonous filth in that pond. Basically the waste product from the smelters over there." He nodded toward the small company town.

Lane's family ranch bordered the property that was owned by the huge copper-mining conglomerate.

"Tuzigoot," he explained, "was an Apache Indian word that meant "crooked water." They rode along the crooked water of the Verde River toward one of its tributaries, Sycamore Creek. The creek was surrounded by, literally, a gorgeous canyon of vivid rock formations. During their ride, they saw the Verde Valley Railroad pulling out of Clarkdale on its way to the outside world.

They rode back and rested the horses for a short while under some Cottonwood trees near a bend in the river. Lane pulled a wool blanket out from under his saddlebag and unfolded it in the shade of the giant tree. From his saddlebags, he pulled out a small loaf of bread wrapped in paper and a tinplate and set them on the blanket in front of Ashley who was now seated.

He looked into Ashley's cocoa brown eyes and said, "I hope you have time for a little picnic. I packed us a little lunch."

"Oh, Lane, so far, this has been one of the most wonderful days that I can ever remember. Thank you so much for inviting me horseback riding. I absolutely love Martha and Teddy. They're so powerful, yet . . . graceful. Teddy reminds me so much of a palomino we had on our ranch when I was a little girl. His name was Sesame. I don't think there's anything you can do to make this day more wonderful than it has already been."

Lane smiled at the seated Ashley. "Ummm. Well, we're not finished yet." He walked over to Teddy and grabbed something else wrapped in paper. He unwrapped it in front of her. "You can't just eat bread without some nice cheese and grapes to go with it." Her eyebrows rose, and her mouth opened in excitement when she saw the food he brought for their picnic.

"Oh, you've thought of everything."

"Well, there's one more thing." He walked back to the horse and pulled a bottle out of the saddlebag. "I hope you like it. I stole it from my father's wine cellar, but I know he wouldn't mind. It's a bottle of red wine from the Douro Valley of northern Portugal. Pops spent some time in Western Europe with the Red Cross during the war and brought back a few cases of European wine. It's too bad you can't find fine wine in the good old forty-eight states of America. Umm, I'm afraid I don't have fancy wineglasses, but I did bring a couple of clean cups to drink out of." He fumbled with a corkscrew that had been wrapped with the cheese.

Ashley felt a sudden surge of emotion come over her. She looked down so Lane wouldn't see her eyes begin to well up with tears. But Lane noticed and sat beside her.

"Ashley. Is something wrong? I'm sorry if I've said something, or did something to upset you?"

After a moment, she looked up, and her eyes met the concerned hazel eyes of the handsome cowboy. "No, it's I that am sorry. You treat me like a queen, Lane. You know what I do and what I am, but still you treat me with dignity and make me feel like I've never felt before in my life. I'm sorry. I don't mean to cry. It's just that no one has ever treated me like you have."

A tender smile broke on Lane's face. He looked deeply into Ashley's eyes and wanted to tell her the truth, that he was in love with her. But he didn't think she was ready. Instead, he said, "I love how I feel when I am with you.

Your company, I cherish. I don't care what you do. I knew what you did when we first met and got together. It may bother me later, but it doesn't now." He leaned into her and kissed her passionately. For him, it was a moment frozen in time. When he finally pulled back, he didn't know if he had kissed her for a minute or an hour. He just knew that he felt the tears on her cheek on his face.

"What do you say I open this bottle of wine?" He pulled out a small folding knife from his pocket and sliced some cheese, placing the slices on the tinplate. He then opened the bottle of wine and poured each of them a glass while Ashley watched in admiration.

"Lane, I'm sorry I got emotional. I like you very much. That's why I have only seen you two times before. I think about you all the time. I'm sorry. There I go again."

"We'll be all right."

They sat in silence as they munched on the bread, cheese, grapes, and wine. The sun was getting low in the western sky and starting to sink behind the mountain past Jerome.

Finally, Lane spoke, "I reckon we should get back to the ranch so I can take you up the hill. It doesn't matter if it's dark or not. The Cadillac has two sets of lights, so I can certainly see well enough to drive at night. I think you know how much I've enjoyed this wonderful afternoon with you today."

She looked at Lane, fighting hard not to show her true emotions. "And I have had a wonderful time as well."

He helped her up on to the agile Appaloosa after he had put the remains of their picnic back into his saddlebag. She gazed down at him with the eyes of a young puppy. She knew she had deep feelings for the man who reminded her of her father. Now, those feelings were beginning to grow. She was thinking that if she wasn't careful, those feelings would burn out of control, faster than a raging forest fire.

During the ride back up the mountain to Jerome, their conversation was short and awkward. There had been a lot of emotions that spilled out between the two that day. It was clear that they may be walking down the same path in respect to how they felt about each other.

As they neared the Parlor House, it had just begun to get dark. Lane saw a man standing on the corner, smoking a cigarette. *What was this clown doing? What was he waiting for? I know he sure in hell ain't waiting for my girl. It might be Saturday night but . . .*

Lane pulled the Cadillac in front of the Parlor House. He got out and opened the door for Ashley, taking her hand. They embraced and kissed passionately at the front door. He told her not to wait so long before she accepted his offer to get together again. She chuckled and said that she wouldn't.

She walked inside and peeked in the main living area. She didn't see anyone, so she walked up the large spiral staircase to her room. Her tired legs seemed to drag across the floor as she walked toward the French doors. She opened the doors and stepped out onto the balcony, fearing that her days at the Parlor House may be numbered. She thought she was in love with Lane. If he proposed to her, she would accept. She enjoyed being independent, but she could be independent and be married to Lane at the same time. After all, he was much like her father.

Her eyes looked down toward the street where she saw a man looking up at her from the street corner. She was used to men looking up at her from the street. He turned away when she looked toward him and began to walk up the street, once turning his head and looking over his shoulder at her again. The man was probably harmless, she thought, but for some reason, he made her a little nervous.

30

There wasn't much for C. W. to do on the Saturday afternoons when his grandfather worked. He didn't have any close friends. There was Carlos, a boy a year older, whom he played with when he was younger. But the two didn't see each other very much anymore.

C. W. enjoyed going swimming at the swimming pool on the three hundred level not far from the large open mine pit. The swimming pool, however, was a point of contention. The town council had decided that the swimming pool on the property of the Verde United Mine would only be used by the white people during the hot summer months. Except on Sundays. On this day, the pool was open to the nonwhites or Mexicans.

Adding insult to the fact that the white people got to enjoy the pool all week was that the water often got dirty and cloudy by Sunday when the Mexicans were allowed to swim in it. At the end of the day on Sunday night, the pool would be drained and refilled with fresh clean water for the whites to enjoy the following week.

Matters were made worse when the town of Clarkdale built a swimming pool in the Mexican quarter. The Mexicans of Jerome felt cheated and wanted to be treated fairly like their countrymen down in the valley. The town council consented and built the Mexicans their own pool in the foreign section of Jerome.

These actions just contributed to the racial segregation that gave the Mexican people a feeling of inferiority. Sadly, it was this racial segregation that was the cause of tension in the town and a reason why C. W. and Carlos were no longer the close friends they had once been when they were younger.

This Saturday, C. W. grew restless. He thought he might go swimming or play a game of miniature golf at the Dynky Lynx. The sport of golf was getting popular and spreading across the country. The Dynky Lynx had become a

126

popular place in town to putt a golf ball around a small course of little hills and curves. It was located in the heart of town between the town hall and the T. F. Miller Company Store. A lot of boys a little older than him would take their girlfriends or girls they were courting there. He thought that maybe he would ask Chiara if she wanted to go there with him. He had a little money saved. The more he thought about it though, the more he thought it might not be that great of an idea. One—he didn't know if he had the guts to ask her, and two—he didn't know if her parents would allow her to if she wanted to anyways.

He didn't know what to do. It had been hours since his grandfather left to go to work. It would be dark pretty soon. Not that that mattered much anymore. He considered himself grown-up although he couldn't go into pool halls or saloons, nor did he want to. But he was getting restless.

Jake was on the porch, chewing on the ham bone. C. W. pulled three dollars out of a sock where he kept his life savings and walked out the front door. Jake looked up for a minute but then went back to chewing on the ham bone. "You be good, boy. I'm going to go into town for a little bit. I'll be back home real soon."

C. W. walked up Diaz Street and stopped in front of the Mexican swimming pool for a minute. The pool was full of people, mostly children, who were splashing around in the water. The pool provided a sanctuary from the summer heat for many of the people that lived near him. C. W. thought about going home for his swimsuit but decided against it and continue walking up toward town.

When he got to the corner of Hull Avenue, he took a left, walking by the Dicus Motor Company's large garage. As he continued walking east on Hull, he passed an apartment building known as the High House, where many of the Italians in town lived. He had seen Chiara's father going in and out of here before and surmised that this was where her family lived. Their small restaurant was located nearby. He thought how nice it would be to see her and at least say hello.

He walked past a row of businesses on the right-hand side of the street and went into the Jerome Market. He paid the grocer five cents for a large red apple, left the store, and continued walking past Chiara's family's restaurant. The restaurant had a sign in front that he couldn't understand, *Gusto dell'Italia*. Hovering around the front entrance, he looked in and saw that the small restaurant was full of people eating and using their hands emphatically in their conversation. No one was speaking English.

He saw Chiara serving plates of spaghetti to a table near the front of the restaurant. She looked up and caught his eye and smiled. To his surprise, she walked toward him and poked her head out the entryway. "I can't talk now. We're really busy. If you can, pass by here in two more hours, and maybe my papa will let me talk to you for a little while." Before he could reply, she quickly darted back into the restaurant.

More than satisfied with the turn of events, he spun around; then with a little extra hop in his step, he began to walk toward the center of town. The late afternoon sun was beginning to set, and the streets were starting to fill up with enthusiastic people getting ready for another wild Saturday night in Jerome. He wondered what he was going to do for another two hours.

Taking bites out of his apple, he decided he would walk up to the minigolf park and see what was going on there. At least he could sit somewhere along Clark Street and watch the people for a while. On the way, he passed the Safeway grocery mart but didn't see Mr. Baker, so he kept walking.

He remembered the other day when he chased down the handkerchief for that beautiful woman and how nice she was to him. Now, he watched as a big black automobile pulled in front of the Boyd Hotel and an distinguished-looking older man and woman got out and went inside. He passed the Chinese laundry and the Coliseum Theater and stopped to look in the window. A picture called *Scarlet Days* was playing.

He had only been to one motion picture. His grandfather had once taken him to see a picture with a big fat guy and his skinny buddy whom he was always so angry with. It was funny. The skinny guy got kicked out of the boardinghouse where he was staying and found a stray dog. The fat guy ended up with a beautiful woman, the dog found a good home, and everything turned out well. He would like to see another picture, but the picture playing didn't look too interesting to him. He noticed that there were a lot of couples going into the theater.

He began to pass more people along the sidewalk as he got closer to the center of town and the saloons. With Prohibition, most of the saloons were now calling themselves pool halls. There were still saloons and alcoholic beverages to be found. There were still dance hall girls, but the townspeople had made much of an effort to distance itself from the Wild West days. Sure, there was the occasional horse tied to a hitching post on Main Street and horse-drawn buggies riding down the streets, but it was the postwar 1920s. The War to End All Wars was over and a thing of the past.

But while the town was hurling headfirst into the Jazz Age, vices that some town members had wanted eradicated still existed. There was certainly prostitution, liquor was easily available, and gambling was also going on. There were opium dens among certain Chinese establishments. In addition to opium, some people indulged in taking such narcotics as cocaine, heroin, and marijuana.

Marijuana was something that was starting to become popular with the Mexican immigrants in the American southwest during this time. Mexicans often brought marijuana from their native land to their adopted homes in the States. Fueled by Prohibition, marijuana use accelerated, especially in the jazz community, where Jerome had a budding fraternity.

Sniffing cocaine was also not an uncommon practice among some of Jerome's younger citizens, even though it had been banned in 1914, along with heroin.

C. W. always looked into the saloons when he passed by. There was often so much excitement and activity that piqued his curiosity. His grandfather didn't drink alcohol nor did his parents before they died. He didn't see what the big deal was. He often saw miners on the streets coming out of saloons or pool halls staggering and stumbling.

His only exposure to alcohol was when he went with his grandfather to hear the Jack Dempsy championship fight that a friend of his grandfather was able to get on his radio. A couple of miners who were there were drinking from a silver flask, and both ended up getting angry and nearly started fighting each other. He didn't really care. He just knew it wasn't for him.

There was one saloon in particular that had always piqued his curiosity. It was called the Mineflower Saloon & Gambling House. It sat on the northeast corner of Hull Avenue and First Avenue, across the street from the J.C. Penney store. Now he figured that since he had some time to kill before he would return past the Italian place where Chiara worked for her family, he would take the long way around Hull to Jerome Avenue and across the street where the Dynky Lynx was located.

He stopped in front of the Mineflower for a moment as a man, probably a bartender by the way he was dressed, stopped and pulled a watch from his vest pocket and checked the time before he entered. The entryway to the Mineflower had two tall oak doors, embellished with frosted glass, that led into a small vestibule. From here, one would enter the saloon through its impressive set of swinging doors. This was all C. W. was ever able to see. From what he could tell, the interior was always kind of dark and very smoky.

C. W. was across the street, watching as the man paused before the entryway. Another man passed along Hull in a black Ford and yelled, "Howdy, Roy. Getting ready for work?". The man addressed as Roy smiled and nodded his head. C. W. was impressed by how the man was dressed. He had a gold watch hung on a chain that sat in the pocket of a burgundy-colored vest. He wore a bright white shirt under his vest. Both his shirt and slacks looked clean and freshly pressed. His brown hair appeared perfectly groomed under a black derby. His handlebar mustache was waxed flawlessly. His black shoes had a shine that C. W. could see from twenty feet away. C. W. was both impressed and intrigued by this place.

He was beginning to notice women for their elegant beauty and to appreciate the curves of their bodies. The Mineflower certainly had their share of beauties coming in and out of it. He craned his neck around the well-dressed man as he opened the large doors and walked inside. As he opened the doors, the sound of loud jazz music escaped. He thought this place had to be the most exciting social affair in town.

For a moment, he wished he were older, maybe twenty-two or twenty-three. He imagined that he would someday walk into the place and speak with a beautiful lady. They would sit together and listen while the five-member band played jazz music. He would take her hand and escort her out onto the dance floor.

He caught himself in his fantasy and let his thoughts return to the present day. He was glad to be seventeen years old. He was having a fun summer. He had a crush on a nice Italian girl who had asked him to come by her family's restaurant so they could talk. She must have liked him too. *Jeepers creepers*, he thought. This was going to be the longest two hours of his life.

31

Pazrosky was seated in an uncomfortable wooden chair in the small paltry crib. The place was a real dump. Lucille had just brought him a glass of hooch that made Homer's hooch taste like expensive French champagne. Nearly vomiting, Pazrosky, in a stifling voice, said, "This is a little rough. Where did you get this shit?"

"Oh. I'm sorry, monsieur. Maybe you heard that there's a law prohibiting the sale of alcoholic beverages. This is the best I could do. Maybe Mr. Bigshot knows a supplier who can help me and the girls around here out with some better-tasting stuff. Something not out of someone's bathtub that leaves you sick and hungover for days."

"Well, I know where you can get some giggle juice a lot better than this swill. In fact, I'd be happy to provide you with a jug. Why don't you come with me, and I'll get it for you tonight?"

"You do? Well, maybe that's not a bad idea." Lucille reached onto the table and grabbed a Lucky from a pack of cigarettes. Hesitating in order to give the man she had met as Henry a chance to light it for her, she finally struck a match disgustedly and lit it herself after it became obvious that he wasn't going to light it for her.

"I'm sorry you don't like my drink. If you rather, I've got a few jujus if you want to smoke one with me."

"I don't smoke much reefer, but I might take a puff or two just to be sociable."

Lucille got up and walked over to a shelf where she kept her marijuana cigarettes, shaking her hips in a lewd attempt of feminine guile. She was rather short and unassuming. She was certainly not an unattractive woman, especially to Pazrosky. Short bobby blonde hair. Nice features. From what Pazrosky could tell, she had firm hips and legs.

Admiring the view, Pazrosky licked his lips, "You know, kitten, you got a nice pair of gams on you. That's probably why you cost a little more."

"Ha-ha. Thanks for noticing." She set her Lucky in a small metal ashtray that was in need of dumping. Holding the marijuana cigarette to her lips, she didn't wait for Pazrosky to stand up like a gentleman and light it for her. Like lighting a cigar, she took a few deep puffs before she held out and shared it with Pazrosky. He took a couple of puffs and returned it to Lucille, who sat down across from him at the table.

Pazrosky enjoyed playing the role of a man with some cash in his pocket. But after a few drinks of the rotgut and three or four puffs off the marijuana cigarette, he quickly reverted back to his misogynistic self.

The effects of the marijuana was making him feel paranoid. He began to worry that the friend of the girl he had taken for a ride a couple months back—*what was her name?*—may suddenly appear and begin screaming at him. He wanted to step outside for some air but thought that he may expose himself to the other girls who were starting to come out. And he was sweating.

"Hey, kitten, you got a sister who might want to come with us up to my buddy's place? I told him earlier that if I found two good-lookin' shebas, that we would have a little party up at his place."

Lucille looked at Pazrosky carefully before she spoke, "Well, you ain't too hard on the eyes. You're better groomed than most of the men that come through here. You never did say what it was you did. You don't look like one of the miners."

"I'm a businessman. Now what do you say, do you have a friend who may want to go for a ride up to the gulch and have a drink with a buddy of mine?" *Let's go. I got to get out of here.*

Lucille was somewhat hesitant because either she didn't trust him or was just playing coy. "Well, what is your friend like?"

"Oh, Homer? He's retired but not that old or anything. I think he has some family money. He just lives real simple. Good fella though. You'll like him. I have to go by my . . . the hotel and pick up my flivver, and I'll come back and pick you and your friend up."

"Ummm . . . Your friend isn't a Mexican or a dinge or anything, is he?"

"No. Of course not. He's a little white guy. From Missouri or Arkansas somewhere. A good fella. A real gentleman like me. He just doesn't know how to appreciate a pretty tomato like I do. He's a little . . . how do you say? Bashful."

"Well . . . OK. It might help if you gave me a little dough first."

"Sure. What do you charge by the hour?"

"By the hour? If you're going to take me away from here for an hour or two, it'll cost you $25."

Afraid that she may have chased him away with the high price which was much more than what she usually charged, she asked, "I hope that isn't too steep a price for ya, is it?"

"No. After all, this is a special occasion. Now what's your sister's name?"

"I'll go see if Izzy wants to go. That's $25 apiece up front."

Izzy, wasn't that the girl's name? "Umm . . . what does Izzy look like?"

"Izzy is short for Elizabeth. But she's tall. About five and a half feet tall, I reckon. Long wavy red hair. A real looker. If you haven't been coming around here too much, and I ain't ever seen ya, you probably haven't seen her. She's only been here for a couple of weeks."

This girl was shorter than that with dark hair, I think. It's not her. "How 'bout if you two meet me in front of the Nevada Cafe in thirty minutes? That will give me time to pick up the Ford and come get you girls."

"All right. But you're forgettin' something."

Pazrosky smiled a debauched smile and grabbed several bills out of his pocket. He handed over $50 to Lucille. When she reached for the money, he wrapped his other arm around her and pulled her close to him.

"I know where you live, so don't skip out on me. Besides, we're going to have a swell time."

She looked at him nervously as if the thought had crossed her mind. She wasn't sure if he was joking or threatening. "Are you crazy? Lookin' forward to it. It'll be nice to get away from here for a couple hours."

Holding Lucille tight in his grasp, his right arm slid down her waist and clutched her left buttocks firmly. He kissed her on the forehead and said, "Yes, kitten, I'm lookin' forward to it myself. Now how 'bout one more shot of that hooch for the road?"

32

Marshal Williams walked down Main Street for the second time that day. From the jail, it was a ten-minute walk to the Hogback and the Parlor House. He tipped his hat to the patrons on the street and headed to the brick home on East Avenue just off Main Street. He walked up to the front porch and knocked on the door. After a minute passed, Cecile answered the door. She smiled, noticing the marshal's badge and greeted him kindly, "Est-ce que Marechal de bon apres-midi, comment je peux vous aider?"

The marshal removed his hat and answered meekly, "Uhh . . . I'm sorry, ma'am. I don't speak French. I was looking for Miss Cheavant. Is she in?"

Embarrassed, Cecile replied, "I'm so sorry, Marshal. Sometimes I forget that I'm not in Paris anymore. Come in, please."

He followed her into the home where she escorted him to the waiting room. Cecile pointed to a comfortable-looking couch and said, "Please, have a seat, Marshal. I will let Madame Cheavant know that you are here. Can I get you a cup of coffee or tea perhaps while you are waiting?"

"No, thank you. I'm fine."

Cecile turned and left the marshal alone in the waiting room. He looked around in awe of the fine furnishings, carpet, and tapestries on the floor and walls.

After a minute or two passed, Paige joined the marshal and smiled as she entered the room. "It's so nice to see you again, Marshal. Are you sure you wouldn't like something to eat or drink?"

He stood up, holding his hat in his hand. "No, thank you, ma'am."

She held out her hand. Unsure whether he was supposed to kiss it or shake it, he grabbed her hand gently and bowed his head.

"It's always a pleasure to see you, Paige. How have you been?"

"Oh, other than having a heavy heart with Annabelle's disappearance, I would be doing very well, I imagine. Is that why you're here, Marshal? You know, two of your young deputies were here just the other day."

"Yes, I know, Paige. I'm sorry to bother you again."

"No, no bother, Marshal. I hope I can help you, but I'm afraid that maybe I can't. You see, Annabelle wasn't out on a date the day she disappeared. Your deputies asked me to look through my records, but then I remembered the last time any of us had seen her was on a Wednesday afternoon when she walked into town to buy some perfume. I believe she was going to the J.C. Penney store if I'm not mistaken."

"Oh, so she was by herself with no plans to meet anyone anywhere?"

"Yes, Marshal. You know that I am very careful with whom I allow my girls to escort. I do my best to screen the men who wish to be escorted by my girls very scrupulously. You know that none of my girls have ever disappeared or were kidnapped, which I'm so afraid has happened in this case."

"To tell you the truth, being kidnapped would be the better of two evils right now. I must warn you that there is a chance something bad may have happened to her worse than getting kidnapped."

Biting her lower lip, Paige answered, "Yes, Marshal, I understand."

"You know, Paige, that two girls from the . . . Cribs disappeared. One we found with strangulation marks around her neck."

"Yes, Marshal, I know. I feel terrible for those girls, but my girls, as you know, are different."

"Yes, I know. I want to show you a photograph of a man we suspect may be involved in the disappearance of the women. I'd like to show the photograph, just in case you might have ever seen the man loitering around or anything."

With that said, he pulled the photograph of Joseph Pazrosky out of the envelope and presented it to Paige. She studied the photograph of the gaunt-faced, beady-eyed man and gave it back to the marshal. "No, Marshal. I have never seen this man."

The marshal wanted to ask Paige if she thought any of the girls may have seen him, but convinced that his man had never set foot in the Parlor House, he placed the photograph back in the envelope. "I know he doesn't look like much, but he may have had a lot of cash on him because he's also a burglar."

"Well, if Annabelle had a weakness, it was a man who had a lot of cash on him. I just don't think she would ever gone anywhere with a man who looks like that. She had class. But I know she wanted to make a ton of money and quit . . . living here. She wanted to move to San Francisco, but she wouldn't have left without telling me or any of us. We're like a family here."

"I know the ladies who live here with you are very respectable women. I've never had any problems with you or your girls. I just want to find the one responsible and see that he pays the ultimate price for coming into our town and doing what he did. Uhhh . . . but one other thing if I may ask? Did Annabelle have a pair of ruby red high heel shoes with a single strap, perhaps brand-new?

Paige put her right index finger to her mouth and looked through the marshal thinking. "Annabelle had several pairs of shoes. I don't remember her wearing a pair of ruby red shoes at all. She wouldn't have worn them the afternoon that she went out as she was just going to the store and wasn't dolled up or anything like that. I will ask the girls if any of them have a pair of shoes like those you have described though."

"Thank you, Paige. Me and my deputies will do everything we can to find her."

"I understand, Marshal, and I appreciate what you and your deputies are doing. I'm afraid I can't help you much, but if there's anything you hear about Annabelle, please let me know."

"I will, Paige." He pushed himself from the couch and started walking toward the front door. "It's always nice to see you, Paige. Take care of yourself."

"I will, Marshal. And you do the same."

The marshal walked outside as the sun began to hang low in the western sky over the mountain. There was still an hour or so before it began to get dark. As he began to walk up the road back into town, he thought about Shirley. He couldn't imagine how he would feel if anything ever happened to her. She meant the world to him. Someday she would probably bear him a child or two.

He kept walking up the hill into town. He thought about how he hadn't seen his mother in two years. That had been at his father's funeral. He wondered how she was doing since his father had died. She lived with his sister in a small Kansas town. Maybe next year when he and Shirley got married, he would pay for them to come to Jerome in a nice automobile.

He hadn't written his mother or sister in a while either. Neither were too happy when he decided to take the marshal job in this Wild West town where the marshal before him had been gunned down in the street. He would write them another letter. Let them know that he was doing fine. He wouldn't tell them about the prostitutes that had gone missing with one found murdered. He'd tell them about how old widow Olsen had reported that her pig was stolen and was going to file a lawsuit against the town if they didn't find it. He found it digging up the vegetable garden behind one of the town surgeon's home two days later. Yeah, they could handle that.

33

C. W. had made it up to Clark Street where he sat on a ledge and watched the happy couples playing golf at the Dynky Lynx. It was getting dark, but Jerome, being one of the first towns in the state of Arizona to have electricity throughout much of the town, had two tall lamp posts that illuminated the miniature golf course.

He recognized Will Noble playing golf. Will had been a classmate before C. W. was pulled out of school two years ago, a short while after his father's tragic accident. Will and another young man were playing golf with the Sherman sisters. C. W. had also been a classmate of Dorothy Sherman, the younger of the two sisters. While he was seated along the ledge killing time, he noticed Will and Dorothy whispering about something, then looking up at him. He knew they were talking about him.

He hoped that one day he would return to school. He liked the structure and all the friends he once had. It was just that his mother and father both died so close apart. He was a kid and didn't handle their deaths very well. He still thought of his father every time he heard a loud boom from the open-pit mine.

He didn't like people talking about him. They probably were feeling sorry for him for losing his parents at such an early age. He didn't like that either. He thought he would walk down Clark Street rather than going back down Main Street. Walking east on Clark Street, he passed by the Telephone Building and some apartments. Looking up toward the mountain, he saw the Club House Hospital and the magnificent Chief Surgeon's House.

The hospital brought back memories of when his mother was sick and dying. Like so many others, she contracted the influenza virus, and there was nothing anyone could do to save her.

He started down the winding streets of nice neighborhood homes before coming out on the east side of Main Street across from the Flatiron Building. He wasn't sure if the two hours had passed or not, but his legs were getting tired from all the walking he had done that day.

He sat down on a bench near the barbershop as several people walked past in both directions. After a few minutes passed, he decided to walk past the restaurant to see if it was still full with Italian customers. He was happy to see that it wasn't as crowded as before although there were still people seated at a few tables.

Much to his delight, Chiara looked out and smiled. She held up a few fingers indicating that she would be a few minutes. He smiled back at her and mouthed, "OK."

Five minutes later, she walked out the front door, looking over her shoulder and wiping her hands on her apron. "Hello. How are you?"

C. W. was awestruck by the young girl's attractive features. She was thin and dainty, yet healthy looking with a clear and dark complexion. Her eyes were dark as coal. Perfect white teeth hid behind a thin smile. Her long straight brown hair fell halfway down her back. Her face was as pretty as any he had ever seen. She was more beautiful than he remembered.

"I'm good." At a loss for words he said, "You know, my grandfather and I are going to come in here and have lunch next week. Will that be all right?"

"Yes, of course. You don't have to be Italian to eat here," she chuckled.

"I've eaten spaghetti before, but that's the only Italian food, I think."

"My mama is a magnifico . . . uhh . . . magnificent cook. You and your grandfather will really like it. I promise."

"Oh, I know we will. We don't eat away from the house too much."

"No? Hey listen. I can't talk much. My papa will get angry. I like you. You're a nice boy. I'm finished here tomorrow at three or four o'clock. Maybe you pass by, no? My mama is OK with me talking to you. My papa still thinks we're in Italy."

At that moment, Chiara's father stuck his head out the front door and yelled, "Ottenga dentro qui immediatamente!"

"I'm sorry. I must go now. Maybe I see you tomorrow." As she turned to hurry inside, her long brown hair whipped around wildly behind her.

He said good-bye to no one and turned. What had happened had not quite sunk in. *Did she say she liked him?* What was happening to him? Just last week, a beautiful woman spoke to him nicely and offered to buy him a soda. Now, the Italian girl whom he had a crush on for as long as he could remember told him she liked him. And that he was nice. A smile emerged on his face as far and wide as the open-pit mine.

Someone from above must be looking down on him. He wanted to run home and tell his mother that the beautiful Italian girl told him she liked him and asked him to come by and see her the next day. He knew his mother would not be at home, but he didn't allow himself to feel sadness at this time.

Now, he was looking forward to tomorrow. On Monday, he would start his job and would probably be running into Chiara all the time. Her family's restaurant wasn't far from the grocery store at all. And he would be earning money. Although he had been walking all day and his legs were tired, his feet barely touched the ground as he ran down Hull Avenue, in and out of the people on the streets, all the way to his front door.

34

Pazrosky wasn't sure why he was doing Homer a favor. He wasn't the sympathetic type by any means. His visit in the Cribs could have gotten him in trouble. Besides, he hated whores. Nor was the urge driving him. Maybe he saw it as a business opportunity. He could supply the whores in the Cribs with their hooch since what he tasted was awful.

He walked back to the boardinghouse, went inside, and poured himself a drink. He wasn't feeling the paranoia as much as he had earlier, but he wished he hadn't smoked that reefer with the whore. Five minutes later, he got in the Ford, with its now-peculiar smell of decay and disinfectant, and drove back up to town.

He met Lucille and the other girl, Izzy, just outside the Cribs in front of the Nevada Cafe on Hull Avenue. The smell of their strong, cheap perfume overpowered any strange scent that was emitting from the Ford, at least as far as he could tell. Neither of the girls mentioned it.

They spoke between themselves during the drive along the dirt road up the gulch to Homer's. Pazrosky was inebriated more than usual. He missed the turnoff to Homer's and had to back up. He had never been to Homer's during the nighttime. He didn't care if Homer had tidied up his roach-infested squalid of an abode or not. He had no intentions of impressing these women. And if he was trying to impress someone, he certainly wouldn't take them to Homer's.

He pulled into the area in front of the home. A gas lamp was burning in the window. Pazrosky laid on the horn before the Ford came to a stop. *Ah-oooga. Ah-ooga.* Pazrosky and the two women got out and walked toward the front door.

A man walked out of the home. Pazrosky blinked his eyes in surprise. In the light coming from behind the man, Pazrosky was shocked. The man was Homer. He had shaved and had taken a pair of scissors to his long unkempt hair. His hair was nicely groomed and combed neatly straight back. He was wearing clean clothes and didn't stink.

"Well, hello, Henry. I didn't know if I would be seeing you this evening or not. Who are your lovely guests?"

Pazrosky was wondering if the reefer he had smoked had some kind of hallucinogenic agent in it. "Umm . . . Homer, this is . . . umm . . . Lucille and Lizzy."

"Izzy," the tall girl with the long wavy red hair answered, correcting Pazrosky but not showing any offense by his slight. She held out her hand which Homer accepted and shook considerately.

"It's my pleasure, Izzy. Welcome to my little home. And, Lucille, it's nice to meet you as well. Please come in. Can I get either of you a drink?"

Izzy, a taller-than-average woman of twenty-five or twenty-six, had a round face and was a little on the heavy side. She answered Homer's question first, "I would love to have a drink, Homer. Thank you. Lucille?" She turned toward the shorter woman with the strawberry blonde hair.

"Yes, that would be nice."

Pazrosky stood back and couldn't believe what he was seeing. Homer had got himself cleaned up nice. He had even gone to a lot of trouble to sweep out and clean his home. He had used the cleaning agents that Pazrosky had left to clean up the place too. The home was aired out, and the deodorizer made the place smell fairly decent.

"Henry, I only have two clean glasses for the ladies. You and me will have to use these tin cans. I washed them out, so they're clean. Help yourself to the bread and cheese. I didn't believe Henry when he said he was going to bring two lovely ladies up here, so I didn't have a chance to run by the store and pick up anything else. Sorry."

Pazrosky still couldn't believe his eyes. He realized that he hadn't said a word since Homer opened the door and invited them in. He finally spoke, "Good to see you, Homer. I'd love a drink. I was telling Lucille that you and me know where to get the good hooch. That stuff I had at her place tasted like horse piss."

"Well, excuse me, monsieur. I'm sorry that I didn't have some French champagne for you. I didn't know that such a butter-and-egg man would be gracing my home with his presence." Izzy laughed, and Lucille and Homer joined her.

"I don't know if I'd call Henry a 'butter-and-egg man,' but I know he's a quite a sharp businessman."

Homer was like a different man. Pazrosky didn't feel that he was so superior to the man like he usually did. Homer was feeding the girls compliments about him like no one had ever done before. Continuing, he said, "I don't know if Henry told you, but we've talked about going into some kind of business venture together."

"Well, this hooch is pretty good stuff, goes down smoother than most hooch I've tasted. It even has a nice sweet aftertaste to it," Lucille said. "If you can get your hands on some of this stuff, I know some girls in the Crib . . . our neighborhood who would love to have some around to serve our guests."

Izzy smiled, exposing a missing tooth. "It does go down pretty smooth."

Homer was taking charge as host, which was fine with Pazrosky. Pazrosky was very inebriated. He stood up and said, "Ladies, Henry, how 'bout if we go outside? I've got a couple logs in the fire pit. We can get a fire going and enjoy the stars."

"Good idea, Homer. That sounds dreamy." Izzy appeared to have taken a liking to the pint-sized man. "Lucille, that sounds fun, doesn't it?"

Homer poured drinks all around from his glass jug. He was having the best time he had in years. He smiled at his friend Henry. He was grateful for the company, especially the female companionship. He let Henry know how appreciative he was the first opportunity the men were alone.

Pazrosky never had a good friend before. In his highly inebriated state, he was glad that he came to Jerome. The town had been good to him. He wondered if he could continue living here as if nothing had happened. He had never been a productive member of any community before. He had burglarized, assaulted, and murdered people his entire adult life. He didn't know if he could ever get that out of his system.

The four people sat on stumps around a fire and drank to where they all were dead drunk. No one could walk a straight line, and they had all stumbled with Pazrosky having to pick himself up and dust off his britches. They all laughed loudly when he swayed to his side, lost his battle, and tumbled to the ground, including him. The four were having a grand ole time.

Izzy and Homer made an odd couple, as she was four or five inches taller, but they hit it off and had taken a walk alone behind the shed that he had locked. Neither had mentioned that they had a still on the premises. They were playing roles as businessmen, which provided a false appearance of importance. Hiding behind their guises of respectability, the girls didn't seem to care. They were buying whatever the men were selling. Both seemed to be happy to be away from the Cribs if only a fifteen-minute drive away.

The lights of Jerome shined brightly below Homer's place and, along with the fire, contributed to the calming ambiance of the night. Pazrosky and Lucille found themselves separated from Homer and Izzy who had wandered off somewhere. They walked up the hill and stood looking down on the fire and the lights of the town. Pazrosky lit another cigarette.

"Henry, I thought you said your friend was bashful. He seems like a pretty swell fellow that knows how to entertain the ladies."

"Uhh . . . yessirre," Henry said with slurred speech. "That's my buddy Homer all right."

"Why don't you tell me a little about yourself, Henry?"

He pulled her next to him forcefully. "Because that's not what I paid you for." He spun her around so he was holding her from behind. His hands began aggressively groping her from her neck down to her waist.

"All right. All right. Just take it easy. Not so rough."

"Rough? You call this rough? You ain't seen rough."

She broke from his grip to turn and face him. She looked him square in the eyes. "Please, Henry, you're scaring me. Let's just go slower. I think yer the cat's pajamas. Without the rough stuff."

The drunken Pazrosky was taken aback by her pleads. He thought about striking the woman, but this wasn't the right time or place.

She stepped closer and wrapped her arms around him delicately. "I know that you've paid me and everything, but things still need to be on my terms. I'm having such a nice evening."

Pazrosky wasn't used to a woman speaking to him so lovingly like this and first thought it had to be a con job. He didn't know whether to trust her or not. After all, she was a whore. But in a fleeting moment of coming to his senses, he realized this wasn't the time or place to do something stupid. Or violent. Whore or not, the woman was treating him with something he hadn't experienced before. He wasn't sure what it was, but he thought it might be respect. How was she so different than the other girls he grabbed out of the Cribs?

Pazrosky sat straight down in the dirt. Lucille sat next to him. She rolled into him and kissed him on the cheek. She began kissing him lightly all over his face until he turned his face and returned her passion. Leaning back on his arms, she was now the aggressor. Her hands ran over his chest and up to his face and beard. She ran her fingers through his hair, then stopped abruptly. "What is this greasy stuff in your hair?"

He quickly sat up. He had forgotten that his dark blond hair was now black from the shoe polish. "Uhh . . . it's a hair tonic that my barber recommended for me. I got it the other day when I was in for my . . . monthly haircut."

"I was just asking. No need to get all clammed up."

"I ain't getting all clammed up. Just keep yer fingers out of my hair." He rolled over on top of her; then he kissed her on the lips with no objection. The two rolled between the deer grass and the dirt, sharing their passionate lust. They were oblivious to their surroundings but at the same time soaked up the cool evening mountain breeze and the starry-filled night.

An hour later, when they were finished, Pazrosky stood up, pulled up, then brushed some of the dirt from the seat of his pants. His mouth was dry. He woke up Lucille, and they walked past the now-smoldering fire and into Homer's small hut.

They were greeted with hysterical laughter from Homer and Izzy, who was sitting across Homer's lap at the table, the bottle of hooch in front of them. In between his fit of boyish laughter, Homer managed to say, "There ain't a Chinaman alive that's gonna get them clothes clean. And another thing, you two gonna audition for a vaudeville act with Al Jolson cuz you sure got the black faces for it!"

35

Lilly Rogers had taken the money she had "earned" on her back all Saturday afternoon and early evening and went out into the night. She walked down past the other cribs and through the Mexican section to the outlying district north known as Chinatown.

The stars shined brightly overhead. But the slight breeze, which had been blowing from the northwest, had left a hovering and foggy haze of smoke from the smelters in Clarkdale that burned nonstop, above the lower area of town. This foul smell didn't bother her. Where she was going, the air was likely to be much worse.

Like a moon halo, a prophecy of inclement weather to come, the lone streetlamp cast a forewarning circle of pale light down on the home of the Chinese peoples' front entryway. In lieu of actual moonlight, the streetlamp and the starry sky sparkling through the haze were the only sources of illumination this far outside town.

Confined to her addiction was like being chained to a brick wall. A prisoner to the Chinese people's opium for the last year and a half, her life was beginning to unravel like the hem on a cheap dress. She knocked on the door at the home of Yao Jiang.

Jiang and his brother owned the Laundry on Main Street. They had also constructed an opium den in their basement that only a select few—granted, the dregs of Jerome's society—knew about. The small Chinatown area of Jerome was nothing like the Chinatown in San Francisco or Seattle. It was generally a peaceful and law-abiding area. It had shrunk in size from its heyday after the turn of the century.

Jiang answered the door and let her in. He was a quiet small man with an old ivory face with flat Mongolian features. On this evening, he wore a colorful silk robe of blues and purples with wide sleeves, black edges, and a round collar. His long black hair was braided in a pigtail that hung down his back. He bowed at Lilly. "Ahh, Miss Lilly. Please come in. Where your friend Miss Jenny?"

She had a sad face. "I haven't seen her in a while. I'm not sure where she went."

"Oh, that too bad," Jiang replied sincerely.

Lilly walked into the living area where Jiang's brother, Mao, was seated and reading a newspaper with large Chinese characters. A Siamese cat lay at his feet. He simply nodded as Jiang escorted her through the living area and to a back room. Incense was burning in the front room, a roomful of Chinese carvings and several images covered with gold leaf. A picture of a pouncing tiger on a black background adorned the east wall.

The Yao family had once been the proprietors of a restaurant as well as a laundry parlor back when Jerome was still a mining camp. Yao's parents had come to Jerome via San Francisco in the late 1800s. Earlier generations of Yao worked on the transcontinental rail line and decided to make their homes in the American West. Within the past few years, both parents of Jiang and Mao had passed away.

Jiang placed his hand on Lilly's shoulder. "May I bring you a cup of tea?" She would have liked a shot of whiskey, but the Chinese people generally didn't care for the American whiskey, nor morphine for that matter, which could have been easily purchased.

"No, thank you, Jiang. I won't be staying long tonight. I have something for you." She placed $5 into Jiang's palm.

"Please come with me." He led her to the back room and opened a trapdoor to reveal a stairwell that led into a dim-lit basement. She followed him down into the cramped basement. The small enclosed area was about eight feet by eight feet. The ceiling was barely seven feet high. There were two bunk beds along the far wall, each capable of accommodating two people.

When she had descended into the basement, where she had been several times before but never by herself, she saw two white men lying on one of the bunk beds. A Chinese man lay alone on the other bunk, smoking from a large clay pipe.

The two white men lay on the other bunk facing each other. They rested their heads on the same pillow. Between the men was a small glass lamp that was filled with a colorless Chinese oil. The oil burned without smoke or odor. A small jar made from rhinoceros horn also sat between the two white men. The horn contained about half a shot glass of opium, a dark semifluid narcotic drug.

The men were totally intoxicated by the drug. They did not respond when she came down into the room although both saw her. They had no inhibitions and paid her no attention. She had no fear of being molested by the hopped-up men.

Jiang went to a small shelf that contained several items of paraphernalia and grabbed a ten-inch clay pipe. He placed a small amount of opium in the bowl and handed it to her. "Stay as long as you wish. Here is something 'specially for you." He handed her a small package wrapped in paper. From past experience, she knew that it was a small amount of opium in a pillbox. "I trust you still have that gift I gave you last time."

On the previous time when she and Jenny had gone to Jiang's, she performed a sexual act on Jiang in exchange for a night of opium use in the basement. In addition to the opium, he had given her a gift in exchange for her services, an opium pipe made from cactus wood inlaid with mother-of-pearl. It was a beautiful pipe. She and Jenny used to smoke opium from it in their small crib. She actually preferred to smoke the opium in the privacy of the crib but always got a much bigger rush when Jiang set it up for her in his basement.

From the lamp, Jiang lit a tightly rolled paper and held it over the bowl while Lilly inhaled through the clay pipe. In moments, a gentle, calm drowsy sensation came over her. She sat down on a mat that lay over the dirt floor. Jiang lit the paper again and lit the pipe for Lilly. "You finish bowl if you like, I go back upstairs now." He turned and drifted out of the room.

The Chinese man smoking from the large clay pipe looked at her and smiled, not lifting his head from the pillow. She smiled back at him.

Lilly lit the pipe again and again before it finally would not smoke for her anymore. She experienced a warm flushing feeling of her skin, and her breathing slowed. Her mouth was dry and foul. Her arms and legs felt heavy. She was lying on the dirty mat. *I gotta get out of here.*

A dank dark cloud of stale smoke lingered throughout the small room. In the summer's heat, the basement felt like a dungeon. She now noticed that weathered pictures of dragons and tigers hung on the basement walls and could be seen in the flickering light of the burning lamp.

I gotta get out of this place.

She struggled to detach herself from the wicked surroundings, wiping the dust and soot from her dirty clothes; she floated to the top of the stairs. Reaching the top, she escaped out the back door and into the night.

I gotta get out of here.

In her euphoric state of confusion, she breathed in the heavenly mountain air. She walked home alone in the dark, dragging her heavy legs like she was walking through mud. A false feeling of serenity. The gentle breeze filled her nostrils. When she got near her crib, she saw a tiny white kitten lapping at a saucer of milk. She finally reached and entered her lonely crib, closing the door firmly behind her.

She promised herself that she would never return to the opium den.

36

The marshal finally made it back to the jail. The walk had given him time to think about things. He enjoyed his visit with Paige, but it didn't seem to help in their attempt to locate evidence on who may be responsible for the disappearance of Annabelle James.

He entered the jail and threw the envelope containing the photograph on the desk. Deputy Ray heard him come in from the kitchen area in the back. "Well, Marshal, what did you find out?"

"Not much, I'm afraid. According to Paige, Annabelle wasn't on a date or whatever you want to call it. She was out in the afternoon shopping around for perfume and never came back to the house."

"Oh. Do you want me to ask some of the store owners if they saw her with anyone on the day she disappeared?"

"I reckon if we just keep doin' what we're doing, keepin' our eyes and ears open. Paige didn't remember her owning a pair of red high heels like the one the old miner had told us about, but I bet ya them girls at the Parlor own a lot of shoes."

"I reckon they do."

"Maybe one of us should go by that house and pick that shoe up today or tomorrow. I'd like to show it to that girl in the Cribs. The one whose friend left with a fellow in the suit in an automobile. She may be the only one that can give us any help. I'm still a little worried about her too."

"You mean because she may be able to identify him?"

"Yeah." The marshal got up and poured himself a cup of coffee that Billy had heated on the stove. "Probably better if Jim or Dave go back over there since they've already talked with the girl. They said she was a little loco."

"Yeah, most of them girls are, I reckon," Billy replied. "Jim stepped in while you were out. He'll be on his way back for his evening shift shortly. Dave will be in, in the morning."

"Good enough. I'll be on duty until at least nine or ten tonight."

"Marshal, if things ain't too crazy, maybe you should take your girl out. Me and Jim will be here."

"Thank you, Billy. But Shirl has got to get it through her sweet thick skull that I've got a job to do around here. Two deputies ain't much if there's a shootin' or a bank robbery. Saturdays can get pretty crazy around here. Hell, I'm surprised we haven't had a gang of professionals come through here knowin' how lightly staffed our marshal's office is."

"When was the last time you talked with Sheriff Thompson?"

"I spoke with him on the telephone a few days back. He said he'd be back over sometime next week."

"I went across the street and spoke to Clarence. You know him. He's all ready to get back out and help searchin' for them two girls."

"Good fella, that Clarence Schneider. You should have seen him when he found the dead girl buried under them rocks. Looked like he just walked in on his sister kissin' his cousin. He was perty upset about it. But then, I suppose we all were."

"Where did you want us to look on Monday?" Billy asked.

"I'd like to take it a little farther down the gulch near the slaughterhouse. I was thinkin' that the way the train tracks loop around not too far from there. And that was where the boy had found the red shoe."

"The mystery of the ruby red shoe," Billy chimed in. "It sounds like a Sherlock Holmes story."

"Yeah," the marshal chuckled. "I reckon it does, but that's about all we got. Maybe Jim or Dave should visit that girl in the Cribs tomorrow, come to think of it. We're all going to be tied up on Monday with the search." He took another sip of coffee.

At 7:00, Deputy Evans walked in and greeted the marshal and Billy. "Howdy, gentlemen. How have things gone today? Perty slow, I hope."

"No one's been shot down yet. Maybe they was waitin' for you to come on," Billy quipped.

"It's getting crowded out there. How come people just don't stay home on Saturday nights?" he asked.

"Ahhh . . . come on, Jim. That would make our jobs too easy." The marshal got up from where he was seated behind the desk and walked out toward the front door. "How 'bout one of you fellas take a walk over to the Mineflower a little later tonight? I hear it's been gettin' kind of rowdy in there. See if Roy wants to go on that search with us on Monday morning. That place gets more business than any business in town. I don't think the presence of a lawman is going to scare any away. Probably gonna be a little drinkin' goin' on in there, but don't go bustin' any bottles over anyone's head."

"'A little drinkin'?" Billy grumbled. "What's a saloon without a little drinkin'? Prohibition is the dumbest thing those boys in Washington, D.C. ever come up with. If they want that strictly enforced, they should send a half dozen of them U.S. marshals out here and let them do the enforcin'!"

Trying to calm the now-irritated Billy, the marshal said, "Yeah, I know, Billy. Alcohol has been around longer than the pyramids. Besides, we just won the damn war. They don't expect the boys to want to celebrate? I'm sure you young bucks like an occasional snort just as I do, but the law is the law. Just use yer common sense."

Billy continued to rant, "No booze, no whores, no gambling. What's a man supposed to do around here anyways?"

The men laughed. "I betcha a silver dollar that when one of you deputies goes into the Mineflower tonight, there'll be plenty of booze, gamblin', and whorin' goin' on in there. Ya follow what I'm saying? Just be respectful. Roy's a good ole boy, and the owner—what's his name?—he ain't a bad fella either."

Jim thought for a minute before he spoke, "I better go. With all them perty girls that go in there, one of 'em might just drag Billy out on the dance floor."

Billy retaliated, "Shucks, I remember watching you dancin' at Roy and Norma Lou's wedding last spring. I wasn't sure if you was dancin' or stompin' on a rattler."

The men all laughed again before the marshal interjected, "Like I said, I trust you young men to use your best judgment. I would never have hired you young single men as deputies if I thought you'd be carrying on like that. What you do on your time, I reckon, I don't really care, just as long as you're law-abidin' citizens, which I know you are."

"Pa has been asking me a cart full of questions about what we found out about that James girl," Jim said. "I've got a funny feeling that he may have known her, but he won't admit it. I reckon he knows Momma will beat him like a dog if he did know the girl and she found out about it."

"Well, Jim, yer daddy *is* the mayor. He probably makes it his business to know most of the people in town," the marshal pointed out. "He's an honorable man. I wouldn't worry about him too much. I see him all the time, and he ain't never mentioned that he knew her to me."

"Shit, the way Momma yells at him all the time. It wouldn't surprise me if he did know her."

"Nonsense, Jim. All of our women yell at us and tell us what to do. That's why they're women. You been courtin' your girl for a long time now. Don't she ever yell at you for something?"

"I reckon she does. She sure ain't given me no reason to jump in some other girl's bed though."

Billy just sat back on the two back legs of his chair resting against the wall, listening to the marshal and Jim talk. He broke in, "At least your women didn't up and leave you in the dust for some big shot store owner's son."

Jim groaned, "Hell, that happened so long ago. Don't tell me you ain't got over her yet."

"I'm over her," Billy mumbled under his breath.

37

C. W. was waiting at the kitchen table when his grandfather came home from work late Saturday night. He tossed his hard hat on the floor and grabbed a root beer out of the icebox. "Anyone from the marshal's office been by today?"

"No. I don't think so. I took a walk through town earlier, but I ain't seen the marshal or anyone come by. Why?"

"I was just wunderin'. I talked to Marshal Williams for a few minutes before I went to work. I told him you found a woman's red shoe down in the gulch. He said he would come by and get it. Might help in their investigation. Just make sure we keep it up so Jake doesn't get his paws on it."

The faithful hound lay on the floor near the table where C. W. and his grandfather were seated.

"Well, anything excitin' happen in town?"

C. W. blurted it out, "I talked to Chiara. I told her that you and me were going to have lunch or dinner at her family's restaurant sometime next week."

"You did, did ya?" He grabbed some bread and cheese from the counter while he was considering the suggestion. "Ummm . . . Italian food huh . . . ? I reckon I could go eat a plate of spaghetti or something."

"I can pay for it, Grandpa. I've saved the money you've been giving me for my allowance. And I start my job at the grocery store Monday."

"Oh, don't worry about who pays. We ain't got any problems there."

"I'm going to go back and talk to her tomorrow too."

"What do her mother and father think about that?"

"Her father is really strict. He doesn't allow her to talk to me when their restaurant is busy. I think it is just her and her parents that work there. I hope that if she can get away for a few minutes, we could go for a walk or go have an ice cream soda at the drugstore."

"That doesn't sound like a bad idea. Just remember to be respectful to her and her parents. The Italian people are a might funny 'bout that." Barney yawned and rubbed his eyes. He still had the remains of the mine dirt and dust on him. The men who worked in the mines had a large shower house that they used after a shift and a change of clothes. But dirt seemed to follow Barney everywhere.

"Well, I'm gonna wash up a little and hit the sack." He got up and walked toward the washbasin area, a small wooden table on the east side of the house. He scooped the basin in a large barrel of recently replenished rainwater and a bar of lye soap and scrubbed his face and hands.

C. W. had a long day and was starting to get tired himself. He was still excited about his conversation with the beautiful long-haired Italian girl. He was even more excited at the prospect of seeing her again tomorrow.

Jake had found what was left over of the ham bone he had been chewing on all day. He was lying in his favorite place, on an old rug in the corner of the kitchen. He was very content.

Barney walked back in the house and sat on the divan. "Maybe you should think about gettin' to bed yerself. Sounds like you got a big day ahead of you tomorrow. I wouldn't doubt it if it rained again. It sure has been hot the last few days."

"Aw right, Grandpa." C. W. walked back to the small house's lone bedroom. He partially closed the door behind him. He always left it slightly ajar. Jake always seemed to want to join him sometime during the night. He turned to his grandfather who was stretched out on the divan in the living room, "Good night, Grandpa. See you in the morning."

"Good night, C. W."

C. W. slept soundly when he finally was able to go to sleep. He was thinking about what Chiara had told him about liking him, that he was a nice fella. He saw Chiara as someone who could be a close friend. He wasn't thinking too much about kissing and the other stuff. In time, that would interest him. He had never done any of that. Although the new job would be a welcome change, he knew that he had no close friends. He hoped that Chiara would be one.

C. W. awoke to the smell of bacon frying on the griddle and coffee brewing. That and a few licks across the face from Jake who was anxious for C. W. to get out of bed and join him in a new day. "Aw right. Aw right. Quit lickin' my face, Jake. I'm getting up."

C. W. crawled out of bed and walked into the kitchen, accompanied by the loyal canine. His grandfather was standing over a skillet full of bacon and biscuits. "Well, lookie here. I didn't know if you were gonna join us for breakfast today or not."

"I couldn't get to sleep for a while last night."

"You must have something on yer mind . . . like an Italian girl."

He smiled. "Yeah, maybe. You know, Grandpa, I was thinkin', I just don't have too many friends anymore."

"I know. Have you ever thought about wanting to go back to school in the fall? You can keep your job at the grocery store. Schoolin' would be good for you. You were a perty good student when you wanted to be."

"What about my chores around here?"

Barney was concentrating on a biscuit that he held in his left hand and was buttering. "Between the two of us, we'll be all right. You're seventeen years old now. Maybe I should never have pulled you out of school in the first place."

C. W sat down at the table and tore into a thick slice of bacon. "I saw some people whom I used to go to school with yesterday when I was in town. They didn't say hello or anything, but I knew they were talking about me."

"They probably know that you went through a spell of bad luck and don't know what to say to ya. Besides, I'm sure you'll meet some new friends after you start your job tomorrow." Barney got up from the table and scraped some scraps off his plate into Jake's bowl. "Now, I have to get ready for church. You coming with me?"

"Yes, sir. I think I have a clean shirt."

"That reminds me. Since you start your job tomorrow, maybe when we get back from church today, you can help me wash some clothes."

"Sure, Grandpa. But do you think it's gonna rain again today?"

"Smells like it might. I want to go to the company store after church and look at some boots. My old ones got holes in them and are fallin' apart. That Italian restaurant open on Sundays?"

"Yes, Grandpa. Do you want to go there with me and have something to eat?"

"I don't want to get in the way of yer courtin'," he joked.

"It ain't like that, Grandpa. But since we're gonna have our Sunday clothes on, maybe it ain't a bad idea."

"Maybe it ain't. Well, we got less than an hour before we got to be in church, so go on and get ready."

38

Ashley got dressed and came downstairs for the formal Sunday breakfast. The other girls, including Paige, had all just been seated. Cecile was bringing the several courses onto the large walnut dining table. Ashley was hungry. The entire home had a savory aroma including that of fresh bread, bacon, and coffee.

As the girls were all seated, Cecile announced that breakfast this morning would start with fried fish with bacon and onions, broiled beefsteak, fried mush, fresh croissants and marmalade, and hot pancakes and syrup. As was customary, a place setting at the table was reserved for Annabelle in the ever-decreasingly meager chance that she would appear for breakfast.

Ashley was now accustomed to the lifestyle that Paige had provided for her. She ate the best foods, wore the nicest clothes, had all the furnishings that she ever desired, and hung on the arms of the wealthiest and most prominent men in all of Yavapai County and beyond.

Paige was dressed in a bright yellow gown. She was in good spirits this morning. "I trust everyone all had wonderful Saturday nights. Or Saturday afternoon in Ashley's case."

Gloria, Norma, and Marian all nodded their heads in confirmation, chewing on their breakfasts. Ashley smiled. "Yes, ma'am. I had a lovely afternoon. Thank you."

Paige coaxed the girls, "Does anyone feel like sharing?"

All eyes were on Ashley, and she felt the fixed stares. "Oh, I went horseback riding down in the valley with a rancher. A very nice gentleman, if I must say so. We had a simple picnic of bread, cheese, and wine under a large shady tree. He was wonderful. The horses were wonderful. It was one of the nicest times that I can remember."

The girls all gushed in envy. Then Norma spoke first, "Well, I thought I had a truly wonderful evening, but after listening to Ashley's day, I think my day paled in comparison."

Marian then spoke, "I too had a splendid evening. I must thank Cecile and Paige for their recommendation. Alexander Weiss, the lawyer, took me to see *Carmen* at the opera house."

Paige beamed. "Oh, I'm glad you liked it. It was written by a Frenchman, Georges Bizet. I, too, thought it was a marvelous production."

Norma asked, "What's it about?"

Marian looked at Paige first, then answered, "It's a stunning story about a gypsy with a real fiery temper. She falls for a soldier, Don Jose, then leaves him for a bullfighter. It took place in Seville, Spain. I don't want to tell you any more and spoil it for you, but I absolutely loved it."

Gloria then teased her, "Talk about setting the table for a wonderful evening. What on earth did you do for an encore?"

Marian blushed and giggled. "Oh, he took me to see his home up on Company Hill. It was really quite impressive."

Norma broke in, "What, the house or Mr. Weiss?"

The girls all laughed. Paige said, "Now, girls. Let's not forget that we are all ladies. We must act like ladies at all times. I'm sure Marian represented the Parlor House with all her charm and grace. Although I must say, it was very late in the evening, or early in the morning, when I heard you return."

The girls all laughed again. Marian's cheeks began to turn a rosy red. "I fell asleep after a couple glasses of wine. What about you, Gloria? What did you do?"

"Well, I escorted Dr. Roscoe Tanner to dinner at the Bartlett Hotel. I had a lovely steak dinner, but nothing compared to how Cecile cooks around here. I was in bed early."

The girls all chuckled at her innuendo.

"Great," Paige said. "I'm glad everyone is happy. After breakfast, Cecile and I are going for a drive to Prescott to pick up some supplies. So we won't be going to church. Hopefully, we won't get caught in the rain. We won't be back until dark. Does anyone need anything? Or does anyone want to come along?"

Norma spoke, "Oh, I would like to go for the ride. I have nothing planned for today."

"Fine. Anyone else?" Paige asked.

Ashley spoke, "I think I will just stay and finish reading my book, *The Age of Innocence*. It's actually very good."

Gloria and Marian both declined also.

"Very well. I hope you three have a lovely day. Oh, I almost forgot. Dr. Ellison wants to see everyone this Thursday for your monthly physical exams."

When the girls all groaned, Paige responded, "Now, girls. It really is for your own good. I can only screen out prospective clients so much. I'm positive that, like always, everyone will pass their exam."

39

It was the middle of the night when Pazrosky drove the two women back to the Cribs. He and Lucille had scrubbed their faces, but their clothes remained filthy, stained with dirt and boot polish. A town that never sleeps, Jerome still had several night owls walking on the streets. There was some bustle in the Cribs as well, making Pazrosky nervous.

He pulled up in front of the Nevada Cafe where there were a number of people dining at this hour. He was dead tired and wanted to return to the boardinghouse and sleep. Lucille baited him with smoking a reefer in her crib, but he was not interested.

He felt awkward as the girls got out and thanked him for a nice time. He hated women, especially whores. They had conned him his entire life, starting with his momma who was the biggest whore of them all. Lying with his uncle, and who knows who all else, every time his daddy went to jail, which was more often than not.

He had felt some anger. He always took it. And if he paid for it, it was his to take as he wished. But he liked the way Lucille had made him feel that night. When Homer and Izzy had laughed hysterically at them after they had been rolling around in the dirt, they weren't just laughing at him but her too. And they deserved to be laughed at. He thought he might take it a little easier with the boot polish, but he felt more safe knowing he had committed all his crimes, including murder, with his natural dark blond hair. He thought he may have to make a trip back to the barber. But there was a chance that one day, the cops might go there asking questions, so he ruled that out.

He drove up Jerome Avenue where he planned on taking a left on Main Street and down Main to his boardinghouse. In front of the Miner's Tavern, across the street from the English Kitchen, he saw her. The whore from the cribs. *What was this broad's name?* He felt a jolt of panic that she may remember the vehicle. He then relaxed, realizing that black Ford Model Ts were everywhere, and his appearance had changed since he had last seen her—or more importantly, since she had last seen him.

And there was something else that made him breathe easier. She paid no attention to him as he drove past her slowly. She was acting very strange. She was like walking dead. Then it hit him. She was hopped up on some kind of dope. She was acting far too strange to be drunk of alcohol or doped up on reefer. He guessed that she was likely high on opium or morphine. This was certainly not an unreasonable deduction, considering the number of whores who had opium addictions in Jerome.

He looked over his shoulder and watched Lucille and Izzy walk down Hull Avenue into the Cribs District. They were talking while they walked and paid him no attention. He looked around and saw that no one was paying him any attention.

He pulled the Ford over, near the Hotel Conner, keeping his eye on the girl, who had her head tilted upward as if she was watching the sky and mumbling something to herself. She continued to walk up the street as she stared at the sky. He got out of the car and walked around it. She was preoccupied with something when Pazrosky approached her. With an aristocratic accent, he said, "Pardon me, ma'am, I was wondering if you may be able to help me. I'm looking for my brother. I'm afraid he may have drank too much here at the hotel and went for a walk, and I can't seem to find him anywhere."

With a look of confusion in her cloudy eyes, she looked through Pazrosky like he was an apparition. Her pupils were nonexistent. "Wha . . . what did you say, mister?"

"I beg your pardon, ma'am, I'm not from here and was hoping you could help me find my brother. We got into town late—"

"Uhh . . . I don't know." She tried to focus on his face, and then her gaze lowered her eyes to his soiled clothing. "I don't know how I can help you."

Looking around, making sure no one was watching this conversation, he didn't feel tired anymore. He glanced up to where a man walked out of the hotel, crossed the street, and walked past them without noticing them.

"Well, if you could help me, I would be happy to give you $20."

"Huh . . . $20 . . . to find your brother?"

"Yes, ma'am. Could you use the $20?"

"Twenty dollars? Uhh . . . yeah."

"I just need you to come with me and drive up and down the street for a couple of minutes. That's all. Then I'll take you to your home. Do you live near here?"

"Uhh . . . yeah . . . yes . . . I live over there." She pointed toward the Cribs.

"Oh good. Not too far. I can have you back home in just a few minutes."

"OK . . . you'll give me $20?"

Getting impatient, he answered, "Yes, my wallet is in my car. Come with me."

"OK." She followed him to where the Model T was parked nearby. He opened the door for her. He walked quickly around the back of the Ford and slipped into the driver's seat.

"I really appreciate this. What did you say your name was? My name is Jeffrey Davis."

"Umm . . . Lilly. My name is Lilly." *Lilly, that's it!*

Pazrosky pulled away from his parking spot and turned right in front of the Hotel Conner. He peeked over her into the hotel as if he was looking for someone and continued driving west. He took the loop around Clark Street and continued eastward.

"I'm sorry, Lilly. You don't look well. Are you feeling all right?" He kept talking to her as she just sat there like a zombie. Her head was beginning to nod forward.

"Uhh . . . what?"

Pazrosky grinned an evil sneer. He remembered riding in the boxcar as a skinny sixteen-year-old kid running away from home when, plied on alcohol, the bum in the railcar had cornered him like a cat and a mouse as he fought to get away. While the train rumbled over the tracks—*Click clack click clack*—the stinky old man with the rotten breath had him pinned up against the metal wall. *Click clack click clack.* Through the Texas countryside, the train continued on. *Click clack click clack.* "*What is it, boy? Yer not afraid of old Ernest, are ya?*" *Click clack click clack. Click clack.*

He looked over at the doped-up whore as she appeared to be sleeping. Her breathing was slow. He watched her chest area as it slowly expanded and deflated. He continued the drive along the winding road, with headlights shining straight ahead on the cut cliff walls. He had taken this drive with the classy whore not long ago, but it wasn't pitch-black with darkness then like it was now.

He drove along the bumpy, snaking road for a few more miles while the girl snored quietly. After driving several miles, he found a place where he pulled the Ford off the roadway and cut the lights. He began to defile the woman as she struggled to open her eyes. "Wha . . . what are you doing?" she shrieked.

"What do you think I'm doing?"

"Get off me!"

He dragged the woman by the neck outside the driver's door as her legs banged over the metal floorboards of the Model T. Wrestling combatively in the dirt and brush, his hands found her throat and tightened around it while her hands pulled at his greasy hair with futile results. Feeling the rush of adrenaline that he so craved, he finished squeezing her throat until her lifeless body ceased to defend itself any longer.

He dragged the woman in the dark, up onto a knoll of high grass where he consummated his act of insane violence. Afterward, he threw her slender body over his shoulder and walked blindly into the mountainside. After walking for what seemed like twenty or thirty minutes, he tossed her dead body next to a fallen log. Using his boots, he "shoveled" some dirt away, then grabbed the woman's limp body and tossed it into the shallow hole, partially covering it with rocks. He then retraced his tracks back to the Ford. Carefully, he looked around the immediate area for anything that may have been left behind during the vicious assault. When he was completely satisfied that there was nothing at the scene of the crime, he got back in the vehicle and turned it around toward town.

As he neared Jerome from the southeast, he could see the sun begin to rise on the eastern horizon. Like a lion after a kill, he began to come down from the rush of his kill. He couldn't believe how easy this one was. Hopped up on dope, she was so frail and defenseless. It was too easy.

He entered the town limits and noticed that it had become very quiet. He saw one or two people walking along Main Street. Now he felt tired, but he would sleep all day. He had a feeling of satisfaction knowing the only person in town who might have been able to identify or describe him to the law was gone. He hoped it would be awhile before anyone will find her. Maybe a bear or mountain lion will finish off her remains, so she would never be found.

He parked the Ford and entered the boardinghouse through the side stairwell. He made it to his room and quickly found the bed. He didn't even need a drink or a smoke. He was that tired. He went to sleep having a good feeling about himself.

40

The marshal poured himself a cup of coffee and stepped outside the jail to have a sip. He was grateful that when he returned to the jail following his night out with Shirley, there was no one occupying the holding cell. He still wanted to check with the main jail, but apparently, Saturday night came and went without any serious trouble.

When he left the jail in the hands of Deputies Ray and Evans around nine on the night before, things had been peaceful. They knew how to contact him if there had been anything serious, and they didn't. Deputy Evans had nothing to report when the marshal returned to the jail before midnight. Evans had gone into the Mineflower Saloon and spoke with Roy, but everything there was uneventful. Good crowd but the presence of the lawman may have had something to do with that.

Every now and then, Deputies Evans and Zalensky would catch some ribbing from some of the older men, especially if they had too much to drink or if they felt the deputies were out of line with their lawful responsibilities. This was of course due to their age, both being in their midtwenties. Plus the fact that they were both good-looking and confident young men. Evans, in particular, would catch the occasional flak because his father was the mayor. Zalensky, as some people knew, was a veteran of the Great War and was highly respected by those who knew this.

Deputy Zalensky, now twenty-six years old, had served his country proudly in the war. He was well respected among the townspeople for his service to the country. Originally from Prescott, he served in the 327th Tank Battalion under the command of Ranulf Compton. He was one of the fortunate survivors of the Meuse-Argonne campaign that took the lives of many men and lasted right up until the cessation of hostilities on November

11, 1918. He was a strong-minded man who appeared to have returned from Europe shortly after the war with no emotional scars.

All the marshal's deputies were responsible young men who took their duties seriously. They understood that they had the right to use lethal force if the cause ever presented itself. All were skilled marksmen who carried Colt .45s with standard barrel lengths of five and a half inches in their holsters. A gun locker at the jailhouse held five Remington .38-.40 rifles with several hundred rounds of ammunition.

The marshal stood in front of the jail and sipped on his hot coffee. Deputy Zalensky strolled up to the jail around nine. "Mornin', Marshal."

"Good morning, Dave. How ya been?"

"Not too bad, Marshal. Anything happen around here yesterday?"

"Nope. Perty quiet. Jim went inside the Mineflower last night. The place was busy, but no fights broke out. He didn't stay too long. Talked to Roy a bit. They had one of them jazz bands with a saxophone player, piano, perty girl singin'. Jim said they sounded perty darn good too. That fella must be makin' money hand over fist."

"Shit. Have you seen some of the barmen he's hired there to keep things peaceful? I swear three of 'em are your size. They're like gorillas swinging from trees. I don't know how that place ever gets so rowdy with all those Brunos in there."

"Well, I reckon when you combine alcohol with women and all those men in town, sometime yer gonna end up with a powder keg that's gonna explode."

"Yeah, I reckon."

"Anything you want me to do this morning, Marshal?"

"It's still a little early over in the Cribs. Maybe around noon, you can go back to that girl's place that you were at last week with Jim. Take the photograph of our suspected killer and see if she remembers seeing the palooka anywhere. That helps us if she can identify him, but that still leaves us the job of findin' him."

"Sure, Marshal. I'm gonna have to take a look at my report unless you can remember what her name was."

"I had it out. Her name is Rogers, Lilly Rogers."

"Oh yeah. That was it. She would be kind of a perty little thing if she wasn't so gosh dern nasty!"

"I follow ya. Some of them girls ain't too hard on the eyes. But it's like you say. They're just so filthy nasty."

"I reckon it's perty sad though. I don't know why they can't get jobs waitressing or laundering or something. They take the easy money."

"That's why it's the world's oldest profession," the marshal pointed out.

"That reminds me, Marshal, I was in the J.C. Penney store last week with my girl when one of them girls from the Parlor House came in there to buy some clothes or something. I thought Suzanne was gonna knock the shit out of me 'cause I looked at her. I mean to tell you. I think this gal was pertier than anything I seen when I was in Paris. Dark brown hair, a face like an angel, and a chassis that . . . ," he whistled. "Sure made me glad I was a man, but Suzanne was so dern jealous, she didn't speak to me for over an hour."

"Sounds like the same gal I seen at the opera house once. Shirl acted the same way. Elbowed me in the ribs so hard, I was afraid she might have broken one."

Finishing his coffee, the marshal had forgotten to ask Dave to help himself to a cup. "Why don't you help yerself to a cup of joe. I was thinkin' about cleanin' our rifles before you head over to the Cribs. I need to walk down to the jail and see if anything's going on down there. I thought I might also go by a house down near the Mexican quarters where a boy found a brand-new woman's red high-heeled shoe down in the arroyo the other day. Sundays are perty quiet round here, thank God."

"Thank you, Marshal. A cup of joe sounds good."

Shortly after noon, Shirley poked her head in the doorway. "Knock, knock. Anyone home?"

The marshal and Deputy Zalensky were sitting around the marshal's desk discussing something. They both looked up and smiled. "Hi, honey, come on in," the marshal insisted.

Shirley had a wicker basket covered with a checkered red-and-white cloth in her right hand. "I brought you fellas some lunch. I thought you might be getting hungry."

"Well, ain't that sweet? Thanks, dear." The marshal got up and removed some paper from the desk. "Go on and set that down right here, hon."

He looked at Deputy Zalensky. "Dave, why don't you stick around for a bit and have something to eat. It looks like my beautiful fiancée here has packed enough for a small army."

"Thank you, Shirley. Marshal."

"Here, you boys sit down. Let me get it fixed for you." Shirley took several sandwiches out of the basket and filled two bowls of vegetable soup for the lawmen and set them on the desk.

"Thank you, Shirl. You didn't have to go to all the trouble."

"No trouble at all, Marshal. I thought you fellas were working up an appetite around here."

"Thank you, Shirley," said Deputy Zalensky. "But so far, things have been rather quiet around here."

"So, Shirl, how was church?" the marshal asked.

"Oh, Father Murphy had a wonderful service. You're going to have to get away next Sunday. His sermon was really invigorating. So, Dave, how is Suzanne?"

"She's doing fine. We went to the opera house last night."

"Oh, did you see *Carmen*?" she exclaimed.

"Yes, we did. I was happy that she enjoyed it. The whole thing was boring to me."

After a few minutes, Deputy Zalensky stood up and wiped his mouth with a napkinette. "Thank you, Shirley. That was really a nice lunch. I need to get over and talk to that girl in the Cribs."

"The Cribs?" Shirley asked, shooting a glance at the marshal.

"Yeah, part of our investigation." Zalensky grabbed the envelope with the photograph off the desk and started for the front door. "Thanks again, Shirley. Marshal, anything else you want me to do while I'm out?"

"Why don't you see how Deputy Burns is doing and a little foot patrol around town. I'll catch up with you and you can take that red shoe back to the Cribs. Show that girl, uhh . . . Lilly, the photograph, and anyone else you see hanging around, and see if she can come up with anything else that can help us out."

"Will do." Deputy Zalensky tipped his hat to Shirley and walked out the front door.

Shirley asked, "So which girl is this?"

The marshal answered, "She was with Jenny Richardson the night she got in some fella's Ford and hasn't been seen since. She saw the palooka perfectly but so far hasn't been able to help. When Dave and Jim spoke with her last week, she was all hopped up on reefer, so maybe Dave can get something from her today."

"Oh, is it just you and Dave today? Where's Billy and Jim?"

"Jim will be in later. Billy is off duty today."

"Oh. Well, in case you're interested, Momma is fixing a nice pot roast this afternoon. Are you coming over to the house tonight?"

"You know I am, darling. What time do you want me to come over?"

"Whenever you can get away from here. I'll just be home waiting for you."

The marshal pulled Shirley close to him and embraced her. "I wish I could come over right now, but I have a few things I need to do first."

Shirley loved being in her fiancé's powerful arms. He never touched her when he was in her house, afraid that her mother or father might catch them in a rare public display of affection. She looked up, and her lips met his. After a short kiss, he allowed her some space and looked into her eyes. "I'm so glad you dropped in. I'll get out of here pretty soon and will come up and see you."

"That would be nice. Maybe after dinner, we can sneak back down here, and you can let Jim go home early."

"I like how you're thinking." He grinned suggestively. "Let's see how things go. I want to hear what Dave finds out from that girl in the Cribs."

41

C. W. and his grandfather walked out of the Haven United Methodist Church and gathered with a small group of people outside near the corner of School Street and Center Avenue. A bent-over older man with thin gray hair and a cane walked up to C. W. and his grandfather, extending his right hand and speaking in a soft voice, "Good to see you again, Barney, C. W., I hope this Sunday morning finds you both in the best of health."

C. W. shook his hand and replied, "Yes, sir, Mr. Wickman. We're doing fine? How have you been?"

"I'm not doing too bad for a man of my age, I suppose. I've been a little under the weather the past few weeks with a small touch of grippe, so I haven't seen you gentlemen in church, I'm afraid."

Otto Wickman, a man of seventy-four years, had lived in Jerome since the days when it was just a mining camp. He and his brother had staked a claim that they later sold to the large mining company for a pretty penny. He later ran a saloon in town before selling that business too. He and his late wife, Thelma, had one son who moved to California with his family several years before, leaving Otto to live by himself in his twilight years.

Otto looked at C. W.'s grandfather. "Barney, how are things going at the mine? I'm glad that the slowdown didn't put you out of work."

"Things have certainly slowed down a bit, but they're still keeping me busy," Barney answered.

The rest of the small congregation flocked out of the church and gathered outside, stopping to shake Barney and C. W.'s hands and asking how everything was going. Ethel Schuster, a widowed old woman, grabbed Otto's arm and invited him to her home for a piece of apple pie, giving Barney and C. W. the opportunity to break away.

After a few minutes of talking about Reverend Krueger's sermon, the Harding administration, and the expectancy of rain that afternoon, C. W. and his grandfather separated themselves from the small assemblage and began to walk down Center Avenue on their way toward the center of town.

"What do you say, C. W., if we see if the company store has a pair of new work boots? I hate to buy a new pair, but the holes have worn clear through, and I got to shake the dirt out of 'em a couple times a day. Maybe we should look around and see if you need anything too."

"I'm all right, Grandpa. I don't need anything."

They walked along until they hit Main Street, then continued up toward the company store. The first floor was long and narrow. Two counters ran down the length of the store on each side. A long rectangular island ran down the center. Glass-enclosed cases displayed shirts, pants, socks, underwear, overalls, handkerchiefs, jewelry, and other articles of clothing. There were racks for ties, belts, and suspenders. Layer upon layer of shelves containing boxes of men's hats and shoes were stacked on the sidewalls. A tall ladder on wheels ran next to the shelves as they were stacked twelve feet high. A section in the back had items the miners would need for work: hard hats, eye protection, work gloves, boots, and other accessories.

A salesman—dressed sharply with dark plaided trousers, white shirt with the sleeves rolled up, a black tie, and suspenders—approached them as they entered. "Is there something I can help you men with today?"

Always polite, Barney answered, "Yes, sir, I need a pair of new work boots."

The salesman smiled. "Come this way, please." C. W. and his grandfather followed him to the back of the store. Three or four other customers were browsing at articles in their display cases.

The back of the store contained several shelves of work boots: slate gray, brown and black, high and low cut, some fancier than others. The salesman pointed at a couple sturdy wooden chairs and asked them if they would like to sit down. After the long walk from the church, Barney was happy to. The salesman said, "I would be happy to show you some boots. Can you tell me what it is you have in mind?"

"Well, the pair I have at the house I've worn for ten years. I believe the brand name of those boots is Wolverine if I'm not mistaken."

"Ahh . . . Wolverine, they make a very strong, durable work boot. What size and color?"

"I wear a size 10 and black if you got 'em," Barney answered.

C. W. just sat and stared at the volume of men's clothing that filled the store. Like his grandfather, he didn't own too many clothes. One pair of shoes, one coat, three shirts, two pairs of pants, three or four pairs of socks, and underwear. He didn't care too much. So long as he and his grandfather had food on the table and enough scraps to keep Jake eating, he was happy.

Barney agreed to the first pair of boots that the salesman showed him. He tried them on, and they fit perfectly. The boots cost $4, but he was entitled to a 25 percent discount as an employee of the Verde United Mining Company. The salesman put the shoe box in a bag. Barney looked at C. W. "Now are you sure there's nothing you need while we're here? Anything you need for your job tomorrow? What kind of shape are your shoes in? You're going to be doing a lot of walkin'. What about a haircut?"

"I don't need anything, Grandpa. My shoes still have several miles left on 'em. And I don't mind you cutting my hair."

Barney was proud of C. W. He never asked for anything. He weathered the tough times considerably well after his parents died. He never asked for new clothes or coat because some other kid had one. He never complained about eating pork stew for five days in a row. He was a good kid. A fine young man.

"Well then, did you want to go home and see how old Jake is doing, or you got some business of your own?" Barney asked.

"We can go on home, Grandpa. That was such a big breakfast this morning. I'm kind of tired. I'll get back out in a little while to visit with Chiara."

"Sure. My dogs are getting a little tired too. Let me give you some money."

"No thanks, Grandpa. I don't need any. I still have some money saved at the house."

"Well, I'm still gonna pay you an allowance."

"You don't have to, Grandpa. With my job starting tomorrow, I'll have all the money I need." Seeing some pain in his grandfather's eyes, C. W. added, "I'm seventeen years old now, Grandpa, and I just want to start doing more stuff for myself. You have taken good care of me. I appreciate it, but I want you to be able to do more stuff with your money than spendin' it on me. I know how hard you work for it."

"Well, C. W., if you ever need anything, you just ask yer ole grandpa, and I'll do whatever I can to see that you get it."

"I already know that, Grandpa."

They walked to their home down on the end of Diaz Street. As they neared the front porch, they were given a warm welcome from Jake. He could barely contain his excitement at seeing his two masters after they had been away for what must have seemed like an eternity to the faithful hound.

Barney walked into the front door first and got two bottles of root beer out of the icebox. "Want a bottle of root beer?" he asked C. W.

"Yeah, Grandpa, that sounds good." Barney popped the cap off a bottle of Ma's Old Fashioned Root Beer and handed the open bottle to C. W.

Barney took a swig from his bottle, then set his bottle down. He began to pick up some soiled shirts, pants, and towels that were lying indiscriminately around the house. Sunday was generally the day that he and C. W. took a few minutes to gather laundry, wiping dust and making sure the house was clean.

If the wind were blowing right, or wrong, the sooty smoke from the Clarkdale smelter would drift up the mountain and hang over the town of Jerome, particularly the northern edge of town. The smoke would leave a filthy film of a smoky residue on clothes, bedding, furniture, and just about anything else—even the dog.

Barney went around the side of the house and grabbed a large metal tub. He poured some cold water from the barrel into the tub and grabbed the box of Snow Dust Washing Powder. He then dumped some detergent from the box into the tub. C. W. came out the front door with an armful of dirty clothes that he threw in the tub. They would let the clothes soak in the cold soapy water, then take a brush to the stains. Afterward, they would rinse the clothes thoroughly in a tub of clean water and hang the clothes on a line to dry.

When the laundry was hanging on the line, C. W. cleaned up himself and got ready. He told his grandpa that he was going to go by the Italian restaurant and maybe see if he could get an ice cream soda with Chiara, that is, if she was able.

He started walking up the street back into town. He passed the Mexican swimming pool but didn't stop. He had a good pace going as he neared the restaurant, only slowing down when he neared it. When he got to the restaurant, he hesitated out front. Chiara waited on the table and saw him standing outside. She smiled at him and held up one finger. He saw her speak with her mother who then looked outside, smiled, and nodded her head.

Chiara took off her apron and came outside. "Buon giorno, C. W."

"Bon . . . jor . . . no, Chiara." She laughed at C. W.'s attempt to speak Italian.

"It means 'good day.' My mother says I can spend a few minutes with you if you like."

"That's swell. Do you want to walk up to the drugstore and have an ice cream soda?"

"*Buona* idea," she giggled to herself. "I must speak English with you. When I'm around my parents, everyone speaks Italian."

"That's OK with me." C. W. was completely infatuated with the beautiful long-haired Italian girl. This was his first crush, and it felt as if a building of bricks just collapsed all over him. He thought she was the prettiest girl he had ever seen. And he remembered what she had said about liking him. He was bouncing from cloud to cloud in this girl's company.

He and Chiara entered the drugstore and took two round swiveling counter stools in front of the long counter. In front of them was a gooseneck tap, blenders, and a blackboard with the ice creams and soda pops available. After a few minutes, a soda jerk wearing a white apron came to wait on them. Wiping his hands on a towel, he smiled, recognizing C. W. from previous visits. "Back again, I see. You're the chocolate ice cream soda man, if I'm not mistaken." Looking at Chiara, he said, "And, miss, I don't believe I've seen you before in here."

Shyly, she answered, "No. This is my first time here."

"Well, let me know when you're ready, and I'll whip something up for you."

C. W. was a little nervous on his first date. He looked at Chiara, and she looked back at him, catching his eye. "I reckon he remembers me because I was in here the other day. I ordered the chocolate ice cream soda. It's my favorite."

"Well, if it is your favorite, then that's what I'll have too."

C. W. couldn't wipe the silly grin from his face. He needed to relax. He had never been in the company of a girl before, except at school. And he thought to himself, *There wasn't anybody in school like this girl!*

42

Pazrosky slept until past noon on Sunday. When he finally crawled out of bed, his head was pounding and squeezed as if it were in a vice. His mouth was as dry as if he had been walking in the desert for the past week. His body was trembling. Scratching his head, he had slept late but not necessarily well. It took him a few minutes to realize what day it was and where he was.

He got up and poured himself a drink from his jug. With drink in hand, he sat back down on the edge of his bed. He rehashed the night's events in his cloudy head. He had a difficult time trying to concentrate, so he got up to open the window, thinking that some air might be able to clear his head. The bright afternoon sunlight blinded him. He felt nauseous. He thought he was going to vomit, so he hurried down the hall to the common bathroom, grateful that it was not occupied.

He disgorged the contents of his stomach, trying to keep the offensive loud retching to a minimum. Afterward, he threw cold water on his face and returned to his room. One miner who shared a room near the end of the hallway by the bathroom poked his head out his door as Pazrosky proceeded slowly back toward his single room. "Hey, Bo, is everything all right?"

Without looking at the man, Pazrosky continued forward. "Yeah, sorry about that. I must have had too much to drink last night."

The man shook his head knowingly and disappeared back into his room.

Pazrosky returned to his room and took another drink from his can. He grabbed his pack of Chesterfields, put a cigarette in his mouth, and lit it. He took a long drag off the cigarette and blew smoke rings toward the ceiling. Returning to the window, he looked out over the cloud-covered valley. Rain. *That would be nice if it rained*, he thought.

He sat on the edge of the bed. *That was some dream I had.*

He looked for some clothes to throw on. He noticed where he had discarded the clothes he wore the night before—into a littered heap in the corner of the room. He rummaged through his slacks and removed twenty dollars from his pants pockets. He saw that his wrinkled trousers and shirt were covered in ground, in dirt, and grass stains. "Huhh . . . what the hell did I do last night?" he muttered to himself.

He sat back down on the edge of the bed and tried to focus his attention on the events of the previous evening. He remembered the women at Homer's place. *Was that Homer?* He looked back at his pile of dirty clothes. He had a vague recollection of rolling around in the dirt with a woman. *Or was it two women?* He had difficulty establishing what was real and what was part of his dream.

He returned to his closet and found another pair of trousers and one clean shirt. He threw them on and walked out to the Ford. It was parked under a tree where he always parked it. He looked inside and found nothing out of the ordinary. He dug in his pants pockets to make sure he had transferred the cash from the other pants into these pants and got behind the wheel. He was still not sure what he wanted to do but felt the need to get away, let his mind clear up.

He drove down the street to the market, parked the Ford outside, and went inside. He came out a few minutes later with coffee, eggs, bacon, bread, and a pack of Chesterfields. He got back in the Ford, setting the sack on the front passenger seat. He looked all around the seat and the small backseat compartment. Nothing. The automobile still had a funky smell to it.

He headed out to the gulch and up the dirt road toward Homer's. A big breakfast and a cup of coffee would help. A late breakfast, but then Homer was a night owl who slept through the morning every day anyways.

He pulled the Ford next to Homer's home, grabbed the grocery sack, and walked up to the front door. As was his habit, he walked in and set the sack on the table without knocking or announcing his entrance. *What's mine is mine, and what's yours is ours.* He saw a jug on the small wooden table and poured himself a drink in a familiar tin can. He noticed that there were four drinking utensils on the table.

He opened the curtain separating the "bedroom" from the kitchen area and looked inside. Homer was snoring but appeared to have a look of contentedness on his shaved face, maybe even a smile. Pazrosky caught himself just as he was about to bellow for Homer to get out of bed. While it was customary for him to awaken Homer with some rude form of greeting, this day, he let him sleep while he got breakfast and the coffee. Acts of kindness weren't something he was known for.

He had bacon and eggs frying in the same skillet. The coffee was beginning to percolate in an old coffeepot. Stepping outside, he lit a cigarette. He walked by a fire pit with the remains of three burned-out logs in it. He remembered drinking around the fire with Homer and two girls he picked up from the Cribs. *The Cribs. Lucille, that's right. And Homer's girl, Lizzy?*

He walked past the shed with its padlocked front door and back in the house where he flipped the eggs and bacon. Taking the coffee off the stove, he heard a stirring coming from the bedroom area. "Is that you, Henry?"

Pazrosky poked his head through the curtains with an evil grin. "Who the hell did you think it was? Clara Bow?"

"Ha. Wouldn't that be something?" Yawning and stretching his short arms over his head, he rolled out of bed. "Something sure smells awful good. Hey, pal, that was some kind of evening last night. I want to thank you, Henry, for setting me up with Izzy. That's one of the best times I've had in a long, long time. I ain't been dizzy with a dame in years."

"It was nice of you to get yerself all shaved and dolled up for her," Pazrosky said.

"Yessir. I figured if you can get yerself all groomed with your hair all dyed and everything, that the least I could do was get myself a haircut and a shave."

Pazrosky had completely forgotten about the boot polish he had used to blacken his hair and beard.

"I thought I was gonna split a gut at you two coming in from outside with that boot polish smeared all over yer faces. And yer clothes. It looked like you rolled from here all the way into town," he chided.

It was coming back to him now. Pazrosky took a sip of the hot coffee. "I gotta tell you, Homer. I really don't remember too much from last night."

"I'm glad I remember," Homer said. He walked past Pazrosky out the front door to the corner of the house and began to urinate. While urinating, he continued talking over his right shoulder, "That's the best time I've had with a woman in I don't know how long. Sure would like to see her again."

"They were whores, Homer. Do you remember that?"

"I know they were whores," spat Homer in disgust. "I was just trying to say that was one swell evening that girl and me had last night, whore or not."

"Well, if you want to see her again, I'm sure you can. It'll probably just cost you $10, that's all."

A dejected Homer poured some coffee into a dirty cup. "We got along perty good, if you know what I mean."

"Good for you. You remember what time it was when I left last night?"

"I reckon it had to be two or three o'clock, why?"

"No reason," he snapped. "I was just wunderin'. I told you I didn't remember too much from last night."

The men sat in silence eating their breakfast of scrambled eggs, bacon, and dry bread.

After several minutes, Homer said, "You said something about drinkin' some really bad hooch when you went to pick up the girls last night. Think we can maybe sell them girls in the Cribs some of our hooch and make a little money?"

Thinking that it was probably the liquor he had drank at Lucille's place earlier in the evening that had made him sick, he recalled, "Yeah. I forgot about that horse piss. I bet we can sell them whores some hooch. As many men as they got going through there every day."

Pazrosky was thinking about the Cribs and the money they could make selling their hooch. Then it hit him. His dream. Maybe it wasn't a dream after all. He searched the depths of his mind for any recollection of what happened after he dropped the two whores off in town. Homer said something, but he wasn't listening. He remembered having a good feeling when he returned in the morning. If he left Homer's at two or three o'clock and the sun was coming up when he pulled in and crawled in bed, then what did he do for those other two or three hours?

"Henry, you ain't listening!"

"Huh . . . what?"

"I was saying that if you pick me up some more ingredients and some more of them glass jugs, then tomorrow night I could whip up another batch. Me or you could go to Lucille's or Izzy's place and see 'bout selling a jug of our hooch for $20 apiece. That's gotta be a nice little profit for you and me."

"Yeah, sure, Homer." Trying to concentrate, Pazrosky added, "Yeah, not a bad idea, Homer, that's what I was just trying to figure in my head, our profit margin."

"Shit, Henry, I was thinking," Homer said excitedly, "I ain't done all the deciphering, but you and me can split $100 a week if we expand our business."

"Yeah, sure." Pazrosky was thinking about something else. Without saying anything else, he got up and went outside. He lit a cigarette and walked over to the edge, looking down into the expansive Verde Valley below. It was coming back to him now. The girl on the street. The "sister" of the girl he had taken for a ride a month or two back. A drive out of town. Pulling off the road. Dragging her in the dark. Burying her under rocks and tree branches.

"What in tarnation is on your mind, Henry? It's like you ain't even here."

Trying to remain composed, he replied, "I'm just thinkin' about all the money we can make moonshining, that's all."

"Well, we're partners, don't forget. If you got some highfalutin ideas, I sure wish you'd bounce 'em off me rather than go running off by yerself."

"I follow ya, Homer. Say, you own all this property up here, right?"

"I sure enough do. Paid for it ten years ago when I was workin' in the mines. I stayed in town during the week. I had a buggy for a while, but when my old nag died . . . Why do you ask?"

"I thought you and me might build another wooden shack up here, and I would live here for a while. Same size as your main house here. I'd pay for all the wood and nails. Then someday when I'm gone, you can have it for whatever you need. I think it might be helpful for our business."

"I reckon that'll be aw right," Homer answered. In fact, he thought it was a fantastic idea. He had no friends to speak of, or to speak to for that matter. Henry was his only friend. There was the prospect of actually making a decent living. Henry was much more polished and sophisticated than he was. He had slept with a woman for the first time in nearly ten years, thanks to Henry.

"I was just thinkin'. I still got money left. I mean . . . I still have plenty in my savings. Nothing fancy of course. Just small and simple. Maybe we can see about a well. I don't know. I was just thinkin'. It's yer property and all."

"Where are you thinkin' you . . . we should put it?"

Pazrosky looked up the hill to the flat area where he had taken Lucille the night before. "Maybe up there, I couldn't help notice last night when I was rollin' in the grass with that girl that it was nice and flat up there." He turned and gave Homer a devious smile. "Come on. Let's go inside and pour ourselves another drink."

43

After feasting on the bountiful lunch that Shirley had brought them, the marshal thought he would head over to the old miner's house to pick up the red shoe. He didn't like it when there were no deputies at the jail in case of an emergency but he figured he wouldn't be too long.

The marshal left the jail and headed down First Avenue. He stopped by the jailhouse and visited briefly with his jailer, Deputy Burns. Two young Mexican men were locked up in separate cells. "Well, Will, what do you got here? Deputy Zalensky been by yet"

The lawman stepped outside. "Ain't seen him. This here ain't too serious, I reckon. Those fellas were fighting over some senorita last night down on the end of Juarez Street. I thought we'd write 'em up for fighting or being disorderly and kick 'em out of here but wanted to talk to you first."

"I'm headed toward a home at the end of Diaz. Why don't I stop by and try to speak with the senorita first. I'll stop back by here in less than an hour, and we can probably cut 'em loose."

"Good enough, Marshal, let me go get her name and address for ya."

With name and address in hand, the marshal decided to go by the home on Juarez Street first to see if he can find out more about what happened with the two Mexican men before stopping by Barney Parker's place.

At the small home on Juarez Street, he knocked on the front door. After a minute, a man around fifty years old wearing a sleeveless white undershirt opened the door. He looked up to the enormous lawman standing at his door. "Si?"

"I'm *el* marshal. Usted habla ingles, sir?"

"No," he answered curtly.

"OK. Bueno. Es Maria casera?"

Again, the Mexican man's answer was short, "No."

"OK." Thinking for a moment, he continued with his rudimentary, limited Spanish. "Usted sabe los dos hombres yo tener en mi carcel? My jail?"

"No." He kept a stern face with no expression. It was clear that he had no intentions of being any assistance. The marshal was beginning to get frustrated.

"OK." In English, he said, "Listen, amigo, you probably understand everything I'm telling you. I don't appreciate your attitude. I got two men in my jail for fighting over a woman. I'd like to let them out so they can go home, but I wanted to ask Maria what the hell happened first. So for now, I guess they'll stay locked up." He turned to go, and the man spoke.

"I find Maria and have her speak to you."

The marshal smiled and nodded his head. "Thank you, sir. I will be at the jail."

He walked the short distance to the Parker house, wondering why the Mexican man had been so uncooperative. The Mexican people had some animosity toward the law, but the marshal generally didn't have too much trouble with them. He had sent a couple of them to prison, but they had committed rather heinous crimes and certainly deserved to go away.

He walked up to the Parker house and was greeted by a friendly hound dog. "Well, howdy, pup," the marshal said, stroking the dog's head. Barney walked out the front door.

"Afternoon, Marshal. Come on in."

"Thank you, Mr. Parker." Making friendly conversation, he said, "Sure thought it was going to rain today, but now I'm not so sure."

"Yeah, I did too. Still might, I reckon. Awful hot out here. Come on up, Marshal. Don't mind ole Jake. I'll get that shoe for ya."

Moments later, Barney came back out of the house with the red shoe in his hand. "I sure hope I'm not wasting your time, Marshal, but me and my grandson thought it was in too good of condition to be just thrown away. Kind of strange too that it would be down in the gulch. I know there's a couple girls that gone missin' from what I hear or I wouldn't have even bothered you with it."

"Well, I reckon the only way we'll know is if we show this to some other girls who might have seen one of the missing girls wearing it." Taking the shoe and examining it in his hand, the marshal added, "Yeah, yer right. Except for this broken strap, it looks brand-new. You say your grandson found it down in Deception Gulch near the slaughterhouse?"

"Yessir." Barney pointed down past the Little Daisy mining operation. "I'm not rightly sure if he was allowed to be down there, but that's where they found it."

Jake gave the marshal a curious look to why he was holding his toy and quickly was in a playful mood.

"Jake, is it? Well, thank you for your help too, but I got to take this with me." He began to head back out of the front yard area. He extended his right arm and shook Barney's hand. "Well, we oughta know soon enough if this helps us or not. You'll probably see some of my men down in that area sniffin' around tomorrow. Thanks again, Mr. Parker, for your help."

"Don't mention it, Marshal. I hope it helps. If there's a killer going round town, he needs to be locked up."

"I couldn't agree more." He tipped his hat and started his short walk back toward the jail.

He stopped by the jailhouse to speak with Deputy Burns. Deputy Zalensky was standing outside speaking with one of the town's businessmen. He handed him the red shoe. "Dave, can you take this with you and ask some of the girls if they know who it might belong to?" The deputy took the shoe and tipped his hat to the businessman, excusing himself. Deputy Burns asked from inside the jailhouse, "So the fella wasn't too helpful, yer saying? I reckon that don't surprise me too much. You'd think he might want us to let them boys go home unless the girl they were fightin' over was his daughter or something."

"He acted like he couldn't give a dern, but we might be seeing the senorita, or him, later today. I'll check back with you later or call me on the telephone. We'll get it squared away. Besides, don't things get perty lonely down here without any company?" he joked.

"Not *that* lonely, Marshal." Burns spat out a stream of tobacco juice and went back inside the jailhouse. He stuck his head out as the marshal turned to walk away and smirked, "I'm sure Deputy Zalensky looks awful perty in a pair of them red shoes, Marshal."

The marshal continued up to the town hall. Deputy Evans was sitting in a chair reading the newspaper. "Howdy Marshal. I was passing by and saw that you and Dave were out so I thought I better stick around for a little bit." The marshal rehashed his negative experience at the home on Juarez Street and the two young Mexican men who were locked up down at the jailhouse for fighting over a girl.

As Deputy Zalensky entered the Cribs District, two young women passed him, walking the other direction into town. There was some foot traffic as several men took advantage of their day off on the Sabbath to pay homage to the working girls.

He walked up to the crib where he and Deputy Evans met with Lilly Rogers last week. The front door was ajar. Relieved not to smell the heavy lingering scent of marijuana burning, Deputy Zalensky knocked on the door. He stepped closer, sticking his head through the open door. "Miss Rogers? Lilly?" He knocked gain. Speaking louder, he called, "Miss Rogers, are you home?" He poked his head in farther without stepping into the crib and took a look around the small apartment.

He knocked again, then stepped into the crib. He didn't see any sign of the young woman. There was a half-full glass of a beverage on the small wooden table. He bent over and smelled the strong smell of cheap alcohol. He looked at the phonograph and saw that the needle had stopped at the end of the record of bandleader Paul Whiteman's "Whispering." The record continued to spin. He thought this was strange, making a mental note.

At that moment, he heard a female voice from the front doorway startling him. "Excuse me," the high-pitched voice sassed. "Do you mind tellin' me what yer doin' in Lilly's place?" He turned, and the petite woman with flaming red hair froze when she saw the tin star on his shirt. She wore a loose white dress that hung from her shoulders. She stuttered, "I'm sor . . . sorry, Deputy. I didn't know you were the law."

"It's all right. I'm looking for Miss Rogers. I wanted to ask her some questions regarding the disappearance of Jenny Richardson. By chance, have you seen her today?"

"Ahh . . . no, I haven't seen her today as a matter of fact. Kind of strange too." The young woman's eyes focused on the red shoe the deputy was holding in his right hand. "What are you doin' with Jenny's shoe, if you don't mind me asking."

"Have you seen this shoe before?"

"Ahh . . . I think so. It looks like one of the pair that Jenny bought not too long before she disappeared. She liked to dance. She was wearing those red shoes on the night she didn't come back."

Deputy Zalensky looked around. "I would like to ask you a couple more questions, but I'm not real comfortable here without Miss Rogers present. Can we step outside?"

"I just live next door if you would like to come over there."

When she saw Deputy Zalensky hesitate for a moment, she continued, "It's really not any inconvenience, Deputy. I live there alone, and I have no appointments or plans for this afternoon."

Deputy Zalensky collected himself. "Thank you, miss. I'm Deputy Zalensky. And you are . . ."

"My name is Dorothy. Come this way." He followed her to the apartment next door and went inside. The place smelled of sex and stale cigarette smoke. He was careful to leave the wooden door open. There was a screen door that let light and a small breeze blow through. "Please sit down, Deputy. You were saying you wanted to ask me some questions?"

"Yes. Thank you . . . Dorothy." He took a seat on a hard wooden stool. "What can you tell me about the shoe? Are you sure it belonged to Jenny?"

"Oh yes, of course. She was always wearing glad rags and fancy shoes. She and Lilly went to the J.C. Penney store over there and picked those out a little over a month ago. She and Lilly were plannin' on going dancing that night at the Mineflower. There was a jazz band playin'."

"So were you and Jenny friends?"

"She was an OK girl, but she and Lilly were just doing too much dope for me. I don't mind a little reefer but when you're hanging around the Chinamen as much as they were. Those two were always so hopped up on the opium or cocaine. Way too much for me and a lot of the other girls around here too."

"It looks to me that Lilly didn't mean to be away from her home too long, leaving the door open. Does she do that a lot?"

"No, it's not like her at all. She and Jenny didn't trust people around here stealin' their stuff. It's not like they had anything anyone would wanted to steal either."

"I want to show you a photograph of a man that may or may not been around here. You look at the photograph carefully and tell me if you've seen him around, OK?" He took the photograph out of the yellow envelope and handed it to her.

"Creepy-lookin' fella." Studying the photograph, she grimaced. "No, Deputy. I really don't think I've seen him. I know he hasn't been in here. Is that the guy whom you think is responsible for Emma's death and Jenny's disappearance?"

"We're not really sure, Dorothy. Maybe not." He got up. "If you see Lilly, can you tell her that I stopped by?"

"Sure. Anything to help you lawmen out."

He left Dorothy's home, tipping his hat to the woman. He knocked on three or four more doors in the Cribs District showing the photograph to a total of seven young women. None of the women recognized the man in the photograph. He put the photograph back in the envelope. Still carrying the red shoe in his left hand, he was anxious to get back to the marshal and let him know what he found out. He knocked on Lilly Rogers's open door one more time before giving up.

As he was leaving the Cribs District walking up Jerome Avenue, he passed the same two women that he had passed earlier when he was entering the district. They were occupied in their conversation and didn't pay him attention, nor did he pay them any. He didn't bother to show them the shoe or the photograph he was holding.

44

As the days passed, C. W. grew to love his job, delivering groceries and dry goods for the Safeway Store. It didn't take long for him to earn Mr. Baker's favor with his hard work, dependability, and attitude.

He would stop for a second every time he passed the Italian restaurant and wave at Chiara. She would always respond with a friendly smile. He made deliveries all over town, from the Hogback to Company Hill, from the business offices of the executives at Little Daisy and the Verde United Copper Company to the hospital. He delivered goods to several of the businesses around town, including the Mineflower and the mansions out on Sunshine Hill.

He worked from 10:00 until 6:00 every day except Sunday. He was always happy to get home at the end of the day, with weary legs, to spend time with Jake. He continued his chores around the house. He even learned how to prepare some simple meals and would have a late dinner with his grandfather when he returned tired and hungry from the mine.

His grandfather went to work just before 2:00 every day, so except during the afternoons, either he or C. W. would be at the house to keep Jake company. His grandfather told him about seeing the marshal, his deputies, and a couple other men searching the Deception Gulch area on the first day of his job.

According to C. W.'s grandfather, a rumor circulating around town suggested that the search team may have found the remains of another missing girl. And there was another rumor that yet another girl from the Cribs was now missing, a young woman who shared an apartment with one of the girls who disappeared.

C. W. heard people talking when he was making deliveries and sensed their fear. He wasn't a night owl, nor he did he frequent the Cribs at night, although he had made some deliveries there during the day. Had he been in the town during the night, he would have felt what the townspeople were truly feeling. Panic. There was a wild animal on the loose who preyed on the working girls. People were afraid, especially the girls who sold their bodies for a profit.

The girls from the Cribs continued working, but it was far from business as usual. Unless they had known a trusted client for a very long time, none of the girls left their home with a man. The girls were rarely seen alone. And many of them now owned small handguns. There was not a crib that wasn't home to a Browning M1911, Star 9-mm, or Remington 51.

Dorothy, who lived alone, had a new best friend. She never left home without Ruby. Ruby was a gift from a miner and loyal customer of her service for the past two years. A veteran of the Great War, where he served in the 158th Infantry, her suitor had given her the Ruby. The Ruby was a semiautomatic pistol that was best known for being the sidearm used by the French soldiers during the war.

It was basically a flawed pistol, but for an emergency situation, she was told that it would do the job. Her Ruby had a nine-round magazine, but she had limited rounds of ammunition. It was only to be used during a life-threatening situation. She was also advised by her suitor that the pistol wasn't particularly accurate and had little stopping power.

One bright note for the Cribs District, however, was that they found a new supplier for the hooch they drank and served their guests. Lucille was now the main supplier for the majority of girls who lived in the Cribs. She was sworn to secrecy and never let any of the girls know where she was getting it. The women and their male guests drank hooch more than they drank water. There had been a demand for a good-tasting hooch that didn't leave one feeling sick afterward, and business for Lucille was brisk.

Toward the end of July, C. W. was making a delivery to the Parlor House in the Hogback. He thought it was a very elegant home where the boarders were all young beautiful women. He had failed to make the connection to how the girls there had made their comfortable living. To him, the place reeked of high class.

He made a delivery there of fruit, produce, toiletries, and other items when the housekeeper invited him in for a minute while she searched for cash to pay him for the delivery. While waiting, he was surprised to see the beautiful brown-haired woman who was so kind to him one day coming down the spiral staircase.

C. W.'s eyes lit up, and his mouth fell wide open when he saw her. Ashley had smiled at the reaction, for it wasn't uncommon for a young man or boy to react to her attractiveness. But she looked a second time and realized that he had looked familiar for some reason or another. She held her right index finger to her lips while she stared at the boy and tried to place him. Cecile came back out from a back room and gave him some cash. She said, "I'm sorry you had to wait. Here is $15. Thank you very much. You keep the rest."

C. W. smiled and began to excuse himself when Ashley approached him. "Don't I know you from somewhere?"

C. W. shyly looked at her before looking at the floor. "I think so. I chased your handkerchief one day when the wind blew it out of your hand."

"Of course. I remember. That handkerchief was once a gift from my mother. I was so happy you were able to run that down for me. So what's your name?"

"My grandpa calls me C. W. My whole name is Charles Winston Taylor."

"Well, I'll call you C. W. then. Is that what your mother and father call you too?"

He frowned. "My parents are dead."

"Oh, I'm sorry. I shouldn't have said anything. I know what it's like to lose your parents. Both of mine are gone too. Any brothers or sisters?"

"No, it's just me and Grandpa. We have a dog too."

She had felt some type of sympathetic bond with the boy. "How about if you stick around for a minute, and I'll cut you a piece of chocolate cake?"

C. W. had a weak spot for anything chocolate. It was rare for him or his grandpa to ever have any sweets or desserts at the house. This was considered a luxury beyond their means. Even though he wanted to hurry back to the store in case there was another order for him to deliver, he accepted her offer, "Well . . . OK . . . That would be nice, thank you."

"Why don't you sit down, and I'll run into the kitchen real quick."

He took a seat on a heavily padded leather divan. He hoped that he wouldn't get in trouble, but he would only stay for a couple minutes. He only waited for a minute before the incredibly beautiful woman in the black gown returned from the kitchen.

She came out with a round silver platter holding a piece of chocolate-layer cake and a big glass of milk. "Here you go, C. W. By the way, my name is Ashley. I didn't know you were a delivery boy for the Safeway Store. How long have you been working there?"

He swallowed a large bite of the moist cake. "Not long. Just a few weeks or so."

"So how old are you?"

"I'm seventeen," he said.

"Seventeen? So do you go to school too?"

"No. Not anymore. I had some trouble concentrating on stuff after my parents died, so my grandpa pulled me out. It's OK, I reckon. I'd like to go back someday though." He felt her staring at him as he enjoyed the chocolate cake. He didn't mind. He felt something that he couldn't distinguish from sympathy or maternal, but she was likely the most beautiful woman he had ever seen in his entire life. He didn't like people feeling sorry for him, but she was different. She knew how things were when both parents have died.

Ashley didn't know why, but she liked this kid so much. She knew that she felt sorry for him, but he just seemed like a very nice boy. "Well, every now and then we need someone like yourself to come around here and do some simple chores, like chopping wood for the fireplaces and doing yard work. I may speak with Paige, she owns the house, and if you need the work, I know where I can find you."

"Thank you, ma'am. That would be nice." He finished his cake and drank the glass of cold milk. Lifting his self off the sofa, he said, "Well, I better get back to the store. Mr. Baker is going to be wondering what happened to me."

She walked him to the front door where he said, "Thank you very much for the chocolate cake and the milk. It was really good."

"You're so welcome, C. W. You come back and see us any time you want, OK?"

"That's awful swell, ma'am. Thank you."

"You're welcome. And call me Ashley. We're friends now."

45

Pazrosky had made some changes in the last week. He sold the Model T for $700 and purchased a used Model T pickup for $500. He had moved out of the New State Boardinghouse and, with Homer's help, was building a small shack on Homer's property. He kept his long hair and beard neatly trimmed but only used the boot polish when he went into town for supplies and in the company of Lucille and Izzy.

Lucille was buying six to eight jugs a week from Homer and Pazrosky. She made little profit for her work but was rewarded with a jug every week for her services. He had also picked up a few other customers. They were brewing their hooch three nights a week.

Pazrosky and Homer were selling their hooch for $20 a gallon jug and $10 for a large Mason glass canning jar. They immediately began to see a profit in their clandestine operation.

Homer had undergone a complete metamorphosis. He kept up a much-neater appearance since he first met Izzy. His self-esteem had transformed to where he wasn't as submissive toward Pazrosky.

The two men pounded away on the new shed, all the while staying liquored on their home-brewed whiskey. They had no visitors except two men whom Homer had sold hooch to prior to Pazrosky getting involved. Pazrosky managed to stay away when those men were on the property. He had politely instructed Homer to keep their business short and send them on their way.

The crude outbuilding was completed in just under a few days, right before the weekend. Homer suggested that they pick up "the girls" and have a cookout. Pazrosky reluctantly agreed. He no longer gave them $50, now only offering $25 that the girls agreed to split. This, he figured, was a lot of dough for the girls from the Cribs.

While Homer and Izzy seemed to have a budding romance going, he was growing tired of Lucille but kept the charade going as she was proving to be a valuable asset selling their hooch through the other whores in the Cribs. She had always been just a whore to him, and he treated her accordingly. But he liked the power of being someone's meal ticket.

In addition to his lack of sentiment for Lucille, he was consumed by his fascination with the beautiful brown-haired woman that lived in the fancy home in the Hogback. He had learned that the house was owned by a French madame. He had also learned that it was once the home of Annabelle, a young woman whose biggest fault was a weakness to refuse an easy $100.

Pazrosky didn't feel the paranoia that had gripped him so tightly in weeks past. After his head had cleared after the first weekend that Lucille and Izzy first came up to Homer's property, he realized that what he thought was a drunken dream was not a dream at all. He had taken care of the only person in Jerome who could have identified him to authorities.

The previous Saturday night, he drove into town and picked up Lucille and Izzy. They had mentioned that there was a state of terror in the Cribs after two girls from the same crib had disappeared. They also mentioned that the gossip in the Cribs was that one of them, Jenny, may have been found strangled to death like Emma had been. Like all the girls in the Cribs, Izzy and Lucille now each carried a loaded handgun.

Pazrosky told them that carrying handguns was probably not a bad idea. He tried to convince them that whoever committed such atrocities had to be hundreds of miles away. He was careful not to say too much however.

On Friday, the two men combined their inferior carpentry skills and finished applying metal panels to the roof. Pazrosky had done some home construction as part of the many jobs he had briefly held and had lost. His real experience came when he was at Huntsville, building work sheds on prison grounds as part of their forced-labor program.

The shed was very simple, but adequately constructed. It had no electrical wiring or plumbing, but appeared sturdy enough to withstand the high winds that swept across the mountain and high hilltops.

They laid the metal roof down over hot sticky tar, securing the panels with long screws. It was grueling work under the Arizona sun. As Pazrosky wiped the sweat from his neck and face, Homer came walking up, holding a coffee can half-full of hooch. He handed it up to Pazrosky, who was standing on an old wooden ladder. He gulped it down in a large swig. Homer spoke, "I'd say we just 'bout got it licked."

Pazrosky got down off the ladder and exhaled a deep breath. "I believe yer right, Homer." Looking up at the cloudless sky, he said, "Sure is a hot son of a bitch out here today."

Homer agreed, "It's got to be a hundred degrees in the shade today."

Pazrosky joked, "Maybe we ought to build a cement swimming pool."

Homer laughed loudly as he was accustomed whenever Pazrosky joked about anything. "Hey. What do you say we bring them girls up here for that cookout I was talkin' 'bout?"

"Yeah, yeah, sure. Ain't you getting tired of that broad yet?"

"Hell, I ain't seeing her that much. Oh, come on," he begged. "I know neither of 'em ain't no Clara Bow, but you got to admit they're fun girls."

"I hate to keep reminding you that they're whores. They're fun girls because we pay them to be fun. You ever wonder how many other fellas they're 'fun girls' with during the week?"

Feeling downtrodden, suppressed by the superior intellectual power of his only friend, Homer whimpered, "Now why you always got to go and do that? Izzy has got enough class for me. It's not like yer bringing up them classy Parlor House dames."

With the mention of the Parlor House, Pazrosky immediately thought about the beautiful woman he had seen coming home in that Cadillac awhile back. He had been thinking about her a lot lately. "What makes you think I can't get together with one of them tomatoes? They're whores too. They just cost a lot more dough, that's all."

"I don't know, Henry. I've heard that the men that go out with them ladies have to pass some kind of inspection or something."

"Inspection? Where did you hear that nonsense? With the kind of dough yer bringin' in now, who's to say that the new and improved Homer can't walk up to their door and have the pick of the litter?"

"New and improved? What are you talkin' 'bout? I've always been able to romance a woman."

"Sure, since you've kept that mangy beard and hair shorn and keep the stink scraped off yerself, you're a regular Rudolph Valentino."

"Ha ha ha. Listen, I'm getting tired of listening to yer shit. I think I'm gonna lie down and take a siesta. I want to have a cookout or go into town or something. I ain't been in a saloon in a long while. Maybe we can find us some more customers. That's what we need to be doin'. Supplying them saloons and restaurants with some of our hooch. I bet we could. You're the big cheese, why don't you try talkin' to one of them saloon owners or something?"

"Why don't you go take your nap? I need to go town and buy me a little bed somewhere. I think there's a furniture store near the barbershop. Maybe I'll go by and see if I can spend some time with Izzy."

"You better stay away from my girl." Pazrosky liked to get Homer riled up by teasing him.

"I'm just funnin' with ya," he laughed. "It's just if I get myself a bed, I'm gonna have to break it in with one of them whores."

Homer was walking toward the main home. Over his shoulder, he hissed, "Just stay away from my girl is all I'm askin'."

46

The search team was a little smaller than it had been then during the last search. J. R. stayed back to watch the family garage. Only one deputy, Deputy Zalensky, was along as the other deputies had other duties to attend to. On the Monday morning that the team set off, they gathered in the area near where they found the body of Emma Lewis, just below the Mexican quarter.

The marshal spoke to the men, "Again, I just want to say I appreciate you men helping me and my deputies out. I think it helps to have some extra pairs of legs and eyes out here to cover more ground. Not far from where Clarence found the remains of Emma Lewis, a woman's red shoe that appeared to be fairly new, if not brand-new, was found by a boy and his dog Saturday morning. When we found Miss Lewis's body, she was wearing both of her shoes, so it wasn't hers. I want to search down the canyon a little farther toward the slaughterhouse. I understand the woman's shoe was found down that way. Do be careful, men, scan the ground in front of you carefully. Be cautious when you reach down to pick anything up. I don't want anyone getting bit by any rattlers. I got a snakebite kit just in case, but just be careful, and nobody will get bit."

The men fanned out under the new home built for one of the family members of the proprietor of the Little Daisy Mine on the northwest edge of town. Scattered brush and tall yucca plants were the only vegetation down in the sparse rocky canyon.

No clues were turned up during the first few hours of the search. The marshal scoped the area, plotting in his head how someone could be able to dispose of a human body so far down the canyon. It certainly wasn't impossible. A dirt road snaked through the Mexican quarter. Someone could have driven a vehicle past the Mexican quarter and dragged a dead body through the brush during the night. The Little Daisy Hotel was near the edge of Sunshine Hill not too far away. Two strong men could have dragged or carried a woman's body easily down into a canyon that wasn't too steep but was rocky in some areas.

The sun began to rise higher in the sky. The marshal took off his hat and wiped the sweat from his brow and neck. He looked over at Clarence who was doing the same. Roy and Deputy Zalensky were down deeper in the canyon.

Time was moving slowly until early that afternoon when Roy found a rusty miner's pick down in a small ravine. He carefully reached down and grabbed the pick. Aside from the rust, the pick appeared to be in good condition.

He searched the immediate area approximately twenty feet in diameter from where he had found the pick. That's when he saw something that didn't seem right. Didn't seem natural. Several rocks were clumped together as if they were placed that way by hand and not by the elements.

He took a deep breath of the warm, dry air and slowly approached the area. The rocks were massed together over a small mound of earth that looked as if it had been cleared away from the rest of the rough desert landscape. The area looked like a grave.

He saw the marshal about one hundred feet to the east and whistled loudly. When the marshal looked up, he motioned for him to join him. The men were far enough down in the canyon where no one at the Little Daisy or those who lived in the Mexican quarter would have paid them much attention.

"What do you got, Roy?" the marshal asked when he made it over through the rocky canyon to where Roy was standing. He had the Pocket Brownie camera hanging around his neck.

"Maybe nothing, but I wanted you to see this first." Roy pointed to the group of rocks that appeared to be clumped together unnaturally. "I found this pick lying over there about twenty feet away. Then I saw these rocks. Looks to me like it may be some kind of grave."

The marshal stood and stared at the anomaly for a while. Looking around the immediate area, he noticed the same thing that Roy had. That it just didn't look right. Finally, he said, "You know, Roy, you may have found something here. Let me get a photograph of this." He stepped back and pointed the camera toward the cluster of rocks.

The marshal then moved closer to where he was standing above the cluster of loose rocks. "Come on, let's move some of these rocks away. I'll need to take a few more photographs if it's what we think it is. Sheriff Thompson will want to see 'em."

Roy helped the marshal remove the rocks away from the smoother area of flattened dirt below them. After several of the rocks were kicked or tossed away from the site, the men stopped and stood up. Both men were sweating in the hot sun. The marshal shot Roy a glance, getting down to his knees. "Well, I reckon this is the moment of truth." He began to shovel the dirt away with his cupped hands. After removing the top three or four inches of soil away from a two-square-foot area, he began to uncover what appeared to be some type of cloth. He looked up at Roy who could only watch, hands on his hips.

After a few more minutes of careful excavation, the men saw what they were there to uncover, yet didn't want to see, human remains. Decaying human flesh. The discovery of the remains was preceded by the smell of putrefying decomposition.

"Oh shit," Roy said. "We found another one."

The marshal shook his head and took a breath away from the corpse. He took the handkerchief from around his neck and tied it around his face like a bank robber, continuing to remove the loose dirt from the grave. He got up and was prepared to take another photograph. Instead, he hesitated. "My hands are getting a little dirty. Do you see Dave anywhere?"

Roy looked up the canyon and to the east and spotted Deputy Zalensky's white shirt and black cowboy hat. "Yeah, Marshal, want me to get him?"

"If you would, Roy. I wanted to spare Clarence from another dead body. After all, he ain't used to all this. Not that you are either, I reckon."

"I'll be all right, Marshal. Just give me a minute. I'll go and get Dave over here."

Roy hurried up over the rocky embankment to where he found a position to wave over Deputy Zalensky.

The deputy came quickly to where Roy was standing and followed him down to where he saw the marshal on all fours. "Aw shit, Roy. Y'all find something?"

"I'm afraid we did. The marshal wants you to take some photographs."

When the two men returned to the site of the shallow grave, the marshal stood up and handed Dave the camera. "I think Roy found another one of our girls. My hands are dirty. If you can get a photograph of this, I want to dig some more of this dirt away by hand." The marshal then looked at Roy and said, "Roy, if you can do me another favor, I brought a body bag this time. It's in the back of my Ford. I want to get her out of here. Sheriff Thompson will have to look at the photographs and read the report. We ain't gonna wait for him this time."

"Sure enough, Marshal, I'll get it and be right back."

"'Preciate, it Roy."

Deputy Zalensky took a photograph of the fabric and what appeared to be part of a leg sticking out of the dirt.

"I reckon those boys from the U.S. marshal should be advised of this also," the marshal acknowledged. "I wish Roy or Clarence didn't have to see this. Dern if the sheriff's office in Prescott had to take Jim on that transport. Sure could have used him around here today."

The marshal dropped back to his knees and leaned forward, being very meticulous in brushing little by little of the dirt and rock away from the body, like an archaeologist who just discovered a four-thousand-year-old mummy. "Hell, I wish I didn't have to be so damn fussy about this, but I got to be careful. I sure would like to get her out of this hole and give her a proper burial."

"I follow ya, Marshal," Deputy Zalensky said sympathetically. "You want me to go tell Clarence to go on back to town?"

"That sure is a good idea, Dave. He don't need to see this," the marshal responded. "Jist hurry back if you would. I need a couple more photographs before we get her out of here."

"Will do, Marshal."

The marshal brushed and shoveled the dirt away with his cupped hands, exposing the remains of the upper half of the female torso. The body was draped in a lightweight material that may have been a white dress at one time. After a few more minutes, the woman's neck and face was uncovered. The front of the woman's throat was discolored with blue, green, and purple. There was clear evidence of a ligature mark around her neck and throat area. The soft tissue of her face had begun to liquefy, making the woman unrecognizable. One thing was obvious. Like Emma Lewis, this woman was also the victim of a brutal strangulation.

Roy and Deputy Zalensky returned to the scene minutes apart.

The marshal looked up and acknowledged the men by a slight nod of his head. He looked over his shoulder at his deputy. "How did Clarence take it? I hope he wasn't sore, but no one needs to go home at night with something like this burning a hole in yer noggin."

"I think he understood, Marshal."

"Good, I'll go talk to him later."

Most of the dirt was cleared away from the woman. Her decaying face and blonde hair were now visible. The marshal looked up for a minute. "Dumb question but either of you ever seen this girl before?"

Roy and the deputy just shook their heads.

The marshal uncovered the dirt and rocks from her entombed left leg down to her bare foot. He then brushed the dirt away from her right leg. He lifted and turned his head, taking a breath through his bandanna. She was almost completely free of the dirt and rock from her shallow grave. He "shoveled" the remaining dirt away from her lower right leg.

On her foot, she was wearing the match to the other ruby red shoe.

47

Ashley had been longing to see Lane again. She hoped he felt the same way. It had been nearly two weeks since they went for their romantic horseback ride and picnic near the Indian ruins.

On this Friday, Lane arrived early morning in his Cadillac. He visited with Paige in the waiting area as he waited for Ashley to come down from her room. With sincere indebtedness, he spoke of the pleasure he has had in Ashley's company. The subject of payment was handled very discreetly, never mentioned. He spoke of their plans for the next two days and when they would return. Before "dark" the following day. She insisted that the couple take a picnic basket full of fruits, bread, and extra water in case there were any breakdowns, road closings, or unplanned event.

Lane recently read in an *East Coast* newspaper about a businessman from Atlantic City, New Jersey, who, in an attempt to bring in more tourists for the summer months, organized a city festival and parade down the renowned boardwalk. The festival featured attractive young women who competed in a contest of their beauty. Judging in the pageant was based largely on the women's appearance, her personality, her interaction with the crowd, and her ability to charm the judges. Lane thought that Ashley would have a good chance of winning.

Her flawless entrance couldn't have been more elegant had it been rehearsed. Ashley, self-confident and deliberate, like a contestant in the beauty contest, sashayed down the winding spiral staircase and welcomed Lane with a kiss on his right cheek. In her right hand, she carried a small tan leather Samsonite suitcase. Lane rushed to take the suitcase from her hand and presented her with a bouquet of fresh flowers that he had purchased from the Jerome Floral Company. Paige arranged to put the lovely flowers in a vase, then wished the couple a bon voyage.

Ashley led Lane outside the home to where the valiant Cadillac was parked along the crescent moon-shaped entryway. He opened the passenger door for her, closing it softly behind her. After he tucked her suitcase away in the spacious backseat, he walked around the automobile. He was amazed at how beautiful she was, wearing a light yellow dress that clung to her lean, delicate body.

The plans for their weekend included some family business as well as an overnight stay at a very sophisticated resort. The resort had always been a favorite of his family, a few miles on the other side of Prescott.

After passing over the bumpy strip of road out of town through Walnut Gulch, the asphalt roadway curved over Woodchute, then Mingus Mountain on the way to Prescott. The road was recently paved, but still there were potholes and hairpin curves that needed to be given special attention.

Always keeping one eye on the bending road in front of him, Lane told Ashley that his father had recently expanded their ranch by purchasing a parcel north of their current property. He had some signed documents that needed to be returned to the county offices in the basement of the Yavapai County Courthouse. He also had a surprise for her that was his way of keeping her in suspense.

He told her of the resort where they would share a two-bedroom bungalow for the next two days. "You're really gonna like this place. My parents love it. They took me here when I was a kid. I hope you packed your bathing suit." He had to keep both eyes forward. The road hugged the mountains' edge as canyons fell hundreds of feet on his side. The road straightened out for a short distance. He continued, "It also has a restaurant, a movie theater, tennis courts, and a golf course. And there are three hot spring baths that are said to have therapeutic healing properties."

He paused to focus his concentration on the winding road as an automobile raced around the corner coming in the opposite direction, forcing Lane to jerk the steering wheel so the Cadillac hugged the edge of the mountain. "Damn! Ahh . . . sorry about that, Ashley. I know it's a long way down, but those people got plenty of enough road to stay on their side."

"I trust your formidable driving skills," she said devotedly. "Everything sounds so wonderful. Tell me more about the resort."

"OK." He told her what his father had once told him. That it was given its name from U.S. Cavalrymen who had been chasing off Indians. The area was surrounded by peaks which reminded the soldiers of castles. They named the creek that run at the bottom of a canyon. They named it Castle Creek. After they chased the Apaches from the area, they found the source of the Indians' magical water. This was named the Castle Hot Springs. Years later, a resort was built near the springs. In addition to private bungalows, there was a main house and a home housing the employees. "There's one more thing I have to tell you about the resort. This is absolutely crazy. It was the first place in the state to have a telephone installed. It's telephone number is 1."

"Ha! That is crazy," she giggled.

It was a slow drive to Prescott. Lane and Ashley arrived in the center of town just before lunchtime. They parked outside the courthouse, and they both went inside. In the basement of the Yavapai County Courthouse were the county offices. They entered a downstairs office with a high ceiling. Two clerks had their heads buried in paperwork while two other clerks were standing, searching for records among several large shelves with books and drawers containing official city and county records such as deeds, mining claims, affidavits, and other recorded documents.

The office had a metal pot-bellied stove for heat behind the counter where the employees worked. Large six-inch round tin flues channeled the smoke and heat from the stove along the ceiling where it formed a T and ran out both sidewalls. A copper light fixture hung from the center of the ceiling. A large picture of the governor of Arizona, Thomas Campbell, a Jerome native, hung near a clock on the far wall.

Thick voluminous record books weighing close to forty pounds each sat on the countertop, separating the employees from the people needing assistance. The countertop set a clear boundary between the employees and the patrons.

One of the clerks who was standing approached Lane as the couple walked in. All eyes were immediately on the beautiful lady. Another of the clerks appeared to stifle an instinctual whistle as his lips puckered upon seeing the striking woman.

He smiled and tilted his head slightly. "Hello. How can I help you folks today?"

Lane responded politely, "My name is Lane Walker. I'm returning some documents from my father, Lester Walker. They're title documents for some property that my family recently purchased."

"Oh yes, Mr. Walker." He took the document and took it to a desk where he studied it. He took another paper that was an official receipt of payment, stamping it with a rubber stamp. He filed the documents away and returned to Lane, providing him with a receipt. "Thank you, Mr. Walker. Here is the receipt acknowledging the finalizing of your father's purchase."

Lane folded the receipt and stuck it in his shirt pocket. He thanked the clerk for his help and nodded toward the door. He smiled when he sensed that the clerks were all staring at the back of Ashley as she walked out.

"Let's get out to the resort," Lane said. "I wouldn't mind going for a little swim. It's just a short drive from here. On the way back tomorrow, I have to stop by a meat market and pick up some beef. I thought we might stop somewhere then. You know? About that surprise I was telling you about."

Ashley pouted. "You mean I have to wait until tomorrow for my surprise?"

"Oh, it's not such a big deal, I reckon." He didn't feel comfortable flaunting his wealth like he was holding it under her nose. "I tell you what, we can drive by tomorrow and pick up that beef for Pops. I'll take you to where I have a surprise now. It won't take but a few minutes. Then we can go for a swim."

"Hooray!" she joked.

He turned the Cadillac around on Cortez Street. "I'm putting the cart in front of the horse I reckon . . . but I wanted to tell you that my father is having a hoedown honoring their wedding anniversary in August. I wanted to buy you a new dress for it. It's two weeks away. Would you like me to take you?"

"I love hoedowns. Of course, I will go with you. I have plenty of dresses. You don't have to buy me another one."

"Yes, I do. I had it especially made just for you."

She gave him a warm smile and said, "Thank you, Lane. I can't wait to see it."

A few minutes later, he pulled the Cadillac into a cramped parking space in front of a small dress store. He jumped out and opened the door for Ashley. "Come on, I hope they're finished with it."

Faye Loveland came out from a back room. A sweet short woman, closing on sixty years, her gray hair was wrapped tightly in a bun on top of her head. Her face brightened when she saw Lane.

She had been in the fashion business since before the turn of the century. There had been quite an evolution in the fashion of 1894 until the fashion of the day. She opened the dress shop on the corner of Third and Shelton fifteen years earlier. A hardworking woman, she had two women who worked for her. She made dresses for his mother on occasions, from funerals to special galas like the one coming up.

"It's so good to see you, Mr. Walker. Tell me. How is your mother doing?" she asked.

"Ma's doing fine. Thank you, Mrs. Loveland. She and Pops got their fortieth wedding anniversary next week. Pops wants to have a big hoedown with square dancing, a fiddler, big beef cookout—it's really going to be a good time. We're expecting about fifty people."

"I haven't been to a hoedown in years," she laughed. She smiled at Ashley. "So this must be the lucky woman that you've been talking about."

"Yes, she is," Lane said embarrassingly.

"She really is as beautiful as you said."

Ashley blushed. "I haven't been to a hoedown myself in a few years. I am so excited that Lane's invited me." She shot a glance at Lane.

Faye had been in this position so many times. A woman and a man looking at each other, as if hypnotized with so much affection for each other. She was a widow. But she remembered the feeling. She turned to go into the back room. "Ashley's gown," she declared. "Excuse me please for just a minute."

Ashley admired a dress that was on a mannequin near a front window. "This dress is absolutely beautiful."

Lane whispered in her ear, "My mother really speaks highly of her."

Faye came out of the back room carrying a large white box. She set it on a table near the front counter. "Here we are, Ashley." She took the box and opened it. "Would you like me to take it out and show it to you, or perhaps you would like to go to a changing room and try it on. I could then make any necessary alterations."

"Oh please, Faye. I'm dying to try it on."

Faye removed the dress from the box and held it above her by the shoulders. The soft green gown had many buttons down the front. The skirt was long, designed to hang down to her lower calves. The dress had a pointed waistline, big sleeves and a princess-line bodice. "It's beautiful!" she said loudly. "It is absolutely beautiful. I love it. Can I try it on?"

Ashley dashed to the back room with Faye to try on the beautiful gown. Faye spoke with Ashley around the door as she changed into the gown.

"Did you know, Ashley, that princesses always wore green in the days of Henry VIII?"

"No, ma'am, but I feel like a princess wearing this. Thank you."

She stepped out of the changing room and stood before Faye. "I think it fits wonderfully!"

"I must give your beau some credit. He described your figure down to the fingernail," she chuckled.

"He did, did he?" Ashley asked, surprised. She then broke into a wide smile. "Maybe we should let him wait until the dance to see me in this. What do you think, Faye?"

"I think that's a wonderful idea."

Ashley quickly changed back into her clothes. She handed the emerald-colored gown to Faye.

Faye folded the gown and placed it back in the box. She closed the lid and gave the box to Ashley. The two women then walked out to the front of the store where Lane waited patiently. He asked, "Did it fit all right?"

"Yes. Thank you. It helped that you were able to give Faye my exact measurements."

Lane's face perked in a flash of embarrassment. He was able to brush off the comment when he realized she was not the least upset with him. He reached into his pocket and nodded nonchalantly toward the back of the business. Faye saw that he wished to be discreet and said, "Please come this way, Mr. Walker." He followed her to the back room where they disappeared. "I know Ashley loves the gown. She will be the most beautiful girl there. She and your mother, that is. I'm still working on your mother's dress. I'll have it ready next weekend."

"Thank you, Mrs. Loveland."

After he paid her $15 for the gown, they met Ashley and walked out toward the front door.

"So are you two on your way back to the other side of the mountain?"

"No, ma'am," Lane answered. "We have a two-room bungalow at the Castle Hot Springs Resort. We'll return home tomorrow after lunch."

"Be safe, you two." Faye closed the front door and watched as the enchanting couple got in a big automobile and drove away. She then returned to the back room where she continued sewing on Mrs. Walker's dress. She was thinking what a beautiful young woman Ashley is. She wondered what it was that she did. Nurse? Schoolteacher?

Lane pulled out of the parking spot and turned south. Catching Main Street, he abruptly turned the behemoth vehicle into a cramped parking spot.

Ashley laughed, "What are you doing?"

"An ice cream parlor. Come on," he coaxed her, "I want an ice cream cone."

After both had finished their ice cream cones at the ice cream parlor, they got back in the Cadillac.

They drove south out of Prescott for a short while before they hit a bumpy dirt road. The resort was only a few minutes down the road. Ashley had been quiet. She felt herself getting emotional again about this man and his kind ways. She finally said, "Thank you for the wonderful gown, Lane. I love it very much. I want you to know that you never have to buy me another thing in your life. That's not why I like you so much."

"I enjoy doing nice things for you. I'm lucky that I'm able to. My father works me real hard on the ranch. Harder than the ranch hands, that's for sure. He pays me well, and of course, our family has some wealth. But I have to work for what's mine. I'm just having a hard time waiting for the day when I come home to you every night after a hard day's work," he teased.

Stunned by the compliment, Ashley responded, "Well, maybe that's something we'll have to talk about this weekend."

48

C. W. left for his job at the grocery store early that Friday morning. He had planned on loitering by the Italian eatery in his hopes to see Chiara before he went in to the store. He hadn't seen her for a few days. He hoped to avoid her father, a short-tempered, cantankerous little man whom he didn't think cared for him much. He was very friendly with his customers, but when he needed something from Chiara or her mother, he would bark at them, holding his curled-up fingers close to his mouth and waving his arms.

Their restaurant was always filled with Italian patrons, from breakfast through dinner. C. W. hadn't eaten there in fear of her father, despite the coaxing from Chiara. That, and the food they served was so different than what his mother and father, and now, grandfather, have always eaten. Chiara explained to him once that a traditional Italian breakfast was merely a small cup of hot coffee with milk and a couple of cookies. They also served bread, butter, and a fruit jam, but no bacon or eggs or biscuits and gravy.

Chiara couldn't get away from the restaurant much. C. W. kept himself busy with grocery deliveries that took him all across town six days a week. He would pass by her family restaurant at every opportunity. She would smile his way every time she saw him. They had walked up to the drugstore for ice cream a couple of times, but he hadn't seen her as much as he would have liked since he started his job.

On the morning of this memorable day, he enjoyed a brief stroke of fate, a false prophesy of things to come. As he neared the restaurant, Chiara was standing at the front entrance, as if she was taking a break, craning her neck up and down the street like she was looking for someone. When he approached the restaurant from the east, she saw him and stepped out. He returned her smile.

"Mornin', Chiara. How are ya?"

"I'm very good," she replied in her Italian accent. "How are you, C. W.?"

"I'm doing fine," he replied. "Thank you. Looking for someone?"

She blushed as if she were a little embarrassed. "Uhh . . . no. Why do you ask that?"

C. W. suddenly realized that he had put her on the spot, so he backed away. Stumbling over his words, he said shyly, "It's just that you're always so busy. That is . . . umm . . . every time I walk by here to see you, your restaurant is full of people, and you're so busy." Unable to keep looking into her mesmerizing brown eyes, he stared into the restaurant where he saw only a few people were seated. "Anyways, it's nice to see you."

"It's nice to see you too." She took a nervous glance over her right shoulder toward the restaurant. "I wanted to tell you that my mother said it's fine if you wanted to do something together this Sunday. She thinks I've been working too much and should have some fun sometimes. That is . . . OK with you, no?"

C. W. could not suppress the ear-to-ear smile that broke out across his face. "That is very OK with me! Whatever you want to do."

The cute girl with the long straight brown hair beamed happily at the tall, lanky boy. "Well, I better go." She turned to walk back inside, then stopped. "I don't care what we do. Maybe we can go swimming since it is has been so hot outside."

"Swimming would be nice. You're sure to see me delivering groceries the next couple of days. I'm usually running around quite a bit on Fridays."

"OK, I'll look for you. Bye-bye. I have to go."

After Chiara hurried back into the restaurant, C. W., having the sensation of sinking in quicksand, finally picked his now heavily laden feet off the cement sidewalk and turned to walk up the street. After he walked a few paces, he turned around toward the restaurant in time to catch Chiara's father peeking out at him with a bitter look of irritation. C. W. nodded his head, turned his shoulders up the street, and continued walking.

He thought to himself, *What a grouch.* He wondered why the fiery man had such a negative disposition. He had a nice wife and beautiful daughter. *Probably has something to do with having a beautiful daughter,* he thought.

He walked the few remaining paces to the Safeway Store and was greeted pleasantly by Mr. Baker, "Good morning, young man. I hope you are well today. You know Friday is typically one of our busiest days around here."

"Yes, sir. I'm fine, sir."

"Well, that's good," he replied. "I got a few calls last night after you went home, so we're going to have a busy morning. Come on in, and we'll get the first deliveries ready to go."

He walked in and greeted Grover and Myrtle. The store had only one customer, Mrs. Walgreen, the English teacher at the high school. She was a spinster who was an unpleasant corpulent woman who looked down the bridge of her nose at Mr. Baker whenever the fruits, vegetables, or bread didn't pass her rigorous inspection. Mr. Baker always managed to remain calm but had been overheard on more than one occasion reminding her that there were two other grocery stores in town who might be able to serve her better.

The Safeway Store had two other employees in addition to C. W. and Mr. Baker. Grover Ross had worked there for the past three years. He was a cheerful balding man in his midforties of average height and weight. When his wife was offered a nursing position in Jerome three and a half years ago, they moved from Prescott where they had both worked for her family's small produce store for a number of years. Like Mr. Baker, he wore a long white apron over dark trousers, white shirt, and a tie.

The other employee was a nice woman who lost her husband in the war. Myrtle O'Hanlon had worked at the store for the past two years. C. W. had seen her around town delivering groceries prior to his start of employment. His hiring had evidently relieved those duties from her. Tall and slender, she reminded C. W. of his mother when she was younger. Mrs. O'Hanlon, a widow for the past three years, had many admirers, but she shunned all offers from the men who were eager to get her "back on the correct path" with her life again. She stood between the long countertop that held a scale and a large roll of brown paper and an eight-foot-high shelfful of canned goods. She worked the cash register when the store got busy.

C. W. was the only one who did the deliveries except when Mr. Baker delivered groceries himself in his automobile. This didn't happen much. Only when the order was unusually large or if it was on the outside of town.

C. W. loved to breathe in the smells of the grocery store with its tantalizing fresh and dried fruits, vegetables, mouth-watering chocolate candy, baked items, coffee, spices, sugar, syrup, cereals, and meats all contributing to an aura of aromatic bliss.

He was given a short list of customers with their respective addresses that he glanced at and stuck in his pants pocket. Mr. Baker then transferred a large box filled with six brown paper sacks full of various groceries from his arms to C. W. "These three orders are all up on Company Hill. When you get back, I'll have you drop off some soda and some other things at the Mineflower Saloon. You know the place, don't you? It should still be rather quiet, I would think, before noontime," he surmised.

"As soon as I get these groceries delivered, I'll hurry back, Mr. Baker."

"Oh, take your time, C. W.," he insisted. "It's gonna be a long day."

"Yes, sir," he said and walked out the front door. His small journey to Company Hill would be a ten-minute uphill walk from the store. He was able to see just over the box containing the grocery sacks, piled high with celery and long loaves of bread.

C. W. passed by the Chinese laundry and saw the two Chinese brothers working inside. He remembered that there had been many more Chinese people in town when he was a kid but now not nearly as many for some reason. He figured the townspeople likely ran them off. When he walked by the town hall and saw Marshal Williams standing outside, he wanted to tell the marshal that it was him who had found the red shoe down by the slaughterhouse. He wanted to ask the marshal if he and his men found anything down in the gulch but thought he better dump this heavy load of groceries off first. Besides, the marshal would think that he was just a kid.

He enjoyed delivering groceries to the Company Hill District. The homes were nice and big, and the people were friendly. You could see the whole town and Clarkdale below from there. The people would often pay him a half dollar for his service, which Mr. Baker allowed him to keep.

There were a lot of people out and about on the streets of Jerome this morning. Motor cars were passing by in each direction. C. W. thought he saw Ashley get into a large automobile in front of the Conner Building when he was coming back down the hill.

He was thinking about the brief conversation he had with Chiara that morning. He felt lucky that she didn't have any other close male friends like him or a steady beau. As pretty as she was, he thought it was strange that no other young man in town had tried to court her.

He wondered why her father hadn't tried to get her together with one of the Italian business owners' sons. Somehow, her father had allowed him to sneak through his front line of defense. Now, she had her mother's permission, but probably not her father's, to spend some time together on Sunday afternoon.

C. W. tried to get his mind off Chiara. He had always wanted to see for himself what it was like inside this famous old saloon, where it was said that Wyatt Earp and one of his brothers stopped in one day. He remembers stories his father would tell his mother about the place, reading from one of the town newspapers about men getting shot or poked with a big knife there over faro or poker games, too much drink, or some woman. His mother would shake her head in disgust and look at C. W. sternly as in displaced anger. He knew later that she was only upset with the violence and criminal conduct and was worried that he would someday be exposed to it.

He walked into the store carrying the empty box. He gave Mr. Baker the money he received for the groceries and receipts of payment. Mr. Baker would then put the money and receipts in the cash register. C. W. saw another box on the main counter full of soda bottles. Mr. Baker directed C. W. over to the box. "This is the delivery I was telling you about to the Mineflower. Be careful in there. Stay away from the billiards and the card games and the young women."

C. W. grinned, not certain how serious Mr. Baker was to imply that he would actually do something like that. "Nah, Mr. Baker, I am a little curious to what it looks like in there. But I'll just get in, help them with their groceries, get paid, and get out. Is there anything else while I'm out?"

"There's been a couple of telephone orders that came in while you're out. Grover is filling them now. He'll have them ready by the time you get back from the Mineflower. They are both out in the Hogback. So after you finish with those, come back, sit down, and have a Coca-Cola and relax for a few minutes."

"Ah, thanks, Mr. Baker, I'm all right," he said with certainty. He didn't mind walking deliveries to the Hogback because that meant a chance to pass by the restaurant where Chiara worked. He didn't want to upset her father, but at least he had a job and was working.

He took off with the box filled with soda bottles. Mr. Baker placed a written receipt in the box as C. W. walked out.

Sensing his trepidation, Grover looked up from where he was getting canned goods from a bottom—row shelf. "Be careful, lad," he warned. "It's Friday. With the mines being all shut down, there might be some ornery fellas in there."

Mr. Baker looked at Grover and said, "C. W. is a big, strong kid. He knows how to handle himself, but I really believe at this time of day, it shouldn't be so wild in there." He pulled his watch out of his apron pocket and looked at it. "Hurry back, and we'll have two more orders ready when you get here to take out to the Hogback."

"Yes, sir," he said as he looked over his right shoulder, carrying the heavy box that contained several bottles of ginger ale, lemonade, soda, and tonic water, along with some bananas, apples, and oranges. He headed out the front door and looked up the street for any automobile or buggy traffic. When he saw a break in the traffic, he hurried across the street, lugging his heavy cargo. He had to be careful to watch his footing. There would be a few angry people if he took a spill and dumped the contents of his box. He made sure he had a tight grasp of the hard-to-carry box and walked quickly up the sidewalk.

49

Before Pazrosky drove into town, he combed a small amount of the boot polish through his hair and beard. He knew of a furniture store on Main Street that sold cheap furniture. He shouldn't have a problem finding a cot that he could take back to his new home out on the gulch. He also wanted to go by the bank.

He parked the pickup in front of the furniture store and stepped out. Taking one last drag from his cigarette before tossing the butt down on the street, he walked by the display window that featured a living room set, complete with matching round throw pillows.

When he was inside, he saw that the entire sales floor was covered with dressers, armoires bureaus with mirrors, lamps, end tables, dining room tables, stoves, tinware, and other furnishings. A salesman, who was dawdling by some bedroom furniture, sauntered over and asked Pazrosky if he could assist him in finding what it was he was looking for. After showing him two cots, Pazrosky chose the ten-dollar cot over the twenty-five-dollar cot, along with a blanket. He quickly paid and was on his way out the door. After tossing the folded cot into the back of the truck, he headed across the street to the grocery store.

Here, he purchased bread, potatoes, four cans of beans, two bags of sugar, cornmeal, yeast, a bottle of ginger ale, potatoes, carrots, and a few other things from the tall, slender woman at the cash register. The grocers had seen him before. He always reeked of cheap liquor. Now, there were four or five other customers in the store, but it was his presence that made Myrtle and the two other grocers uneasy. He reminded her of a mole with his minute, yet penetrating, cold dark eyes. The eyes that examined her shamelessly whenever he came into the store.

He paid for his groceries and carried them to the Ford truck parked on the other side of the street. When he was gone, Mr. Baker, who was now helping a Spanish-speaking man on the far side of the store near the dry goods section, and Myrtle's eyes met as they each took a deep breath, glad that the man who exuded such a dark aura of lechery was gone.

To them, he appeared to be more of the crooked-businessman type than an out-of-work miner, but then there were a lot of both around. Mr. Baker suspected he may be a moonshiner because of some of the items he had purchased before in the store.

C. W. was there once when the man with the darkened hair and beard was in the store. After the man left, Grover made the statement that "that's a cat that shouldn't come out during the day."

Pazrosky drove the Ford back out to the gulch, taking the two sacks of groceries into Homer's house, placing them on the table. He heard Homer snoring from his bed. He yawned and thought he might lie down on his new bed after he fixed himself a drink.

He got the cot out of the Ford and unfolded it, then poured himself another drink from a glass jug. Inhaling from a cigarette, he wiped the polish from his hair and beard with an old burlap potato sack and tossed the sack back to the ground. Feeling tired from the sun and drink, he finished his large glass of hooch and lay down on his small bed where he fell fast asleep.

He was soon immersed in a dream where he was being chased by several men somewhere in Mexico. He was running all across town in the rain with men chasing him screaming, "Get him!" and "There he goes!" Running down a rain-soaked road, he heard a gunshot and felt the bullet hit him in the back shoulder. It didn't hurt like he thought that it would. He dove into a ditch near the road that was full of water in the rain. Five or six men ran past where he was lying in a foot of water.

"Come on!"

"This way!"

"Kill him!"

"Vamos!"

When Pazrosky abruptly woke from his nap, Homer was in the small shed with the still. With some items Pazrosky picked up while he was in town, he was able to get a small barrel of mash mixed up. Pazrosky rubbed his eyes and tried to shake the bad dream from his mind. He started walking toward Homer when he smelled something good cooking in the main house, the beans and collard greens on the stove. He entered the small hovel and took a whiff at the supper that Homer had cooking on the stove. In addition to the beans, potatoes, carrots, and collard greens he picked up at the grocery store, a skinned rabbit was boiling in another pot.

Grabbing the jug from the table, he poured himself a large mixed drink with ginger ale, then stopped to light a cigarette. With his drink and cigarette now in hand, he stepped back outside.

Homer was stirring the mash like he was churning butter. They had mash prepared in another small wooden barrel that was ready for brewing later that night. He turned to see the man he knew as Henry Joseph block the setting sun standing in the doorway.

"I'll be damned if it isn't Sleeping Beauty awoken from her spell."

Ignoring the unamusing little man, he said, "I see you got some supper on the stove. It looks like it's ready."

"Well, let's go sit down then. It'll be dark perty soon."

The two men took their seats at the small wooden table. Homer lit an oil lamp and set it on a stool near the table. "I shot us a jackrabbit while you were asleep the past four hours. I seen where you picked up some beans and greens and figured I'd throw them all in together."

Pazrosky nodded. "I can see you will make some man a lovely housewife someday."

"Ha-ha. Funny man." Homer poured himself another drink. Looking at Pazrosky, he said, "I'm tellin' you, Henry. We've got a mighty good business brewing, and I mean that jist as it sounds."

Ripping the meat off the leg and stuffing it in his mouth, Pazrosky said, "I was thinking that we should start to cut our product down a little, ya follow? Maybe water it down a little."

"Gee, I don't know, Henry," Homer responded. "With the girls in the Cribs and our other regular customers . . . I'm already dilutin' it with the Jake. I don't want to get a reputation for having bathtub swill."

"I was thinking about just a little more watered down. That's all."

"What I think we need to do is keep brewing quality hooch and get us some more customers." Getting excited, Homer continued, "This is the most money I've ever made in my life! I don't want to mess around with a good thing too much. That reminds me, are we going to see the girls tonight?"

"I thought that we would see 'your girls' tomorrow night. No sense wasting this good supper and hooch on them whores tonight."

"Yeah, I reckon yer probably right," Homer conceded. "I just want to see Izzy. How 'bout a cookout tomorrow night?"

"Sure. Maybe you can shoot us another rabbit. I didn't know you were such a good hunter," he said sarcastically.

"I'm a hell of a good hunter," Homer boasted. "I've shot quail, rabbit, possum, and rattlesnake before. And four or five years ago, I shot a wild pig right over there," he said, pointing toward the east. "It tasted perty damn good, I remember. Ain't you a hunter? I thought you said you did some bird or game hunting in Texas."

"Oh, I'm a hunter all right," he said coldly.

"I keep my rifle under the bed in there if you ever feel like shooting at a bird or something."

Pazrosky was climbing to that level of intoxication where his speech was hard to understand. He had always thought of himself as a hunter or a predator. When he was a stupid kid, he enjoyed killing animals but not to eat. Just for the fun of it. Cats, dogs, chickens. His prey now was foolish women who sold their bodies to the night.

He had convinced himself if he cleaned up a bit more, he may have to pay a visit to the Parlor House and arrange for a night out with the lovely woman he was starting to obsess about.

50

The marshal was sitting with his both feet up on his desk, reading the latest edition of the *Jerome Mining News*. In a column near the bottom of the far right corner, he saw an article of interest:

ANOTHER JEROME YOUNG WOMAN DIES

Jenny Lynn Richardson, aged twenty-three years and native to Albuquerque, New Mexico. The immediate cause of death has not yet been released to public record, according to Town Marshal John Williams. Miss Richardson was reported missing by her close friend, Lilly Rogers, approximately one month ago. She is survived by her mother Charleen Rantzen; her stepfather, Edwin Rantzen; and brother, Paul Richardson, aged twenty-five—all of Albuquerque, New Mexico. Mr. Richardson is en route to Clarkdale to accompany his sister to her final resting place, interment at the Our Lady of Sorrows Cemetery in Albuquerque. R. J. Stanford, undertaker, yesterday prepared the remains for shipment which will take place today. Deceased resided in Jerome for three years. Her former occupation was as a waitress at the English Kitchen.

He wanted to smile knowing how his girl Shirley would have reacted to the last-known occupation, which was working as a waitress, although the girl had been seen in there a lot. He was tight-lipped with the fellas from the newspaper. He had also taken his grand old time with finalizing the case and transferring his reports to the public record. He didn't want to alarm the townspeople more than they already were. The newspaper also mentioned

Lilly Rogers. Her piece was in the very right-hand corner below the obituary piece for her former crib mate:

ANOTHER JEROME YOUNG WOMAN MISSING

Friends have reported that Miss Lilly Rogers, aged twenty-two, of 462 N. Hull Avenue, has not returned to her address in approximately two weeks. Friends are concerned she may have been the victim of foul play. Anyone who may have information regarding the whereabouts of Miss Rogers is to contact the town marshal's office located in the town hall.

The marshal angrily tossed the newspaper on his desk. He had dragged his feet and was not giving the killer the respect that he deserved. He should have put deputies on Miss Rogers at night and random hours of the day. She had seen the killer. He didn't do enough, and now she was likely dead too. He and his deputies had known that she had seen the killer. Any first-year deputy should have known that she would have had a target on her back. If he had watched her more closely, maybe they could have caught him, saved her. He would make sure that his deputies would patrol the Cribs District and the homes of ill repute more and keep their eyes open for some lunatic lingering around.

He had discussed the case with Sheriff Thompson in Prescott a few days earlier. He in turn had been contacted by the U.S. marshal's office out of Phoenix who requested he share information about the case with them. They were sending some of their deputies back to Jerome. This didn't bother the marshal much. From his experience with federal lawmen, they were generally respectful. Sure, they would at times be condescending, but they turned up the heat on the gamblers and bootleggers when they were in town, which only made his job a little easier.

When Deputy Ray came in at noon, the marshal went for a walk around town. When he walked through the Cribs, he was met by derogatory comments that spewed out from behind open windows and doorways from a few disgruntled women.

He heard comments like, "Yer a little late, Marshal!" and "It's about time you got here!" He had a lump in his throat when he thought of the oath he swore to protect these people, and now three of these girls were likely dead. All killed in the last few months. The girls that never wanted his presence before were now mocking him for his inability to keep them safe.

He walked down through the neighborhoods just below the Cribs. He wanted to go for a short walk, then come back through the Cribs on his way back. He decided to pay a visit to the old miner who had dropped in to the jail after his grandson and his dog found a shoe. He knocked on the door, and the dog came running out barking. "Shut yer trap, Jake!" Barney came out the front door. "Oh, afternoon, Marshal."

"Good afternoon, Mr. Parker. I was just doing a little foot patrol and thought I'd pay you a quick visit. Maybe you read where another of the missing girls was found dead. Your evidence was helpful. Thank you."

"I'm glad I could help. I sure hope you find that fella soon, Marshal."

"Me too. It's getting quite bothersome, but we're turning the town inside out and upside down, looking for the man responsible. That is, if it is just one man. We'll find him. I just hope it ain't too late when we do. One other thing while I'm here. Do you ever have any problems with your neighbors? Any loud arguments or fighting?"

"Nah. You mean the Mexicans? I don't hear too much. I work from two 'til ten, thank God, so I don't see too much around here. My grandson has never said anything."

"That's good," the marshal replied. "I had a couple young men who lived near here be guests of mine in my jailhouse a week or two ago."

"We've never really had any trouble with anyone from around here. I reckon there's got to be some jealous people out there since I was one of the very few not to lose my job this past year. But it's not like I'm a scab or anything like that."

"I reckon you are lucky to still have a job in the big mine. But I've heard that copper prices are going up, and the mines will open up again. Seems everybody's got electricity these days. You got to have copper if yer gonna have electricity. I don't know, maybe you've heard different."

"Nah, Marshal. I've heard for a while now that things would soon get back to normal. I reckon I won't believe it until I see it."

"It would be a nice change for the town." The marshal turned to leave, patting the friendly dog on the head. He tipped his hat. "Nice to see you again, Mr. Parker."

"Thanks for stopping by, Marshal. Good luck finding that crazy fella who's murderin' our girls. Personally, I haven't paid any of them a visit in the years that my beloved has been gone, but who's to say if I wasn't a younger unmarried man away from home. Those girls up there don't need to be treated like that."

"I agree. Have a good afternoon, sir."

The marshal stopped back through the jailhouse, which was unoccupied now, to speak with Deputy Burns. The marshal was given a brief written report regarding the transport of a man wanted for crimes in the western part of the state that morning. He had been held there for a couple of days after his arrest up in Indian country. It was determined by state officials that the prisoner would be held no longer than two nights in Jerome while the deputies from Yuma arrived. It had been discussed that the prisoner be taken from Jerome by train, but that was decided to be less safe than the thick patrol transport vehicles.

The prisoner was transported in a Ford stretch automobile with steel bars separating him from the deputies. He was chained to a metal base anchored to the floor of the automobile The three deputies who transported this dangerous man halfway across the state were later rewarded with a night's lodging at the Bartlett Hotel with their meals paid for, until they returned the following day.

There had been some fear that a jailbreak may be in the works. Players held their cards close to their chest and didn't discuss the transportation plans very much. It made for a nerve-rattling two days for the marshal and his men. There was always one of the marshal's deputies there to back up Deputy Burns, just in case someone tried to break him out.

Late that morning, three deputies from Yuma County picked up their man from the jailhouse. The marshal and Deputy Evans assisted Deputy Burns and the lawmen from Yuma by having their guns ready.

The transfer went smoothly. The prisoner was on his way over the mountain with a stopover in Prescott. It was a relief getting him out of town. The marshal saw that Deputy Burns was also glad to see the violent thug gone. The prisoner's false warnings that six men from his gang were on their way to shoot it out with him had made the deputy jailer quite anxious. He would finally get some sleep this evening.

The marshal stopped into the Mineflower and saw Roy serving soda drinks behind the bar. The marshal knew that some of the customers were spiking their root beers and Coca-Cola drinks with alcohol, but he did not feel like checking everyone's drink. He told Roy, loud enough to allow one or two overly curious people to overhear, that the U.S. marshals would be sending deputies to the town in the next few days to make sure everyone still adhered to the Prohibition law.

Roy told the marshal the truth, that he never serves an alcoholic beverage. What happens to the beverage once the customer buys it isn't his concern. The Mineflower was mainly a billiard parlor now with five elegant pool tables. A

Victrola played phonographs during the day. The evenings were filled with live entertainment. It was a beautiful place with a high ceiling. It had lost a little of its charm with Prohibition. People still enjoyed going there to watch the jazz bands and orchestras that included Jerome in their traveling schedule.

The marshal soon walked, with both eyes straight ahead, out of the Mineflower. He walked through the Cribs one more time before he circled back to the jail. With the disappearance and killings of the prostitutes, he felt that he needed to be more conspicuous. He wanted him and his deputies to be seen more. He didn't know if it would deter future kidnappings and murders, but he was sure in hell going to show the town that he will do whatever it takes, like cooperating with other agencies, including the federal men, to find the man responsible for the killings.

When the marshal returned to the jail, he took his hat off and sat down at his desk. Deputy Ray stepped in from the back room. "One of Sheriff Thompson's men just called. A Ford packed with four U.S. marshals just left from Prescott. It sounded like they wanted to poke their noses around a bit. Try to blend in with people."

"It doesn't surprise me to see those fellas again. I thought we'd be seeing them sooner than later. We'll help them out all we can, and they'll give us nothing, but right now, we ain't got much to go on ourselves. Blend in with folk, huh? Maybe they can stay for the Labor Day parade!"

Deputy Ray laughed, "I don't know what they'll be up to. Probably gonna stir up a hornet's nest. Get everyone all riled up."

"Oh, I don't know, Billy. I've already been getting a lot of manure thrown at me. The whole town thinks that there's a maniac out there. None of the young women feel safe at all. I reckon whatever it takes to catch this character, if he's even still around, we could use the help," the marshal replied solemnly. "We'll see what happens." He started walking out the front door, muttering to himself, "Jist another Friday night in Jerome."

51

Lucille was having a mixed drink in her small crib when Izzy knocked on the door.

"Come in. It's not locked."

Izzy walked in. "I don't leave my front door unlocked anymore. Not with that lunatic on the loose."

"I follow ya, sister. I usually do, but I was hot. Besides, I was expecting you to drop in and have a drink with me."

"You was, was ya?" Izzy replied mockingly.

Lucille poured Izzy a drink. "Hey, it's Friday night. Let's loosen up," she cried.

Izzy collapsed onto the bed. "It has been the longest day!"

Lucille was rolling a marijuana cigarette at the table. As she licked the cigarette and rolled it closed, she looked over at Izzy lying on the bed. "Oh, how long of a day was it?"

Izzy rolled over and sat up on the edge of the bed. "Twenty-four dollars. That's how long a day it was."

They both laughed. Izzy took the lit cigarette from Lucille. "And how long was your day, Miss Pickford?"

"I made $8 today. But I sold four gallons of hooch, that's $80. I've just about got that fool Henry conned enough where we're going to raise the stakes, take a bigger slice of the pie."

Izzy took another drag and handed the reefer back to Lucille. "I don't know, Luce. We got a pretty sweet deal going right now. I hear what you're saying though, sister. We got those two fools thinkin' that we're nuts about 'em. I bet ya we can hustle 'em for a little more dough, but I don't want to mess with Henry. He gives me the heebie-jeebies."

"He scares me to death. I thought he was going to give me the Broderick one night. He looked at me with those insane little eyes like he wanted to kill me. I jist hope he doesn't go off the track."

"Yeah. Those fellas are both such maroons. Little old Homer is harmless, but I bet ya we can get him on our side. Maybe we can make them a deal that if we can sell a little more hooch, they can give us a little dough along with our drink."

"We can sure use a little more dough around here. I heard from a girl who was at the Mineflower that the marshal was in there and told Roy to make sure there was no hooch flowing because there would be U.S. marshals in town, arresting people. Maybe I'll tell that queer fella with the boot polish in his hair that we're gonna quit sellin' their stuff because we're afraid of getting nailed by the feds, see what he thinks about that."

Izzy laughed, "You ever ask him why he wears that shoe polish in his hair? Maybe he thinks it makes him look like Rudolph Valentino."

"I ain't never asked him. I jist don't know how he would react. He'd probably give me a goog or a kiss on my yap."

Lucille walked to the front door and looked out, taking a drag off the reefer. "I saw the marshal earlier today walking through here. Some of the girls were giving him some chinning."

"Well," Izzy replied, "he does get paid to protect the people, and we're part of the people. But it ain't his fault that some girls are dumb enough to get mixed up with some goofy palooka. That's why we need to be packing heat."

"It's either we pack heat or be sent home like Emma and Jenny in a wooden kimono."

Izzy laughed, "I don't know where you come up with some of your stuff. You should take your act on the road."

"Yeah right, me and Charlie Chaplin. Jist what we need, a woman with a smart mouth." She walked back inside and poured herself another drink. "I hope that patsy Henry gets his arse back through here soon, we're almost out of hooch." She took the last drag from the reefer and smashed it in the ashtray. "Not only that," she whined. "I'm gonna have to lay down for Hector too. It's Friday night, and we're out of reefer!"

52

Ashley and Lane had a fantastic time at the resort. They went for a swim and played tennis. Then they finished their evening with a delicious steak dinner where they discussed their future. When they returned to the bungalow, they cuddled together on the divan. She had told him that if he wanted her to find another profession, he need only ask. They both fell asleep soundly while they held each other in their arms. Lane woke up first and carried the weary Ashley to her bed in a separate bedroom.

He told her the separate bedrooms were because he didn't want her to think of him as just another paying customer. They had discussed waiting to consummate their relationship until a day in the near future. Ashley didn't second-guess his intentions, which she knew were honorable, but she had an aching desire for him as he did for her.

After a late breakfast by the swimming pool, they placed their bags in the Cadillac and left the resort, driving toward Prescott. Ashley looked at Lane and said, "Thank you for a wonderful weekend. I know it's not over yet, and I'm looking forward to the trip back to Jerome, but in case I forget."

Lane laughed, "The weekend is not over, my dear. There's still some things I'm trying to find the nerve to tell you. I always have a wonderful time when I am with you." In a more serious tone, he added, "I hope you don't think it's too queer that we haven't shared the same bed yet. It's not as if we were living in the days of our grandparents, by God. I'm not overly in religion or anything like that. I just want you to feel the respect that I have for you." After a pause, he continued, "I truly believe that someday perty soon we'll be waking up every day in the same bed, same house, same ranch."

Ashley teased him seductively, "My, you certainly sound like a man with a load of confidence on his back."

He laughed, "Yes, maybe too much in this case."

"I admire the way you carry yourself. I don't mind waiting. I think we both feel the same way and want the same thing. But . . . I hope you're not talking about waiting for . . . years . . . or . . ."

"Oh heavens. No," he blurted. "As beautiful as you looked last night. I could never wait that long. I'm not saying I didn't think about how wonderful it would be. I just want to be different. I want you to have respect for me like I do for you."

"What about your parents? What makes you think that they will like me?"

"We talked about this at dinner last night. Don't you worry about my parents liking you. They will. It's like I said though. We'll have to think of something to tell them about what you do for a living. I don't ever want to lie to my parents, but we may have to come up with something in this case. You and I are going to have more money than we can ever spend someday. We are going to be happy. Let's just no worry about my parents for now."

"OK, whatever you say." She was looking out the window. "I'm just a little nervous about meeting them. I hope there won't be someone at the hoedown who knows of me."

"I hope not either. But let's don't worry about that too much now either. I don't care where I found you or how I met you. I'm not going to ask that you quit what you're doing. At least not right now, I won't. I have to admit that I've thought about it sometimes. I know how you feel about me."

She interrupted, "I'm sorry, Lane. I don't want to cause any problems for you. I knew that my moral character would be judged the day I accepted Madame Cheavant's offer to live in the Parlor House. I told you I have a savings account. You and I can buy some ranch property somewhere of our own. You can still help your parents out, we won't be too far. Or if you want to live farther away where no one will ever know who I was or what I did."

"It's not like that, Ashley. Maybe you don't have a bad idea there about buying our own ranch. Just forget that I will ever be ashamed of you or anything like that. I never will be. There is no reason to be."

They pulled into Prescott where Lane found a place to park the Cadillac in the shade of a willow tree near the Brinkley & Patton Meat Market. Ashley offered to wait in the car while Lane hurried in. He came out five minutes later carrying a large box overflowing with cuts of beef wrapped in white paper.

He opened the trunk and placed the box down into it. Several chunks broken from a block of ice had been placed on top of the beef. He hurried back in. "That box weighed half a ton," he joked. "It's full of fresh beef. Pop's has got an icebox big enough to keep it under ice until the big party. I reckon we better hurry and get it to the ranch."

They left Prescott on the paved road back to Jerome. The drive out of Prescott was fairly smooth. It seemed the board of supervisors always managed to see that the roads in and out of Prescott were always well maintained. The road ascended up the mountain, hairpin curves and the short cliff hanging straightaway made for perilous travel.

As they were halfway up the mountain, Lane said, "You know something? Behind you in the backseat is that sack that Paige insisted we take. Can you reach into the back and grab it and fix us a sandwich?"

"I would be happy to. Is the drive making you hungry?" she asked. She turned her upper body around and grabbed the bag with the bread, cooked potatoes, and cheese.

"I'm going to find a nice shady tree, and we can pull over and check on the beef. We can have a quick picnic break by the road. We're actually making perty good time."

Near the top of the mountain, he found a shady place off the roadway tucked into where the side of the mountain had been dynamited a few years earlier. He turned off the ignition and walked to the back of the Cadillac. He opened the trunk compartment. The big chunks of ice had melted some but should easily last for the remaining two hours of the trip.

Ashley cut up the bread, cheese, and potato on top of a clean handkerchief on the automobile's slightly rounded hood. Paige had also packed a canning jar of apple juice. The picnic gave them a chance to stretch their legs. It also proved timely as Ashley was getting tired from the travel.

After thirty minutes, they got back in the Cadillac and continued their trip back. They got stuck behind a slow-moving truck and couldn't get around it until they were half the way to Jerome. It was after six o'clock when they pulled in front of the Parlor House.

Lane jumped out and carried Ashley's bag while she clung to the box with her dress for the hoedown. They both disappeared inside the front entrance. They were welcomed by Paige and Cecile who were curious to hear about their trip. Norma was also present and asked Ashley to tell her all about Prescott.

After Lane excused himself, Ashley followed him to the Cadillac. They embraced for a long time as they silently rehashed every whimsical event that they had just shared in the last day and a half, each not wanting to let the other one go. They kissed passionately for a few minutes when Lane forced himself to break away and get in the automobile. She followed him around and stuck her head inside his window. "Thanks for another wonderful time. Will I see you before the hoedown?"

"I'll try to reach you by telephone beginning of the week."

He drove out of the driveway as she walked inside. He always had mixed feelings dropping her back off at the Parlor House. He was excited for how he felt about her and he thought she felt about him. He couldn't wait to see her again. There was the matter about telling his parents about her. He wasn't sure how he would handle that. Consumed by his thoughts and feelings, he turned the corner and began to head down the mountain toward the Walker Ranch.

He didn't pay any attention to the dark-haired man smoking a cigarette, who was standing in front of a nearby boardinghouse watching the farewell spectacle from across the street.

53

C. W. had to set the boxful of bottled drinks down so he could free a hand up to open the door into the Mineflower. With some difficulty, he managed to hold the door open with his foot while he carried the heavy box through the front entrance.

The monumental saloon had several patrons playing billiards and card games. Most of the people were men, but C. W. saw three or four young women in the saloon, all paired up with a man. "The Gallows Tree" by Bently Ball played from a Victor VI Victrola phonograph. The man whom he had seen so impeccably dressed entering the Mineflower a couple weeks back helped him unload the box onto the bar.

"You must be C. W.," the man said. "I'm Roy."

"Yes, sir. Let me get your receipt for you." C. W. pulled two pieces of paper from one of the bags and handed one to the man.

"Thank you. Let me see what I owe you." He looked at the total of the delivery circled on the bottom of the piece of paper and said, "I'll get this and be right back."

While the man disappeared for a moment in a back room, C. W. watched the people, almost all had a cup in their hand. He wondered if they were all drinking alcohol at this time of day. He heard the loud clack where a man just started a game of pool by breaking the pool balls from their tight triangle rack.

"Here you go, C. W. Here's $15. You keep the change."

He thanked the generous man who just left him with more than a dollar's change. He reached for the empty box and began to turn around.

"By the way. You come in anytime you like. Just ask for me if you need anything."

"OK. Thank you," he replied timidly.

He left the Mineflower, impressed with its grandeur. He could see where it would be a fun place to be, with a loud band playing and pretty women dancing and frolicking around the place. His father had once told him a story about how a tinhorn from out of town once had to carry his winnings out of the saloon in a potato sack after a day of heavy gambling. He had been accused of cheating which resulted in a gunfight that left three men dead on the street. There were also gunfights over women. Another thing his father told him was that Wyatt Earp and one of his brothers had stopped in for some drinks and gambling once when C. W. was still a crawling baby.

Upon returning to the grocery store, Mr. Baker waved him over to where he had filled a grocery order and placed four sacks in the box. "C. W., Take these two sacks to the Reynoldses's home and drop these two off at the Parlor House on your way back." He dropped the paperwork into one of each customer's grocery sack.

C. W. lifted the box off the table. "Yes, sir." He turned and carried the box down the street. When he left, Mr. Baker looked at Grover, nodded, and smiled. Their new delivery boy was working out quite well.

C. W. crossed the street before he was in front of the Italian restaurant. He was hoping Chiara's father would see him carrying this heavy boxful of groceries and think he was a hardworking young man, worthy of his daughter's friendship. He would look for Chiara on his way back.

He had delivered to the wealthy Reynolds family several times before. Mr. Reynolds owned a lot of real estate around Jerome, including one of the hotels. Mrs. Reynolds was a nice older woman who always offered C. W. a glass of lemonade when he delivered groceries to their house. He would accept the drink, as he was allowed to do, but never stayed long to shoot the bull, as Mr. Baker liked to say.

He left the Reynolds home and got on East Avenue. He loved the Parlor House because the women there were all beautiful and always treated him very kindly. He adored Ashley and hoped that he would see her when he was there. She always greeted him with a warm, "Hello, C. W. How do you do?"

He delivered the groceries to Cecile who paid him for the groceries and gave him an extra half dollar. When he asked her to pass along his best wishes to Miss Ashley, he was told that she was out of town for the weekend but that his greeting would be passed along when she returned.

He smiled and walked out the front door, carrying his now-empty box. Walking past the Italian restaurant, he noticed that there were only a few customers, Chiara looked up at him and smiled. She ran to the front door and said, "Hello, C. W. How is your day going?"

He briefly told her about his deliveries when she had to hurry back inside. She was able to sneak in "see you Sunday" before her father motioned for her to get back to work.

He continued walking up the street. When he was near the grocery store, he saw the man with the slicked-back coal black hair getting into a Model T pickup that was parked across the street. He remembered the man from when he was in the store last week. There was something eerie about him. Something dark. He made everyone in the store feel uncomfortable for some reason. C. W. watched as the man drove off down Main Street.

There were four or five customers in the store when he returned from making deliveries. Mr. Baker walked over to him. "Why don't you sit down and have something to drink? You've been on your feet all day."

"Thanks, Mr. Baker. Hey, I saw that man with the greasy slicked-back black hair getting into his Ford."

"Ah . . . yes. He was in here again."

"He sure is a creepy fella," C. W. said.

"I must admit there is something about him that makes me a little nervous. He isn't really the friendly type."

C. W. grabbed a seat and was drinking a bottle of Dr Pepper when a man wearing a dark suit and tie walked into the store. He saw C. W. seated and began walking toward him. "Excuse me. Are you C. W.?"

"Yes, sir, I am."

Mr. Baker and Grover watched the man as he spoke with C. W.

"My name is Robert Calhoun. I am a production engineer with the Verde United Mining Company. I'm afraid there has just been an accident involving your grandfather. Now before you get upset, let me say that he'll be all right. We just dropped him off at the hospital. We think that he broke his leg."

C. W.'s mouth flew open, and he shot up from his chair. "What happened?" he asked.

"The elevator cage that took the men down into the mine must have malfunctioned. It dropped several feet. Your grandfather and another man were in it when it dropped. He told me I could find you here and not to worry about him."

"Well, I'm very worried about him." He looked at Mr. Baker who had overheard some of the conversation and was hurrying toward C. W. and the mining engineer.

"Did I hear you say that C. W.'s grandfather was hurt at the mine today? Maybe C. W. should go up to the hospital and see him?"

"That will be fine. The accident occurred right at the start of the 2:00 shift. Like I said, C. W.'s grandfather is going to be OK. I'm not so sure about the other man. I'm sure the doctors will let him see his grandfather, but he's in some discomfort."

C. W. looked at Mr. Baker. Before he could even get a word out, Mr. Baker said, "Go! C. W., by all means. Don't worry about us here. In fact, come with me. I'll drive us up there."

"Yes, sir. Thank you, Mr. Baker."

"Now, don't you worry none. It'll be just like the man here says."

Mr. Calhoun was standing near C. W. "I'm also on my way back up to the hospital. You men can both come with me if you like, or I will meet you there."

C. W. jumped in Mr. Baker's Ford that was parked in front of the store while Mr. Calhoun followed them to the hospital up on the hill. It took less than five minutes for both vehicles to arrive at the Verde United Hospital. After they parked, C. W. and the two men all walked briskly through the front door. Mr. Calhoun rushed up to the nurses' station and where a stuffy-looking older woman was seated at the desk wearing a white nurse's hat. He advised her that they were there to see the boy's grandfather, Barney Parker.

When the woman got up from behind the desk, the men saw that she was dressed in white from her hat down to her stockings and shoes. "Please have a seat. I will check on the status of Mr. Parker," she said bluntly.

The Verde United Hospital was one of the finer medical and surgical institutions rivaling many of the hospitals in the eastern part of the country. Only a few years earlier, the most highly trained doctors were few and far between and only practiced in the largest of American cities.

Most of the older hospitals had no laboratories for urine or blood to be examined and were very crude compared to the VU Hospital. In addition to general practitioners, the VU Hospital employed quite a few specialists. No matter what the medical issue or emergency one brought with them to the hospital, the various afflictions were now cared for by a specialist.

The nursing staff of the VU Hospital was also of the utmost quality. They were very much in line with the doctors when it came to diagnosing some of the injuries or illnesses. Their judgment and tenderness with the patients went a long way in establishing the trust and comfort that was so valuable for the patients.

After ten minutes passed, the nurse from the front desk returned and approached the men who were seated in a small waiting room. She said, "I've spoken with the doctor attending to Mr. Parker. Mr. Parker has been given a sedative and is now relaxing comfortably. He asked that only the grandson, which I assume is you"—looking at C. W.—"be allowed to visit and to keep it brief. Mr. Parker will be staying here at the hospital for a few days. Now, if you will follow me, I will take you to his room on the second floor."

C. W. got up uneasily and followed the woman in white down through closed doors and down a corridor bathed in bright lights. The phenol smells and chemical disinfectants filled the corridor, giving the hospital a distinctive odor that contrasted greatly with the smells from the grocery store.

Midway down the corridor, there was a stairway off to the right-hand side. With C. W. following closely behind, the nurse walked up the steps in a slow and cautious manner. She took a left at the top of the stairs without ever looking back or speaking with C. W. It was understood that he was just to follow her.

At the end of the hallway, she walked into a room where C. W.'s grandfather was lying on his back in a bed. His left leg was in a plaster cast and elevated in a sling. He looked drowsy and half-asleep. He smiled with difficulty when his eyes met the worried eyes of his grandson. C. W. edged near the bed. It was painful for him to see his grandfather in this position. "Grandpa. Are you OK? I mean, how are you feeling?"

Barney was sedated but could still see the distress in his grandson's eyes which pained him just as much. He said quietly, "Don't you worry 'bout me, C. W. I just hurt my leg. But I'm lucky that the doctors were able to save it."

"What happened, Grandpa?"

"Oh, the cage collapsed with me and another man in it. Dropped about twenty feet, I reckon. From what they tell me, I'm in a whole lot better shape than he is. The doctors gave me something, and I'm a real tired, but I don't want you to worry. I'll be fine."

The nurse remained by the door standing silently. She took a few steps closer to the bed. "Mr. Parker, the doctors want you to rest. I'll give you another five minutes with your grandson. Can I get you a drink of water?"

"No, thank you, ma'am."

The nurse walked outside the door, giving the injured miner some privacy to speak with his grandson. "You and Jake got plenty of food at the house, so you'll be all right until I get back home. I'm feeling a little tired. Jist don't worry about me none, I'll be down for a little while, that's all. The company will take care of me. I'm perty sure about that."

"Yes, sir," C. W. replied. "Mr. Baker and a Mr. Calhoun are downstairs. They both came with me, but the nurse only let me come up and visit."

"You tell those men thanks for coming but not to worry."

The nurse returned and took her place by the door. This was her signal that the visit was over.

C. W. could see that his grandfather was very tired. "I reckon I better go and let you get some rest, Grandpa. We sure are going to miss you at the house tonight." He bent over and kissed his grandpa on the forehead, tears beginning to well up in his eyes. He didn't want his grandfather to see him crying, so he quickly turned away. He looked at the nurse who was waiting impatiently by the door. "Is it all right if I come back tomorrow and see him?"

She nodded her head slightly without smiling. "Yes, young man. Why don't you stop by sometime after lunch. I'm sure your grandfather will be feeling a little better by then."

He began to leave. Before he left, he looked at his grandfather with moist, reddened eyes and said, "I love you, Grandpa."

"I love you too, C. W. Now you go on home and take care of that dog for me."

54

Pazrosky and Homer devoured the rabbit stew, washed down by hooch that they had the sense to now dilute with a soda beverage, at least with their supper. After the sun had set, an evening breeze blew through the hills, providing a cool reprieve from the day's heat.

Homer started a fire in the fire pit, and the two men sat around it like a couple of hobos. Pazrosky lit another cigarette and walked over to the northern edge of the property. He looked down on some of the homes in the Hogback, with their lights now on, thinking about the Parlor House. His obsession with the place and the long-haired brunette that lived there was growing.

He was now drinking straight hooch from his cup. He had dozed off earlier but had drank without slacking since he had awoke from his afternoon nap. He looked over at Homer who was staring into the fire, entranced. He said, "That wasn't a bad supper you cooked up, old-timer. Maybe we *should* have invited a couple of girls from town to join us."

Homer scratched at his bearded face. "I follow ya, partner. This hooch has got me wishin' I had some dame to keep me company tonight. Not that yer company is too bad," he added awkwardly. "You know what I mean."

Picking at his yellowed rotting teeth, Pazrosky said, "That wasn't a bad rabbit stew at all. Maybe you can shoot us another one tomorrow, or a yard bird, and we can get some girls up here for a cookout like you was saying." He took a drag from his cigarette. After he exhaled, he finished his thought, "We can cook it over the fire this time."

"That ain't a bad idea. I got some brewin' to do tonight. Good idea to have a fire burning on nights that we're brewing. But I don't suppose those U.S. marshals would ever come out here. It's those moonshiners brewing that swill in their bathtubs and makin' everybody sick, thems the ones that the feds are coppin'."

"As long as that girlfriend of yers and Lucille keeps their yaps shut, we ought to be all right," Pazrosky offered.

"As fond of me as that young lady is, I don't see 'em doin' nothin' that would get 'em in trouble with us. Besides, they're getting all their hooch paid fer," he said confidently. "And I thought you were takin' good care of Lucille."

"I don't trust a broad as far as I can throw one. They see how good a business we got goin', and they're gonna wanna have more dough. You just watch," Pazrosky said bitterly.

"Ah, Henry, I don't think so. They're making plenty of dough already. As good-lookin' as those two are, I bet ya they're making $25 a day."

"Five dollars a day, more like it. Those girls get paid a dollar a pop. It'll cost you at least $100 to be with one of them Parlor girls. I don't know where they go and think that they're so special like they're some kind of movie star or something. No dame is worth that much money!"

"There ya go again, talkin' 'bout them gals at the Parlor House. I wish you'd leave them gals alone. Jist because you or me ain't got that kind of money doesn't mean that there ain't some fella out there with deep-enough pockets wantin' some broad with all her teeth and perty dresses and everything."

"A whore is a whore," Pazrosky said rudely. "They're all only good for one thing."

"I ain't gonna argue with ya. All I know is before you came up here to Jerome from wherever you says yer from, I hadn't been with a woman in year—quite a while. I forgot how good it was to spend time with someone soft and perty who smells real good and everything."

Homer got up from the tree stump that he had been sitting on. "Well, Henry, if you'll excuse me for a minute, I got to get the brew goin'."

Pazrosky struggled to stand up, the effects of the hooch pulling him to the side. He tripped over a log and fell face-first into the hard pan of the ground.

Homer turned around with a big smile on his face. He didn't care because it was dark outside, and Henry wouldn't see the huge grin he was wearing across his face. "You hurt yerself, Henry?"

Pazrosky was angry. "No. I tripped over this log you had sittin' here."

Satisfied that Henry hadn't hurt himself, Homer chided, "Hell, I thought you were doing one of them fancy cowboy dances or ballet or something. I seen ya go down out of the corner of my eye."

Not about to make light of himself falling down, Pazrosky stood up and brushed himself off. "Damn it! Now I'm gonna have to take these clothes down to the Chinamen so they can be laundered."

"Well, that's the problem," Homer joked. "If you was wearin' yer Friday-night drinkin' clothes instead of yer Sunday—go-to-meetin' clothes, you wouldn't have to go give yer good clothes to the Chinamen."

"Very funny. Why don't you jist drag your arse in there and get our hooch brewin'. I'm gonna go lie down for a while." He vanished into his newly constructed abode and slept off the hooch and rabbit stew.

Homer shook his head and walked into the shed where the still and a barrel of mash was waiting. He enjoyed a laugh when he was inside. While Henry's dance step was one of the funniest things he had seen in a long while, he knew how capable Henry was of losing it. He had never forgotten how he socked a large Irishman in the kisser on the first day that he had met the man. There was something about Henry that was frightening.

The next morning, Pazrosky got up from his cot and lit a cigarette. Stepping outside, he shielded his eyes from the sun that was beginning to rise in the eastern sky. He walked over to the shed and stepped inside. The hooch was dripping drop by drop from a spout off the worm box into a large filtered metal bucket. The filter, being a square piece of cloth, was much like a handkerchief. He wanted to water down the finished product in order to increase their profits but decided against it. His head hurt.

He walked into the main hovel to get some coffee going. Homer was snoring behind the curtain. The table was still full of vegetable scraps and garbage from the night before. The hovel had recaptured its body odor stink. Stepping on a cockroach that he nonchalantly knocked off the table, he tossed his cigarette butt outside and grabbed the tin can that he used to drink. He then walked back outside toward the shed where he found a jugful of hooch and poured himself a drink.

With his cup in hand, he walked over to the northern edge where he could look down toward the smelter in Clarkdale. From this vantage point, he could also see part of the Hogback. He was getting bored and feeling anxious. He hated women but couldn't live without them for too long at the same time. He thought he would drive down to the Cribs, see if Lucille wanted to go for a drive. He might even go to one of the pool halls, see if there were any other women that may pique his interest.

He walked back to Homer's hovel and poured himself a cup of coffee. Then he walked back into the shack where the hooch was dripping. On the floor in the corner were three unfilled jugs and a boxful of empty canning jars. He picked up one of the glass jars and dipped it into the large metal bucket. He tightly screwed on a lid and took the jar with him back to his shed. He would bring this jar with him into town and present it to Lucille.

First, he needed to wash up and find some clean clothes. He reached under the cot where his cigar box contained some cash and jewelry. Most of his stolen money was safely being kept at the bank where he had opened an account, the first bank account he had ever had. He examined the .45-caliber handgun that he also kept loaded in the box. Ironically, he didn't like guns too much. He put the gun back in the box and grabbed the pocket watch. He examined it thoroughly. It was a fourteen-carat yellow gold Paul Ditisheim with the name "Vincent J. Panivini" printed in small characters on the face. He wondered who Vincent Panivini was. He turned the watch over to see that it had an engraved monogram of "SW" inside a blue enamel circle. He wound the mechanical hand wind and placed the watch back in the box. He knew it wasn't wise to keep the stolen jewelry.

Pazrosky lit another cigarette, set it on the edge of the cot, and took another drink from his coffee. As he now alternated between drinking his coffee, his hooch, and smoking his cigarette, he thought he would make things easier and poured the remains of his hooch in with his coffee.

He counted out $20 of paper money and replaced the box under the cot. He grabbed the tin of boot polish that set on his homemade dresser, his only piece of furniture other than the cot. He picked up his less-conspicuous watch that he had also stolen, somewhere in Texas, and saw that it was already past one in the afternoon. He had slept longer than he thought. His dismal wardrobe hung from a broken broom handle wedged in one of the corners. Dirty laundry was clumped together on the floor in another corner.

Hungry, he decided to go into town and have lunch at one of the restaurants. After he was cleaned up and had combed the polish through his hair and beard, he grabbed the jar he had filled with hooch and headed into town.

He drove up East Avenue past the Parlor House two times but didn't see anyone coming in or going out. The house was clearly one of the nicer homes in that area. He parked the Ford nearby and walked into town.

He entered what appeared to be an Italian restaurant and sat down. There were a few other people having lunch, none who were speaking English. He began to turn around when a beautiful young woman with a striking dark complexion, whom he figured to be seventeen or eighteen years of age, waited on him. She smiled and led him to a vacant table. After he sat down, she placed a menu in front of him. She returned a minute later with a glass of water.

The girl stopped at a nearby table where she spoke something in a foreign language that he was able to determine was Italian. When she returned to his table, she spoke English, not figuring him to be Italian. She was warm and friendly. "Yes, sir?"

He looked into her brown eyes, then her mouth before his lecherous eyes slowly roamed from her face down the front of her thin torso to her waist. The girl held her hands protectively in front of her and turned away from the pathetic man. His eyes finally returned up to hers. He said coldly, "I'll have spaghetti and meatballs."

She wanted to get away from the man who had made her feel so filthy and dirty. Turning to return to the kitchen and the security of her mother and father, she sensed his swinish eyes follow her degradingly as she walked away.

When she entered the kitchen, her mother knew something was wrong. She looked up from the stove where pasta was boiling. In Italian, she asked, "What is it, sweetie?"

The girl shook her head and looked down at the floor, rolling her eyes. "That awful man out there. The way he just looked at me. I think I'm going to be ill."

Her mother wiped her hands off on a towel and walked to where she could see the man who had been so offensive to her daughter. She immediately knew why her daughter was so upset. The man had oily black hair combed straight back and had a dark, apathetic appearance. She returned to her daughter. "Your father won't be back for another few minutes. He ran to the store. So you have to go back out there. Don't worry, I'll watch out for you."

"Mother," she protested. "That man is a wicked creature, a snake. You should have seen the way he looked at me, up and down. I've never felt so disgusted in my whole life."

Her mother hugged her quickly and gently. "Honey, we have *perveritos* back in Italy as well. Men like that are everywhere. As a beautiful young woman, there are going to be men that look at you without respect."

The young girl had calmed down some. "OK, Mother, but if he looks at me like that again, I swear I am going to throw his spaghetti all over his head!"

"Go on back out there, Alfredo and Lucia are looking for you."

Reluctantly, the young girl went back out to the restaurant. She ignored the miserable man and waited politely on the other customers. With her back turned toward him, she took the old couple's money and thanked them for coming in. While they were both in the middle of voicing their gratitude for the delicious meat-filled tortellinis and her kind service, the man rudely interrupted, "Can I get some bread over here?"

The pretty young girl looked toward the back of the small restaurant at her mother, who was watching hidden in the small kitchen area, before turning her gaze at the man. "Of course, sir, right away." The old couple shot the loudmouth man a loathing look before they left the restaurant.

She hurried into the kitchen and looked at her mother. Before she could say anything, her mother said irately, "You're right. Quell'uomo e a figlio di puttana." She immediately blushed as she had never used such harsh language in front of her daughter before. The young girl giggled at her mother.

"Let's just hope he eats and gets out of here."

She brought the man a plate with a half loaf of bread. "Anything else, sir?"

"No, unless you have some vino?" he asked flippantly.

"I'm sorry sir. We do not have vin . . . wine." Before he could reply, she turned and hurried to the kitchen area. Aside from a young Italian couple and their small boy, the irritating man was the only customer in the restaurant.

The girl took the plate of spaghetti and meatballs to the man as her father returned from the store with a sackful of vegetables. She asked the man, "Is there anything else I can get for you?"

He muttered something under his breath that she could not understand. She assumed correctly that it was something vulgar and walked back to the kitchen where her father had sat the sack down.

Her father was always suspicious of those people who were not Italian. "What is that man doing in here?" he asked.

Not wanting to enrage the quick-tempered head of the household, the girl's mother said, "He's just someone with poor manners. He'll pay and be out of here soon." She did not mention how he had looked at their daughter earlier with such degradation and indecency. "*Marito caro,* Chiara, and I will get these vegetables prepared. Why don't you wait on him until he leaves?"

55

It was close to five when the large automobile carrying four U.S. marshals pulled up near the town hall. They all wore big hats with their guns strapped into leather holsters. There were three big men and one that was not so tall. Oddly enough, it was the shorter man that walked in first. He introduced himself as Captain Rawlings. He introduced the other deputies to the marshal and Deputy Ray. Before he started speaking, he turned to one of his deputy marshals and asked him to secure their rooms at the hotel across the street.

He took a seat opposite the marshal while Deputy Ray stood in the doorway to the back room. "First of all, Marshal Williams, I want to apologize for getting here so late. We blew a tire in Prescott, then our damn jalopy overheated on the way over here." he laughed. "That's some view, I must say." He nodded at one of his deputies. "A little too much for Deputy Owens here. I reckon he didn't like his lunch that much anyways." The other federal marshals laughed as Deputy Owens smirked and looked at the ground.

"Can I offer you, gentlemen, some coffee or a soda drink?" the marshal offered.

"No, thank you, Marshal Williams. We're going to sit down and have us a nice dinner perty shortly. Maybe you can tell us a nice restaurant where we can all get us a nice steak? I want to explain why we're here and why we ain't. I don't reckon there is too much we can do, but we're hoping jist being here might help let the townspeople know we mean business in findin' this character responsible for the disappearance of some of your finest ladies."

The marshal wore a look of disappointment on his face. "We don't mind your assistance, Captain. Frankly, the whole thing has got so damn messy. I wish we had more clues or something to go on. We'll be happy to share everything we have, but I'm afraid it ain't much."

"Appreciate it, Marshal," Captain Rawlings stated. "We sure would like to help you find the man responsible. If nothing else, our presence in Jerome may drive him out of town, if nothing else. Like I says, what we ain't here to do is step on anybody's boots. We know yer doin' everything you can. I also know yer a little shorthanded. Y'all the fourth largest town in the state. You should have more money for more deputies. Maybe the state wants them wealthy mine owners to do more, I don't know, any how, there are two dead women and two more missin' and probably dead too. I spoke with Sheriff Thompson, and he has promised to provide you with more manpower. Now, Marshal, I hope you don't mind, but me and my deputies plan on making our presence known this weekend. Lovely town you got here, but we ain't here on vacation."

"I understand that, Captain," the marshal assured. "We can pull the files on the deceased and what we got on the other two girls, but like I say, it ain't much."

"Thank you, Marshal. My plan tonight is for me to come back here after we get us a bite to eat and go over some things with you while my deputies take to the streets and look into some of the pool halls. We ain't planning on fillin' yer jail cells up at all. Nothing like that. We don't want to stir up any trouble." When he began to stand up, his deputies fell in behind him. "I want to discuss the man whom we think may or may not be responsible. I know you spoke with a couple of our special agents awhile back. They likely informed you of a man we've been lookin' for."

"Yes, sir. They did. We've taken his photograph around town, but nobody seems to have seen him."

"Well, I doubt we'll find that slitherin' yellow belly either, but if he's here, he'll sure in hell hear that there's more law enforcement in town. We'll either smoke him out or chase him into California or Nevada somewhere. Now, can you tell us where we can get us a good meal?"

After the U.S. marshals left, Deputy Ray took the seat where Captain Rawlings had been seated. Deputy Zalensky walked in soon after and stated, "Geez, it looks like I missed something. I seen three men wearing U.S. marshal badges just walk into the hotel." He was quickly brought up-to-date on the business of the federal lawmen. "Well, Marshal, the way I look at it, they can't really hurt anything. Make a few people mad though, I reckon."

"I reckon they may do that," the marshal acknowledged. "At least they were respectful. Said they weren't here to do any arresting or anything. One thing for sure, they ain't here for the gamblers or moonshiners. They're here to help us find that no-good son of a bitch."

The marshal looked at Deputy Ray. "Billy, why don't you pull everything we got, the photographs we took, any notes, reports, things like that. I don't know how helpful they'll be though."

"Will do, Marshal."

Deputy Zalensky sat down at a desk in the back room and began to run a steel cleaning rod through the chambers of his revolver. He leaned back and spoke to the marshal, "I'll be done here in a minute. Is there anything you want me to go and do?"

"I reckon you can go out on foot patrol, see if Deputy Burns needs anything. It's starting to get dark outside. You may want to check with the Wells Fargo Office for any telegrams. I forgot to go by there today. Later, stop in at the Mineflower, speak with Roy for a minute. I don't want any hooch in there with all them federal lawmen poking their heads around. Myself, I'm going to stick around here and wait for Captain Rawlings to come back."

Deputy Ray had gathered several files and set them on the marshal's desk. He had a forlorn expression on his face. "Four women gone missin', two of whom we found dead, and this is all we got on the whole damn case."

The marshal looked up. "Now, Billy, I'm beating my head against the wall enough for all of us. We need to stay positive and focused. Myself, I feel like I've let a lot of people down. Sure them girls were all loose women, but they're people too. They're just trying to survive like the rest of us. They got family. Hell, you should have heard all the bull that was thrown my way when I walked through the Cribs this afternoon. It's gonna be tough for all of us until we find this man. Why don't you go out and take a little walk, ask the people if they've seen anything out of the ordinary lately."

"Will do, Marshal" He grabbed his hat and walked out the front door.

The marshal began to look through some of the files Deputy Ray had laid on his desk. After nearly an hour had passed, Captain Rawlings returned. He had a leather pouch in his right hand. Rubbing his stomach, he smiled. "You sure was right about that restaurant in the hotel. That's the best steak I've had in a long time." He took the vacant chair across from the marshal. "Mind if I take a look at some of these reports?"

"Go ahead, Captain. Me and my deputies were just shootin' the bull about not havin' dug up much on these girls that were abducted. Two of them shared the same apartment. One has already been sent home in a box. We found her buried under some dirt and rocks not far from where we found one of the others. We ain't found her crib mate. My deputies had spoke with her shortly before she disappeared. She was a little loco from dope. One of other deputies found out that she also spent time with some Chinamen, hitting the opium pipe. What makes me real sore is she was the only one whom we spoke with who had seen the man. Here, it's in this report." He handed a file over to the lawman.

Captain Rawlings accepted the file and tossed his leather pouch on the desk. "I brought some things I wanted to share with you too, Marshal. But I wanted to ask you something. Have you ever investigated a multiple-murder case before?"

"No, not where one man is suspected of killing more than one person, no."

"I have much experience in this area," Rawlings noted. "I believe the type of murderer that we are now playing cards with is someone motivated by lust and power. He is aware that his actions have terrified the community, at the same time, his ability to leave law enforcement totally confused adds to his feeling of power. I could go on and on, but we still feel that Joseph Pazrosky is the main suspect in the kidnapping of these four women and murder of at least two of them."

"We've had murders in Jerome since I have been here, but they were basically cut-and-dried. Someone knifing someone in front of witnesses after they felt they were cheated, men killing their wife's lovers, killing someone and stealing their property—things of that nature. Before this happened, we had no unsolved killings in Jerome."

"I see," said Rawlings. "Marshal, is that invitation for a soda drink still on the table? We have quite a bit to discuss, and my mouth is already parched."

The marshal stood up. "Of course, Captain." He walked briskly to the small icebox in the back room and grabbed a bottle. "How about Dr Pepper?" he asked.

"Fine, thank you," Rawlings answered. He took a swig from the bottle. "Ahhh, hits the spot, thank you." He looked through the reports for a minute before continuing. "Now, before we discuss this fella Pazrosky in particular, is there anyone who may be responsible for these crimes who has a general knowledge of the area?"

"I must say, Captain, other than what we were told about Pazrosky, we don't have any person of interest. We don't have another suspect."

Rawlings looked over the photographs taken at the scene of where the two bodies were found. "Were you able to find any tire tracks or shoe imprints?"

"Captain, we sure tried. The bodies were found in a gulch several hundred feet away from the closest road. That roadway was in the Mexican sector where most of the residents are Mexican and employed by the Little Daisy Mine. And as you probably know, this is the time of year for heavy rains, and we've had quite a bit of rain in the past month or so which certainly hasn't been very helpful in our investigation. We photographed and tried to record everything the best we could. I don't know whether they're relevant or not."

Rawlings nodded his head. "I see here that you've interviewed some of the girl's friends and family members. Very good. Everyone's alibis have been verified?"

"Yes, we pursued a couple of gentlemen callers and jilted lovers or whatever you want to call them. There's some names listed in the reports. None of them seem to be solid suspects however as there alibis were verified."

"I see." He took another drink from his soda bottle. "Well, another reason why we feel it may be Pazrosky is we have wired several law enforcement agencies in the surrounding states, and it doesn't appear that he has been locked up anywhere in the past year or less. We have also made contact with those agencies where there have been young women, prostitutes or not, kidnapped and or murdered. All eyes are focused in this area, particularly Jerome."

Rawlings grabbed the pouch and removed several papers, including copies of Pazrosky's photograph that was taken while he was a prisoner at Huntsville, Texas. "Marshal, what do you think about posting this man's photograph up outside town hall here and handing a few out to the brothels and saloons?"

"Well, Captain, I reckon it wouldn't hurt and may be helpful. I've certainly got the townspeople on my back, and I don't blame them. They're concerned that there is a killer on the loose. I've also heard that young women are losing sleep in fear that they may be the next target. It's very unsettling for me personally."

Rawlings smiled sympathetically. "Personally, I feel that the man responsible is someone driven by compulsion. He likely has some knowledge of the area." He sifted through the photographs of the two victims as they lay in their shallow graves.

The marshal's expression on his face was as if he had just been stung by a scorpion in his boot. "You'll read it in my report, Captain, and in a couple of those photographs, but the thing that I find the most gruesome about those deaths is in the body we found most recently. Jenny Richardson. Her body was shipped out to some family members in New Mexico this morning. We got a lead from a boy who had found a brand-new woman's shoe down in the gulch. When we found the girl's grave nearby, she was wearing the match to the shoe. If I may see those photographs, I'll show you what I'm getting at."

Rawlings handed the marshal the file containing Jenny Richardson's photographs and reports. The marshal pulled a photograph out of the collection, then said, "There are just some things that I don't want the townspeople to ever hear about." He handed the photograph, a close-up shot taken of the victim's hands, to the federal lawman. "The photograph didn't turn out as well as I had hoped. But if you were to use a magnifying glass, you can see that there are a few broken fingernails. The fingers where the nails weren't broken all had dirt encrusted under the nails."

Rawlings let out a low whistle. "So she was buried alive."

56

T hat Friday night when C. W. returned from visiting his grandfather in the hospital, the empty home felt strange and lonely. C. W. had always waited anxiously for his grandfather to come home from working at the mine. On this night, he wouldn't be coming home at all. C. W. was torn between feeling sad that his grandfather had got hurt and grateful that he was still alive, knowing good and well how dangerous it was to work in the mines.

He remembered the day his grandfather came to Jerome for the funeral of his father. His grandfather had told him that things were going to be difficult for a while but that he would move to town, find work, and take care of him. Together, the two of them would get by. And they always have been able to get by. They had each other and little more.

To see him now, sedated and lying in a hospital bed, tore C. W. up. He said a prayer, thanking God for not taking his grandfather away to heaven and to help him recover quickly so things could get back to normal. He boiled a potato for supper but found that he wasn't even hungry enough to eat that. He tried thinking of beautiful Chiara to get his mind off his grandfather, but his grandfather's injury had put a damper on even his thoughts of her.

Jake also sensed that something was wrong with C. W. The dog followed him everywhere he went. C. W. thought about taking the dog for a walk, but it was nearing 8:00 and would soon be dark. As there were no table scraps on this evening for poor Jake, C. W. had fed him from a can in the cupboard. After the war, horses and mules were being replaced by the automobile and trucks. Therefore, canned horse meat was cheap. On nights where there were no table scraps, the dog would be fed the canned horse meat. The playful pooch was always thankful and well cared for. C. W.'s grandfather would also purchase Milk-Bone dog biscuits from the grocery store whenever they had them and get cheap cuts of offal and raw meat from the butcher. Indeed, Jake was part of their little family. He too felt C. W.'s pain and knew something was not right in their home on this night.

C. W. could hear the sounds of jazz music and laughter radiating from the Cribs behind his home. He remembered how wild it used to be when he was younger. His mother and father would get so annoyed at the loud noise and drunkenness of the men and women who would party all through the night. He figured the slowdown at both the large mines and the federal law that prohibited people from getting drunk of alcoholic beverages had something to do with things not being as wild as they once seemed.

No one in his family had ever been interested in drinking or getting drunk. He remembered his folks drinking a glass of wine or champagne on two or three occasions at Christmas or once when they celebrated on the day they had been married. He didn't see what the big deal was about it, but understood that adults often get drunk as an escape from the blahs of their day-to-day lives.

He thought about wandering the streets, which he often did at night before his grandfather would come home from work. He was bored and worried about his grandfather. He wondered what Chiara was doing, wishing they were closer friends as he really needed some companionship. Looking down at Jake, the dog tilted his head in a show of concern for his friend and master. C. W. patted the dog on the head. "What's the matter, boy? Can you tell that things jist ain't right around here with Grandpa in the hospital? Don't worry, he'll be all right." He decided against going out to walk the streets tonight. He would stay home. He and Jake would keep each other company.

It was odd not having Grandfather there when he got out of bed the next morning. He could hardly wait until lunchtime when he would go to the hospital and visit him. He wanted to take Jake too but thought that the nurse at the front desk wouldn't likely appreciate that too much. He was going into the grocery store. He enjoyed his job and was hoping it might keep his mind off his worries. He knew Mr. Baker would allow him to visit his grandfather.

Without breakfast, he left home for work early. He patted Jake on the head and threw him a couple of dog biscuits. "You be good, boy, I'll be home in a little bit." He was hoping to see Chiara again. Taking the long way to work down Hull Avenue, he walked by the Italian restaurant and looked inside. The restaurant only had two tables of patrons at this time. He didn't see Chiara as he paused in front of the restaurant. However, her mother saw him and smiled. He smiled back and continued walking to the store.

As he was walking up the street, he heard someone call his name. There was no mistaking the Italian accent; it was Chiara. He stopped and turned around. She was walking toward him. "My mother said that she saw you. How are you?"

"I'm fine. I'm just on my way to work," he answered.

"I'm glad you're fine. Are we still going to do something tomorrow?" she asked.

"Yes, of course," he replied. He frowned and looked away. "Sure."

"Is something wrong?"

"Well"—he hesitated a second—"my grandfather is in the hospital up there," he said nodding toward the hill. "He had an accident at the mine yesterday. He broke his leg. I'm not sure when he is coming home, but I'm going to want to be around to help him."

Chiara immediately could feel the concern in C. W.'s voice. A look of sadness materialized on her face. "Oh, C. W., I'm sorry. That's too bad. I hope he is going to be all right."

"Yeah, me too," he said. "Last night was strange with him not being home. I'm hoping Mr. Baker will let me go see him after lunch today."

She gave him a caring look and touched his arm. His body responded to her touch in a way he had never felt before, as if it radiated from his arm and shot in all directions throughout the rest of his body. She took her hand back and looked over her shoulder back toward the restaurant as if she was expecting her father to come out and holler at her to return. "If you like, maybe I can walk up to the hospital with you today."

Surprised, C. W. said, "Are you sure? What about your father? I don't think he would allow you to leave the restaurant and go with *me*."

"Don't worry about my father," she said insistently. "My mother and I have been talking to him lately about a lot of things. Sometimes, it's us against him. He is very . . . how you say . . . stubborn . . . Is that the word?"

C. W. smiled affectionately. "I'm sure your father is a good man. He only has your best interests at heart. You know, this is the longest we've talked in a while."

"I know. I need to get back to the *ristorante*. Pass by if you go to see your grandfather, and maybe I can go with you." She turned and hurried back down the street before he was able to say how much he would enjoy that.

C. W. watched her dash off. He had a good feeling about that girl. He wondered where her father was and why he didn't come out like he always did. Shrugging it off, he turned and continued to the store arriving at exactly 10:00. There were no customers in the store.

Mr. Baker, who was standing behind the counter, pulled his watch from his apron pocket and looked at the time. He looked at C. W. "I wasn't sure if you were coming in to work today or not. You're always early."

"Umm . . . yes, sir."

Grover was taking some fresh vegetables out of a crate and putting them on the shelf, making sure to place the older vegetables toward the front and the fresher vegetables in the back to prevent waste. Myrtle was stocking the back shelf with canned goods, turning the cans so the labels all pointed to the front. Both looked up and cordially greeted C. W. They were always polite to him, but today, he felt their sympathy.

Mr. Baker was loading some items in a box. He said, "We've got a few deliveries this morning. What time did you want to go and visit your grandpa?"

"Uhh, well," he stammered. "The nurse said to come back sometime after lunch."

"We'll have to manage without you for a while then. It won't be a problem at all. We want you to spend as much time with your grandpa as you like, or as long as that nurse lets you anyways."

"Thank you, sir. It sure was strange him not being home last night. I sure missed him."

"I bet you did," Mr. Baker said considerately. "Your grandfather is a good man. We all feel bad that he hurt himself, but those big shots at the mine, I hear, are real good about taking care of their men. He'll be all right."

"I hope so. I'm afraid he's going to be down for a while until his leg gets all healed up."

"He's gonna be just fine, don't you worry. Now, let me get these orders ready, and you can take 'em to the customers. The Hudsons and Greelys up on Company Hill. You been to both their homes before. And then there's a sack here that needs to be dropped off at the warehouse. I hope it isn't too heavy. There's a lot of milk bottles in here."

"Not a problem, Mr. Baker." C. W. felt that he was being treated differently today, perhaps a little patronized because of what happened to his grandfather, but he didn't mind. He liked Mr. Baker and the others. They were kind to him. He grabbed the heavy box off the counter and lugged it out the front door.

57

When Pazrosky left the restaurant, he returned to the pickup that was parked down the street. The pretty young Italian girl had stirred up the lustful desire that had been smoldering in his loins, giving him a tingling sensation. He lit a cigarette and decided he would drive up to the Cribs where he would pay Lucille a visit.

Parking the pickup in front of the Liberty Theater, he got out and walked down to the Cribs, which was quiet with only two or three men around. He pulled his fedora low over his eyes. A few girls stood in their doorways attempting to drum up some afternoon business.

He knocked on the door to Lucille's. She answered the door on his third attempt, smiling when she saw him. "Good afternoon, Henry. I was hoping I might see you today."

He barged in to her home. "You was, huh?"

She watched with a perturbed expression as he rudely walked past her into the small dining area and made himself at home. He pulled a chair from the small table and sat down.

"Is there anything I can get you? I was going to tell you that I'm all out of hooch. I was hoping you brought some with you."

"I did," he said bluntly. "But I left it in the crate."

"Oh, well, do you want to get it so we can have a drink? I was able to get some reefer today. Maybe you want to smoke one?"

"Nah," he replied. "What do you say we go for a ride out of town, find some shade somewhere, and have a few drinks?"

"Well, I guess that would be OK. I thought you might want me and Izzy to come out to Homer's tonight and have some fun. I wanted to talk to you about moving more hooch through here. I can sell a lot more than what you've been givin' me."

Impatiently, he answered, "Sure, we can talk about it later. Let's go for a drive."

"All right. Let me run next door and tell Izzy that I'll be gone for a little while."

With indignity, Pazrosky said, "What you want to do that for?"

She looked at him. "Because until they find that killer, all the girls around here have been letting each other know when we're going somewhere so nobody worries."

"But you'll be with me. Nuthin's gonna happen to you."

"I know that, Henry. I jist don't want Izzy to worry about me. Everyone has been on edge since Lilly disappeared. I can tell her that we're all gonna go up to Homer's tonight too. You know how much she likes Homer."

"Sure she does," he said sarcastically. "All right." He dug his hands in his pocket, took out some money, and handed it to her. "Why don't you give her some dough so she can run and buy some groceries when we're gone? Some stuff for a cookout."

"That sounds like a good idea," she said excitedly. "You wait here. I'll be right back." She turned to walk out but then pivoted and approached Henry. She wrapped her arms around him and kissed him passionately. "You know, you can be a really sweet man sometimes when you want to be." As she turned away and walked out the door, he wiped his mouth with his hand, a disgusted expression on his face.

She returned a few minutes later. "OK. Everything is hunky-dory. I don't know about you, but I'm gonna grab a reefer for the road."

"You and your reefer," he said. "Come on, I need a drink."

The two left the Cribs and got into the pickup. He took one last drag from his cigarette, then threw the butt out the window. They turned right, driving by the Conner Building and circled around Clark Street past the minigolf. Lucille looked across Henry, down to the miniature golf course. "That looks like fun. Why don't you and I ever play?"

"What do you mean, like go on a date?" he asked.

"No. Not go on a date," she repeated with a mocking tone. "I'm just saying that it looks like fun, that's all."

"I don't golf."

"Tsk-tsk." She looked straight ahead as Henry drove out of town on the twisting, turning road.

Reaching back behind him, Pazrosky grabbed the canning jar that he filled with the hooch from the still. He twisted off the lid and took a drink before handing it to Lucille. She disregarded his lack of manners and took a long sip. "I don't know where you and Homer get your shine, but it's better than any homemade brew I've tasted."

"A friend of Homer's gets it for us," he lied. "Yer right. It ain't bad." He took the jar away from her and took another gulp. He handed it to her, then placed his hand high on her left thigh, caressing her.

Lucille lit a reefer. She handed it to Henry who took a drag before handing it back to her. "Where do you get this shit?" he asked her.

She took another drag from the marijuana cigarette and held in the smoke. A moment later, she answered him, "From some Mexican that lives down behind us. Why?" She placed the reefer in the ashtray, feeling a little dizzy.

"I was jist wonderin' if there was any money to be made sellin' the shit. It ain't like you can jist run into the grocery or drugstore and pick up a deck, ya follow?" he replied.

"If you want to peddle reefer, you got to deal with the Mexicans. Jist like if you want to peddle opium, you got to deal with the Chinamen. I don't know if that something you want to do quite honestly," she said condescendingly.

He removed his hand from Lucille's lap and fumbled with a cigarette, the jar of hooch between his legs.

"Be careful that you don't kill us both by drivin' us over a cliff," she warned.

He got his cigarette lit and took the curve fast, his two right tires leaving the roadway, nearly scraping the cliff wall. "You did that on purpose!" she wailed.

Never one to laugh around women, Pazrosky smirked proudly. They drove in silence for another mile or two before he pulled the Ford off the road. The cigarette dangling from his mouth was dropping ashes on his shirt. Stopping the car under the shade of a cottonwood tree, he placed the cigarette in the ashtray and took another gulp from the almost-empty Mason jar. He handed the jar to Lucille, smiling where his crooked yellow teeth were displayed. She took a big gulp and handed him the rest. He finished the last few sips and placed the jar in the backseat.

He closely leaned into her, intruding on her personal space. His hands began to grope all over the front of her body. His foul breath was wheezing all over her. Oh, how she was starting to loathe this man. "Hey, watch yer flippers! Why do you always have to play so rough? I may be a whore, but don't forget I'm also a woman, ya follow? A human being?"

"Sure you are," he said. "But playing rough is the only way I know how to play."

58

It was past 10:30 when Captain Rawlings retired to the hotel across the street from town hall. The marshal was sitting in the jail with Deputy Zalensky when Shirley stepped in. "Is it all right if I come in for a minute?"

The marshal quickly came to his feet while Deputy Zalensky sat up in his chair. "Yes, Shirl. Come on in," the marshal said. "I'm sorry I haven't stopped by the house. We've got some U.S. marshals in town from Phoenix. Been busy goin' over some things with them. How have you been, dumplin'?"

Deputy Zalensky was about to excuse himself, but Shirley stopped him. "Oh no, Dave. You don't have to get up or go anywhere. I'm not staying long. I understand you men have some work to do. I just wanted to say hello before I go home and hit the hay."

"Are you sure, Shirley? I don't mind," Deputy Zalensky stated.

"No, you're fine. I've been busy myself. Me and the other teachers have been meeting with the superintendent and the principal, discussing the curriculum for the fall. Juanita and I had a cup of coffee over at her apartment, and I was going back home."

"I was gonna say. It's getting a little late," the marshal observed.

"I've seen some big lawmen walking around down the street. They must be the U.S. marshals you were talking about."

"Yeah," said the marshal, somewhat bothered. "They're here to establish some presence, I reckon. As you know, the whole town has been a little rattled, to say the least, with all that's been goin' on with all the kidnappings and . . . you know."

"Yes, I know. But you fellas are doing everything you can. Some of the teachers were talking about that tonight at our meeting. Some were saying it was divine intervention for living their lives in sin, but I don't think that's fair."

"No, dumplin', that isn't fair. That isn't fair at all," the marshal replied. "No women, and I don't care if they're nuns or whor . . . ladies of the evening, deserve to be killed like the two we found were. I understand that people are going to be scared until we find the man responsible, but saying that these girls have got what's coming to 'em jist ain't fair."

The marshal stood up and put his hat on. "Dave, if you'll give me a minute, I'm going to escort my fair lady to her home. I'll be right back."

"Yes, sir, Marshal. You take your time. Billy should be coming back through shortly. I can go back out when he comes in if you want."

"Why don't you stick around. I'll be back in fifteen minutes."

Shirley said good-bye to Deputy Zalensky. She and the marshal left the jail and walked up the concrete steps to Clark Street. Arm in arm, the marshal said, "I'm sorry I've been out of touch lately."

"I must say I've been a little worried. You've been so distant. I know you're concerned about the girls. I wish you wouldn't take it so personally. I know it must be part of the job. It comes with the territory. I still love you, and I always will."

They passed several people out on the streets as they walked up to Company Hill. Several of the people acknowledged the marshal politely. "You see, darling, the people respect you too, like I do."

"I just want to get you home, Shirl. This man, he functions on sadistic power. The last thing in the world that I want is for some insane killer to know who the love of my life is. He may be crazy enough to try something. I want to speak with your father. He has a gun in the house, right?"

"John! Don't talk like that," Shirley said, animated. "Those poor girls have all been prostitutes. You don't think the killer will come after me, do you?"

"No, I don't. I'm sorry I even said anything to worry you. I would never let anything happen to you. I just want this man, dead or alive, I don't care which."

When they reached Shirley's house, he kissed her. "I've got to get back to the jail, honey. It doesn't look good for the town marshal to be out gallivantin' about town with his girl on a Saturday night with all that's been goin' on with that maniac on the loose."

Shirley looked up into the eyes of her tall beau. "I'll be so happy when you do catch this monster. I can't wait until things get back to normal around here." She kissed him on the lips. "I love you. Please be careful."

"Don't worry. Things will be back to normal. I promise."

"I'll bring you some breakfast tomorrow before we go to church, if you like?" she asked lovingly.

"Thank you. That sounds like a great idea."

The marshal hurried back to the jail, where Deputy Zalensky was waiting. "Sorry about that, Dave," he said. "I haven't seen too much of her lately with all this shit goin' on."

"Don't mention it, Marshal. Things between me and my girl have been a little strange too lately. What do you suppose those federal deputies are up to tonight?"

"I'd like to know. Maybe Billy knows something. I spoke with Roy, let him know the feds were going to be in town and to keep a close watch on the booze. I don't think those federal deputies are as concerned about that so much. At least not on this trip."

"We got anybody locked up in the jailhouse?" Deputy Zalensky asked.

"Not as of about 7:00." The marshal took his watch out and looked at the time. "Why don't you go on down there and see how Deputy Burns is doing, get out some more. I'll stick around until Billy gets back, then I'll get out. You know, I was thinkin' too, we'll need to get our search team back together next week too."

"Yeah, yer right. You would think Prescott would send some deputies over to help us out so we didn't have to expose drugstore owners and bartenders to half-naked strangled women buried in two-foot graves."

"I'll get on the blower with Sheriff Thompson tomorrow, see if he can do anything to give us a hand."

Deputy Zalensky placed his hat on his head and strapped his holster around his waist. All right, Marshal, I'm headin' back out. Any place in particular you want me to give particular attention to?" he asked.

"If you would, I would like you to spend some time in the Cribs. Of all the nervous people we got in town now, most of 'em got to be those girls. Make sure there's still a vacancy down at the jailhouse before you arrest anyone for public intoxication. If you have to, you can bring someone back here and put 'em in the holding cell. Hopefully, you won't have to, but it *is* Saturday night."

The marshal thumped a pencil on the desk. "Oh, one more thing, Dave, I want you to take this Wanted poster of our chief suspect and nail it on that post next to the old Miner's Tavern."

"Will do, Marshal." With that said, Deputy Zalensky took the Wanted poster of Joseph Pazrosky and headed out into the night toward the Cribs.

59

When C. W. returned from delivering groceries on Company Hill, Mr. Baker had another delivery boxed and ready to go. C. W. gave Myrtle the money from the delivery, and she promptly placed it in the cash register. She smiled at C. W. and said, "I sure feel bad about your grandfather's accident. I'm sure he is anxious to leave the hospital and get back home to you and your dog."

"Yeah," he replied shyly. "Me and Jake will sure be glad to get him back to the house too. It sure was different with him not being there last night or this morning when I got up."

Mr. Baker looked up from the box he had finished packing. "Well, I think this is everything. This goes to Ethel Schuster. She just lives up behind us a little ways on Fifth Street. I'm gonna warn you too. She will talk your ears off if yer not careful."

C. W. laughed, "I know Mrs. Schuster from church. You got that right, Mr. Baker. She sure is a talker. Me and Grandpa take off running whenever she comes around. She's a nice lady though. Jist lonely, I reckon."

Grover had been idly standing behind the counter. "Oh yes, Mrs. Schuster. I've heard all about her. Where elephants go to die," he whispered.

"What in God's glorious name do you mean by that?" Myrtle snapped.

Chuckling, Grover continued, "Oh, me and the missus live just down the street from the widow Schuster. She is a sweet old lady. Always trying to lure old men to her home with her baked pies and cookies. The old-timers are never seen again."

"Oh, what nonsense," Myrtle fired back. "You shouldn't speak of old women like that."

"I'm just warning C. W.," he said. "You know what happened to Hansel and Gretel."

Myrtle shook her head while the men smiled. Mr. Baker chimed in, "Well, C. W., just be sure and leave a trail of bread crumbs so you can find your way back." The men laughed while Myrtle, who failed to see any humor at the expense of the older woman, turned away disgustedly.

Changing the topic which had left Myrtle a little irked, Mr. Baker stated, "Anyways, C. W., when you do make it back, it will be lunchtime. If you want to go and visit your grandpa up at the hospital, that's fine."

"Thank you, Mr. Baker. That will be nice." He grabbed the box and started walking toward the front door.

As C. W. was about to exit the grocery store, Grover looked up and, further aggravating the already visibly disgruntled Myrtle, said, "We bid you Godspeed in your quest."

C. W. walked up the curling road to Mrs. Schuster's home, still sniggering about what Grover and Mr. Baker had said. He would make a point of being nice to Myrtle when he got back to the store so she wouldn't think he was taking sides against her.

He knew that Mrs. Schuster's home was the modest one-story gray house surrounded by the white picket fence. He balanced the box on his knee as he opened the gate and walked up the front porch. Mrs. Schuster opened the door as C. W. was about to ring the doorbell. "Well, hello, C. W.," she said warmly. The short, slightly bent-over woman, with her gray hair bundled into a net, was wearing a colorful flower-printed dress, covered by a white apron. "Come on in, I just baked some chocolate brownies." His acceptance of her offer was always a foregone conclusion.

He followed her into the home where she headed straight for the kitchen and the tray of freshly baked brownies. "I know you'll like these. I got the recipe from the *Sears, Roebuck and Company* catalog."

"Thank you, ma'am," C. W. obliged. He entered the sparsely furnished home, immediately smelling the sweet smell of baked chocolate coming from the kitchen. The smell, a further reminder of his mother and how she so much enjoyed baking nice things for him and his father. He took the two sacks of groceries out of the box and set them on the kitchen table. "Here you go, Mrs. Schuster."

"Oh, aren't you sweet, sonny? Sit down, sit down. Tell me, how is your grandfather doing?"

"Well," he replied clumsily. "He was doing pretty good, I reckon, until yesterday when he hurt his leg at the mine. He's up in the hospital right now. I don't know how long they're going to keep him there. The nurse said it might be a couple days or more."

"Oh no! What on earth happened?" she asked, wincing with worry.

"For some reason, the metal elevator that they ride down to the mine shafts gave way, and he and another man fell like twenty-five feet down. My grandpa broke his leg in the accident."

"That's terrible. I bet you were worried sick!"

"Yes, ma'am. I was," he answered sincerely. "I don't know what I would do if anything ever happened to him."

"My, my, my," she said as she scooped the brownies from the pan. "I should let Reverend Krueger know. He will want to pay your grandfather a visit."

"That would be fine, ma'am. When I get back to the store, Mr. Baker said it would be OK if I visited him."

"Well, I'm sure he's going to be well. Our doctors in Jerome are really as good as any around." She walked to the icebox. "I have milk, and I have lemonade. Which would you rather have to wash your brownies down with?"

"Umm, a glass of milk would be very nice, ma'am, thank you."

As he sat in the small kitchen munching on a delicious brownie, he looked into the quaint, old-fashioned living room area where two pictures hung on the walls. A bookshelf held several books and some knickknacks. On the top row of the shelf, two framed photographs of men in uniform flanking another photograph of an older gentlemen caught C. W.'s attention. Two of the photographs were of an older period while the other looked fairly recent.

"If you don't mind me asking, Mrs. Schuster, who are those men in those photographs?"

Mrs. Schuster's face lit up like the sun as she walked from the kitchen the few feet into the living room. C. W. got up from the table and followed her. "These are my boys," she said proudly. She picked up the first picture of a stern-looking man with his dark hair parted down the center. He appeared to be in his midtwenties. "This is my oldest, Robert Schuster. He was named after my beloved husband. He was twenty-three years old when that photograph was taken in 1897." She looked at the photograph fondly in silence for several uncomfortable seconds before continuing, more quietly, "He perished aboard the USS *Maine* on February 15, 1998, in the port of Havana, Cuba, during the Spanish-American War. He's buried there."

She looked as if the tears would flow any second. C. W. finally spoke to break her agony, "I'm sorry, ma'am."

She sat the photo back on the shelf carefully and grabbed the other one, again taking several seconds of repose. "This was our youngest, Donald Schuster. He's been gone for almost three years now. He perished in the Battle of the Argonne Forest in the Great War. He was thirty-two years old when he died in 1918." After a few more moments of silent repose, she continued, "Both of our boys were heroes who gave their lives for their country. She said mournfully, replacing the photograph on the shelf, "I am very proud of my boys."

She grabbed the center photograph and smiled. "This is their father. He was also a great man. He passed away shortly after our youngest was killed. His heart was broken, as was mine." She returned the photograph to the shelf as C. W. watched respectfully.

She turned to C. W. and smiled softly. "I know that you too know how it feels to lose the people who are the closest to your heart."

C. W. looked from the photos to Mrs. Schuster. "Yes, ma'am, I do." After a moment, he slowly turned and returned to the kitchen, picking up the empty box.

"Here," she said, "let me get my purse. What is it I owe you today?"

C. W. suddenly felt heavyhearted. "Umm." He pulled the receipt from his pants pocket and looked at it. "Only $2.89."

She grabbed her purse that was sitting on a coffee table in the living room. She dug through it before giving C. W. three one-dollar bills. He returned her change of $0.11 against her objection for him to keep it, and said, "Thank you for the brownies and the glass of milk. I haven't eaten brownies that good since my mother used to bake . . . for me and my father." He looked at the ground.

"You're welcome. Do give your grandfather my best. I'll say a prayer that he gets better and is home where he belongs soon."

"Thank you, ma'am. I will." He began shuffling toward the front door. As he began to walk out the front door, he said, "You must be awful proud of your sons, ma'am."

She nodded her head gently. "As proud of my sons as your mother and father were proud of you."

C. W. left Mrs. Schuster's home with a whole different feeling for the lonely widow. She displayed such class through the immense pain from losing her family. Now, living a sheltered life with her family shrine—her altar.

He also had great respect for the men who fought and lost their lives lying in the trenches with the planes flying overhead dropping poisonous bombs. When he was still going to school, a favorite subject was always history. George Washington. Abraham Lincoln. Ancient countries on the other side of the ocean bickering and going to wars. He had read the gruesome stories and would imagine what it would be like to be a soldier.

He wasn't far from the hospital and resisted his desire to rush there and tell his grandfather about his visit with Mrs. Schuster. He thought about Chiara too. He wanted to tell her about the feeling of respect and sympathy he now had for the elder woman, especially after Grover and Mr. Baker had made fun of her.

With the sun now high in the sky, he returned to the grocery store. Grover was helping a customer take her groceries to her automobile while Mr. Baker was stocking apples in the inclined shelf outside the front doors. He looked up as C. W. walked by, "I see you made it back all right."

C. W. smiled. "Yes, sir. I'll go and give Myrtle the money." He continued walking without stopping to the front counter where Myrtle was returning change to a lady holding a sack of groceries in her arms. He waited a minute for the lady to turn and leave; then he approached Myrtle. He dug the money from his pants pocket. "Here you go Myrtle, $2.89."

Myrtle took the money from C. W. and rang the cash register up for the amount. Stalling in front of the counter, Myrtle looked up with her eyebrows raised, waiting for C. W. who looked as if there was more he wanted to say. "Yes?"

"Umm, I just wanted to tell you that you were right about Mrs. Schuster. I really like her. She was very nice."

Myrtle smiled at C. W. "Yes, I know Mrs. Schuster too. She is a wonderful lady. I met some really kind people when I was running groceries all over like you do now. She was always nice to visit, offering me pieces of cake or pie. She doesn't go anywhere except church."

Mr. Baker finished his project at the front of the store and walked in. He pulled his watch from his apron pocket and looked at the time. "It's after one o'clock. Why don't you go and see how your grandpa is doing. Come on back whenever you like. That nurse isn't going to let you stay around too long, I would reckon."

C. W. nodded his head and smiled. "Thank you, Mr. Baker."

Walking out the front door, Mr. Baker was jostled by something he just remembered. "Oh yes, C. W., I almost forgot, a young lady stopped by here when you were up at Mrs. Schuster's. She wanted me to tell you that she wasn't able to get away from the restaurant and go to the hospital with you today. Something about she was not going to be able to leave her job."

"Thank you, Mr. Baker."

"She didn't tell me her name. She just figured you would know who I was talking about," he said snidely.

"Her name is Chiara. She works at her parents' restaurant. She's nice. We're friends."

"Just friends, huh?"

From the back of the empty store, Myrtle chuckled, "Now, Mr. Baker. Mind your own business!"

60

Pazrosky dropped off Lucille, with her messy hair and wrinkled dress, near a wooden post next to the once-thriving Miner's Tavern. He held a ten-dollar bill in his hand and told her to make arrangements with one of their friends to give her and Izzy a lift to the road leading into Homer's lair later that night. He said he and Homer would expect them around nine o'clock, which was in just over four hours.

A little worse for wear with boot polish and grass stains on her dress, Lucille had a friend with an old automobile that she knew would give her a ride out to Homer's place for a couple dollars. She tried to haggle more money from the man with the polish in his hair, and now on his face. He argued that he had already given her ten dollars for groceries. After balking for a time, he took the ten-dollar bill and placed it securely in the breast pocket of Lucille's blouse. "I'll give you some more cabbage when you come up tonight," he assured her.

Their plans were made for the girls to bring the grocery items up to Homer's. Homer would get supper started while they all enjoyed some mixed drinks under the stars. The girls would be paid a yet-to-be-determined fee for their company. The next morning, he would either drive the girls back into town or give them some cash to split and make them walk or hitch a ride into the center of town.

As he pulled out onto Jerome Avenue, he was thinking that if he had money when he was younger, he wouldn't have got in so much trouble. He thought that if you didn't have enough, or any, money to live a comfortable life, then man is only naturally going to do everything he can in order to survive. And then there were the women. The women that wronged and ridiculed him his whole life.

Shaking his head, he turned left to return up to Homer's property, passing the town hall and its first-floor jail unit. The powerfully built tall town marshal was standing outside the door of the jail, looking up Main Street at the incoming town traffic from the Prescott highway.

Minutes later, a large black car with a driver and three large badge-wearing men as passengers pulled into town.

On his way out of town, Pazrosky passed near the Parlor House where he found a parking place and pulled the Ford over. He stepped out onto the sidewalk and lit a cigarette. With his body squared facing down the street, he tilted his head to look over his left shoulder. His eyes fixated on a top-floored bedroom balcony. The breeze felt good standing in the shade. He finished his smoke and tossed his cigarette butt to the street. As automobiles passed in both directions, he looked up at the balcony window and wondered what the beautiful dark-haired woman was doing.

Pazrosky got in and drove the pickup out of town toward the gulch where he now shared Homer's property. He pulled in the drive and parked the truck. Homer was wandering about the property when Pazrosky arrived. He walked toward Pazrosky and said, "Where ya been, Henry? I ain't seen you all day."

"That's because you sleep all day," he replied rudely.

"Yeah, but that's because I'm working at night," Homer said, deflecting the barb. "Come here, I want to show you something."

Pazrosky followed Homer to the shed where the still had just produced a new batch of the home brew. Homer opened the door and stepped inside; Pazrosky followed him in. He watched as Homer pulled an old blanket from their inventory. "That's what we got," he said with a tone of arrogance. Several gallons of moonshine was distributed into gallon jugs and canning jars. "If we can get this unloaded real quick like, same good price, we'll be in the money!" he said merrily. "Oh, I got something else to show ya. Come on, we got a jug in the house."

Pazrosky again found himself following in the footsteps of the diminutive man. In a show of species dominance, Pazrosky cast another stone. "You know the girls are coming up tonight, and you still ain't got yourself all dolled up like you usually do, still smelling worse than a Kansas City stockyard."

"I'll get dolled up all right. I'm going to clean up the place. What the hell? Come on."

Pazrosky followed Homer into the home. On the small table were six freshly cleaned and feathered plump Gambel's quail. The hearts and livers were set to the side. Pazrosky was impressed but still managed a contemptuous tone in his voice, "Nice work, Bo, it looks like you been busy shootin' yard bird all afternoon."

"What time are the girls comin'?" Homer asked as he grabbed a full jug of hooch off the table and poured drinks for him and his partner.

"Expect the girls around nine o'clock. I gave Lucille money to buy groceries so you can get some vegetables cookin' later. I'm going to have a drink and go lie down and get an hour or two of rest."

Pazrosky left Homer and retired to his new home. He lit a cigarette, thinking he was glad that he built the tiny outbuilding on Homer's property. He had a safe place out of the town to lie low and spend most of his time, an unlimited supply of alcohol that was bringing in good money, a loyal friend, one who could shoot birds and rabbits and prepare nice meals.

While part of him wanted to run away west, he felt that he belonged here. No one could ever finger him for those girls or the home in Tucson. Still, he needed to stay one step ahead of the law, or he'd sure enough be locked up.

At times now, he fretted about why he felt compelled to do what he does, wondering if he ever could go straight. That is, straight enough to where he was through killing people. Not that straight where he wasn't peddling moonshine or drinking enough homemade alcohol to drown a Copper Creek catfish. After all, he was starting to cozy up to Lucille, and he just knew that she was loco about him. Maybe he would take her away from here.

He sat on the edge of his cot and removed his boots. Grabbing a dirty towel off the cot, he wiped off the boot polish that was still in his hair and beard. He would get cleaned up after he awoke from his siesta. He flicked his butt out the door into the dirt and lay down on the small bed.

After drowsing off after a few minutes, the killer fell into a dream of when he was a boy in Texas. In his dreams, he was always getting chased or fighting where he always got beaten up. By his father, his uncle, or mother. There was the man on the train appearing intermittently. Sometimes it was Mexicans. Lately, when he went to sleep, he dreamed of lawmen chasing him. He would wake up and want to jump in the Ford and go west. Maybe come back through some other time.

Homer was cleaning off at the side of his house where he had a half-filled barrel of a mix of rain and creek water. With a bar of soap in his right hand, the naked man bathed himself, washing his hair and taking a sharp blade to his whiskers. An old mirror hung from a nail on that side of the house now since Homer began taking a concern about his appearance. He made sure he always had a clean pair of underwear, trousers, and shirts on hand for when Izzy and Lucille came up.

As the shadows began to grow longer, he got the fire pit going. He then put the skewered quail far from the fire for a slow roasting. He had cleaned himself up, even taking a brush to his teeth and a rag to his ears. He was locking up the shed when Pazrosky came outside, lighting a cigarette. "Hey, old-timer, how 'bout a drink?"

"He'p yerself, in there."

Pazrosky saw the birds cooking over the fire, emitting a savory aroma. He had the spaghetti and meatballs early in the afternoon, but he was now getting hungry. He poured himself a drink and walked back outside. Like a hawk gazing over a valley for prey, he looked down on the lights of Jerome. He had taken sleep for three hours and had vivid dreams that now occupied his thoughts. *Were the lawmen closing in on him?*

With drink and cigarette in hand, he watched as an automobile turned off the roadway hundreds of feet below. It wormed around as it made its way up the winding dirt road in the dark. Minutes later, he heard automobile doors slammed down off the road. As the vehicle turned and returned down the way it came in, Lucile and Izzy walked into view. "Hey, fellas, we're here!" Izzy cried.

Homer came out from his hovel. "Evenin', ladies. I hope you got here all right." Seeing that Lucille was carrying two sacks of groceries, he rushed to her assistance and grabbed the bags. Pazrosky finished his cigarette and stamped it out. "Ladies," he said, less than warmly. "Anyone like a cocktail?"

Homer spoke up, "Sure they do. Well, come on in. How 'bout I mix some drinks? Y'all like ginger ale?"

"Sounds swell," Izzy replied. "Hey, what smells so good?"

"That's our supper. I hope you like quail."

"I love quail," Izzy said excitedly. "Let's get some potatoes and some greens boiling."

Lucille smiled at Henry while she waited for Homer to prepare her beverage. He swirled his drink around in his mug, his eyes focused on the lights below. Lucille walked out to where he was standing. "Hello again," she said quietly.

"Howdy. I take it you found someone to give you a ride without any problems?" he queried.

"My friend Bonnie charges me a whole six dollars to drive me and Izzy up here, three dollars apiece," she whined.

"I've been drinking, and I don't see well at night," he vowed.

"Anyway, that quail sure smells good," she said. "Izzy and Homer got some vegetables boiling on the stove. And we brought some nice bread. It should be a real nice dinner. Thanks for inviting us."

"We enjoy it when you and your friend come to visit on Saturday nights. It's good for Homer to have some feminine contact."

"What about you, don't you enjoy feminine contact, as you call it?"

Hesitating, he said, "Sure I do. What about that picnic we went on this afternoon?"

"You call that a picnic? I wanted to talk to you about that. I wish you weren't so rough on little old me," she complained.

"You call that rough?" he said unsympathetically.

"Yes, I do. I have some boundaries, ya follow?" she said self-righteously.

After a moment spent standing and looking down into the town and valley lights below, she said, "You gotta match?" She pulled a reefer from behind her right ear. Pazrosky struck a match and lit it for her.

"You can keep that stuff to yerself. It makes me want to go to sleep," he protested.

Laughing, Izzy and Homer came outside and took the roasted quail away from the fire. Homer looked at Henry and Lucille and hollered, "Supper will be ready in about ten more minutes."

He and Izzy disappeared into the kitchen area, talking loudly.

Pazrosky downed the last gulp of his drink, then lit a cigarette while looking at Lucille. He couldn't understand his attraction for her. She was a whore. He hated whores. He killed whores.

Finally, as she was starting to feel the effects of the marijuana, she asked him, "What? Why are you looking at me like that?"

"Like what?" he replied.

"I don't know. It was like you were just looking right through me for the last couple of minutes, kinda creepy."

"Oh? Sure it just isn't that shit yer smoking?"

"No!"

"Yer jist real perty, that's all," he mumbled. "I was going to tell you that if you could drum up some more customers, that is, customers for me, then I could kick you a little more dough. I'm sure we can get it on this end."

"I sure could use the dough, but with all those U.S. marshals in town, maybe we should lie low for a little while."

Pazrosky did well to control his emotions. "U.S. marshals?" he asked, unexcited.

"Yeah. They're all over town tonight, at least three or four of them. Big fellas carrying guns and wearing badges. The word is they're looking for the killer of those girls. The paper is calling the killer 'the Jerome Strangler.' It's scary down there sometimes. That's why I always take my purse with me," she said, patting it and the small handgun she carried in its inside pocket.

"Good idea. What else did you see or hear about these federal marshals?" he said, trying hard to contain his nervousness.

"The town marshal, Marshal Williams, and his deputies have been walking up and down our streets a lot more lately. Now, you got these large federal fellas all over town. They been goin' in the Mineflower and the Kitchen and everywhere else. I heard they been asking some people to look at their suspect's photograph. I haven't seen it."

"Seen what?" he asked uneasily.

"You know. The photograph of the fella whom they think has been killing the town's women. They say that they might be close to nabbing him."

Their conversation was interrupted when Homer yelled over to them that supper was ready to be served. "It's on the table," he cried out.

Pazrosky needed another drink. He was suddenly nerve-wracked knowing the federal lawmen were closing in on him. He realized that he hadn't colored his hair that night, wanting to stay in the dark and eat outside. He was wondering about the photograph that the lawmen were circulating all over town. Worried if it was his photograph from Huntsville or El Paso, New Orleans or Houston for that matter, where he could now be identified. The more he thought about the U.S. marshals, the more panic-struck he became and wanted to flea.

"Are you coming?" Lucille asked.

"Go ahead. I'll be right there." He watched her walk into the kitchen as he walked toward his place. He sat down on the edge of his bed, reached beneath it, and grabbed his tin of boot polish. He was careful not to put too much on. After Lucille told him that she thought it was a little queer from him to color his hair, he lied and told her his hair began to gray a few years ago, and he's afraid he looks too old. She tried to convince him that he didn't need to do that, telling him how handsome he would look with gray hair.

He was beginning to think that he had outstayed his welcome in the town of Jerome. He got on his knees and saw that his cigar box was there. If he were found with the dead man's belongings, he would hang for sure. He was glad to have the loaded pistol though. He ran the comb through his hair and beard. He now knew for sure that he had to take his circus on the road. He would enjoy a nice supper, the soft feminine companionship of Lucille, a few more drinks. Then later, he would disappear for a while.

61

The marshal awoke and came out of his living quarters. Saturday night had been relatively quiet. Like wildfire, word spread through the town that U.S. marshals were there. The town was on its best behavior. The bootleggers stayed away, did their peddling somewhere else. The gamblers either took the night off or found a safe place to have their game played. There were plenty of people intoxicated on moonshine alcohol or hopped up on dope. But they went home early on Saturday night.

Deputy Zalesky had a pot of coffee on the stove from early that morning that the marshal heated up. He tucked his shirt in his pants and walked into the main part of the jail. He was pleased to see that there was no one in the holding cell. The lawmen worked split shifts with at least one deputy staying on well after midnight and another through the entire night. Deputy Ray finished his duty until 2:00. Deputy Zalesky had been on duty during the night. He usually went home shortly after sunup, or when the marshal got out of bed.

There were people walking up and down Main Street when the marshal stepped outside to drink his morning cup of coffee. He watched as the two Chinese men opened their laundry for the day. He thought that they were brothers or something; he was never quite sure. He had spoken with the men before when he was visiting with all the local business owners. They had been very quiet, apologized for their inability to speak the language well. He was always a little suspicious of them, and they were distrustful of him.

The restaurants and cafes were open, ready to dish out a plate of biscuits or pancakes with bacon and eggs. Automobile doors were closing as parking spaces were beginning to get filled. Many of the parishioners of the Catholic Church nearby parked along Main Street. The morning congregation was beginning to gather.

He leaned against the entryway, like he was accustomed of doing, and sipped from his cup of hot black coffee. Out of the corner of his eye, he saw Mr. Hudson's mammoth red Packard pull into a parking space near the town hall. Shirley popped out holding a large tray that was covered by a red-and-white checkered cloth. Her parents waved from inside the large automobile. He opened the door for Shirley as she walked up. "What do you got there?" he asked her.

"Your breakfast," she answered, setting the tray on his desk. "I'm glad you have coffee because I didn't bring anything for you to drink." She looked around to make sure they were alone, then pecked him on the cheek. "I gotta get going. Daddy wants to go for a drive out of town for a while while it's still nice and cool before church and breathe some fresh air as he likes to say."

"Thank you, dumplin'," the marshal said as Shirley hurried back out to her father's automobile. He gave a friendly wave to her parents before ducking back in to devour Shirley's lovely breakfast. Removing the checkerboard cloth, his eyes widened at the sight of the six-course breakfast his girlfriend had prepared for him. He sat himself down at his desk, in front of the banquet in front of him.

Starting with the sunny-side up eggs, he worked his way through pancakes and syrup, biscuits and gravy, sliced-up bacon accompanied by fried potatoes, and a bowl of diced-up fruit. He was able to enjoy his breakfast uninterrupted, washing it down with his second cup of joe.

With a stomach full of breakfast, the marshal sluggishly stepped back outside to feel the morning breeze. After a few minutes, he saw Captain Rawlings walking his way. "Good morning, Marshal," he said politely.

"Morning, Captain. I hope you and your men got a chance to get some of your investigatin' done last night without any problems. Come on in. Sit down."

"No problems or anything like that," the captain said as he took a seat in front of the marshal's desk. "You've got some nervous young women in town, that's one thing for certain. And most of these women are carrying handguns. I hope you don't have a case where an innocent man gets shot because one of these girls gets a loose trigger finger."

"I had heard that some of the girls living in the Cribs District had purchased guns," the marshal replied sternly.

"Well, let me fill you in on some things from last night," Captain Rawlings said. "First of all, we didn't make any arrests. We had a few men empty out their flasks onto the street when they were flaunting themselves too much.

There were a few people who reported that they may have seen Joseph Pazrosky in town, but no one has seen him in the last couple of months or so. There was a man who thinks he may have worked at the Little Daisy Mine. Me and one of my deputies are going over there to speak with someone after lunch. Just to let you know, Marshal, me and my men will likely get on out of town sometime tomorrow. We want to follow up, take a look around outside town. We'll share anything we have with you and Sheriff Thompson. If you do the same, maybe we'll catch up with this fella. I think it's important we keep all our lines of communication open."

"We certainly will, Captain," the marshal stated. "I want this town to get back to normal where no one is all scared and nervous. It really is one hell of a town."

"Oh, I bet it is," Captain Rawlings exclaimed. "You sure gotcha a lot of nice folks up here."

"We got a couple theaters for motion pictures, an opera house with a fresh act every couple or few weeks, musical bands, comedy troupes, some nice stores and restaurants, good schools, swimming pools. It's a crying shame that for some stroke of bad luck, this fella had to come through our town and stay a bit."

"Well, Marshal, I must say it has been mighty big of you, and you already *are* a big man, to let me and a few of my men dig around a bit, find out anything we can. Some marshals may have got a bee in their trousers about having another agency working on a murder case. I sure appreciate it."

The marshal said, "I don't care if my men find this fella or your guys find him. And I don't care if we get him dead or alive. I just want him off my streets."

"I understand that, Marshal," Rawlings replied. He stood up and started for the front door. "I'll stop back through later in the day. Let me know if there's anything I can do for you while I'm here."

"Thanks, Captain." the marshal nodded.

Around noon, Deputy Evans walked into the jail. "Howdy, Marshal. What's been going on around here? I heard about the U.S. marshals in town asking people a lot of questions."

"That's right. Their captain was in here earlier. They're here to help us smoke out the killer."

"Well, I hope they're doin' some good," Deputy Evans conceded.

"The way I figure it, they can only help us," the marshal said. "I don't know if the people are going to rest any easier or not. Probably not until we catch the skunk."

The deputies in town with the U.S. marshal's office walked through the Cribs late that Sunday morning. Like their counterpart lawmen in Jerome, they weren't able to find anything out on their chief suspect, even though they spoke with over a dozen of the young women. There were only a couple of girls who did not appear to be at home. The deputies made a note to return later in the day to the homes of those girls who weren't in at this time.

Other deputies drove through the Mexican sector where the two murder victims may have last been seen. They spent the afternoon driving along the outskirts of town, speaking with people and showing them the photograph of the man they suspected was responsible for the deaths of at least two women in Jerome. No one they spoke to said they had seen the man in the photograph.

They holed themselves up in pool halls and hit the boardinghouses and hotels. Somebody from the Valley View Hotel thought he had seen a man who looked similar to the man in the photograph, but he wasn't positive, said maybe he saw him late winter. At a boardinghouse, the deputies were asked to come back later and speak with the owner, who was in Prescott for the day. That person had said that there was someone who resembled the subject in the photograph who had rented a room there for a month or two, moved out not long ago.

It was at the Little Daisy Hotel midafternoon when the deputies got their first solid identification verification from a man who worked there. The night old watchman said that he had seen the man pictured in the photograph a few months ago. He thought he had stayed there for a little while. He said that he thought the man's name was Henry, not too friendly of a fellow, he added.

The deputies later met up with Captain Rawlings in their hotel's restaurant where they discussed the information they had dug up in the last twenty-four hours. That late in the afternoon, the restaurant was quiet with few other customers other than the table that seated the four lawmen from Phoenix. They spoke discretely between themselves but not loud enough for anyone else to hear what they were talking about.

Captain Rawlings ripped a piece of bread from the common loaf at the table. Before shoving it down his mouth, he said, "I believe we are dead-on with our chief suspect. It seems that he used the name of Henry Joseph while he was in town. No one has seen him for a while, so maybe he has left town or just lying low. He worked as a mucker at the mine for approximately two and half months. He just quit showing up one day, according to the payroll clerk."

One of the deputies spoke up, "The way he likes to hunt cheap prostitutes, he's got it made here. Hell, he's like a pig rollin' in slop. I think he's just lying low waiting for the heat to cool down on 'em. Then, he'll come out again. He probably already has a woman in mind who he's going to attack next."

The captain swallowed down a spoonful of beans and said, "I believe you're probably right, Deputy Hill. I wish we had another day up here. By the time we get back and finish up our reports, they'll send us back up here, at least a couple of us, I reckon. The question remains. Is he still here?"

62

C. W. and Jake spent another quiet Saturday night at home after C. W. returned from seeing his grandfather in the hospital.

His grandfather was still in some pain, tired and disoriented from the sedatives he was getting. The nurse only allowed him five minutes with his grandfather before she asked him to return the following day.

C. W. was saddened to see his dear grandfather so uncomfortable. The nurse said it would still be a couple days before he would be released. He was told that he would be needed to help his grandfather get around when he gets released. He was very happy with helping him get around. He would check in with him when he was working his grocery deliveries. Jake could provide the companionship while C. W. worked.

After getting out of bed in the quiet, empty house on Sunday morning, he ate some stale dry bread and washed it down with a bottle of warm Coca-Cola. He threw a couple dog biscuits to Jake and made sure he had a bowl of drinking water. He thought about going to church, seeing the Reverend Krueger and Mrs. Schuster. Everyone would want to talk to him, ask him how his grandfather was doing. He decided against it. He had never gone to church all by himself before.

Today was also the day that he hoped to spend some time with Chiara. He thought he would visit his grandfather first, then pass by the restaurant and see Chiara. He hurriedly combed his hair and brushed his teeth, washed up, patted Jake on the head, and started for the hospital.

On this afternoon, he was pleased to see his grandfather sitting up in his bed finishing his lunch. He was much more responsive. His face lit up when C. W. walked into his room. "Hey, buddy. It's good to see you. I don't remember too much from your visit yesterday. I must have been real tired. I feel better today. My leg hurts, but it's gonna for a while, I reckon."

"Ole Jake really misses you, Grandpa. Me too. We'll both be glad to help you get around when you come home. I got the bedroom all cleaned up and ready for you."

"I think the doctor is gonna let me go home tomorrow sometime. He has to teach me how to use them crutches. I just got to stay off my legs for a little while. The mine's paying for all my bills here. We'll get by all right."

"Sure we'll get by all right," he echoed. "My pay's perty good, especially with the tips the people give me."

"I have a feeling someone from the mine will be by the house to make sure we have everything we need," he said confidently.

"As long as your leg mends up real nice and you do everything the doctor says. That's the important thing." He told his grandfather about his friendship with "the Italian girl," as his grandfather liked to refer to her.

"Yes, the Italian girl, Grandpa. I think she's perty sharp to be able to speak her country's language and learn another one too."

"I'm sure she's a very sharp girl. She likes you, doesn't she?" he teased.

"I think so. I think I'm going to take her to a three-reeler playing at the pictures. With Harold Lloyd, Grandpa. He's a real funny fellow. I wish you could come long. You and me haven't seen a picture in a while."

"One of these days. Say, you and Jake got enough food at the house? You've got groceries for us before. I have some money at the house. I'll tell you where to find—"

"I have money, Grandpa," C. W. blurted. "I'll make sure that we have a lot to eat when you get home tomorrow. Is there anything special you want me to buy, like an apple pie or a ham or something?"

"No, no," he said. "I reckon we should be celebrating the fact that I survived that accident to see another day. I don't think my workmate made it."

"You mean, he's dead?" C. W. asked bewilderedly.

"I'm afraid so. I broke a leg. He broke his neck is what I've been told," he replied sadly.

"That's terrible, Grandpa. Good thing you only broke yer leg. At least yer gonna be all better one of these days soon, and yer still here with us," he was saying until the nurse walked in. She told him to return the following day for a report on his grandfather's progress.

He kissed his grandfather on the forehead and told him he loved him. "I'll come see you tomorrow, Grandpa. The house is cleaned up and ready for your return home. I'm sleeping on the divan, and the bed is already for you and your bad leg."

The nurse hurried him out of the hospital room and escorted C. W. toward the front doors. On the way, she told C. W. that his grandfather suffered a severe bone break of his leg and that he may be a couple more days at the hospital. She also told him that he would be down for a long time before he is able to walk around on his own. This had burst his hopes.

He hoped Chiara could get away so they could talk. He was anxious for her company again.

Passing in front of the restaurant, he was surprised to see an older woman working there. He had only seen Chiara and her parents there before. Chiara walked out the door a moment later. "Hello, C. W., how are you today?" she asked.

"I'm well, thank you," he responded. "How have you been?

"I'm doing well. How is your grandfather?" she asked.

"He's doin' better, but the nurse said he broke his leg perty bad and that it was gonna be awhile before he was able to get around on his own."

"Oh no, is too bad," she said sympathetically. "I'm sorry, C. W."

"The other man in the accident died, so I reckon I'm kind of lucky." To take their conversation to a more cheerful level, he asked, "So. What would you like to do?"

"I don't care what we do. You pick," she said considerately.

"I wanted to ask you. Who was the other woman working in the restaurant today?"

"That's Signora Zerbini. She is a friend of ours. Her family was having some problems, so my father will let her work some hours at the restaurant. That is the reason why I am able to get away for a while."

"Swell," he said genuinely. "There's a couple of Harold Lloyd motion pictures playing in one the theaters in town. I think you will enjoy them. He's very funny."

"I haven't been to the cinema in a long time. It sounds like fun," she said.

"It's been awhile for me too. Come on." He paid the fifty cents for the two tickets, and they entered the small theater. They laughed and giggled throughout the two short films. When the curtain closed after the final showing, they walked outside. He suggested they cross the street and have an ice cream cone or sundae.

They laughed as they went over their afternoon at the cinema. He spoke of how nice it was that she was able to get away from the restaurant for a while. The conversation turned to where Chiara was thinking about something. "Oh. I wanted to tell you something. You know my parents don't let me get away yesterday, so I go and talk to Mr. Baker to tell him."

"Yes, he told me," C. W. remembered.

"Anyways, there was this strange man, not Italian," she said. "He came into the restaurant yesterday. He was like some of kind of sex pervert or something. I got real nervous when I look at him. I don't like the way he was looking at me too. Yuuchh! He was saying things real low, so I don't hear him, but I know the things he say are real bad."

"Where was your father?" he asked. "I can't believe he didn't bop the fella in the nose."

"My father was out for only a few minutes when the man walked in. The man ordered spaghetti and meatballs. I told Momma that I was going to dump everything on his head if he kept looking at me like he was doing. She laughed, but the man was scary-looking."

"Jerome has some men like that," he offered.

They left the drugstore after they finished their ice cream. Chiara suggested that they walk around the long way back to the restaurant. She wanted to see something about the films they had seen, so she ran across the street to the theater, gazing at the marquee in the window. "Thank you for taking me here. It was funny."

The young people began their long slow walk back to the restaurant where she would be put to work. They weren't far from the theater when Chiara stopped suddenly. C. W. couldn't tell what it was that she was looking at. "What is it Chiara? What are you looking at?"

"There. On the post. The photograph of that man." She pointed at the Wanted poster that had been nailed on the post recently. "His face. He looks like the *figlio del diavolo* who was in the restaurant yesterday. The man I told you about."

"Are you sure?" he asked supportively.

"I'm not for sure, but I think so. This man in the restaurant had dark hair, real black and shiny. But his face and his . . . eyes." She spat toward the ground. "I think this is the man I saw. What is the poster say he's wanted for?"

"It doesn't say exactly, but I would bet it's got something to do with the girls who were found killed."

"Girls who were found killed? What are you talking about?" she gasped.

He looked at her for a second. "You mean you haven't heard about the two women? They were prostitutes who lived in the Cribs. They were found buried down over there somewhere." He pointed out past the Little Daisy Mine. "There is also one or two more girls that are missing and maybe dead," he added. "I can't believe you haven't heard about that. The whole town is on the edge. Everybody has guns. It's like a powder keg getting ready to explode."

"My father reads an Italian newspaper that comes out every two weeks. Maybe he read something but he don't want me to know." She looked up at the man's photograph on the wooden post. "They think this man killed some women?" *Momma mia.*

C. W. focused the photograph. Now he thought that he too had seen this man. "You were saying the man had long dark black hair, real greasy or slimy?"

"Yes. His hair was dark black, like his beard."

"His beard?"

"Yes. He had a black beard too."

"I have seen the man whom yer talking about," C. W. said. "I've seen him in the grocery store. He is always very rude and impolite. Myrtle has said that she doesn't like the way the man looks at her. I'm sure we're talking about the same fella. I bet it is this fella too. That's probably why he darkens his hair and beard. Some kind of disguise while he's on the lam."

"On the lamb?" she asked.

"On the run. You know. On the run from the law. I'm going to say something to Mr. Baker. He can talk to the marshal for us. They're friends. Come on."

They walked down the street. When they got closer to the restaurant, she stopped and said, "I must tell my parents about that man." She looked up at the young man whom she was growing very fond of and kissed him on the cheek. "In my country, a man and a woman kiss two times, one time on each cheek when they see and another when they leave each other."

"That's good. I'll have to remember for next time," C. W. joked. "I can't believe your father allows men to kiss you at all. He seems so protective of you."

"He is protective. Too much perhaps. So what he doesn't know about you and me won't harm him. He'll find out about us someday, I'm sure. Bye-bye." She kissed him again on the cheek, just brushing her lips barely over his, then hurried into her family's restaurant.

63

Pazrosky filled his tinplate with quail, bread, apple sauce, and an assortment of boiled vegetables, then took a seat on a tree stump next to the fire. Lucille soon joined him while Homer and Izzy dined inside. "You and Homer eat better than most people I know," she mused. "What will it be next week? A pig? Venison?"

Eating his bounteous dinner with a whiskey drink, he said, "Ole' Homer is perty good around the house. He knows how to hunt and fish, all those things you need to survive. Which he has done, survived."

"I could see him working as a cook in one of the nicer restaurants in town," she speculated. "He would do well in the kitchen."

Pazrosky may have appeared calm and relaxed on the outside, but inside, he was as frightened as last week's rabbit or tonight's quail before they were gunned down. Jerome was a big town, but it wasn't that big where a team of lawmen couldn't track him down. He took another drink from his can and set it down. "Homer is a good cook," he bragged. "Like I said when I first met ya, he's jist the type of man who likes to be out on his own, away from people, ya follow?"

"How did you fellas ever meet anyways?" she asked.

"Oh, I can't remember," he said, not wanting to tell her about the day he met Homer in a rowdy pool hall. "I think it was outside the barbershop one day," he lied. "He said he knew someone who could get us some booze, and the rest is history."

"You fellas sure know where to find the good hooch, that's one thing for sure," she said candidly.

"That reminds me," he said. "If I' m not here, make sure Homer gets you everything you need tomorrow. I met a man who lives down there in the valley. I may spend a day or two down there looking over some business proposals," he told her.

When they finished their meals, Lucille took Pazrosky's plate and empty can that he was drinking from and walked into the small kitchen area where Izzy and Homer were engaged in a hearty conversation. She put the plates aside and mixed drinks for her and her date, leaving Izzy and Homer discussing the Harding administration or whatever it was they were so captivated with.

Pazrosky lit a cigarette, looking down into the lights of the town below. He couldn't see any automobile traffic that left the roadway headed in their direction. He half-expected to see an automobile with federal lawmen speeding toward him at any minute.

Lucille returned and handed him his drink. "I wanted to thank you for the marvelous dinner. There's a lovely cake too whenever yer ready." She wrapped her arms around Pazrosky's neck and gave him an affectionate kiss on his lips. "What was it you were saying about leaving for a couple of days?"

"Oh, that. Yes, jist want to look at drummin' up some more customers to sell our bosses' hooch, some other business, that's all."

"Oh, take me with you," she begged.

"I'll think about it," he told her. "So what about this afternoon. That was a fun time, wasn't it?"

"Fun? I reckon so, but it's like I say, I need you to treat me more delicately, more gently. You are much too rough with me. Savvy?"

He grinned a wicked grin. "You think I'm a little rough, huh . . . ?"

"I'm just saying that I like it when you treat me more gently. And another thing, I told you that I think you would be handsome with your gray hair. I don't think that greasy stuff makes you look that much younger. Besides, it's so messy when we're kissing and everything."

"I jist don't like all the gray hair, that's all." He looked and could see Homer and Izzy drinking at the table. Taking Lucille by the arm gently, he said, "Come on, let's take our drinks for a walk." He walked her near the edge of the ravine.

"Be careful, Henry," she warned. "You need to be careful walking round here, especially after you been drinkin'."

"You sound like my mother," he protested. Then he thought for a moment and said, "Well, the truth is, my mother never gave a damn about me. She didn't care enough to ever tell me what to do."

"My mother didn't ever care too much about me neither," she added. "That's why I ran away from home when I was still a kid. My father would attack me, and my mother never did a thing about it."

"I'm sorry. It sounds like both of us grew up in rough homes," he said comfortingly.

"It was rough all right," she said bitterly. "Let's don't talk about things like that. I like to come up here, get away and enjoy your company, a nice dinner and a couple of drinks. I shouldn't tell you about how things were when I was a little girl. That would just spoil the mood."

"Well, I reckon we're jist two people who have had to play through a horrible cold streak, had life dealt to them from the bottom of the deck." He tossed his cigarette butt to the ground cooly.

"I reckon so." She walked up next to him and placed her arm around his waist. From the house, they heard Homer yell something about coming in and getting a piece of cake covered with strawberries. "Did he say strawberries?"

"It sounds good whatever it is, come on."

The girls purchased a flat pineapple cake from the bakery covered in creamy strawberries. Homer, who was mixing drinks when Pazrosky and Lucille walked in, quickly replenished their drinks. Big slices of the mouth-watering cake were cut and placed on plates at the table. "You two better get a slice of this cake," Homer mumbled.

Lucille sat on Pazrosky's lap eating her piece of cake. "Ain't this some cake, Henry? The girls got it at the bakery," Homer said.

"It is a scrumptious cake, Homer," Pazrosky admitted. "It was a lovely dinner also." He held out his tin can and proposed a toast, "To Homer, for the wonderful dinner he prepared." Everyone took swigs from their drinks.

Homer followed his buddy's lead and held his drink out. "I want to propose a toast for our lovely guests. We are thankful that you're here and that you bought and carried all those groceries up here. So my toast is, 'Thank you, girls for your company this evening.'"

Lucille crawled out of Pazrosky's lap after she finished with her dessert. She stepped outside followed by Pazrosky, who lit up another cigarette. She put her arm around his waist to help keep her balance. "Look at all the stars," she said, tipsy.

He wrapped his arms around the woman as they both struggled to keep their balance. "Yes, the stars are beautiful. I jist wish they would quit spinning around," he stuttered. The couple swayed back and forth in each other's arms. He coaxed her into his private shed, where he dragged her down to his cot. After a few minutes, they both fell fast asleep.

Pazrosky dreamed that he was locked up in prison. In his dream, he shared a cell with the bum on the train that attacked him when he was only a scrawny seventeen-year-old kid. The bum kept looking at him and licking his mouth. He kept saying over and over, "We're going to get you. You can't hide. We're going to get you."

64

Ashley hurried downstairs to take the telephone call that night. Lane was calling with Saturday plans. The plans called for him to pick her up in the afternoon at 2:00. She hung the phone in the receiver. From the back room, Paige stood, looking at Ashley, with a tender frown on her face. Before she had a chance to speak, Ashley rushed up the steps to her room.

She flung her closet doors open, took her new gown out, and held it in front of her before her full-length mirror. She looked over at the shoes she was going to wear. A nice match she thought. The hoedown at Lane's family ranch was going to be loads of fun. She loved folk dancing and loud fiddle music.

Lane hadn't said anything about the subject of her occupation. She was worried that his parents would not want him to be near her. Even after he promised her that his parents would like her. She was putting the gown back in the closet when there was a knock at her door. "Come in," she called.

Paige opened the door a few inches and peeked in, "Getting ready for the ball?" she asked.

Ashley turned around to face her. "Yes, ma'am."

"Your gown is really a thing of beauty. I love the work the seamstress did. Beautiful craftsmanship. With those gorgeous shoes? Magnificent! You will be the belle of the ball, Ashley."

"It should be a grand time. I haven't been to a hoedown in a while. They're a lot of fun."

"Yes, they are," Paige answered. "And Mr. Walker? He is a very nice gentleman, no?"

"He is a very nice gentleman, Paige," she said. "Why do you ask?"

Smiling, Paige said, "Why? I hope you don't think that you're the only girl who has lived under my roof to fall for a man who was courting her?"

"I'm not?" she asked.

"It has happened before," she said brightly. "I can see the way you look at this man. You just spent the weekend together. He buys you this beautiful dress. Then there's the men who were Annabelle's suitors. They want to spend time with you, but you refuse. I think you may be hearing wedding bells pretty soon," Paige said.

"I don't know. He is a wonderful man, Paige," she beamed. I don't know whether to accept if there is a proposal or not. You take real good care of us here. We're like a family where the sisters all get along. You pay me as if I'm some Hollywood actress. It's all in the bank where it's safe, I hope."

"I would be the happiest person in the world if you and Lane married. Don't worry about things here at the house. You never signed any lifelong contracts with me. But if you decide to leave, the girls and I will have the best bon voyage party for you with special food and drink. It will be the most special of occasions," she said joyfully.

"I reckon I haven't thought it all the way through, but I think I would be happy with having horses and cattle on my own ranch. Lane said he has a beautiful ranch he wants to buy about twenty miles north of his parents' spread. The ranch belongs to a close friend of his parents. A gentleman, I'm afraid, is getting too old to keep ahead of the ranch and no family to help. Lane says it's beautiful. The dirt is all red, and the ranch is surrounded by red rock cliffs."

"Well, my dear Ashley, that is not too far away. I can get there in my roadster in two or three hours for croissants and tea." she laughed.

"You would always be welcome to come down and go horseback riding," she said. "I really shouldn't be putting the cart in front of the horse. The subject of matrimony may not even come up in our conversation."

"I'm sure no man could resist you in your magnificent new gown," Paige boasted.

"I'm a little nervous to meet his parents. Lane hasn't told them how he knows me. He said it wasn't a big deal. I'm afraid they may not like me."

"Quel non-sens," Paige said defensively. "You are a savvy woman with good business sense. How can they not like you?"

Ashley smiled nervously. She walked toward the gas lamp and lit it, adding some light to the room after the sun had set. She opened the French doors to her veranda. She then poked her head out and looked in both directions.

"Is something wrong, dear?" Paige asked, puzzled.

"No. No. It's just that on a few occurrences, I've looked out my balcony and seen this man standing down there watching me. He smokes a cigarette and faces the other way, but I know he's looking at me. I've seen him there for a while. He's creepy."

"Oh my," Paige said alarmed. "I wish you would have told me that before. The marshal brought over a photograph of some thug a couple weeks ago, but it wasn't anyone I had seen before. It was certainly not a man whom I would have ever allowed to spend time with any of you girls. But if it is the same man, he is obviously very dangerous. I will telephone the marshal and tell him about that man so he can have a deputy keep his eye on things around here."

"Thank you, Paige. I'm sure that that's a good idea."

"It's better to be on the safe side," Paige reasoned. "The monster who took our sweet Annabelle from us. Maybe it is him, maybe not. I can't ever have anything like that happen again. You girls are too important to me. Just in case anyone like that ever comes around here, I have a rifle, and I know how to use it!"

"The marshal and his men should keep us safe, don't you think?" Ashley asked.

"I hope so, Ashley. Did you know that of all you girls, Annabelle was the only one that I was ever a little afraid may be a little too greedy or do something foolish. I'm not blaming her for being kidnapped, don't misunderstand. It's just the rest of you are all so smart. Perhaps she was just too trusting of people."

"Annabelle was the sweetest girl I've ever known. Will she ever come back, Paige? I don't know if we'll ever see her again," she said, nearly weeping.

"Jerome is a tough town," Paige proclaimed. "But what's been going on around here with ladies being kidnapped and killed. That's just lunatic. It's horrible."

Paige started toward the bedroom door. "Back to happy thoughts," she said. "You have the hoedown on Saturday, and you will look ravishing. I wish it were me. I'm so envious." She stopped and turned to Ashley, closing the door behind her. "Good night, child. I will see you for breakfast in the morning."

"Good night, Paige. Thank you for coming up to talk with me. It's always so nice."

Paige's warm smiling face vanished behind the closed door. Ashley looked at herself in the mirror. She appeared to be very healthy and happy. She walked back to the veranda and looked from side to side. There were a few people walking in each direction, but she could see no sign of the cigarette-smoking man with the long black hair. She wondered if the strange man whom she had seen looking up at her was the killer. A terrifying chill bolted up her spine. She quickly closed and locked the door.

Ashley closed the curtains and got ready for bed. She was reading a book, *This Side of Paradise*, by F. Scott Fitzgerald. She grabbed the book and sat up on her bed where the lamp could provide adequate lighting for reading. The book was able to keep her mind off the disappearance of her friend Annabelle and the other young women. She read a few pages before her eyelids began to get heavy. Placing the book on the nightstand, she reached over and turned off the lamp. She was sleeping soundly within minutes.

65

The marshal was glad to see the U.S. marshals return to Phoenix. They had made their presence known but made no arrests the entire time they were in town. Deputies did pour out liquor when it was displayed too openly in a flask or other container. The cocaine and opium users were left alone. It was hard to tell if the town were any safer.

There were reports that the man in the photograph had been seen in town recently in the Safeway grocery mart and the Italian-owned restaurant. He once worked at the Little Daisy Mine and lived in the New State Boardinghouse. He had not been seen much since he checked out of the boardinghouse about a month earlier.

It had been nearly a week since Deputy Zalensky nailed the Wanted sign of Joseph Pazrosky to the post outside the Miner's Tavern. There had been a few people who pass by the jail to report that he may have been in the furniture store or the barbershop; they couldn't say for certain.

Paige made a telephone call to the marshal on one night where she said one of the girls who live on the second floor has seen a strange man watching her from the street on more than one occasion. He had slicked-back black hair and was always smoking a cigarette.

Tom Baker came by the other day to say that a man who has come into the grocery store resembles the man in the photograph. His hair is different, Tom said. According to Tom, the man made some purchases like cornmeal, yeast, and sugar that may have suggested he was a moonshiner and gave their female employee the heebie-jeebies whenever he was in the store.

Through information gathered from the federal lawmen, he was advised that Pazrosky was driving a Model T four-door but had been seen more recently in a Model T pickup. He had been seen at the Bank of Jerome and thought to have a bank account there.

Maybe the killer was lying low. There were two more girls still missing. At least no one has been reported missing since Lilly Rogers disappeared. The marshal knew that hadn't been too very long ago. The girl was on dope and may have just went away since her best friend had been found dead. She felt responsible for not doing more to keep her away from the man who killed her.

He shook off the urge to be defeated. It tore into him like a dull knife when he thought how the killer had taken four women right under his nose.

He and his men were following up on some leads the U.S. marshals shared with them but could not locate any tracks leading to Joseph Pazrosky. They searched every hotel and boardinghouse in or around Jerome.

The tension of the town remained tightly wound. The marshal and his deputies thought their man was lying low. He may have left town. They couldn't wait for him to make a mistake. It was a race to find him before he struck again. He and his deputies continued to make themselves more conspicuous as they patrolled the Cribs, up and down Main Street, and down around by the Parlor House. They knew the man they were looking for now had long black hair combed straight back.

The marshal was afraid the pressure applied by the federal lawmen the previous week may have compelled the killer to make a rash decision. He was afraid there might be more victims. There was something about cornering an insane monster like Pazrosky that was a concern to the marshal.

The marshal and his men organized more searches but never found any clues to help them find the missing girls or their killer. He vowed to never stop looking for the killer. Clues turned up from time to time, but the trail never warmed.

The Labor Day festivities were well attended. The town's various ethnicities all carried on harmoniously. There were no knifings, no assaults. Everyone joined the parade. The mood of the town was relaxed on that day. Rumor was spreading that the mines would soon be back to operating at full capacity with the price of copper increasing.

Paige Cheavant and a few of her girls watched as members of the Automobile Club slowly drove by, with its proud owners sitting high and mighty behind the wheel. Paige had given some thought about joining the all men's club. She enjoyed taking her automobile on holiday excursions, just as the men did, but had been discouraged whenever she attempted to vie for membership to the exclusive fraternal organization.

The men driving these beautiful automobiles smiled and waved at the women as they passed. Except for those men whose wives were with them.

Most of these men were smart enough to act like they didn't notice the beautiful young women standing by the street. One unfortunate man who must have forgotten his wife was with him received a hard punch to his right shoulder when she didn't approve of how he had waved so enthusiastically and tooted on his horn for the girls. It didn't help the man's cause when Gloria called out his name. Paige found this to be particularly humorous.

The volunteer Fire Department marched past the Parlor House girls, followed by a few chanting members of the Apache Indians with their jingling bells and florid-feathered headdresses. Moments later, the mayor waved to the crowd that had swarmed to the edge of both sides of the street from the backseat of a convertible roadster driven by local attorney, Eric Beltowski. An accompanying vehicle threw candy sweets to the children.

Like the previous year, the marshal and his deputies opted out of doing anything with the parade, but all deputies were on duty and scattered about among the day's full schedule of events. The marshal stood in front of the jail, occasionally tipping his hat to those who passed by in the parade and those that stood along its route. He smiled a phony smile, torn between anger and a low feeling of self-worth. Two girls had been boxed up and sent home on a train like freight. Two more girls were likely buried under rock and dirt not too far away from where the town was now celebrating, right under his nose.

The timing of word that the mines would soon be back to full capacity again helped alleviate some fears the marshal had that a small gang of out-of-work miners would stage a protest march or get together to voice their grievances and stir up trouble. There was also a group of men who were associated with union activities who walked together in the Labor Day parade. This year was no different.

The day was full of contests and festivities that got started after the parade had passed by. Men gathered for foot races while children were organized for traditional events like the three-legged race and the attempt to catch the greased pig. For women, there were contests where their pies and cakes were judged.

A large picnic held in city park near the town hall was getting under way. Several people with baskets of chicken, potato salad, and watermelon, carrying ice buckets with Coca-Cola and lemonade, congregated under a large awning.

Mayor Evans gave a short but rousing speech praising past accomplishments and the need to meet future challenges. His wife sat stone-faced near his side as he delivered the boring oratory to the hot, restless crowd.

The town council had hired a New Orleans—style band that was in the middle of touring through some Western states. The five-man Negro band featured a trumpet player who also played the tenor sax, a pianist, a double bass, a trombonist, a clarinetist. A shapely, full-figured woman in her thirties with black hair and a deep, mournful voice belted out sad blues songs. The band's resonating beat bounced off the hills and echoed down to the houses below.

The town's enthusiasm for Labor Day was their way of moving on past the summer. A summer where the bodies of two girls were found and two others went missing. Now the summer was over, and the fall was upon them. It was nice to see the smiles on the people's faces as they ate dessert and listened to the jazz band. Children ran barefoot in the grass.

Shirley met the marshal in front of the jail. "Hi, handsome, you have a chance to eat anything today?" she asked.

"I ate the wonderful leftovers you packed for me last night. It was very good."

"I'm glad you enjoyed it. Where are all your deputies?"

"They're all on duty, I reckon. Things can get rowdy on Labor Day sometimes," he answered briefly.

"Well, I wanted to tell you something while we're alone."

"Oh?" the marshal teased. "Whatever can it be?"

"If you're going to be a smart alec, then I won't tell you," she said playfully as townspeople walked by and watched the town's town marshal and his fiancée play the coquette.

"Oh, come on. I'm just teasing you. Tell me your big news."

"Well, OK then if you're going to be a gentleman," she said. Continuing, she said, "I wanted you to know. My father is taking my mother and my sister to visit Aunt Lillian in Wickenburg next week. They'll be gone for a few days. I can't go because classes start Wednesday."

The marshal looked straight ahead as several people walked along the sidewalk up and down Main Street. The sound of the band's horns could be heard blowing not far away. "So don't tell me you're gonna be home all by yourself?" he quipped.

"No, *I'm not* going to be home by myself because my big tough, rugged fiancé is going to take care of me," she retorted.

"He is, is he?"

"He better want to take care of me," she said angrily. "Why do you always have to make me so mad?"

He laughed, "Because, you're so beautiful when you get angry. You're like a mountain lion. I just want to roll around and play with you, but I'm afraid you might bite my neck off."

"I'll show you a mountain lion," she replied bitterly. "I'll scratch you so hard you won't be able to sit down for a month."

"Now, honey, stop being so feisty. You're scaring me."

"I better scare you," she said threateningly. "You better be nice to me."

"I *am* nice to you. Don't fret. I will make sure to take care of you, until the day I die, or you die. Whoever dies first," he stumbled.

"Nice try," she responded coldly. "Sometimes you can be so darn ornery, John Williams. You're so cold and unaffectionate. I don't believe you when you tell me you love me."

"What? Why did you have to go and say that? There ain't no truth to that," he said sternly. "You know what you mean to me."

"Well, sometimes a girl likes to hear that she's wanted, you know, desired, loved."

Two young women in their midtwenties were walking straight ahead toward the jail where the marshal and Shirley were engaged in a heart-to-heart talk. They crossed Main Street. The marshal looked down at his pouting fiancée and quickly said, "You are all three."

The women approached the marshal. The taller, thinner, and least attractive of the two women asked, "Are you Marshal Williams?"

"Yes, ladies. I am Marshal Williams. What seems to be the trouble?" he asked.

The two women both looked at Shirley nervously. The same thin woman asked, "Is it all right if we step inside?"

"Of course, you can," the marshal replied.

Both girls refused the marshal's offer of sitting down. Shirley waited outside but held the door ajar with her foot. She tried to listen in on what had been such an important problem for the two women. She heard the marshal say, "Well, all right then. What is it that's troubling ya?"

The same girl acted as the designator speaker for her and her short, curvy friend. "OK." She shot a quick look at her comrade. "We ain't sure, but we just wanted you to know that we ain't seen a couple of our girlfriends in the last few days. We thought for sure if they went somewheres that they would be back in time to throw a little Labor Day party like they had been mentioning."

Shirley brought her hand to her mouth to suppress a gasp. She knew how the marshal was feeling right now, with his guts all torn apart with worry. She heard him say, "Where do you ladies make your residence?"

The same female voice answered, "On Hull Avenue. You know. The Cribs."

Like a cloud of mustard gas dispersed above the battlefield and being blown away by a strong wind, the marshal had hoped he had heard the last of Joseph Pazrosky. He was determined to track the monster down until his last day. Little did he know at the time that Joseph Pazrosky would never be seen again in Jerome.

The marshal grabbed a lead pencil from his desk. He looked up at the two women and said, "First of all, why don't you give me the names of the girls and why you think they might be in some trouble?"

66

C. W. was thrilled to have his grandfather back home. Getting accustomed to getting around on the wooden crutches and the plaster cast that covered his entire leg was still a struggle. The doctor said it would be several months before his leg would mend. He also told C. W. to keep his grandfather off his feet and that it was important to keep the injured leg elevated.

Since the day he was first released from the hospital, C. W. took good care of his grandfather, making sure he was always comfortable and looked after. He cooked hearty breakfasts before he went to his job at the grocery store in the mornings, then run by the house to check on him two or three times a day. Supper was on the table at seven every night. C. W. loved looking after his grandfather, and his efforts were appreciated.

C. W. and his grandfather lived by simple means but were never in any serious danger of starving or losing their house. In addition to the earnings and tips C. W. was making, an executive from the mine had been to the house with an envelope full of cash. Barney had been contacted by lawyers who tried to convince him to file a claim for the elevator accident, but he wasn't sure he wanted to. The mine has already paid for the hospital stay and medical services. The executives had always treated him well, even keeping him employed during a slowdown where two-thirds of the workforce had been laid off. He would give it some more thought but didn't think he wanted to cause any trouble for the mine. He had enough money. As long as they were going to keep paying him.

On Labor Day, C. W. brought over Chiara to the house to meet his grandfather. She and his grandfather immediately formed a close rapport. Barney told her to stop by the house and visit whenever she felt like it. She assured him that she would.

They left his grandfather and Jake at home and walked into town to watch the parade. Then they went to the park where they listened to the band from New Orleans play their new jazz sound. Chiara and C. W. found themselves swaying to the beat of the exhilarating music. Chiara had to speak directly into C. W.'s ear in order for him to hear a word she was saying. She told him thanks for taking her to the park and parade. Other than Italians in the community, she didn't know many people. Later they joined some of the townspeople at the picnic and had their fill of watermelon and ice cream. They listened to the arresting sound of the band's music in the park until they played their last song.

Jerome was a town with very few black people. Those few were often the unfortunate victims of racial harassment. On this day, there was little tension among the various ethnic groups and cultures. The all-black Southern band was received a vociferous ovation for bringing their new sound to Jerome, a town whose population consisted of a majority of white miners, businessmen, and cowboys.

As Chiara and C. W. walked from the park, the two talked about the criminal whom they had seen in town. Neither of them had seen the man since they saw the Wanted poster nailed onto a post near the Cribs. "I wonder if he was the man that killed them two girls," C. W. said as they walked by the poster.

"Ahh, he was awful. I hated the way that man looked at me that day."

"I'm sorry. You should have came and got me," he replied sharply. "I would have punched him in the nose."

Chiara laughed, "Oh, I didn't know you were such a violent man."

Embarrassed for how he reacted, he said, "I don't mean to sound so angry. I knew how that man treated Myrtle in the store. I can imagine how he looked at you."

"Hopefully, you and I will never see that stupid man again, ever."

C. W. wanted to get off the subject of the wicked man. "We should probably start walking back to the restaurant. Your father probably doesn't want you away too long. But do we have to time to check on Grandpa first? We've been away for a few hours. Maybe he needs something."

"That's fine. Should we bring him something to eat or drink?" she asked earnestly. "That's too bad he can't come with us and eat the . . . ohh . . . how do you say . . . *anguria and gelato?* Ice cream and . . ." Getting frustrated, she said, "Ahh, you know, the green vegetable with the sweet red—"

"Oh, you mean the watermelon," he interrupted laughingly.

"You think is funny," she sighed. "My English is not too good sometimes. Do you know that you are the only one I ever speak English with? You and that . . . terrible man. Sometimes I don't even know why I bother to learn your language."

"You speak very good English," he said as they continued walking toward his house. "I think you must be the smartest person I know to be able to speak another language. I've never really asked you how you learned to speak English so well."

"It's nothing," she replied. "My parents make me learn English when we were still in Ferrara, my home in the north. There were some American people there, missionaries they were called, that teach me during the war. My father lost his two brothers in the war, and my mother also lost her brother. It was only the three of us there, and my father wanted to come to America and start a new restaurant. It's long story. I promise I will tell you one day."

They walked up the porch where they were greeted by the ever-friendly Jake, who shook like a leaf in a tree at the sight of C. W. and the new friend. "Come on in. I'll see if we have anything cold to drink."

Chiara followed C. W. into the house that hot Labor Day afternoon. C. W. peeked into the bedroom and saw that his grandfather was sleeping, so he shut the door quietly. "Grandpa's asleep. Want to go back into town and get a lemonade or soda drink somewhere?"

"Whatever you like is fine. I should be getting back to the restaurant soon though."

"Sure. Come on."

Chiara patted the faithful dog on his head as she and C. W. walked out of the yard. C. W. rubbed Jake's ears and said, "I'll be right back, boy. You make sure Grandpa is OK."

The dog turned its head back to the house at the mention of "Grandpa" as he understood what C. W. was telling him perfectly.

"That is a real nice dog," Chiara said. "I had a dog when I was a little girl back in Italy—Paolo. I miss him a lot."

Looking back at the panting Jake, C. W. said, "I'm sure you do. I love that dog. I don't know what I would do without him."

When the young couple came upon Hull Avenue, C. W. saw the well-dressed bartender, Roy, examining his pocket watch, getting ready to enter the Mineflower Saloon. He saw C. W. and gave him a friendly wave. C. W. smiled and waved back. Roy hollered across the street, "How ya doin', C. W.?"

C. W. and Chiara crossed the street. "Fine, thank you," C. W. replied. "Going to work?"

"Yeah. I took a little break to take my girl to the park, watched the parade, you know. We generally get a good crowd in here on Labor Day. I reckon this year won't be any different." Roy smiled at Chiara and said, "Who's your friend, C. W.?"

"I'm sorry. This is Chiara. Her family has the restaurant down on the end of Main Street."

"Nice to meet you, Chiara. That's the place that serves the Italian cuisine, isn't it?" he asked.

"Yes, my family has owned it for the last two years, since we came over from Italy."

"Well, I must admit I've never eaten there, but one day I would like to try it. My mother used to be a pretty good cook with pastas, spaghetti, and all those thick sauces. It was some kind of good. The kind of food that makes you fat," he said rubbing his belly. "It's just about 5:00. I reckon I should be getting inside. Say, can I buy you two a Coca-Cola or a sarsaparilla?"

"Sassa perilla? What's that?" Chiara giggled.

"Sarsaparilla. It's a soft drink. Like Dr Pepper or Coca-Cola. Come on in and have a cold drink. It ain't very crowded in here yet."

C. W. and Chiara looked at each other for a moment before Chiara said, "I have time for a cold drink. I want to see what it's like in here. Come on C. W."

They followed Roy through the frosted glass outer doors into the saloon with its several pool tables and phonograph playing ragtime music. The saloon smelled of cigar smoke. There were a handful of men playing pool and an older couple sitting in a corner table. Two young women were seated at another table engaged in a pleasant conversation. One man who was bent over getting ready to make a shot straightened up and inquisitively watched Chiara as she walked in. A brawny barman stood with arms crossed inside the front doorway, ready to throw somebody to the street if they were out of line.

C. W. and Chiara took a seat at the magnificent bar that ran parallel to the eastern wall. Roy exchanged some friendly banter with a couple of the men, then walked behind the long polished bar. "So what can I get you two?" he asked.

C. W. smiled at Chiara. She smiled back at him bashfully. "I don't know. C. W., what are you having?"

C. W. looked at Roy. "A Coca-Cola will be fine for me, Roy, thank you."

"I'll have a Coca-Cola also please."

"Two Coca-Colas it is then." Roy turned and grabbed two clean glasses off the back shelf. As he did so, Chiara scanned the saloon. She noted the saloon's high ceiling and spacious interior, the large wooden dance floor surrounded by tables and chairs. Roy returned to the two young adults sitting alone at the ornately carved cherrywood bar. "Here you go, Miss Chiara, and, C. W. On the house. If you two were to stick around a bit, we've got a woman coming in tonight. Sings like a canary."

C. W. and Chiara thanked Roy for the cold drinks. Chiara took a sip from her glass and continued to visually explore the saloon. The other walls were filled with colorful advertisements for beer and tobacco products featuring beautiful and often scantily clad women. There was a small bandstand stage at the north end. A Bush & Gertz Louis XV baby grand piano sat near the west wall to the side of the stage. Another sign on the wall featured a photograph of the attractive woman who was advertised to sing at the saloon later that evening.

A smaller adjacent room contained another billiards table. Spittoons were placed strategically every ten or fifteen feet apart on the wooden floor.

C. W. took a sip from his glass and put it down. He looked at Chiara. "Well, what do you think of this place?"

"I like it. It's very nice," she marveled. "My father probably wouldn't be too pleased if he thought this was a place that I visited often," she whispered.

"No, I reckon not," C. W. responded. "We don't have to stay very long. I've made a few deliveries here. Roy is a good fella."

"He seems nice." She looked around. "There's no one in here that's our age," she pointed out.

C. W. laughed, "No, that's for sure." He finished his drink and sat down his glass. After Chiara finished her drink, the two got up to leave. They thanked Roy politely for the drinks and said good-bye. The outdoor air was a welcome blessing compared to the smoke-filled saloon.

"I hope my clothes don't smell of tobacco smoke. I wasn't going to tell my mother or father that you and I went in there for a cold drink."

C. W. took a long whiff of his shirtsleeve. "I don't know if we were in there long enough or not. I sure don't want you to get any trouble with your parents. They may not let you see me anymore."

"I'm not a little girl anymore," she protested. "I love my parents and don't want them angry with me, but they both like you, so not letting me see you again is not going to be a problem," she assured him. As they walked down Hull Avenue, she continued, "I had fun today. Thank you for taking me to the parade and to listen to the music in the park. It was nice to meet your grandfather. The saloon was fun too."

They walked by the High House on Hull Avenue. "This is where I live," she said.

"I know," he admitted. "I've seen your father come out of here sometimes and thought this must be where you and your parents live."

"Someday you must come over. I know my parents would like to speak with you, through me of course," she giggled. "They don't speak any English."

They continued past the High House to the restaurant. They looked inside and saw that there were only two tables with customers. Her father waited on the two tables with the regular Italian customers. He saw Chiara and motioned for her to come inside.

She looked at C. W. affectionately. "Thanks again, C. W." She looked again into the restaurant. "I want to give you a little kiss, but maybe is not the right time," she said girlishly.

C. W.'s eyes grew large. "That's all right. I mean, you know I like you a lot and everything, but there will be the right time and place. I want your father to like me."

At that time, her father poked his head out the front door and did something that C. W. had rarely seen; he smiled. He said something politely to Chiara in Italian, then looked at C. W., and said, "Grazie, C. W."

C. W. graciously returned Chiara's father's act of kindness with a respectful nod of his head and smiled. He turned to Chiara and said, "Thank you. I better go." Slowly turning to walk away, he said, "I'll see you again. Maybe we can go see another picture next week."

"I would like that," she answered. "Thank you, C. W." She walked into the restaurant as C. W. began to walk up the street.

He was astonished that her father had treated him kindly for once. He popped into the grocery store and said hello to Mr. Baker and Myrtle. Grover wasn't there. Both warmly greeted him on his day off and asked how his grandfather was doing. He told them that his grandfather was doing all right and that he would see them both in the morning.

Trying hard not to walk with a skip in his step like a little boy, he returned home to his loving grandfather and Jake. He considered himself a very lucky and contented young man.

67

With his head pounding and bathed in sweat, Pazrosky peeled himself away from Lucille's clutches. He walked outside into the dark night where the enormous star-filled sky above radiated down on him.

He walked over to Homer's hovel and walked inside. He opened the curtain and saw that he and Izzy were sleeping tightly in Homer's cramped bed. He walked back outside to the northern edge of the property where he could look down on the Verde Valley and the edge of Jerome with all its lights.

His head was foggy from all the hooch he had drank earlier. He had a splitting headache. *What was that Lucille had said? Was that part of a dream?* He had a hard time remembering the events of the evening. After a few minutes, he had some memories of an enjoyable dinner with drinks. He was together with Lucille in his tiny shed. *What else?*

He knew that something significant had been said during the course of the evening that had caused him to worry. He just couldn't remember or thought that it was something he had dreamed. He walked over closer to the edge of the small canyon. He needed a cigarette but had to return to the shed to get them. He walked back to the shed still in a zombielike state.

Lucille was lying on the cot, snoring quietly. He grabbed his pack of Chesterfields from the hastily constructed end table, shook out a cigarette, and lit it. Taking several puffs off his cigarette, he still couldn't relax. He walked around outside for a while trying to quell his fears and paranoia, continuing to sweat profusely.

After several minutes, his mind began to clear. He tossed his cigarette butt to the ground and walked back to Homer's hovel to pour himself a drink. The events of the evening were beginning to become more clear to him as his headache began to go away. He took a sip of straight hooch, swirling it around in his mouth before letting it slowly go down his gullet.

Now he was starting to remember what Lucille had said. The town was swarming with U.S. marshals looking for him. He had stayed a couple of steps ahead of them, but he knew that he couldn't stay ahead of them forever. He couldn't let them give him the buzz. They had a photograph of him and were showing it to all the townspeople. That meant that he couldn't buy food or supplies in town anymore. It wouldn't be long before Lucille and Izzy, and perhaps even Homer, would see his photograph. Maybe there was also a reward for whoever turned him in to the lawmen.

Yap, it was time to go. *What about Lucille, Izzy? Homer? Would they recognize him from the photograph being circulated of him? Now they would all know why he tried to disguise himself. Did they need to be silenced?*

He returned to his shed where he had earlier gathered his things, including all the cash, jewelry, and gun. He looked at Lucille sleeping peacefully. She had been nice to him. He was her butter-and-egg man. She treated him like a real man. She made him feel like a man and not some chump. He didn't *want* to kill her. Sure, she was a whore. She was in a better position now since she met him.

Thoughts filled his head as he stared down at the sleeping woman. He stuffed his clothes in a potato sack along with the ammunition for his revolver. He took the expensive gold watch and hurled it far into the dark canyon. He stuffed the cash, about six thousand dollars, in his pockets and grabbed the potato sack. He opened the chamber to his revolver. It was loaded. He tucked it into the front of his trousers. He returned to his truck and threw the sack in it. He then retrieved his suit from the shed and tossed it in the truck.

He returned to Homer's hovel and refilled his tin can with hooch from the jug. After taking a large swig, he grabbed the key to the still that hung from a nail. Walking out to the shed housing the still, he unlocked the door and grabbed a jug for each hand, placing the jugs on the floor of the pickup. That was everything. *Or was it?*

He slowly pushed his Model T pickup down the bumpy dirt road, away from the others who were sound asleep. He approached the front of the vehicle and began turning the hand crank until the engine turned over, then walked back to where the others were sleeping off a night of heavy drinking and feasting.

EPILOGUE

In the weeks and months following Jerome's Indian summer of 1921, the days became shorter, and the nights became cold. As the skies turned gray, the townspeople turned inward, making the transition from summer to fall. The change in temperature and increase in wind always came suddenly for the town that lie on the edge of a mountaintop two thousand feet above the Verde River below.

The townspeople of Jerome had begun to overcome their fears that a mad man was still in their community among them. The kidnappings and murders of the call girls abruptly stopped. Although there were still issues of violence involving the women, that was thought to be merely the nature of the business. The newcomer with the greasy black hair and beard was never seen around Jerome again.

For some, the summer of 1921 will be remembered for the romance that blossomed from seeds planted earlier in the season. A teenager's first love and a wealthy young rancher taking a wife out of the town's prestigious Parlor House.

At the Walker family hoedown, Ashley accepted Lane's marriage proposal. She moved out of the Parlor House the following week. She moved into the cozy home that was on their large ranch in the Verde River valley near the farming community Carl Schelby named for his wife, Sedona. Here, she and Lane loved to go horseback riding at the base of the beautiful red rock mountains.

Married a month later, Ashley and Lane took the Cadillac to Payson shortly after their wedding where she visited her parents' grave and her family's old ranch. She wept at her parents' grave and when she saw her horse. All in all, it was a very emotional time for Ashley. She made arrangements to take her horse back to their ranch. She was happy and felt blessed.

Despite the pleading of his betrothed, the marshal was unable to forget about the horrific events for which he remained wrought with guilt for the rest of his life. He would never grasp how one man would chose to come through his town like a deadly disease and wreak so much havoc with his murder without having to pay a price for it.

He and the former Miss Shirley Hudson were married during the spring of 1923. A year later, he resigned the position of town marshal to Deputy Zalensky. Through the help of his father-in-law, he accepted a position of superintendent of security with the large mining company.

During the summer of 1924, Shirley gave birth to their beautiful baby daughter, Cherylynn. She stayed home with her until Cherylynn was six years old. Then, she returned to teaching school while Cherylynn spent more time with her grandparents.

The marshal, his wife, and daughter lived comfortably, even through the hard times of the Great Depression. He retired before he was too old of a man. He spent the rest of his days in the company of his family. As hard as he tried, he was never able to forget the two young women he uncovered from their graves, strangled to death by a mad man. Nor the other women who disappeared and, for all he knew, likely suffered the same fate. The events of his tenure as town marshal, just over four years of loyal service, haunted him until the day he died.

When he was sixty-three years old, the partial skeletal remains of an unidentified woman were discovered by a man hunting a rogue mountain lion that had been killing some of the locals livestock. The man said nothing of the finding but gave the remains a proper burial, marked to this day by an unidentified gravestone. These were the remains of Lilly Rogers.

The Verde United Mining Company took good care of Barney during the two years it took him to recover from his leg injury. When he was walking well again, albeit with a noticeable limp, the mine found an office position for him in the mail room. He worked until the Great Depression. He was a man who always felt very fortunate. He had a growing family and a faithful dog who kept him company.

C. W. loved working for Mr. Baker. In 1923, he became assistant manager after Grover left the grocery store. Years later, Mr. Baker made a deal with C. W. making him general manager and part owner.

At the age of twenty-two, he married the love of his life, Chiara. She stayed behind with her new husband after her parents sold their restaurant and sailed back for Italy. She found work as a translator and teacher for her ability to speak fluent English and Italian. She also worked in Jerome's nicest restaurant as a waitress or hostess. She was very happy.

In December of 1926, a son was born to Chiara and C. W., named Christopher. The proud parents' hearts would break nearly twenty years later when they receive word of his death in Germany during the last days of World War II. Chiara had difficulty coping with the loss of their only child. She passed away peacefully in her sleep three years after Christopher's death.

Widowed and childless in his early forties, C. W. never remarried. He sold his half of the Jerome Safeway grocery store and moved down into the valley where he worked at a Cottonwood grocery store until he retired in 1972. The rest of his life was rather sad and lonely. His distant memories of teenage love, his faithful dog, his loving family, and the horrific murders that paralyzed the town during the summer of 1921 had faded away.

C. W. died on October 3, 2001, a lonely, but happy man.

"I've been trying to tell you if you can jist get the dirt out of yer ears! I dropped the girls off outside town. Izzy didn't want to wake you up." Pazrosky took a big puff off his cigarette, a cup half-full of hooch pinched between his legs. Exhaling, he said, "Like I said, we're all in big trouble. Big trouble. We all need to lie low for a while. Our lives are in danger. When we started selling our hooch in the Cribs, we infringed upon some big-time bootlegging operation, and they want us all dead."

Homer had a frightened look on his face. "Holy Toledo! Do you reckon they'll come lookin' for us?"

"I reckon they will," Pazrosky answered. "Listen, while you were sawing logs, I loaded our entire supply in the back of the truck, covered by that tarp. The still is all locked up. My buyer in Flagstaff is gonna pay us $300 for our hooch. That's $150 apiece. And on top of that, I'm getting a new roadster. What do you think of them marbles?"

"Sounds swell, I reckon. Why didn't you tell me earlier, why so all of a sudden? It's still dark out," Homer whimpered. "And it's raining."

"It ain't all of a sudden. I just decided to take you with me, that's all. Ya know, I . . . we gotta be careful with all this hooch. Relax, we'll be in Flagstaff in a couple hours. When was the last time you had $150 burning a hole in your pocket?"

The two men sat in silence for a while as the sun began to rise over the ponderosa pines of the higher country and illuminated the stunningly majestic red rock cliffs of the Mogollan Rim.

Homer twisted around in his seat and saw where the sunrise had broken through the clouds over the sleeping town. He hadn't been away from his home in the gulch in over a decade. He didn't travel well. His head ached, and the bumpy road made his stomach churn. His face was soaked with perspiration.

Pazrosky sensed Homer's discomfort. Breaking the silence, he said, "Up here a few miles, we'll be able to get a cup of coffee, maybe some breakfast."

"If I can make it that far," Homer moaned. "You may have to let me out for a minute."

"Try not to make a mess in the jalopy," Pazrosky snarled. "We're getting ready to trade it off for a new one in Flagstaff."

"I'll do my best, Henry," he replied softly.

"Good," Pazrosky answered stiffly. "I gave the girls some money and told them to get out of town for a while."

"Good," Homer replied. "So we stole all their business and some people got burrs in their bonnets."

"Yeah. That's right. These people are from Kansas City or Chicago back east. They're serious," Pazrosky said with rare emotion. "'Angry' isn't the word to describe these men. They will kill us for sure. We cost them hundreds of dollars at least."

Pazrosky glanced over at his travel companion and took a drag from his cigarette. "Don't worry 'bout nuthin', after we unload all this, we'll each have $150 in our pockets. I thought we would take the new roadster for a drive out to Californi'. You ever do any oil work?"

"The only work I know how to do these days is moonshinin'," he snapped angrily.

"Say! That ain't a bad idea. There will always be customers to buy our reputable shine—*your* famous secret family recipe."

"Yer right. It ain't a bad idea. How long you reckon we gotta lie low?" Homer asked.

"Don't know for sure. A month maybe," he lied. "We'll set up shop somewhere, get some brewin' goin'. I may look for work in one of them oil wells or something."

"Sounds all right, I reckon. I'll miss my girl Izzy," he moped. "I can't wait to see her again."

"Someday," he lied again. "Don't you go cryin' over no woman either. They're all jist whores anyways. Where we're goin', you won't believe your eyes. We'll get us some new clothes. You ever seen the ocean?"

As their automobile drove in the light rain along the rutty, muddy road along Oak Creek, Pazrosky pulled out his watch and looked at the time, ten o'clock. He looked at Homer. "Two hours. We're only two hours away from sellin' this automobile loaded with hooch for a new roadster and three hundred clams. That's a hell of a deal!"

Lost in thought, Pazrosky had his loaded .48 handy so nothing was fishy during the transaction. Once they headed west out of Flagstaff, he would breathe a little easier. He didn't suspect any roadblocks. He tried not to think too much about what he did to the two whores back at Homer's place. He was released from his trance when Homer spoke loudly, "I said, do you think they will go after Izzy and Lucille too?"

"Who?"

"You know. The mobsters."

"Oh yeah. Them guys. I reckon they will. The girls won't be found for a while. I mean . . . I gave them each a hundred bucks. Who knows, we'll probably see 'em in Californi'."